THEY SEEMED TO COME
OUT OF NOWHERE ...

... four MiG-25 Foxbats flying fast and high. Hawk Hunter quickly identified the MiGs' strategy.

"They're chicken bastards," he yelled back to the gun crew. "They wouldn't know a fair fight if they fell into it. All weapon bays ... *activate!*"

Two MiGs came into together, their sights lined up on the fat part of the *Bozo's* left side fuselage.

Hunter counted to three, then yelled: "All engagement weapons ... *fire!*"

Instantly, the left side of the huge Galaxy erupted in a sheet of flame as all of the Gatlings, all of the AA-guns, all of the field artillery pieces fired at once.

The MiG pilots never knew what hit them.

THE WINGMAN SERIES

#2: THE CIRCLE WAR	(2120, $3.95/$4.95)
#3: THE LUCIFER CRUSADE	(2232, $3.95/$4.95)
#4: THUNDER IN THE EAST	(2453, $3.95/$4.95)
#5: THE TWISTED CROSS	(2553, $3.95/$4.95)
#6: THE FINAL STORM	(2655, $3.95/$4.95)
#7: FREEDOM EXPRESS	(4022, $3.99/$4.99)
#8: SKYFIRE	(3121, $3.99/$4.99)
#9: RETURN FROM THE INFERNO	(3510, $3.99/$4.99)
#10: WAR OF THE SUN	(3773, $3.99/$4.99)

WINGMAN

#11 THE GHOST WAR
MACK MALONEY

ZEBRA BOOKS
KENSINGTON PUBLISHING CORP.

ZEBRA BOOKS are published by

Kensington Publishing Corp.
475 Park Avenue South
New York, NY 10016

First Printing: July, 1993

Printed in the United States of America

PART ONE

Chapter One

Captain "Crunch" O'Malley was exhausted.

For the last ten hours, he had been flying his RF-4X Super Phantom in a wide search pattern over the eastern sector of the Philippine Sea. Under normal circumstances, he would have quit for the day a long time ago.

But there was nothing normal about today's recon.

What Crunch was looking for, what he was actually hoping *not* to find, was nowhere to be seen. Except for the occasional green dot of some obscure, uncharted island, all that stretched before him were thousands of square miles of empty ocean. Water, water everywhere.

"But not a drop to drink," O'Malley muttered.

A quick glance at his control panel's fuel quantity indicator told him that the Super Phantom was getting critically low on gas.

He banked to the left and set a new course.

"Time to head for the barn," he thought.

His new destination was a place called Xmas Island. Located approximately 400 miles southeast of Luzon, Xmas Island had nothing to do with Santa Claus or Divine Birth. Just the opposite, in fact.

Xmas was owned and operated by the Triad Holding Corporation, a collection of some of the most greedy and cutthroat wheeler-dealers on the planet. Absolutely anything could be had for a price on Xmas—it was capitalism gone amok. Any kind of operation was allowed on the twenty-square-mile island: prostitution, drug manufacturing, weapons running, money laundering . . . and jet refueling. Just as long as Triad got its cut—usually 50 percent—anyone could do business there. It was all strictly cash and carry. If the payment was short one penny, justice was swift. No trial, no jury of peers, no appeals—only execution. Sometimes as many as ten a day. All in all, it was definitely not a place for the faint of heart.

O'Malley had been to Xmas Island dozens of times over the past few years and knew it well. None of the squalor, filth, and disease that was rampant in this part of the world existed on Xmas. The reason was simple: despite their econo-authoritarian ways, the Triad Holding Corporation poured a substantial amount of their profits back into development and maintenance of the island. So, oddly, Xmas boasted the best living conditions in the Pacific Rim—a nice place to live, but you wouldn't want to visit there.

The island itself was beautiful. Except for the harbor, where much of the importing and exporting went on, the entire coastline was covered by gorgeous beaches of pearl white sand. Fishing was ideal and plentiful, wild fruits and vegetables grew everywhere, cattle and exotic game hunting provided the meat, five state-run distilleries provided the booze. And it was said that the power surfing there was better than any other place in the world outside of Hawaii.

But Crunch wasn't going there to fish or eat or surf or get drunk. This time is was simply a fuel-up stop for a tank of JP-8 and maybe a bottle or two of scotch. Then it would be up and out again for another 2500-mile loop, this time south, skirting northeast New Guinea, continuing his search for a nightmare.

He activated his radio and set it to the regular hailing frequency for the control tower on Xmas Island.

"Triad One, Triad One, this is Phantom Zebra-Adam. Over."

Crunch continued to eyeball his fuel status while waiting for a reply. But none came. He radioed again.

"Triad One, Triad One, this is United American Air Force Phantom Zebra-Adam. Are you receiving me?"

Nothing. The island was just appearing through the haze on his southern horizon. Crunch dialed over to the Xmas tower's emergency frequency.

"Triad One, I am approaching at 28,000 feet, about sixty-four miles east of you. Request permission to land and purchase refueling services. Over."

All that came back was an earful of static.

"What the hell is going on?" he thought. "These guys go out of business?"

He brought the RF-4X down to 10,000 feet, tried the radio again, and got the same results. He quickly double checked his own UHF set system—maybe something was busted on his end. But everything came back green. The island was now looming in the distance about forty miles away.

Gradually reducing his airspeed, Crunch descended through the cloud cover preparing for a visual fly-by over the island. He also armed his weapon systems—just in case.

He was down to an ass-scrapping 1,000 feet when he streaked over the island's outlying barrier reef and immediately headed inland. A bad feeling began to rise in his stomach. His gut was telling him that something was *very* wrong on Xmas—a correct assumption as it turned out.

He broke through the last cloud cover about a mile in. He wouldn't soon forget what he saw.

Gone was the lush green vegetation that had covered the island. Now the landscape below consisted of nothing but hundreds of smoking craters. No buildings. No roadways. What few trees remained were only charred stumps.

What the hell happened here?

He banked towards the main town and was over it four seconds later. It was a pile of rubble and smoking debris.

The high rises, the casinos, the barrooms, and the brothels were all gone. All that was left were thousands of bodies and body parts lying everywhere. It was astonishing—Crunch had never seen such utter devastation. The entire twenty square miles of the island had been completely leveled.

It was the Bingo Bell that snapped Crunch out of the shock of viewing the hellish vision below. Reality returned. He was running out of fuel—fast. He needed gas, and he needed it now.

He nosed the RF-4X toward the airfield, located at the island's southern tip. It too was completely devastated. All that was left of the control tower was its foundation. Every other major structure around it was little more than a pile of twisted steel and busted concrete.

Suddenly Crunch got lucky: Most of the auxiliary runway still looked serviceable. That was the good news. The bad news was that right smack in the middle of the usable part was an airport maintenance truck, laying on its side, burning wildly.

Crunch quickly assessed the situation. His fuel gauge was buried past bust—he was flying strictly on fumes. He had to put the Rhino down before it put itself down, and he had only once chance to do it.

He roared back around, this time at a right angle to the runway, lined up dead on with the overturned truck. His weapons control system up and running, he let loose his single offensive weapon, a Maverick air-to-ground munition. The missile shot out from under his right wing and Crunch banked hard starboard as soon as it cleared. Twisting in his cockpit, he turned to see the AGM hit the truck square. Its warhead exploded as advertised, scattering chunks of the burning vehicle everywhere.

The runway was now as clear as it was going to get.

He came around a third time, even as he heard his last fuel reserve tank click off. The Phantom hit the runway with a bone-jarring thud. Crunch immediately deployed his drag chute, but the landing proved to be like driving through an obstacle course. He fought with the stick, careening the big jet away from chunks of concrete, steel, and debris scattered across the concrete ribbon. Finally he got passed most of the wreckage and gradually brought the Phantom to a halt.

He popped the canopy and slowly climbed out of the cockpit, his 9-mm pistol in hand. The devastated landscape was like something from a science fiction movie. And absolutely quiet. He jumped from the plane and cautiously began to reconnoiter the immediate area. It wasn't long before he was convinced that not a single soul had survived whatever the hell had happened. He slipped his sidearm back into its holster. Except for the occasional squawking of a couple of vultures fighting over a piece of flesh, the silence was deafening. It was so eerie Crunch started to get a major case of the creeps. He had to find some fuel—quick.

The gas storage tank area was destroyed and still burning—he knew he'd find no usable fuel there. However, through the smoke and haze, he could see the remains of two of the island's defensive fighters still burning further up the runway. They had crashed, apparently on takeoff. Acting on a desperate hunch, he began walking along the edge of the strip, and in less than a minute, he found what he was looking for. The fighters had obviously scrambled at the onset of the disaster, letting go of their drop tanks in the process, just to get the hell off the ground as quickly as possible. Buried nose down about three feet into the mud in front of him was a 1300-liter drop tank from an old French-built Jaguar. O'Malley rapped it with his knuckles. It was full.

It took one hour and forty-five back-breaking minutes, but Crunch finally managed to get the fuel out of the drop tank and into his fighter. But while scrounging around in

11

what was left of the hangers nearby for rubber hoses and the makings of a hand pump, he discovered some intriguing evidence. There was almost nothing of any value left inside these bombed-out shells of buildings. Just about anything that was not tied down had been cleared out; sinks, toilets, electrical wiring, doorknobs, pipes, windows. As strange as it seemed, it looked like everything had been taken *before* the buildings were destroyed, including, he was sure, any usable weapons and ammunition. This told him something he didn't know before. The place had been stripped clean first. And *then* it was leveled.

Xmas Island did not die a natural death. No hurricane, earthquake or tsunami could have caused such complete and utter destruction. No—he was convinced the island had been attacked, and attacked so ruthlessly that it defied comprehension. In all his years of combat, he had never witnessed such total and wanton devastation. The big question was: Who was responsible?

He was afraid that he already knew the answer.

He climbed back into the fighter and quickly took off, overflying the island twice, the cameras in his nose cone working frantically to capture the entire ghastly scene below. Then he kicked in his afterburner and rocketed away to the east.

He'd found his nightmare.

Chapter Two

San Diego Harbor
48 hours later

United American Armed Forces Captain Ben Wa scanned the pile of black and white photographs spread out in front of him and felt his jaw tighten.

"Unbelievable," he whispered. "Just incredible . . ."

He was sitting in the conference room aboard the aircraft carrier, USS *Mike Fitzgerald*. The ship, battered and hurting from a recent campaign in the Pacific, was now in dry dock for major repairs and refitting, a project expected to take a year or more. But because the carrier still held a lot of important communications gear, the United Americans were using it temporarily as a base of operations.

The photo prints before him were so recently back from the darkroom, Ben could still smell the developing solution. When he first saw them, he actually thought they were shots of the lunar landscape. There was photo after photo of nothing but desolation and craters. But when he learned they were of Xmas Island, a place he was familiar with, he was simply astonished. The once-beautiful haven of captlistic hedonism was now as barren as the moon. Absolutely nothing was left.

And one thing was clear: Whoever was responsible for the devastation was a very dangerous force indeed.

"We sure as hell don't need this," Wa whispered again. That was an understatement.

It had been a tough past few months for the United American Armed Forces. The USS *Fitz* and the men aboard had taken a terrific beating in the all too recent confrontation with their latest enemy, the Combined Greater East Asian Warrior Society, otherwise known as the Asian Mercenary Cult.

This fanatical, quasi-religious organization had successfully invaded the American continent just over a year before. Occupying most of the territory west of the Rockies with fifty infantry divisions, the Cult also had two very dangerous aces up its sleeve—a pair of nuclear-armed submarines, known as the *Fire Bats*, which continually patrolled the waters off California, their sixteen-megaton ballistic missiles ready to be fired at a moment's notice.

The United American forces couldn't readily attack the occupying Cult forces as long as these submarines cruised offshore. On the other hand, the Cult did not have the military or logistical ability to expand eastward over the Rockies and beyond. The result was a stand-off—a "Phony War"—existing between the two sides for several months.

Then American intelligence sources learned that the Cult was preparing for a nuclear first strike against the helpless American citizens held captive by the occupying forces. The United Americans had to act and act fast before a million or more innocents were immolated.

The Americans' counterplan was to stage a preemptive air strike called "Operation Long Bomb," using the *Fitz* as its launching platform. Modeled after the famous Jimmy Doolittle Raid during the early days of World War II, the idea called for bombing a number of key targets on the Cult-controlled Japanese Home Islands, one of which had also been high on Doolittle's list: *Tokyo*.

The strategy was to do away with the Cult's leader, Hashi-Pushi, a drug-crazed madman who exercised absolute control over a brutally repressive, far-flung Pacific empire. The hope was that with the head of the snake eliminated, confusion would cascade down to the highly regimented Cult officer corps and quickly diminish their fanatical willingness to die—or to order the launch of a nuclear warhead on their own.

Incredibly, the bold American air strike worked.

Using an ungainly collection of land-based jet fighters adapted for carrier service, the United Americans nearly burned the entire city of Tokyo to the ground. The destruction was so swift and so widespread, Hashi-Pushi chose to do the Americans a favor and blow his brains out.

But the battle was far from over.

Unbeknownst to the Americans, the Cult had created a tremendously efficient underground factory on the nearby island of Okinawa, dedicated to manufacturing World War II-vintage kamikize airplanes. Hundreds of explosive-packed Mitsubishi-type A6M Zeros were being turned out twenty-four hours a day by this facility, mainly with the labor of enslaved natives.

Faced with this unexpected threat and their own diminishing resources, the small American fleet—consisting of the *Fitz,* two supply ships and the Norwegian-manned battleship, USS *New Jersey*—eventually staged a brilliantly conceived air-land operation which resulted in the total destruction of the huge Okinawa complex, freeing thousands of slave laborers in the process.

When news of this defeat flashed around the world, the *Fire Bats* disappeared and the Cult ground forces began withdrawing from West Coast. With this stunning victory, the American continent was totally free of foreign invaders for the first time in years.

But a final confrontation with the Cult was still to come.

Massed around what was once called Pearl Harbor, the Cult was tricked into expending its entire aerial strength on the destruction of a United American "phantom navy." The result was the bulk of the Cult's forces were either killed or isolated on the island of Oahu, their food and water supplies obliterated. There, they were left to the unheroic fate of mass starvation, cannibalism—or suicide.

But now, as Ben scanned the photographs once more, he realized the fight was not yet over.

He was not alone in this conclusion. There were three other men in the conference room with him, and by the grim look on their faces, Ben knew that they silently agreed.

Sitting to his left was JT "Socket" Toomey, one of the most experienced and capable fighter pilots in the United American Armed Forces. Next to Toomey was Major Pietr Frost, the Free Canadian pilot who served as military liason officer between the United American Armed Forces and the democratic government of Free Canada.

And sitting at the far end of the table was Major Hawk Hunter, known to all as The Wingman, the greatest fighter pilot who ever lived.

It was to him they turned to now.

Hunter shifted uncomfortably in his chair. For once he was well-rested, but hardly by design. Shortly after the defeat of the Cult forces at Pearl Harbor, he had returned briefly to Okinawa. On the return flight, he somehow ran out of fuel and was forced to ditch on a deserted island at the very western end of the Hawaiian chain.

He was officially listed as "missing in action," until his friend, Stan Yastrewski (aka "Yaz"), had a sudden vision from his bed in the sick bay of the *Fitz*, shortly after coming out of a deep hypnotic coma. From this, Yaz was able to lead rescue forces to Hunter's small tropical island, where they found the Wingman living the life of Robinson Crusoe, well-tanned, well-fed, and well-rested for the first time in years.

In retrospect, Hunter was glad that he had taken advantage of the down time on the small island to recoup and recharge. Because he knew now, by the photographic evidence before him, that their war with the Cult—or more

16

specifically the evil forces *behind* the Cult—was indeed far from over.

"The good news is this," Hunter began, referring to a message he'd received shortly before the meeting commenced, "despite the fact that Xmas was totally destroyed, we can rule out a nuclear strike. There were no detectable signs of weapons-related radiation on Crunch's flight suit, boots or airframe."

There was a collective sigh of relief from the others in the room. The nuclear-armed Fire Bats had not been present at the climatic battle of Pearl Harbor. In fact they had not been seen since they disappeared from the waters off the West Coast. One initial fear was that the rogue subs, considered "missing but still operational" by the United American strategic advisory unit, had nuked Xmas.

Hunter went on. "The bad news is that Crunch's report also states that three more islands on the eastern edge of the Caroline chain got the same treatment recently."

Another tense silence gripped the room.

"Same M.O.?" Frost asked finally.

"Apparently so," Hunter replied. "None of those islands had any strategic military importance whatsoever. They were simply stripped of anything of value, their populations wiped out, and then completely leveled."

He studied the photos of Xmas again.

"I'm convinced this was done by 16-inch high-explosive shells," Hunter said. He knew that Captain Wolf, the Norse commander of the battleship *New Jersey*—itself armed with 16-inch guns—would have agreed with him. The formidable Wolf was presently en route to Norway to refit his own battered vessel and would rejoin the allies as soon as possible.

"I'd say hundreds of big shells, fired in a barrage that lasted for at least four hours, is the only thing that could have caused these craters," he continued, dropping the prints back on the conference table. "And from the intensity of the firing pattern, it looks like they not only wanted

17

to make sure that everything was destroyed . . ." he paused and looked at the men around the table. ". . . they wanted us to know about it."

"It's got to be them," JT said bitterly, now stating the obvious. "The freaking battleships."

Just before the battle for Okinawa, the United Americans had discovered a second, huge Cult manufacturing facility. Located on a string of islands south of Okinawa, this gigantic complex was dedicated to building World-War-II-style battleships. Though they had spotted scores of them steaming out of the gigantic shipbuilding facility, with their hands full on Okinawa, the Americans could do little about them. By the time the Okinawa operation was over, the battleships had disappeared. But to where? No one knew—so they, too, were officially tagged "missing but operational".

These battleships made for a formidable enemy. With a displacement of 58,000 tons fully loaded, each was more than 880 feet long. Each had a weapons complement of twenty 5-inch guns, sixty pairs of 40-mm Bofors, and nine gigantic 16-inch cannons, whose powers of destruction were quite evident to all in the room. In fact, the concentrated firepower aboard one of the highly automated battleships could nearly mimic a nuclear strike. And there were twenty-four of them. With a maximum cruising speed of 30 knots and a range of 15,000 nautical miles, this fearsome extension of the brutal Cult slash-and-kill doctrine could go just about anywhere—and do just about anything it pleased.

Hunter was as much in the dark about the exact whereabouts and intentions of the battleships as everyone else. But obviously at least one of them had paid a visit to Xmas Island recently.

"If they are establishing a sphere of influence in one particular area by leaving their calling cards," Hunter went on. "The populations down there must be close to panic. There's no military good *or* bad to protect them."

18

"Easy pickings," Toomey summed up.

Again, everyone in the room nodded in grim agreement.

"If they are intent on destroying island after island," Toomey added, "they could be down in that part of the world for months."

"Is it enough time for us to get our act together?" Frost asked. "We have to do something about it. After all, we're the only power in the world that could come to the defense of these people in the South Pacific. If we don't do it, who the hell else will?"

"Wait a minute," JT interrupted, "maybe we need to take a step back and consider one thing."

The room fell into silence.

"Is it really *our* job to stop them?" he asked. "We dealt with them here in America, and we finally got rid of them. What we're talking about now is a danger that is all the way around the other side of the planet," he paused, then quietly asked, "Is it really our job to be the policemen of the world?"

No one said a word for a long time. It was Hunter who finally addressed the hypothetical question.

"Freedom is the most cherished thing anyone can have," he began. "After what we've all been through, we here know that better than anybody. We have to fight for it, constantly. As Americans, we *have* to know its value."

Hunter stared into the eyes of each man seated at the table, then looked downward. "For me, it's simple. If one person in the world is not free, then no one is entirely free."

Every man in the room, in turn, nodded without the slightest hesitation.

"It's true," JT said quietly. "But you know what that means . . ."

They all did. They were going to war. Again. Yet another leaden silence enveloped them.

"So what the hell do we do?" JT finally asked.

For the first time in a while, Hunter's face actually brightened.

"I think I might have an idea," he replied.

Chapter Three

Fiji

Colonel Ubu Ikebani strode briskly through the lush garden of the heavily guarded compound, heading toward an elaborate grass hut.

The morning dew made the thousands of red flowers lining the path glisten in the dawn's early light, and their sweet scents perfumed the air. But Ikebani did not revel in this natural beauty. Instead, he was doing the best he could to suppress the fear boiling in the pit of his stomach. He had a right to be nervous—he was on his way to deliver important information to the man named Soho, the rather irrational Supreme Warlord of the Asian Mercenary Cult.

As each guard he passed snapped to attention and saluted briskly, Ikebani knew the authority he had over these men was absolutely nothing compared to the power of life and death that his leader inside the hut possessed. Ikebani reminded himself to stay on his toes, to keep his mind razor sharp. For though the news he was bringing was good, what mattered most of all was the mood of the man to whom he was delivering it. So as Ikebani raised his hand to knock on the wooden door of the hut, he steeled himself by saying a small prayer to whatever gods were listening, beseeching them to allow him to live to see the sunset.

21

* * *

"This is really unbelievable," Soho mumbled. He took another long drag on his hashish pipe and patted the head of the beautiful island girl who was kneeling between his legs performing the best fellatio he had ever experienced.

"Unbelievable," he moaned again as he raced faster and faster to a glorious climax. "Just incredible . . ."

But suddenly a sharp knocking on the door shattered his impending moment of bliss. His euphoria quickly disappeared. The island girl slowly raised her face up to Soho; it showed nothing but fear at what she thought was her failure to please her master.

He lightly stroked her cheek. "Don't worry, little one," Soho said benignly. "There will be another time for you."

She smiled, gathered up her grass skirt, and hurriedly tiptoed out of the room—before he could change his mind.

Soho leaned back and took another long drag on his pipe, causing the rock-sized chunk of hashish to glow brightly in the darkened room. Once again, he became lost in thought, pondering the events that had brought him to this moment in time. They seemed so far away and so long ago.

Okinawa, where he was stationed, was under heavy attack by the United Americans. He was a pilot of a Sukki Me-262 jet, and like everyone else on the island fortress, he was ready to die to protect the Supreme Commander of the Asian Mercenary Cult, the beautiful young woman with red hair named Aja. At the height of the battle, he was summoned to Shuri Castle to appear before her in her private quarters. Fully prepared to receive his suicide mission orders, she instead ordered Soho to drop his pants. Then this great woman commanded him to enter her. An ever faithful and obedient soldier, Soho obeyed immediately.

When he was done, she ordered him to fly to Island Facility Number Two. Then, to his utter astonishment, she plunged a sharp knife into her stomach, killing herself in the most horrible, ritualistic way.

He was in his jet within minutes, streaking through a hail of deadly gunfire thrown up at him from the ground and from the American aircraft carrier floating offshore. He eventually made it here, as ordered, to Military Manufacturing Facility Number Two, which wasn't a manufacturing facility at all. Rather, it was the tropical paradise of Fiji, a place devoid of the thick dense industrial smog that covered Okinawa; a place with very little military activity.

But it was here where things began to get *really* strange for him.

Upon his arrival, he was immediately treated by the island's top Cult military brass as *their* Supreme Commander. His jet, the Me-262, was painted a sickly pink and mounted on stilts at the edge of the cliff overlooking the main beach. It was covered with fresh flower petals and multicolored blossoms. Six smoking urns were placed around it, their firepots constantly billowing cinnamon incense that mingled with the smoke from the five hundred candles that also surrounded the jet and which burned twenty-four hours a day.

But that was not all.

Hundreds of beautiful island women were instantly put at his disposal to do with as he pleased. Alcohol flowed like water; the drugs, the best in Asia, were plentiful. Incredible feasts of wild game, fruits, and vegetables were brought to him whenever he wanted. He lived like a king—in fact, he *was* their king. But despite the royal treatment and their attendant pleasures, many things still troubled him.

One was the disturbing memory of Aja, who, right before she killed herself, seemed to transform from a bloodthirsty leader into a young innocent girl. From the moment he had landed on this island—an island where his every whim was catered to—another thought had constantly replayed in his mind, over and over again: *"Why me?*" Why had he been chosen to be the Supreme Commander of the Asian Mercenary Cult?

But what had bothered him the most was the distinct feeling that he was no longer sure of his own identity. As time went on, he felt less in control of his destiny. In reflection, this feeling seemed to begin right after he'd completed his coupling with Aja—it was almost as if some being had entered *him* as well. At first he thought maybe it was the drugs, or the booze, or the constant sexual pleasures that he enjoyed so often since arriving on Fiji. But now, he had no idea what was happening to him. It was as if someone—or something—had stolen his very soul from him.

Even stranger, it was bothering him less and less as the days went by.

Another loud rap at the front door broke Soho away from his thoughts.

"Enter!" he barked.

Colonel Ikebani double-timed into the hut, stepped before Soho, and gave a smart salute. Soho returned the gesture by exhaling a cloud of hashish smoke right into the Colonel's face.

"Colonel Ikebani reporting, sir!"

Soho did not respond. He simply sat there, taking his time, looking the soldier up and down, much to the discomfort of Ikebani. Then he reached over, lifted up a pitcher and refilled his coconut cup with a sweet alcoholic drink.

"Would you like a drink, Colonel?" Soho politely asked.

"No thank you, sir, I'm on duty." he replied, hoping that his answer would please his leader.

Soho grunted, and then drank the entire contents of the coconut cup in one long swig. He put the cup down, wiped his mouth with his sleeve, folded his arms across his chest, and looked up at the Cult officer.

"Well?"

"A radio message for you, sir. It just came in over the

secure frequency." Ikebani produced a red envelope, sealed with black tape, and handed it to Soho.

Soho looked at the envelope and the words TOP SECRET stamped across its front. He wondered why they constantly bothered him with this crap instead of leaving him alone so that he could enjoy himself. He snatched the envelope out of Ikebani's trembling hand, tore it open, and quickly scanned the decoded cable. He then looked back up at the officer.

"You thought *this* was important enough to disturb me?" he hissed.

"Ahhh, yes . . . sir." Ikebani stammered.

"Well, Colonel," Soho corrected him. "You were wrong."

Ikebani's small prayer was indeed granted by the gods. He *did* live to see the sunset. But it was only after being tied to a post at the edge of the cliff, partially skinned, and left as a delicacy for the scavenger birds. By the time the sun finally dipped below the horizon, Ikebani was quite nearly picked to death. He was grateful then for the cold steel blade that was finally drawn across his throat.

He did not live long enough, however, to see the people who sent what he thought was such an important message. For one hour after Ikebani died, two Fire Bats nuclear-armed submarines broke surface in the island's inner harbor.

Chapter Four

Edwards Air Force Base
Southern California
Three weeks later

The A-37 Dragonfly appeared as a dot on the eastern horizon, its silver body glistening in the rising sun.

The small jet circled the huge airfield once, then touched down for a picture perfect landing on the longest runway in the world.

Less than a minute later, the Dragonfly rolled up to its hardstand and stopped, its canopy open. General Dave Jones, Commander-in-Chief of the United American Forces, unhitched himself and climbed out.

"Been flying a desk too damned long," he said, taking off his crash helmet and rubbing his stiff arm muscles. "Got to get up more often."

A white HumVee pulled up to the Dragonfly just as the General stepped down to the hot asphalt. Hawk Hunter was at the wheel.

"Welcome to Edwards, General," Hunter said with a salute as Jones climbed into the passenger seat. The two men shook hands. "How was the trip out?"

"It's always a gas to fly out here," Jones said, studying the vast expanse of the high California desert. "I love this place. I saw everything from the X-15 to the Shuttle land here. Lot of aviation history has been made in these parts."

Hunter put the HumVee in gear. "Well, General," he said, with a wry smile. "I think we might be working on another chapter."

They took off with a squeal and were soon traveling across the acres of tarmac towards the back side of a long row of enormous hangers. It was there that Hunter was going to show Jones the fruition of the idea he first proposed back in San Diego nearly a month before.

Everyone in that conference room that day agreed that the Cult's rogue battleships posed an enormous threat not only to the defenseless people of the South Pacific, but to the world security as well, as shaky as it was. Yet they were also in agreement that to organize an American naval fleet, arm it, train its crews, and then sail halfway around the world to counter the Cult threat would take at least six months—much too long to do anybody any good. The problem called for the quickest response possible.

Hunter's idea that day was simple: if we can't float a force to check the Cult battleships, then let's fly one there instead.

Now, General Jones was about to see firsthand how that concept had been turned into reality.

The row of hangers seemed to stretch for more than a mile. Hunter swung the jeep around the corner of the end barn and brought it to a halt.

"Well, here they are, General," Hunter said after he killed the engine. "The First American Airborne Expeditionary Fleet."

Jones' eyes grew to twice their normal size. "This is incredible," he finally managed to say.

What he saw was a long row of gigantic C-5 Galaxy cargo jets. There were at least two dozen of them, sitting wingtip-to-wingtip in the hot California sun. Each one was surrounded by scores of support trucks and dozens of ground personnel, flight mechanics and cargo handlers, all working at a feverish pitch. Each one was painted in the strangest way.

The C-5 Galaxy was the king of long-range heavy military cargo transports. Indeed, it was the largest airplane ever built in the free world. Powered by four turbofan jet engines capable of 41,000 pounds of thrust, the C-5 could cruise at 440 knots and climb as high as 50,000 feet. The airplanes were simply enormous. At 250 feet long, they were a scant 50 feet shorter than a football field. Their wing span was 222 feet, encompassing 6,200 square feet in area. Most important, the C-5 could carry nearly 150 tons of equipment, military gear, weapons, people—whatever—in its gigantic hold.

Jones let out a long, low whistle.

These monstrous airplanes, dug up from all corners of the American continent by the well-known used-airplane salesmen, "Roy From Troy," were the cornerstones of Hunter's latest brainstorm.

They started coming in three weeks before, just hours after Hunter put the call out to Roy to find as many of the giant airships as possible. As always, the intrepid salesman came through; he began finding them everywhere. For five days they were landing at Edwards, some from as far away as Nova Scotia, others from the hellish sun of nearby Arizona. All were in various states of disrepair. Several were barely flyable; others were in such bad shape they could only be cannibalized for parts. Those that were repairable were slated to be overhauled from stem to stern, a massive undertaking considering the ever-shrinking timetable.

Hunter knew from the beginning the amount of technical service the C-5s would need would be awesome. So he put out a call for volunteers. From all across the country they came, some with the airplanes themselves, others by car or truck, some even on foot. All offered their services for free. From aeronautical engineers to those who only knew how to tighten a screw, each and every one of them had been put to work. Between the scorching desert heat, the cold nights and frequent dust storms, it made for back-breaking, dirty, hard labor.

Yet not one person dropped out.

But the sight of the long line of enormous cargo planes alone was not so mind-boggling for an old Air Force buck like Jones. Rather, it was the fact that each plane looked, well, . . . so *damn* different from anything he'd ever seen before.

"I never expected this," Jones said, actually rubbing his eyes in order to take it all in. "These things look like hot rods. . . ."

It was true. Each C-5 was done up in its own, individual design and color scheme. Some were subdued, some pretty garish. It made for either a treat, or a nightmare, for the eyes.

The first Galaxy was done up totally in black camouflage, except for its enormous nose which was painted over with a huge shark mouth, open and showing rows upon rows of sharp, deadly white teeth, similar to the nose art of the famous Flying Tigers of World War II fame.

The second C-5 was painted bright silver, with the designation NJ104 emblazoned on its fuselage and wings. The third airship was pearl white with broad red and blue stripes running along its hull and on top of its wings, and an immense decal of a football with the number "1" adhered to its tail.

The fourth C-5 was even stranger-looking: it was painted in yellow-tan with scroll designs and highly stylized lettering running from front to back. It looked like an airplane a circus would ride in—and that was the idea. Its name, printed in huge letters on the front, was "Bozo."

Further down the line, a C-5 was painted a lime green camouflage with a graphic nose illustration of a huge Cobra, mouth open, forked-tongue poised and ready to strike.

"It all started with the JAWs guys, sir," Hunter began to explain, pointing to the first in line Galaxy. "They'd been working on their airplane night and day, and the crew needed a diversion. They scared up some paint and designs and . . . well . . .

"Then when the others saw what JAWs did, everyone caught the bug."

Jones was quiet for a few moments. Then he said: "I don't know why, but I like it. Reminds me of the nose art on the B-17 Fortresses during World War Two. Shows individuality, but also unit pride."

Hunter let out a low whistle of relief. He wasn't quite certain how the rather straight-shooting senior officer would take to the elaborate detail work on the huge airplanes. Now, with the initial visual shock out of the way, he was able to get down to the serious business for which the enormous planes were readied.

They climbed out of the HumVee and began their tour on foot.

The first C-5 they passed—the one with the huge shark mouth on its nose—was being outfitted for the commando outfit known as JAWS. Originally a local police force from Johnstown, New York, JAWS was a twenty-man team that had evolved and expanded into a crack commando unit. Unlike other postwar militia, who tended to specialize in one particular fighting skill, the JAWS team was expert in many of them. From mountain climbing to scuba diving to night-parachuting to tunnel digging, these men were the best of the best. They were trained in getting in and doing the job on any kind of target, either hard or soft. Bunkers, fortresses, buildings, airfields, or any other obstacle were no match for the JAWS team. They had been very useful in the recent attack on Okinawa.

Jones could see crates upon crates of every kind of imaginable gear being loaded by a dozen forklifts into the cavernous hold of the JAWS Galaxy, including several tons of weapons and ammunition. With everything from machine pistols, SEMTEX charges, grenade launchers, and mortars, to anti-tank guns, flamethrowers, and small but heavily armed dune buggies, it was obvious the JAWS team was ready for anything.

Hunter and Jones walked down the line to the next C-5. It was the silver bullet plane that would carry the 100-man-strong 104th Battalion of the New Jersey National Guard—the best combat engineers who ever built *or* blew up a bridge. And the gear that was being assembled attested to that fact.

As Jones and Hunter walked past, they saluted Lieutenant Colonel Frank Geraci, the 104th's commanding officer. Another veteran of the recent Pacific campaign, Geraci was supervising the on-loading of bulldozers, pontoon bridge sections, and small cranes, as well as the tools of destruction—cases of TNT and SEMTEX, light and heavy machine guns, mortars, TOWS, and hundreds of small arms. Both Jones and Hunter appreciated the efficiency with which the engineers' huge plane was being loaded; there was literally no room to spare.

Hunter then brought Jones by the C-5 that belonged to the Football City Special Forces Rangers, now led by Major Donn Kurjan. Known to all by his code name "Lazarus," Kurjan had been jumped in rank from lieutenant because of the heroic role he played in ending the Fourth Reich's occupation of America about a year before.

Parked along side the red-and-blue-striped-C-5—which was christened "Football One"—were more than twenty trucks and several already overworked crews handling case after case of weapons. Heavy machine guns, mortars, howitzers, shoulder-launched Stingers, Blowpipes, Javelins, cases of grenades, hundreds of M-16s, and thousands of 5.56-mm rounds were slowly filling up the belly of the huge transport. The men of Football City Special Forces were experts with all of these weapons. Serving primarily as a SWAT-type Rapid Deployment Force, these professionals were trained to go anywhere, at anytime, to get the job done fast and then fight their way out. Their black combat fatigues and black helmeted visors gave them the appearance of space aliens. For many of their enemies, it was the last image they ever saw.

They continued their walk down the flight line.

"Do these look familiar, sir?" Hunter asked Jones.

Before Jones were parked two C-5s with the unlikely names of *Bozo* and *Nozo*. These two customized Galaxys were the result of the unconventional imagination of their close friend, the late, great Mike Fitzgerald, many years before.

The idea was based on something called Puff, the Magic Dragon. During the Vietnam conflict, the U.S. Air Force had mounted Gatling guns, capable of firing 4000 rounds per minute, on the left side windows of C-47 cargo planes, creating a totally new kind of aerial gunship. These cargo-to-combat hybrids were highly successful, especially for long-time loitering over combat sites. Their characteristic long streams of tracer fire made them look like flying, fire-breathing dragons.

What Fitzgerald did was take the "Puff" idea one giant step further. He had armed the C-5.

Nozo had a complement of no less than twenty-one GE GAU-8/A 30-mm Avenger cannons sticking out of twenty-one hatches located on the left side of the C-5. Each Avenger was capable of firing 4000 rounds per minute, using cannon shells made of depleted uranium, a projectile which spontaneously ignited upon striking its target. And while the outside of the C-5 named *Nozo* bristled with cannon barrels, the inside contained a highly automated, totally computer-driven firing system as well as a remarkable track-feeding system that housed literally miles of belted ammunition.

After seeing the critics put to shame after his idea worked, Fitzgerald pushed it to the max with a second huge gunship, the aptly named "Bozo." He started with six GE Gatling guns. Then he had mounted five MK-19 automatic grenade launchers, complemented by a single Italian-made AP/AV 700, three-barrel multiple-grenade launcher. After that, he got serious—and a little crazy. First, there was the Soltam 120-mm mobile field gun, which fired IMI illuminating rounds, as well as rocket-assisted charges. Then he added two Royal Ordnance 105 mm field artillery pieces and three German-made Rheinmetal 20 mm converted antiaircraft guns. And as a final *piece de resistance*, Fitz installed a 17-ton West German-made LARS II 110 mm Multiple Rocket Launcher, capable of firing 36 six-foot-long high explosive-filled rockets in less than 20 seconds. A specially fitted "rear-end blast" deflector piped the backfire down and out of the airplane. Even after witnessing the destructive powers of these planes in battle after battle, the sight, sound and carnage that they produced was still quite unbelievable.

And in turn, these two airplanes had been Hunter's inspiration for this great air fleet now assembling.

Two Bell AH-1 attack helicopters sat nestled inside the next in line C-5, their main rotors disassembled and attached to racks that lined the inside of the hold. This plane, christened "Big Snake," would be used by the Cobra Brothers, a freelance attack copter outfit with close ties to the United American Armed Forces. Mounted under each of the Cobra gunships was enough firepower to fight a small war—M20/19 rocket launchers, a TAT turret boasting one M-28 minigun and one 40-mm grenade launcher, double racks of QUAD Hellfire missiles, and four M-16 7.62-mm minigun pods. The Cobra Brothers had also rigged under the choppers special platforms to handle Sidewinders, Stingers, and TOW launchers. Besides spare weapons and cases upon cases of ammunition, their C-5 also held a complete maintenance shop with every conceivable spare part to repair combat damage or to adapt the helicopters for specialized missions. Hunter pointed out to Jones the crew in a cherry picker putting the finishing touches on the painting of the Cobra's fangs, bared for the kill.

"Just the sight of that coming at them would make anyone head for the hills," Jones remarked.

The general, who had been noting the special function, cargo, or particular mission that each plane they passed was being readied for, was astounded at what Roy From Troy had provided in such a short time. Of course, it hadn't been cheap. But you get what you pay for, and usually Roy's merchandise was good quality. The general was also amazed at the level of expertise and imagination of the members of the ground crews who customized, reconfigured or rehabilitated each of these planes for their special purposes. And he was impressed by how hard they all had been working. Everything that Hunter had promised, right down to the last detail, was there.

They continued down the flight line.

The next C-5 had the word "Crunchtime" painted garishly along the length of both sides of its fuselage. Piloted by "Crunch" O'Malley, recently back from another long-range recon mission, the Galaxy was basically a flying freighter carrying any weapon, gun, missile or rocket launcher that had been begged, borrowed, stolen, or that just plain didn't fit into any of the other C-5's cargo holds. It also carried extra fuel in special rubber bladders attached to the inside of its cargo hold.

The two Galaxys beyond *Crunchtime* were Football Two and Three. They were exact copies of the red-and-blue-striped Football One, and both as well were under the command of the Football City Special Forces Rangers.

Hunter and Jones then walked by two Galaxys that were surrounded with M-1A1 Abrams tanks, M-3 Bradleys, M-113 APCs, and M-198 155-mm howitzers. Hunter pointed out to the General the operational portholes that were being cut through the sides of the transport to accommodate either the 105-mm guns of the Abrams tanks, the 25-mm cannons and 7.62-mm machine guns of the Bradleys, the 12.7-mm M-2HB Browning machine guns of the APCs, or the big bore 155-mm barrels of the artillery pieces. As Hunter explained, these guns were not only to be used on the ground, but were also to provide covering fire from the air as well.

The general could see that much was still to be done to achieve one hundred percent readiness on these particular airplanes.

"From here on down the flight line, the reconfigurations are still going on," Hunter said, confirming the general's observation. "We've got nine airplanes close to ready, the rest are in various states of completion."

The next C-5 was still in the process of being converted into a flying hospital, complete with operating rooms; another was being transformed into an aerial machine shop/maintenance service plane.

"The gear in there and the boys who'll run it can repair just about anything," Hunter explained.

Their walking tour continued. The next three transports belonged to the 1st American Airborne, led by Captain Lamont "Catfish" Johnson, a towering black man who formerly played defensive end for the San Diego Chargers of the old NFL and was now commander of this airborne outfit. More than fifteen hundred soldiers of this airborne corps were feverishly working at hundreds of long wooden tables, folding parachutes and cleaning weapons, while over a dozen quartermasters inventoried and oversaw the storing of the tons of materials needed to support that many men. Inside the planes, crews were diligently installing an interior deck that would add a second level to accommodate the paratroopers.

The next three Galaxys, painted in sea-gray camouflage, looked dull by comparison. And there was nothing remarkable going on inside their great hulls.

But the work going underneath those C-5s was what Hunter wanted to show General Jones.

They walked up closer to one of them where a very unusual operation was taking place.

"What the hell is this?" Jones asked.

Two Alpha Jets were being painstakingly attached to the airplane's underbelly by a ground crew.

The Alpha Jet-E was a small but powerful trainer. It had a maximum speed of 620 mph, and a range of 273 miles. When configured as a fighter, it boasted one 30 mm cannon and could carry Sidewinders. It was the perfect plane for a very unusual mission.

Hunter knew that the long range force being assembled here could not afford the luxury of air cover. So learning from history, he took the idea from the time back in the 1920s, when bi-planes were attached to the underbelly of U.S. Navy blimps. Blimps could stay up almost forever, and their operating range was far greater than any fighter plane built at that time. But in wartime they were vulnerable to attack from enemy aircraft. By bringing their own fighters along, they wouldn't compromise their long-range capability, and at the same time still benefit from a fighter's assistance when necessary—just as this modern great air fleet would now.

The Alpha's crew consisted of two pilots. But instead of having to have to sit the entire downtime in their cockpit, as the pilots under the blimps had to do, the Edwards' mechanics had come up with an ingenious design. Two flexible, accordionlike loading shoots, attached to the underbelly of the C-5, stretched down to cover the open cockpits of the both Alpha. When the time came, the pilots of the Alphas would simply climb down the flexible internal ladders, close their canopy, and then release the accordion shoots by the gravity switch inside their cockpit. The shoots would then retract back up against the belly of the transport. Then explosive bolts would be set off, breaking the Alphas free of the struts and its mother ship. Docking was a little more tricky. After a system of hooks and clamps were deployed from the belly of the transport, the Alpha would fly under the C-5 and match its cruising speed. Then, much as in the procedure for in-flight refueling, the Alpha would nuzzle into this set of braces and secure itself.

After a quick lockup procedure, the accordion shoot would be lowered for the pilots to climb back up into the hold.

Hunter then brought the general past five more Galaxys in various stages of readiness. Three of these C-5s were being converted into aerial refueling planes, each capable of holding almost 26,500 gallons of jet fuel. The other two were being outfitted to carry tons of ammunition; bullets, bombs, rockets, missiles and mortar shells needed for resupply.

But the tour was not yet over.

They finally came to the last airship on the line. Even though the general had gotten used to the whacky paint jobs on the previous cargo planes, he was not ready for this one.

A painting of a larger-than-life-sized, very attractive, but *very* naked young lady graced the enormous nose of the Galaxy. And how she was posing was exactly the reason this C-5 was named "Triple X."

Formerly called "The Empire State," it had once belonged to the New York National Guard.

The general did not say a word. But Hunter quickly brought him around to show him the interior of the airplane. There he pointed out how the work was going on to convert the hold to carry smaller aircraft.

The sound of an approaching fuel truck caught Hunter's attention and he flagged it down. He and Jones climbed up into the cab and caught a ride back up the half-mile-long flight line to where the white HumVee waited.

Climbing into the Hummer, Hunter and the General then drove out to an isolated part of the runway.

Cutting the engine, Hunter produced a thermos of coffee and two cups.

"Everyone's done a great job," Jones said, pouring a splash of cognac from a small flask into their cups. "A *hell* of a job." The general then stared off in the distance and slowly shook his head.

37

Hunter had seen that look before; he knew bad news was incoming.

Since the big meeting in San Diego, the United American forces had commenced a twenty-four-hour-a-day satellite monitoring service to both watch and listen all over the South Pacific for further activity of the battleship fleet. The United American's top intelligence groups were using these photos and recorded radio transmissions in conjunction with computer analysis to attempt to predict a pattern for the enemy fleet. The ships *were* seen from time to time, but not often—and mostly during inclement weather or nighttime. They were sometimes traveling in packs, sometimes in pairs, sometimes alone. Sometimes they lit up the air waves with ship-to-ship chatter. Other times, they were silent for days. So far, the strategy didn't really make sense.

Jones swallowed back a jolt of spiked hot coffee. "We've got confirmed reports that five more islands have been hit—just as hard as Xmas," the general told him. "We've been feeding the Cray computers every piece of information imaginable: fuel ranges, weather conditions, tides, you name it, but their movement still appears totally random."

"Maybe they're just nuts," Hunter said, taking a swig of the laced joe. "Maybe they're all drugged up and they're just out on a killing spree. No motive. *No* strategy."

Jones gave a quick nod. "I would tend to agree with you, if not for something that we learned just yesterday."

He handed Hunter a single sheet of yellow Telex paper. It was covered with a series of numbers, which to the untrained eye seemed to be just random binary codes. However, Hunter quickly detected a startling pattern.

"Communications satellite readouts," he said to Jones who confirmed with a nod. "Same message over and over."

"Exactly," Jones replied. "It's all in two-digit numerical code, but I'll tell you the translation. It reads: 'Mayday. Mayday. Thousands killed. Can't hold out much longer. Mayday. Mayday.' "

Hunter let out a long breath. There was something frightening about the stark SOS, repeated over and over and over again, perhaps as many as 1000 times just on this page alone.

"Where's it coming from?" he asked Jones.

The general took another sip of his coffee. "We're not exactly sure." he said slowly. "But it's being transmitted from somewhere around the South China Sea, maybe a little further west. Our Signal Intelligence guys are still trying to nail it down."

Hunter just shook his head. "It's got to be linked with the battleships," he said. "Be too much of a coincidence if it wasn't."

"I'm sure its connected," Jones replied. "But there's more."

He took out another piece of Telex paper. "While the SigInt guys were studying the signal, they routinely put the encoded message through the Cray, figuring something in the patterning itself could help in narrowing down the location of the satellite uplink.

"And?"

"And, they found something even more disturbing," Jones replied slowly. "They found that someone was actually tampering with the uplink channel, affecting its transmission time and level, from *another* uplink station relatively nearby. They weren't blocking the Mayday call, or throwing a lot of electronic fuzz around it. Rather, they wanted it to go out—along with their own little message."

Hunter was stumped. "A message like what?"

"Like this," Jones replied, handing Hunter the second sheet of paper. "The frequency of the tampering had its own pattern—it was not at all random or chaotic. They would simply delay the Mayday call for anywhere from one to ten seconds. By doing this, and by using the same binary code, the tampering agent was able to insert their own message in between the Mayday calls. A message that could be understood only by someone looking for it. The message is on that piece of paper. . . ."

Hunter opened the folded sheet and saw it held the same single sentence over and over again.

It read: "Victor is alive."

Dusk

Hunter sat on the summit of the isolated mesa, staring at the sun as it slowly dipped below the horizon.

There was a fire in his heart, unlike any he'd felt in a long time. The days he'd spent on the deserted Hawaiian island *had* given him time to think—but maybe it was too much time. On one hand, he'd convinced himself that despite all the misery that America had gone through in the past few years, there was something to celebrate: the American continent was once again free of foreign invaders.

But on the other hand, he knew the misery index was way off the meter at other places around the globe. The United American Command regularly received reliable reports that Europe was in the throes of periodic anarchy and chaos, and that Africa, South America, and the Middle East were even worse. On the greater Asian continent, China had retreated back to its mysterious, xenophophic ways, as had most of the countries on the subcontinent. And, as much of central Japan had been left in flames and ruin by the recent campaign of United American air strikes, that country was hurtling into anarchy and destabilization.

So while America was for the moment, stable and free, the rest of planet was suffering in most places.

Hunter did not believe in the randomness of events. He'd seen too much—*experienced* too much—to buy in to the notion that the cosmos just grooved along in its own unguided way. No, he believed everything that happened—big or small, significant or not—was related to something and everything else. Everything had a meaning; every event a cause and an effect. That's the way it was in deep physics—and that's the way he believed it was in deep life.

This belief had led him to another conclusion long ago; Evil was not random. It was not something floating in the air, something that just happened to fall on unsuspecting heads at any given moment. No—evil was a bomb whose fuse was usually lit; evil was unnatural. As such, evil could be personified.

And at that moment, it appeared that evil's new name was "Victor."

Victor, aka "Viktorvich Robotov," aka "Lucifer," was a walking, living, breathing human plague—or at least he used to be. Just where he came from, no one was really sure. The most reliable bio said he was a former KGB agent who never got with the program after his ilk was put out to pasture. He first came to America during the massive foreign invasion which touched off the so-called "Circle War." Once defeated by Hunter and his allies, Victor fled to the Middle East, where he adopted the persona of "Lucifer."

Gathering a huge army in the Saudi Arabian desert, Victor attempted to invade the Mediterranean countries via the Suez Canal and relight what was informally called World War III. It took Hunter and a band of fearless RAF pilots to thwart Victor's plans, refloating a disabled nuclear aircraft carrier and towing a small, but effective air armada to Suez where they delayed Lucifer's Legion just long enough for a much larger Free World-sponsored mercenary army to arrive.

Hunter's final confrontation with Victor happened shortly afterwards in the middle of the Arabian desert. To stand face-to-face with the man was to experience pure terror. Victor looked like every person's idea of the devil: sinister eyes and nose, a thin mouth, a stiletto mustache and

41

goatee. Hunter was about to shackle the superterrorist in order to bring him back to America for trial when suddenly a shot rang out. His back, throat, and chest literally blown apart, Victor fell dead at Hunter's feet. Off in the distance, two men armed with long-range rifles, wearing Nazi swastika armbands, hastily drove away.

Hunter had checked Victor's body for a pulse and had found none. He didn't bother to bury the body—vermin like Victor did not deserve a final resting place. Better that the buzzards and the insects eat him.

So on that day, Hunter thought they were finally rid of the human death sentence—but in the past few months, he wasn't too sure. Strange things happened during the recent campaign against the Cult's headquarters in Japan, and the subsequent battle on Okinawa. Little things—a stray radio message here, a sudden disappearance of enemy forces there, bloody messages left on a wall. To a trained eye, these signaled that not everything was kosher with the cosmos.

And there were larger things, too. Entire armies usually don't sacrifice themselves blindly as the Cult did at Pearl Harbor—especially if they were made up almost entirely of paid mercenaries. But that's exactly what happened in the final battle of the recent Pacific campaign. The top staff of the United American Armed Forces was savvy enough to know that when peculiar things happened involving large military forces, then some kind of extraordinary control—be it drugs, brainwashing or both—was probably in play. Not many people had the power to control large numbers of paid soldiers, but Victor had done just that during the Circle War—and in retrospect, his psychic fingerprints were all over the final actions of the Cult grounds forces in the more recent Pacific war.

And then there was the case of Yaz.

Stan Yastrewski was a charter member of the United American Armed Forces Command. His duties usually involved troubleshooting or performing special missions at the bequest of General Jones. During the Pacific campaign, Yaz, a former submarine officer, found himself in charge of the American aircraft carrier, the USS *Mike Fitzgerald.*

While returning from a long-range recon mission, Hunter's airplane had been caught in a typhoon. Running low on fuel and nearly out of electrical power, his F-16XL's nose cameras popped on momentarily just as he was entering the murderous swirl. Some time later, when Yaz reviewed this footage, a vision on the screen literally knocked him into a life-threatening coma, from which miraculously emerged weeks later.

No one ever really figured out what happened to Yaz—why he went into his death sleep, and why he just as quickly woke up. All that was certain was the vision which had triggered the extreme hypnotic suggestion had been the enormous image of a face, possibly projected onto the storm clouds by lasers.

That face, Yaz had said, was that of Victor.

The videotape was now locked in Jones' safe at his office in the Pentagon, under strict 24-hour guard. No one had viewed it since Yaz's nasty experience, and probably no one ever would.

So Victor—or, at least, some incarnation of him— seemed to be back in the world. And nothing would be right again on the planet until this presence was eradicated.

This was why Hunter's mind was now pulsating with rage. In addition to all the misery Victor had unleashed on the planet's population, Hunter also had a personal motive for finding this devil. Several years before, at the height of the Circle War, Victor had kidnapped Dominique, Hunter's lovely girlfriend. In a twisted example of propaganda and mind control, Victor had photographed Dominique in near-pornographic poses and distributed these pictures to his troops, along with vast quantities of mind-altering drugs. The powerful combination of the drugs and her

43

stunning X-rated beauty was enough to make his legions follow Victor anywhere.

So was the superterrorist dead or not? Hunter didn't know. His fingers still stung where he had felt for the man's pulse that day in the desert and found none. But on the other hand, if there was anyone able to convincingly fake his own death, it was Victor. Finding him alive would be the equivalent of finding Hitler alive—maybe even worse.

But there was one thing for certain: someone, somewhere around the South China Sea wanted anyone who was listening to at least *believe* Victor was still alive. And with the recent atrocities committed by the Cult battleships in the same general area, Hunter was convinced something was up—something of cosmically evil proportions.

And he was equally convinced that it would be up to him, and the men of the United American C-5 air fleet, to attempt to stop it.

He took his eyes off the fading sun and turned back to the airbase. The lights were just coming on in the massive hangars, and he could see the outlines of the twenty-five multicolored Galaxys. Time was running out—he could *feel* it. And while the original plan called for all twenty-five of the C-5s to fly to the Pacific together, Hunter knew now that there wouldn't be enough time for that.

They had to go with what they had—or forever lose the chance to do anyone any good.

Chapter Five

The next morning dawned hot and sunny, with low winds and a minimum of dust being blown around.

It was perfect flying weather.

There were nine C-5s warming up on the runway in three groups of three. The first flight consisted of the gunships *Nozo* and *Bozo,* plus the Football City Special Forces Rangers airship, *Football One.* The second flight held the JAWs plane, the New Jersey National Guard Engineers' *NJ104,* and *Football Two.* The third flight was made up of *Crunchtime,* the Cobra Brothers' *Big Snake,* and *Football Three.*

Their engines whining up to full power, their holds jampacked with up to 150 tons of men, weapons, equipment and supplies each, the air fleet made for an impressive, if gaudy, sight.

General Jones and Stan "Yaz" Yastrewski were waiting by a HumVee parked at the head of the column of Galaxys. Behind them were the thousand or so remaining troops and mechanics. Hunter had just completed his walk around *Bozo,* the airplane he would be piloting along with Ben Wa. The Wingman walked over to Jones and Yaz and gave them a crisp salute.

"Everything green, Hawk?" the General asked.

"As green as it's ever going to be," Hunter replied. "If

45

we forgot anything, I'm sure you can send it over with the next wave."

He grinned slightly upon making the statement—it was an inside joke. With the rush to get the first nine airplanes in the air, they all knew that there probably wouldn't be any second wave. The other C-5s would leave Edwards and head for the Far East as soon as they became operational, and this meant individually, if at all.

"For the record, this is a great undertaking," Jones told him, "This country has always stood for freedom, for all people. Just because we've been through our own upheavals, that doesn't mean we can forget exactly what America—and Americans—are all about."

Hunter nodded. "I couldn't agree more, sir . . ."

They briskly shook hands. "Good luck, Hawk . . ."

Hunter saluted once again. "Thanks, General."

He turned to Yaz. "Wish you were coming, old buddy," Hunter said, putting on his crash helmet. "Could be quite a trip."

Yaz just shook his head. With his successful rehabilitation from the hypnotic shock more than a month old, he certainly felt strong enough to go. Yet Jones had forbidden it.

"Don't worry, Hawk," Yaz replied, his voice almost cracking. "I'll be in the sequel."

Hunter shook his hand and then turned and ran out to *Bozo*.

"And tell JT to keep it in his pants!" Yaz yelled after him.

Ten minutes later, Hunter gunned the four massive engines on *Bozo* and ran them up to full power. Slowly, the huge Galaxy gunship began to move down Edwards' long runway.

To the thunderous applause of those assembled, it rose up and off cleanly, followed close behind by *Nozo*, with JT at the controls and then *Football One*. The *JAWs-NJ104-Football Two* troika went next, with *Crunchtime*, *Big Snake* and *Football Three* right on its tail.

The air fleet formed up high above Edwards. Then as one, it roared overhead in a three-chevron formation, turning west, toward the other side of the planet. Toward the unknown.

In pursuit of a ghost. . . .

It took more than twenty minutes for the roar of their engines to completely die away.

Chapter Six

Fiji

Supreme Commander Soho could hardly hold the chisel steady, his hands were shaking so much.

What is happening to me? he heard a voice whisper inside his left ear. *Am I dying? Or am I just going insane?*

It was close to midnight and Soho's ears had been ringing all day. On the table in front of him was a chunk of black Turkish hashish the size of a coconut. In his left hand was a large cold chisel; in his right, a heavy ballpeen hammer. He'd been trying to chip off a smokable piece of the hash for what seemed like hours—but his strength was so depleted, all he could get were slivers, most not big enough for even a couple of puffs.

And he needed more than that.

Finally, he summoned up enough strength to drive the chisel into the center of the hash block, chopping off an ice-cube-size piece. This was more to his liking. He took the chunk of hash over to his small wood-fired stove and dipped it into a pan of clear liquid that had been simmering on one of the burners for hours. This liquid was pure opium. He watched, eyes watering in anticipation, as the hash began to grow in size, absorbing the morphia.

Five minutes later, the chunk of hash was twice its original size. Soho retrieved it from the opium soup, put it inside his water pipe and quickly began toking on it, keeping it lit by means of a hand-held propane torch.

Five minutes of opium sucking followed. Then, suddenly, the candles inside his hut exploded and it became dark as night. Soho found himself on a hill, his mouth full of dirt, his eyes watering, his breathing labored. There were scores of dead bodies all around him, twisted in ghoulish poses. He was looking down on a steel graveyard—there were crashed airplanes everywhere. And there were soldiers, dressed in strange garb, carrying flaming acetylene torches, cutting into the dead airplanes and causing them to shriek with ungodly mechanical horror. . . .

Soho opened his eyes; he was shaking from head to toe. What was the problem? Too much opium? Or not enough? He wasn't sure. . . .

He got to his feet, his knees close to buckling, and headed for the door, pipe and torch in hand. Bursting out into the dark night, he found two guards standing next to the entranceway.

"They . . . they are still here, sir," one stuttered in mumbling Japanese. "They are still on the island . . ."

Soho looked at the man queerly. His face seemed to be melting away. "Who are you talking about? Who is still here?"

The guard gulped loudly. "The men . . . from the Fire Bats, sir . . ."

Soho was stumped. He had no idea what the man was talking about.

He turned to the second guard; he was trembling now as much as the first.

"Explain this . . ."

The second guard bowed quickly, letting out an involuntary grunt. Eyes down, he began to speak.

"The submarines that sail beneath the heavenly oceans arrived here a few weeks ago, Your Highness," the guard began. "Just yesterday, the men within finally came ashore, and by your supreme wisdoms, you ordered everyone on the island confined to their quarters—even yourself, oh, Great One."

Soho wiped a bit of drool cascading from his mouth.

"Why did I do that?" he asked the guard.

The man grunted again. He could barely breathe, he was so frightened. "The men from the boats that sail the heavenly ocean said they had work to do here. Very important work. That is why they finally came ashore. That is why they could not be disturbed."

"Even by me?" Soho asked, his feet suddenly feeling like they were growing roots into the ground.

The man grunted a third time. "By your orders, your Supreme Beingness . . ."

Soho considered this for a moment. "That doesn't sound like me," he said, to which both guards grunted.

"And all our people are inside their houses?" he asked.

"All—except the ones we shot. . . ."

"Shot?" Soho asked.

"On your orders, sir," the first guard said, finally summoning up enough courage to talk. "Anyone outside their hut while the men from the heavenly submarines were here was to be shot. On sight. With no warning . . ."

"And you followed those orders?"

"Yes, sir. Two women. An hour ago. They were bringing flowers to you, sir."

"And you killed them?"

"Aye, sir," came the reply.

Soho thought for another moment. His arms were going numb. Were the fingers falling off his hands?

Suddenly, he was enraged. "And I suppose you also used acetylene torches to kill these women?" he demanded of the stunned guards, the drool turning to foam at the corners of his mouth. "And did you also burn their wings off? Their propellars? Their wheels?"

The guards looked at him. *What was he talking about?*

They didn't know—nor would they find out. Soho staggered away, the small torch cranked up to high, the chunk of opium-dipped hash glowing in the dark night.

He stumbled through the beautiful floral gardens, down the pathway to the cliff and past the body of Colonel Ikebani, still rotting on its blood-smeared wooden post.

Soho had decided he was going to fly—just fly away. He would have to do this without an airplane   all the airplanes had been butchered by the soldiers with the torches. No—he would have fly by himself, using his arms as wings, his feet as rudders. Getting airborne would be no problem. In fact, if he tried hard enough, he might make it all the way back to Okinawa.

He fell twice before making it to the cliff. Here was the Shrine of the Sukki jet, the hideously pink airplane that he may or may not have flown to the island a couple months before. There were at least 500 lit candles surrounding it as usual, and its cinnamon fire pots were going full blast.

But something was different here.

He strained to focus his opium-soaked eyeballs and believed he could see four or five figures huddled around the jet. They were poking inside the cockpit, fussing with something, quietly murmuring among themselves. They were dressed oddly—their neon blue uniforms were actually glowing in the moonless night. There seemed to be halos around their heads. They may even have been floating several inches above the ground.

Soho approached, his torch still ignited. Suddenly one of the men looked up at him.

". . . and you are?" he asked in very heavily accented English.

Soho straightened up. Now all five men in glowing blue suits and white halos were looking at him.

"I am the Supreme Commander of the Asian Mercenary Cult," Soho told them in his own severely fractured English. "As such, I am your god . . ."

The men laughed. "Sure you are," one replied.

They returned to their work, completely ignoring Soho. This infuriated him.

"That is my airplane!" he screamed, "And you are trying to cut it to pieces!"

The men continued their work inside the Sukki cockpit, looking all the world like surgeons, calmly operating on a patient.

"You will not take a torch to my airplane!" Soho screamed at the top of his lungs.

Suddenly one of the men was right in front of him. Soho stared into his eyes. They seemed to be pure white. The man's hair was long and blond, like that of an angel—or maybe a Viking. And his face—it seemed to be glowing. And the halo looked quite real, too.

The man smiled. He looked at Soho's torch and suddenly the flame went out. He looked at his water pipe and suddenly the hash stopped glowing. Soho was now trembling—and it was not just from the opium.

"I am ... I am your commander ..." Soho somehow managed to blurt out. "You ... you must obey me ..."

The man was smiling so benignly, it frightened Soho even more.

"You are nothing but a lowly pilot," the strange being told him, his face but two inches from Soho's. "Now just follow orders ..."

At that moment, Soho opened his eyes.

He was alone on the cliff. It was close to dawn. And all of the candles around the Sukki jet had gone out.

The next morning

The small runway on the western tip of Fiji was lined with hundreds of natives, all of them bedecked in flowers, grass hats, and leis.

Gentle string music wafted through the early morning air, broken only by the occasional blast from a conch shell.

Off in the distance, a choir of children could be heard softly chanting.

The Sukki jet was at the far end of the runway, a new coat of sickly pink paint still drying on its wings. Soho was there, a cup of opium-laced alcohol in one hand, the everpresent hash pipe in the other, sitting on a throne carried by six of the strongest natives on the island.

The young girl who had been living in Soho's hut was also there; her parents were at her side, weeping openly. They were convinced that she was about to be killed by Soho's men as a kind of sacrifice to the higher Cult gods—whoever the hell they were.

A team of Cult flight mechanics was standing around the Sukki—they hadn't done a stitch of work in months, and now they were wondering how an airplane designed more than a half century before could be returned to flying condition without benefit of any specs, design plans, or schematics.

But as it would turn out, getting the old Me-262 down from its shrine on the cliff would be their biggest task. Because though they didn't know why exactly, once the airplane was on the runway, it was quite capable of taking off, all by itself.

Soho clapped his hands twice and two aides brought forward a wooden bucket full of ice water. On his command, they threw it directly into his face, brutally reviving him. He stepped from the portable throne and with wobbly knees, approached the Sukki.

He was dressed in a ragged flight suit, with a leather cap and goggles—the same uniform he was wearing when he arrived on Fiji in the Sukki, several months before.

The music drifted away, and a light breeze came up on the airstrip. Soho looked at the assembled natives and the small troop of Cult soldiers lined up at attention behind them. Once again, a question which had been bouncing around in his debilitated brain since he first made Fiji came back to him: *Who the hell are all these people?*

He staggered over to the Sukki, barely taking notice of the young girl and her distraught parents. He nodded to one of the flight mechanics who took a deep breath. Reading from a small piece of parchment containing the barely decipherable scrawl of Soho, this man reached inside the jet's cockpit and pushed a single red button. Suddenly the Sukki's pair of wing-mounted engines roared to life simultaneously. This even surprised Soho; despite his drugged-out state, he knew that by normal procedure, the Sukki's jets were started very slowly and always one at a time.

But this lucid thought passed quickly. He took another titanic suck on the hash pipe and washed it down with a long swig of his opium-and-alcohol mixture. He knew there was some kind of ceremony over which he was now supposed to preside, but the details of it were lost long ago. The jet was running; it was obviously meant to take off. But to where? And with who?

He didn't have the slightest idea.

But the voices inside his left ear began speaking again, and in one ragged heartbeat, it all seemed suddenly very clear to him.

He smiled and beckoned the young girl to his side. She was dressed in a flowing white gown, her hair braided with flower stems and sprinkled with pine-rose petals. She was trembling—and with good reason. Soho reached out and caressed the young girl's hair. Then he pushed her up against the side of the jet, and to the stunned silence of all, engaged in a quick, exhausting round of intercourse with her.

When he was finished, he drained his coconut cup, and then immediately threw up on himself. The young girl's parents were crying openly now—they were certain their daughter's life was about to come to a grisly end.

But they were wrong.

With the Sukki's engines still screaming, Soho boosted the young girl up into the jet's cockpit, and then threw two levers. One unlocked the jet's brakes, the other lowered its canopy. In one swift motion, the jet began rolling down the runway, the startled young girl its only passenger. To the surprise of all, it lifted off and climbed almost straight up, as if it was under some kind of otherworldly power.

Leveling off at about 5000 feet, the Sukki circled the airfield once, came directly over the crowd, and then, with a wag of the wings, disappeared to the west.

As the noise of the jet engines finally faded away, another stunned silence descended on the crowd. All eyes turned back to Soho, who was standing alone on the empty runway, his dressing gown damp with vomit, his undershorts dangling around his knees.

"Why me?" he cried out, self-disgusted and mortified. *"Why was it left up to me?"*

With that, he produced a small pistol from his pocket, put it against his temple and pulled the trigger. There was a sharp crack and Soho immediately collapsed, half his forehead blown away.

No one moved to help him; no one dared.

All that could be heard was the sound of the wind, the rustling in the trees, and the chorus of children, still chanting in the distance.

Chapter Seven

Adora Atoll
Marshall Islands

There was a time when they called the place "Clark Kent."

It was a small island, barely three square miles in total size, and that included the reefs on its northern and eastern tips. It was 212 nautical miles due west of Bikini, and like that famous island, it was noted for its heavily shark-infested waters, its near-lack of vegetation beyond isolated clumps of palm trees, and its enormous population of goony birds.

And one more thing: its one-time prominence as a top secret American air base.

They called it "Clark Kent" because sometimes aircraft flight-listed to land at other Pacific or Far East bases would take on a secret identity and be diverted to the small, single airstrip island. This was especially true if the aircraft were slated for black op missions or carrying cargo that, for whatever reason, had to remain secret. The base was originally built to conduct secret atomic bomb drop tests in the early 1950s. Later on, in the mid-1960s, it was where the United States kept a substantial number of nuclear weapons, earmarked for use on North Vietnam, should the word ever come down to do so. In the later years, it served as a stopover point for SR-71 Blackbird recon jets that regularly cruised the skies above China, Vietnam, North Korea, and much later, the industrial heart of postmodern Japan.

The base on Adora Atoll had laid abandoned for many years—that was, until a pair of Free Canadian C-141F Starlifters landed there a week before. Contained within these two long-range airplanes was a special unit of Canadian engineers. Their task: get the secret base up and running for the imminent arrival of a force of very large aircraft.

The Canadians worked day and night to do so. Their main project—to extend the runway of the atoll an additional 1000 feet—was accomplished twenty-four hours ahead of schedule. Smaller but no less important assignments—such as installing temporary fuel tanks, reviving a sea water desalination plant, and retooling a small gas turbine to provide electrical power—were also completed on or before deadline.

In fact, the Canadians were putting the finishing touches on, of all things, a baseball field when the first radio report came in. Suddenly, all thoughts of the baseball diamond were dropped. The transitting force they'd been waiting for were now only a hundred miles away and coming fast.

It was *Bozo* that came in first; Hunter's expert touch at the controls put the extended runway to its first test and proved it was a job well done.

One by one, the other great Galaxy airships descended on the base, each setting down nimbly, drag chutes extended, engines screaming in reverse, strange colors displaying proud aerial individuality.

It took but three minutes, twenty seconds for all nine C-5s to touch down and taxi in. Their engines whining down, their cargo doors open, their crews disgorged, the first leg of a very long journey had come to a successful conclusion.

Hunter was greeted by the friendly Canadians, and he

praised them for their efforts and obvious top-notch workmanship. They in turn challenged the Americans to a round of baseball games, to be played on the newly built diamond. Hunter quickly accepted.

Then he went to the Canadians' recently constructed radio shack and sent a microwave burst message back to Edwards, clear on the other side of the globe.

The scrambled message simply read: "The First American Airborne Expeditionary Force has landed . . ."

Chapter Eight

Two Days Later

Two hundred and sixteen miles to the southwest of Adora Atoll, Bobby "Wallybee" Fletcher was sitting in a blind near the shoreline of a long, boomerang-shaped island, known simply as Boho.

It was a perfect location, for he had a commanding view of a narrow but deep strait that ran through the nearby archipelago of small deserted islands. On and off for three weeks, and now for the past twenty-hours straight, he had hardly budged, despite the swarms of mosquitos that seem to cover every square inch of his exposed skin.

He was waiting.

Fletcher was a coastwatcher, and like his father, and his father's father, he was one of the best. Regardless of the dangers or the isolation or the loneliness that came with the territory, Wallybee was able to draw on his enormous reserves of patience, the patience needed to sit through the worst kind of weather, severe hunger, thirst, bugs, and hours of boredom, simply to do his job.

And now this patience was about to pay off.

He heard it first, a kind of sloshing noise, slightly punctuated by a low mechanical throbbing. He took another long pull on the jug of New Zealand moonshine he kept handy to sharpen his senses, and then peered into the inky blackness of the moonless night.

The noise grew louder and louder until it was almost on top of him. In the black night, Fletcher could see a gigantic shadow passing by, like a great black cloud. He instantly knew it was what he had been waiting for all this time. The size of the phosphorescent wake spreading out after it passed was confirmation enough.

Fletcher opened up the wooden carrying case that shielded his World-War-II-vintage radio and quickly plugged in the antenna that stretched between two nearby tall trees. Then he rigged the power line from the battery to the generator and to the axle of a rusty, rear-wheel-less bicycle mounted on a stationary platform. For the next fifteen minutes, he sat on the tattered seat and pedaled furiously, building up electricity. After a quick voltage test, he set the transmitter to the frequency of the day, tapped out a short coded message on the sending key, and waited until he received the return verification signal from the place he knew only as "Clark Kent." Then, as quickly as he had set up his gear, he broke it down, camouflaged it among the vegetation, and disappeared into the night.

Chapter Nine

Dawn

The lone, gray battleship sliced through the deep South Pacific waters, heading southwest. Its engines running at full steam, it was on its way to rendezvous with the remainder of the Asian Mercenary Cult fleet cruising off of Luzon. If all went well, they would join the fleet within forty-eight hours.

The warship was two days out from its last port of call, a small South Pacific tropical island that was once a favorite tourist spot.

Typically, the battleship had left the island in flames.

Met at the dock by the beautiful women of the island, the crew had eagerly accepted the flower leis offered to them. Once ashore, the 1,242-man crew drank every drop of alcohol it could find. And then they went berserk.

First, they looted everything that wasn't tied down, and what they couldn't carry, they simply destroyed. Then they embarked on a killing frenzy that went on all through the night and all the next day. They eventually hunted down and slaughtered every living soul on the island including the elderly, the young, and even infants. Only the beautiful women were spared, but just long enough to be gang-raped and then killed. By dusk that next night, when the crew had finally staggered back to the ship after twenty-four hours of uncontrollable blood lust, they'd murdered more than 10,000 people. Then, with the crew on board, the vessel's nine massive 16-inch guns opened up, splitting the black night with their long, white-hot flames.

Every square foot of the island was obliterated, the great explosions throwing tons of dirt and rubble hundreds of feet into the air and creating craters more than a half mile across. Fires erupted everywhere, and burned wildly out of control. The heat generated was so intense that even steel was vaporized. By the time the battleship sailed away, nothing was left standing on the island, nothing was left alive. For the next day at sea, the crew could admire their handiwork: a huge, thick column of black smoke could be clearly seen rising from below the horizon behind them.

Junior Radio Officer Oka Ueno did not remember much of the raid. The booze and the drugs had flowed so freely through the entire rampage, he'd quickly lapsed into an alcoholic blackout. But he knew that if there was a hell, he surely had a place reserved. For when he finally woke up the morning after, he discovered that his uniform was encrusted with blood, caked brain matter and dried semen. His shipmates later told him that of them all, he'd done the most raping, the most killing. His officers went so far as to commend him for his actions.

Now, this early morning, as one reward for his butchery, Ueno was given the honor of raising the ship's colors and insignia of the Asian Mercenary fleet high up the battleship's mast.

But he would have much rather stayed in his bunk. Even two days later, he was still suffering from the worst hangover of his life.

As he crawled into his dress whites, preparing for this honor, he had to suppress the urge to vomit. And he was not alone. Groping his way up from his quarters onto the deck, he passed the assembled ceremonial guard and saw that each sailor's face was also a pale sea-green. Though they were doing their best to remain rigid and in close order, they too couldn't wait for this ceremony to be over so they could suffer in peace.

In the hot morning sun, Ueno clumsily fumbled with the masthead's clips and rope, finally attaching the Cult insignia of the three red dots on a field of white to the line. Then he slowly raised the huge flag to the sound of the ship's bugle blowing morning reveille. Each note played drilled deeper and deeper into Ueno's rotting brain, and between the broiling sun and the constant pitching and yawning of the ship, he was convinced that he would lose control of his stomach soon. He prayed that the ceremony would be over quickly.

As his eyes followed the flag on its way up the mast, the bright sunlight caused scores of tiny black dots to bounce around his bloodshot retinas. This was typical of people in severe postinebriated state. But no matter how often or how hard he blinked, two dots, two tiny little specks that seemed to be out near the southeast horizon, would not go away. From the combination of his overwhelming feeling of nausea and his confused alcohol-soaked state, Ueno couldn't be sure whether or not the two specks were even there.

But he was soon to find out that they were indeed quite real.

At long last, the flag raising ceremony was completed, and the order to dismiss the crew was finally given. The ranks gladly broke, but Ensign Ueno glanced back in the direction of the two dots. They were still there, but now, not only did they seem to be getting bigger, they appeared to be heading directly towards the ship. Ueno noticed that the rest of the crew had also seen them off in the distance. They too remained on deck, curious to see what they were. As they all watched, the two specks continued to grow in size as well as climb rapidly. Within a minute, they were directly overhead. An anxious ripple shot through those on deck as the two gleaming specks went into a lazy orbit high above the battleship.

The captain was alerted, and he was quickly out on the bridge's gangway staring up at the circling objects through his high-powered binoculars.

Then they began to spiral down.

First one, then the other, seemed to be falling toward the ship. The crew lining the rails were spellbound. They had never seen anything like this before. At that moment, the captain cried out in warning—the ship was about to be attacked. But Ueno didn't hear him. Unable to control his nausea anymore, he had fallen to his knees, clutching his stomach, his body now racked by the dry heaves. In the distance, he thought he could hear the klaxons of the great battleship begin to scream in warning. And through this din, he also thought he heard the tone-deaf bugler try to blurt an off-key call to battle stations, though he couldn't be quite sure.

But when he finally raised his eyes back up to the sky, he saw the objects were now the two biggest airplanes he had ever seen. Their bodies wide, the engines screaming, their wings stretched out, they looked like the twin angels of death.

The Cult's battleship was exactly where Wallybee the coastwatcher had said it would be.

The ferry pilot of the C-5 named *Nozo* had located it quickly. Now as he put his massive gunship into a long wide spiral downward, he swiftly went through the prefiring checklist with each of the aircraft's twenty-one gunners and their ammunition control men. The pilot's voice was level, patient, and firm, like that of a surgeon about to perform a major operation. The responses from the crew members were equally professional.

"Forward firing generators to On . . ." the pilot calmly ordered. Twenty-one separate affirmative responses came back.

"Video screen antiinterference mode secured."

"Check!"

"Power drift stabilizers to on."

"Check!"

"Ammunition engage light lit."

"Check!"

The highly trained crew of the gleaming chrome and silver *Nozo* were men of precision. They moved about the antiseptic hold of the Galaxy as if they were performing in precise choreography to the strains of a world-renowned symphony. Each had a specific task to do, and each was responsible for a part of the loading, targeting, or firing of one of the 21 GE GAU-8/A 30 mm cannons that lined the port side of the cavernous Galaxy transport-turned-gunship. There was no unnecessary chatter, no unnecessary movement. The men methodically went through their lengthy preattack check-offs, dressed in their neat, freshly pressed white coveralls, and speaking in turn through microphones imbedded in the hooded air/gas filters that covered their heads.

"Crew to attack positions," the pilot ordered through the *Nozo* intercom while continuing to turn the huge plane in the steep, leftward bank high above the Cult battleship. Instantly, twenty-one shutters—nine forward of the wing, twelve behind it—snapped open.

"Weapons ready . . ." the pilot called out. Immediately the Avenger cannons, hooked on to miles of ammunition belts loaded with depleted uranium shells, deployed out the twenty-one gun ports.

"All positions ready," the flight chief called forward to the cockpit.

"All positions, stand by," the pilot replied.

He checked and then double-checked the massive airplane's position. It was now 1,100 feet above the battleship, drifting slightly to the south to match the enemy vessel's speed.

He nodded to his copilot and together they pushed down on the control column. Suddenly the big plane was dropping rapidly—down to 1,000 feet, then 900, then 800 ... its engines in full scream, its wings banked left at almost an 80-degree angle, the Galaxy seemed to be falling out of the sky.

When it reached 350 feet, the pilot yelled to the copilot and together they pulled the plane out of the harrowing spiral. They were now at optimum attack altitude.

Banking into a tight orbit directly over the battleship, the pilot braced himself.

Then he keyed his microphone.

"Commence firing. . . ."

Instantly a sheet of flame erupted along the side of the C-5 as thousands of rounds of 30 mm shells poured out of the spitting barrels of the twenty-one Avengers and streaked down upon the battleship.

The first battle in what would be a very long war had begun.

The battleship's crew, caught out in the open on their way to battle stations, seemed to scream in one, ear-piercing, bloodcurdling, not-of-this-earth cry of pure terror as the rain of mechanized lead poured down on them. Some died instantly. Some began to uncontrollably vomit. Others tried to run, only to slip on the blood-splattered deck. Some fell over those who had fallen prostrate. Others were crying hysterically, begging for forgiveness for all the inhuman crimes they had committed.

But as the massive airplane slowly circled the ship, its cannons raking it from forward to aft, across its beam, and then back again, any Cult sailor caught above deck was either chopped to pieces by the intense volume of gunfire, or cut down by the flying red hot chunks of steel torn from the ship's structure. The cannon fire was so intense, it soon penetrated the battleship's thick-steel deck, severing hundreds of cables, wires, and pipes. In a matter of seconds the power was cut off in the aft and midsections of the ship. The battleship was instantly plunged into darkness.

As the huge airplane continued to circle the stricken battleship, electrical fires quickly broke out below decks. The toxic fumes slowly began to spread throughout the bowels of the ship. Orders were given for the air and watertight hatches to be secured—but it was too late. The deadly fumes and suffocating smoke had already spread too fast. The gagging sailors below panicked in the inky darkness. They began to fight and claw their way topside, towards fresh air. They spilled out onto the deck—and into the gunsights of the Avengers. The frighteningly efficient 30 mm cannon fire simply tore them apart. While a few were able to throw themselves over the railing into the sea below, the majority were cut down in midstride. Soon the battleship's decks were awash with blood.

And then, as suddenly as it began, the massive gunship stopped firing. Its engines still screaming but fading, it leveled off and turned toward the eastern horizon.

The sudden silence snapped Ensign Ueno out of his dazed stupor.

He had somehow managed to survive the nightmarish aerial attack. Through the heavy, oily smoke that now covered the ship, he was astonished to see the amount of damage that this one plane had so expertly inflicted on the once-mighty battleship. Though it seemed like forever, the entire attack had lasted less than a minute.

Ueno quickly grasped the grim accomplishment of the plane's surgical strike. In the short time it took for its just five slow orbits, it had succeeded not only in killing most of the crew but also in completely knocking out all of the battleship's major defense systems. Each of the ship's gun directors—the high-tech, computer-enhanced radar systems that sequenced the targeting and firing of the ship's guns—had also been obliterated. Most of the antiaircraft fire control systems were now out of commission. Whatever 20 mm cannons or five-inch guns that the ship was able to fire during the lightning attack had been fired blindly. Not one shell found its mark on the frightening enemy plane.

There was total panic aboard the ship now and insanity swirled all around Ueno. Sailors ran back and forth, some killing anyone who got in their way or any officer who tried to give an order. It was every man for himself. Gasping for breath, Ueno tried to stand but quickly collapsed in a heap. He realized for the first time that his left leg was horribly shattered. He never felt it happen, for the shock of being hit with a 30 mm cannon shell had numbed it completely. Unable to staunch the flow of blood, his leg trailing behind at an odd, twisted angle, he started to drag himself across the deck toward the bow, the only place that was not burning.

But just then a deep sense of foreboding overwhelmed him. He looked skyward to see the second enormous airplane now spiraling down on the ship just as the first one did. This one, though, was painted in bizarre orange, blue, and yellow colors. Ueno stopped moving altogether. He sensed the end was very near.

He was right.

Hunter wrestled with the control stick of the C-5 *Bozo*, trying to bring her around. After seeing *Nozo* break off its attack, it was now time for him to deliver this immense airplane's unique version of mechanized death to the severely damaged battleship blow.

Unlike its sister ship *Nozo*, *Bozo* was quite unbalanced, due to the wide array of weapons on board. The combination of Gatling guns, artillery pieces, grenade launchers and a huge rocket platform distributed unevenly through the hold made for guaranteed aerodynamic instability. But Hunter finally managed to slowly bring the C-5 into something that resembled a spiral. Struggling with all his might to keep the huge lumbering plane in a slowly descending attack attitude, he called back step-by-step instructions for the gun crews to prepare.

With each lopsided spiral, the airplane dropped nearer and nearer to the battleship. At the same time, the gun crew aboard went through the paces of loading and aiming their weapons. When the awkwardly loaded Galaxy reached the proscribed altitude of 350 feet, Hunter pulled hard back on his control column. He was barely able to bring the heavy C-5 out of its controlled fall. The instant it leveled off, he quickly banked it to the left then gave the command.

"Commence firing!"

That's when all hell broke loose.

In a deafening *whirrr,* the six GE Gatling guns poured out rounds at a rate of seventy per second, sending severe vibrations throughout the monstrously clumsy gunship. The heavy thuds of the five Mk-19 automatic grenade launchers rocked the plane violently with each recoil, and when the AP/AV 700 three barrel multiple grenade launcher joined in next, the circus-scrolled Galaxy was further tossed about. Then the Solton 120-mm mobile field gun and the two Royal Ordnance 105-mm field pieces opened up, pumping shell after shell into the battleship, and shaking the C-5 even more crazily with their blasts. Though it seemed that the aerial behemoth would in short order shake itself into pieces, this particular C-5 always somehow defied logic, physics, and aerodynamic law. As before, it held together.

The situation inside the hold of *Bozo* was quite the opposite of its beautiful sister, *Nozo,* however. The shouts of the weapon's officers directing their crews could barely be heard over the incredible roar of the crazy collection of weaponry all firing at once. But when the three Rheinmental 20-mm converted antiaircraft guns opened up, it was deafening.

The crewmen were covered with a grimy layer of soot and burnt gunpowder from the thick smoke building up quickly inside the plane, this despite the fact that a series of exhaust fans were cranking at full speed, turning the length of the massive gun hold into one long wind tunnel. On top of that, empty casings of every imaginable caliber were flying all over inside the hold as they were ejected from their weapons' chambers. Soon a foot thick layer of brass casings and spent rocket charges rattled back and forth along the length and width of the deck. It was controlled chaos.

Down below, it was a second vision of hell.

Rockets, high-explosive shells, and cannon rounds were impacting along the port side of the battleship; the tremendous barrage of explosions was rocking the Cult gun wagon every which way. As Hunter banked the C-5 around to rake the ship's starboard side, he saw the battleship leap forward in speed and turn right full rudder, trying to come around to meet him broadside. It would prove to be a vain attempt at a classic naval maneuver.

The battleship's trio of heavily armored 16-inch gun turrets swung in the direction of the C-5. Reacting immediately, Hunter knew it was time to play his ace in the hole—the 17-ton LARS II 110 Multiple Rocket Launcher.

He banked the C-5 even steeper, maintaining 350 feet of altitude and bringing the airplane around so that barrels of the LARS II were perfectly angled towards the battleship's two forward turrets. He counted down to five, then gave the order to fire.

During the next twenty seconds, thirty-six six-foot-long high-explosive rockets were loosed with a Vesuvius-like roar from the C-5, striking exactly on top the two heavily armored gun turrets. The plane was jolted so hard by the fusillade and the resulting concussions that Hunter had to fight to maintain stable flight. Nearly every gunner and ammo feeder back in the hold was tossed around and thrown to the deck. The LARS crew, scrambling back into position, quickly reloaded their awesome weapon as Hunter coaxed the great plane around towards the bow of the ship—and the third 16-inch gun turret.

"Fire!" he called back again, and another thirty-six rockets streaked down at the ship, once more throwing the crews around the hold of the plane. The second barrage struck on top and all around the battleship's rear 10-inch thick armored turret. In what seemed like one long gigantic explosion, it simply disintegrated.

As the smoke cleared, Hunter grimly accessed the damage. These enormous enemy guns that had leveled island after defenseless island were now reduced to three smoldering craters of twisted steel and broken bodies.

At that moment, *Bozo's* Soltam mobile field guns, which had managed to continually fire its 120-mm rounds, finally found their target—the twin rudders of the battleship. Now the great battleship was locked in its turning degree, steaming at full speed in a tight circle, going nowhere and getting there fast.

That's when the ship's main boiler busted a seam and exploded. Hunter saw the enemy vessel shudder, then drunkenly lurch to the port side. He called back the order to cease fire.

Circling the smoking hulk three more times, the battered ship finally came to a stop in the water. There was no reason to expend any more ammunition; the battleship was dead.

Hunter banked the plane toward the southeast horizon, and gunned its engines.

Their mission was accomplished.

Thirty Minutes Later

Major Donn Kurjan—code-named "Lazarus"—was sitting directly behind the pilot of *Seahawk #1*, anxiously chewing on a wad of gum.

Combined with the two Seahawk choppers behind them, Kurjan was in command of forty-five shock troops of the elite Football City Special Forces Rangers, the men who had come in on *Football One*.

Out on the horizon they could clearly see the shattered, burning hulk of the Cult battleship, a long plume of black smoke rising more than a mile in the sky above it.

"How much longer?" Kurjan yelled into the pilot's ear, needing to be heard over the racket of the Seahawk's engines.

The pilot made some quick calculations. "Two minutes," he yelled back. "Maybe two and a half . . ."

Kurjan tapped him twice on the shoulder and then turned and signaled to his second-in-command riding back in the chopper's overcrowded troop compartment. *"Two minutes,"* he yelled, holding up two fingers. "Get ready."

He turned back to find the battleship getting closer by the second. There were more than a dozen fires burning out of control all over the devastated battlewagon, and every few seconds the ship would be wracked by yet another explosion.

Kurjan had to shake his head in admiration: the combined punch of *Nozo* and *Bozo* had reduced the huge vessel to little more than a floating hulk of burning metal and igniting ammunition. Trouble was, Kurjan had to lead his men on board that piece of hell.

His mission was to look for information—dispersement orders, sailing manifests, codebooks—anything that might give the United Americans some clue as to the strategy of the Asian Mercenary Cult's frighteningly large battleship fleet.

"One minute out . . ." the chopper pilot yelled back to Kurjan. "We'll be swinging around for a north-south approach in about ten seconds."

Kurjan went about the business of checking his own gear when the copilot leaned over and tapped him on the leg.

72

"Just got a Mayday out of the target, sir," he reported. "Sent out on the old long-range general aid frequency."

Kurjan froze for a moment. He had been prepared to hear this news, all the while hoping he never had to. The transmission of the Mayday meant at least someone was still alive on the battleship; maybe many more. Having dealt with the Cult before, Kurjan knew it was an open question as to the tenacity of the soldiers they might meet. Sometimes the Cult troops were incredibly ferocious; other times they were quite timid. It all depended on how much liquor and drugs they'd ingested recently, and also how voracious their immediate commanders were.

"Do you have a good read on that Mayday?" he asked the copilot. The man replied with a solid nod.

"Damn," Kurjan said, checking his ammo clips. "This'll make it interesting."

"We're forty seconds out," the pilot yelled to him. "Hang on . . ."

Kurjan did as the pilot suggested, grabbing the flight compartment frame support. The lead Seahawk went into a sharp left hand turn, momentarily putting the burning battleship out of his view. When it appeared again, the chopper was lined up on the ship's bow, coming down in both altitude and speed.

"We're twenty seconds away," the pilot told him.

"Got another radio transit," the copilot added. "It's another Mayday . . . sloppy, but clear."

Kurjan studied the burning battleship as he fastened his crash helmet. If there was any kind of organized force aboard the Cult vessel it could get very hairy for him and his men.

"Five out," the pilot yelled. "Do you want to do a flyby first?"

Kurjan quickly agreed. Time was of the essence in this landing operation—there was no telling what kind of Cult forces were in the area. But he had forty-five lives at stake here—fifty-two, counting himself and the chopper pilots.

With the Mayday calls indicating someone was still breathing on the ship, he decided he could afford the luxury of quick recon before setting down.

The lead pilot led the trio of Seahawks around the port side of the battered battleship. Just about everyone onboard the choppers stared out at the burning battleship. The destruction caused by the two Galaxy gunships was unbelievable. There didn't seem to be a square inch of the ship's deck, armor, or superstructure that hadn't been perforated by some kind of cannon shot or high-explosive shell. There were no large weapons in any kind of working order; the second attack by *Bozo* had seen to that. Between the fires, the smoke and the multitude of holes in its hull, it was a wonder the ship was still afloat.

"Third transmission," the copilot reported. "Still sloppy, but pretty clear. S-O-S with rough location coordinates."

Son-of-a-bitch, Kurjan whispered, never taking his eyes off the burning enemy vessel. It was eerie, looking at the devastated battleship and thinking there might be squads of fanatical suicide troops waiting from them to land.

The three Seahawks swooped around the back of the ship and along the starboard side. If anything the extent of the destruction was worse. The three huge turrets were all pointing in this direction when *Bozo* took them out, and now they were little more than twisted gun barrels, ripped-apart armor, and deep holes billowing clouds of black and white smoke.

Could anyone still be alive on there? Kurjan wondered.

He tapped the pilot on the shoulder again, and the lead Seahawk immediately swooped down to the cleared area just behind the demolished rear turret. No sooner had the chopper touched down than Kurjan leaped from the troop bay, his Uzi up and ready, his men right behind him. The two other Seahawks managed to squeeze on the stern of the ship too, and their troops were soon pouring out.

"*Fourth Mayday signal* . . ." the copilot yelled out the side window at him. "*Still pretty clear* . . ."

"Any idea where it's coming from?" Kurjan asked the man.

The copilot could only shrug back. "I'd try the radio shack first," he yelled. "Or maybe the bridge . . ."

Kurjan linked up with his squad commanders and made sure everyone was on the same page. Three troopers would be left behind to guard the helicopters; the rest of the force would split into three groups and quickly search the burning ship.

Kurjan checked his watch. He had to complete the entire mission in less than ten minutes, that's how long the choppers could keep their engines running and still have enough fuel to make it back to the base on Adora.

"OK, let's go!" he yelled.

While Kurjan's group headed topside, the two other groups went below deck.

Because of the dense smoke and toxic fumes, each member of these two teams had to quickly don gas masks and turn on their high-intensity lamps. What they saw was a scene straight out of hell. Burned bodies, severed heads and limbs, blood and other body guts were everywhere. They grimly made their way down the cluttered narrow passageways, using the classic leapfrog approach. Three men would secure a forward position and then wave the rest ahead. As they went deeper and deeper into the ship, both groups were amazed at the thorough job done by the Galaxys. It was like being on a ghost ship. They just couldn't imagine anyone being alive.

At midships, Group Three began making its way toward the back end of the ship; Group Two would concentrate on the front end.

Because they met no resistance, Group Three reached the radio room far ahead of schedule. They found it empty—but all of the radios were smashed and out of commission. Whoever was sending the Mayday calls wasn't doing it from here. Group Three went about the business of tearing the place apart, looking for any kind of information that they could get their hands on.

Group Two was also making progress. As planned, they came to a juncture of three passageways, each one of them leading to a forward magazine. Silently breaking up into three smaller units, they advanced down each of the passageways.

The point man of Unit Alpha reached the door of Magazine One. All was still quiet. Covered by the rest of the squad, he kicked in the door. What he saw would give him nightmares for years to come.

There were four Cult sailors; each had a time-detonator strapped to his chest. Obviously they were part of a suicide squad ordered to disperse to the ship's magazines and serve as human time bombs, triggers which would ignite the battleship's ammunition chambers and blow the vessel—and all those aboard—sky high on the given command. But it was just as obvious that the command never came—or it was ignored when it did. The four men, still sitting side-by-side, had chosen to die in a more traditional way—by the ancient ritual of hari-kari. What the squad leader found then were the four men horribly impaled by their own swords, their stomachs and lower abdomen organs running out onto the magazine's floor, their faces identical masks of pure, pale terror.

The squad leader immediately vomited. He was quickly led away by his second officer.

It was this man who discovered that though dead, the time-detonators strapped to the bodies were nevertheless ticking away, the last act of four men who preferred the blade to the explosion as a way to die.

After some anxious, quick calculations, the officer determined the magazine—and the rest of the ship—would blow in less than eight minutes.

Topside, Kurjan and the men of his group had eased down the sides of the smoking superstructure and now surrounded the battered bridge. On cue, one of the commandos fired a burst through the thick greenish plate glass of the front of the bridge and two others immediately lobbed in concussion grenades. The two explosions blew out the rest of the glass, and in an instant, Kurjan and six commandos leapt through the opening, their weapons up and ready.

"What the hell is this?" Kurjan muttered once inside the bridge.

They found the ship's captain sitting in his command chair. The warm barrel of a Lugar was still in his mouth, his brains literally dripping from the ceiling. There was a wry grin on his lifeless face.

A loud electronic noise was coming from a small room off the bridge. Kurjan and two of his troopers cautiously approached the entranceway to the room. The squealing sound was almost like morse code, yet all jumbled up. Kurjan finally kicked in the door—and immediately solved the mystery of who was sending the Mayday calls. The room was a small, auxiliary radio shack, close to the bridge to serve the ship's command staff. Stretched across an ancient COMM-SAT keyboard was a Cult sailor. His hands had been blown away as had his right leg. The man nevertheless had been tapping out the SOS calls with an exposed forearm bone—and had done so until he died, quite apparently from shock and loss of blood.

His body was still twitching though and this was the cause of the jumbled radio messages.

"A ghost . . ." Kurjan heard himself say, somewhat involuntarily. "We're always looking for ghosts."

He walked over to the dead man and dragged him off the COMM-SAT keyboard, thus ending the electronic squealing. Laying the body aside, Kurjan noticed the man's uniform's name tag read: Ueno.

Kurjan's group returned to the bridge and went right to

work, gathering up every scrap of paper, sea chart, and report in the bridge, and tossing them into several duffle bags brought along for the purpose. It was Kurjan who spotted the safe.

"This is really what we're looking for," he called to his men. "Let's peel this sardine can open."

Just then, the leader of Group Two arrived on the bridge. He had bad news.

"They've got the forward magazine on timer detonators," this man reported. "Our electronics officer says he can delay the zero point for another six minutes or so, but there's no way he can defuse or move one without setting them all off."

"Damn . . ." Kurjan swore through clenched teeth. "That means we've got no time to screw around with this thing," indicating the safe.

He turned back to Group Two leader. "Tell your man to delay detonation as long as he can and keep in constant radio contact. And get the rest of your men topside with whatever they've got already." Kurjan then summoned his radioman to call Chopper One, telling the pilot to get airborne over the bridge and drop its steel cable and winch.

"What do you have in mind, sir?" Kurjan's second-in-command asked.

Kurjan looked at the Seahawk taking off and then back at the safe.

"We're going to take this thing with us," he declared.

It took eight men over four minutes to wrestle the safe out of the bridge and onto the outside landing where the cable from the hovering Seahawk dangled. Every minute, on the minute, Group Two's second-in-command radioed up from the forward magazine counting down how much time they had left. It was quickly running out.

With only two minutes to go, Kurjan called all of Group Two topside, and then he ordered everyone to get back aboard the Seahawks.

Kurjan made the final adjustments in locking the aerial

cable to the safe. Then, when he was certain that every one of his commandos was safely in the choppers, he pumped his arm up and down, signaling the pilots of Seahawks Two and Three to get the hell out of there and fast. When they were clear, he hopped on top of the safe, tied himself as secure as he could to the cable with his web belt, and then signaled the pilot of Seahawk One to lift off. The copter slowly climbed until the cable was taut, and then added power, going straight up, plucking the safe and Kurjan off the ship.

They made it with just seconds to spare.

Dangling on top of the safe as it swayed from side to side, Kurjan was only 100 feet above the battleship when he heard a low roar from deep within the ship's hold. The Cult vessel was suddenly rocked from stem to stern by a violent shudder. An instant later, the magazines blew. A great fireball lifted up through the main deck and out both sides of the ship in one deafening roar.

Kurjan was hit with the tremendous shock wave. He clung to the cable with all his strength as he was tossed and spun him around, totally out of control. But he managed to hang on. When the concussion passed and the smoke began to clear, he saw that the battleship had been broken completely in two, each half sliding to its watery grave. In a matter of seconds, there was nothing left but small bits of flotsam churned up by the froth of air bubbles escaping the dead ship.

The huge battleship fleet of the Asian Mercenary Cult was reduced by one.

Now all he had to do, Kurjan thought, his butt dangling out in the breeze, was to relax, and enjoy the ride back to the Adora atoll.

Chapter Ten

Adora Atoll

Hunter, Ben, JT, and Frost were sitting on the ivory white sands of Adora, drinking ice-cold beer and eating pork ribs when the trio of Seahawks appeared over the western horizon.

Hunter saw them first, of course—he was up and at the water's edge in a flash, his extraordinary vision picking up the three dots like a radar screen.

"OK, they all made it back," he said with some relief as the choppers drew near. "No problems on the return flight. That's a good sign."

Five minutes later, Seahawk One was hovering right over the small cove where they had set up their rib spit, Major Kurjan still sitting on the safe which was still dangling from the cable of the bottom of the chopper.

"Those Football City guys are really nuts," JT remarked, as the safe and Kurjan were lowered down. "Who else would bring back the whole safe with them?"

"Looks like they might have hit the jackpot though," Hunter replied. "Who knows what could be locked in there."

The Seahawk finally came down low enough for the others to help Kurjan off and then disengage the safe from the chopper cable. Once released, Seahawk One gained altitude and followed its two companions back to the Clark Kent airstrip, a half mile from the cove.

"Good work, Laz," Hunter told Kurjan as they studied the safe. "How was the ride back?"

"I can always find work as a trapeze artist," Kurjan replied. "I just had the crash course."

JT handed him a beer. "Don't you know its bad luck to say the word 'crash' around pilots?" he asked.

The others were already surrounding the safe, inspecting it.

"It's a double-lock combination," Hunter said, slowly twisting the tumblers. "Could be any sequence of numbers. Might take a while to break it."

"No, it won't," JT said. With that, he pulled his everpresent .357 Magnum from his boot holster and fired one shot, right between the pair of tumblers. The safe burst open immediately, much to the astonishment of his colleagues.

JT dramatically blew the smoke from his gun barrel, and reholstered the weapon. "I'm going to put another pig on the spit," he announced, walking away, "So stay hungry. . . ."

Kurjan and the others just shook their heads. "I'm glad he's on our side," Kurjan said.

Hunter was already pulling documents out of the safe. Some were written in Japanese, others in Korean, still others in Mandarin Chinese. It made no difference; he was fluent in all three.

But right away, the news was disappointing. Nearly all the documents dealt with the rather mundane matters of running a Cult battleship: ration proportioning, pay schedules, work orders. One document spelled out the restrictions on drinking *sake* while on-board. Another detailed with grisly nonchalance a list of looted items pillaged from some unknown location during one of the Cult's island-hopping death-sprees. Still another documented the quantities of mind-bending drugs on board, a large amount being that of the incredibly-addictive superhallucinogenic *myx*.

"Well, they're drinking *myx*," Hunter told the others. "That explains why they're so freaking crazy all the time."

He kept reading, but nothing rang any bells as to what the fleet of Cult battleships were up to.

Then he came upon the last document, a large sealed blue envelope.

Hunter ripped it open and was astonished by what he found.

"Well, I'll be damned," he whispered.

The others crowded around and stared at the document in Hunter's hand. It was a single piece of yellowed onion paper with a little writing at the top.

"What the hell language is that?" Ben asked.

Hunter had a hard time believing it. "It's Arabic," he replied. "A very old dialect. Goes way back."

"What's it say?" Frost wanted to know. "Can you read it?"

Hunter could, but just barely. "It *is* a dispersement order," he said slowly. "Not many instructions. Just some coordinates for a rendezvous point of some kind."

"So they all might be heading to one place, just like we thought," Ben said.

"Looks that way," Hunter replied, quickly taking down the English translation of the longitude and latitude points.

"Any idea where those points are, Hawk?" Kurjan asked.

Hunter closed his eyes and thought for a moment. He conjured up a vision of a world map in his head, calculating over from known longitude/latitude points. He had the answer in less than ten seconds.

"Damn," he whispered. "I don't believe it. . . ."

Ben was practically shaking him by now.

"Where the hell is it, Hawk?" he asked. "Where the hell are the battleships going?"

Hunter looked up at them. "Believe it or not," he said. "I think they're heading for Vietnam. . . ."

Chapter Eleven

The Next Day

It was unusually foggy over Edwards.

General Jones and Yaz were sitting in a HumVee at the side of the longest runway, their eyes straining to see through the unseasonal mist.

"Of all the damn days to be fogged-in," Jones said, his voice uncharacteristically gravelly. "Whoever heard of fog in the desert."

Yaz could only shrug. He certainly didn't know. He was Navy man—oceans, he knew about. Not deserts.

He looked out on the line of C-5s, all of which were in some degree of disassembly. The weather was so bad, Jones had reluctantly called a halt to all flight testing, a critical delay in the timetable for getting more of the converted Galaxy transports over to the South Pacific.

But there was one airplane he had allowed to take off, almost sixteen hours before. They were now anxiously waiting for this airplane's return.

"What time are we at?" Jones asked.

Yaz checked his chronometer. "I've got 1100 hours on the dot, sir."

Jones began fidgeting with his long-extinguished pipe.

"They were due back here forty-five minutes ago," he

half-muttered. "God, if we lose them—and that plane—then we might as well . . ."

He didn't finish the sentence. He didn't have to. Suddenly the foggy morning air was reverberating with sound and vibration. Instantly the two sensations combined into one mighty roar, made by a machine unlike any in the world. It stung their ears as it streaked overhead, still unseen.

They both let out a breath of relief. "They're here," Jones finally exhaled.

Within seconds, the portable lights lining the runway snapped on. The roar went overhead once again, and then got lower in tone. It was coming in for a landing.

They watched as the fog at the far end of the runway suddenly turned bright pink, then bright orange, and then finally deep red. A second later, a sleek black form burst through the colored mist. It touched down not five seconds later, and was soon streaking by Jones and Yaz.

"A good landing," Jones declared. "Good pilots."

It was an SR-71 Blackbird, the near-hypersonic spy plane operated by the famous brother-team of Sky High Spies, Inc. The airplane was capable of speeds close to 2500 mph or more, and could fly nearly eighteen miles high. It had just returned from a flight which took it halfway around the world, literally.

The Blackbird slowed to a crawl with the help of three deployed parachutes, and then taxied over to where Jones and Yaz were waiting.

A ground crew appeared and began servicing the strange airplane even before it rolled to a stop. The double canopy soon popped open and two white-suited pilots climbed out.

Jones and Yaz walked over to greet them. They were Jeff and George Kephart, the Sky High Spies themselves.

"How'd it go, guys?" Jones asked, shaking hands with them.

Brother Jeff pulled off his helmet. "Bumpy the whole

way over and back," he reported. "But we've got a lot of stuff on the cameras. Lot of activity down there."

Brother George had already retrieved one of the Blackbird's video cannisters. He walked over to the small group, holding the large cassette like it was made of gold.

"Let's grab a brew and take a look," he suggested.

Twenty minutes later they were sitting in the main ops room, a large-screen TV/VCR unit set up and running.

Beers were dispensed, and sandwiches brought on. The Kepharts were still in their flight suits, wolfing down roast beef spuckies, drowned with gulps of cold suds.

Yaz inserted the primary videotape and fast-forwarded it through a series of color bars. Finally the screen went from black to white to black again.

Then it turned a familiar shade of green.

Before them was an extreme altitude shot of a crooked-elbow coastline. It filled Jones with an instant forboding. Of them all, he was the only one who had actually fought in Vietnam.

"We've got the old DMZ at the top bar," Brother George explained between bites. "Old Saigon at the bottom."

Both Jones and Yaz were astonished. It appeared as if the entire country was in flames.

"We counted at least twenty major battles going on down there," Brother Jeff told them. "And a lot of little ones. Mostly on the coast. The smoke alone is immense. We've got some infrared stuff, too. It helps on the close-in stuff."

They watched the entire 25-minute tape, the Brothers explaining various points of interest as the footage documented their six overflights over what used to be South Vietnam. It was evident that just about the entire country was under attack.

A second tape was brought in, and this showed the so-

86

called "close-in" stuff. It depicted roads absolutely packed with military equipment—tanks, APCs, troop trucks, mobile artillery. From highways, to smaller roads, to little more than widened paths, there were traffic jams of weapons and troops, all of it looking brand-new, all of it heading south.

"This would almost be comical, if it wasn't so serious," Jones said, more than once. "I feel like I'm looking through a time machine."

"You'd think they'd finally leave that poor country alone," Yaz said. "It's had more than its share of this kind of thing."

Jones finally wiped his weary eyes. "Well, this confirms Hawk's information," he said, referring to the burst message he'd received from the Expeditionary Force 36 hours before. The information culled from the Cult battleship's safe prompted his sending the Sky High Spies on their photo run over Southeast Asia, and particularly Vietnam.

Now it was quite evident that the country was on the verge of total war—again.

"Who the hell would be fighting over there these days?" Yaz asked.

Jones just shook his head. "I know they finally found oil and gas offshore," he said. "Not that that makes much difference. There was little more than rice and rubber there in the sixties. We lost fifty thousand guys fighting for it."

He shook his head again. "What a waste . . ." he said, his voice trailing off.

"Well, someone's got a whole lot of problems over there now," Brother Jeff said.

"And if the Cult battleships are heading there, you can be sure they're on the side of the aggressors," Yaz added.

Jones nodded in glum agreement. "The question is, what can we do about it? We've only got a third of our force deployed in the area. And this looks like a country that needs about a half a million men—again."

Yaz just shook his head and looked at the General.

"There's an underdog over there, somewhere," he said. "With the Cult on its way, you can be sure it's their allies who are doing all the stomping. It's not really our style just to sit back and watch someone get pummeled."

Jones nodded. "So we *are* the world's policemen, again?"

The three other men just stared back at him.

"We're Americans," Yaz finally said. "That's all we can be . . ."

Jones looked over at the younger man. There were actually tears forming in the corner of his eyes.

"OK," he said, after a while. "Get Hawk on the radio."

They were playing baseball when the call came in.

The diamond set up by the Free Canadians was first rate— complete with sod for grass, old parachute packs for bases, and hard sand for base paths. A tourney was in full swing, one team representing each of the nine C-5s versus a like number of squads made up from the Canadian engineers.

As it turned out, the *Bozo* crew had won their round-robin with a 3-0 record, and was playing the Canadian Molson Muscles for the championship. It was 7-7 in the ninth inning, with extra innings looming when Ben hit a double. Then with Hunter at the plate, the radiophone inside *NJ104* began buzzing.

The game was stopped while Hunter took the call. He emerged after twenty minutes and asked that the American crews assemble. With the several hundred men of the First American Airborne Expeditionary Force standing before him, Hunter announced that Jones was sending them into action. Based on the information found inside the Cult battleship safe, and subsequent recon done by the Sky High Spies, Jones had ordered them to deploy to South Vietnam, assess the current situation, and, if possible, help any democratic forces there with their common defense. More of the C-5 fleet would follow as they became ready.

It took a few moments for the news to sink in. The assembled troopers just stood there, not talking, not stunned, not surprised—just simply considering what lay ahead of them.

Finally, someone simply said: "We're going back to Vietnam."

That's when it hit home. They *were* going back. Back to a land that had known literally thousands of years of war. Back to a land where many foreigners had died, fighting for ill-defined goals. Back to a land where more than 55,000 Americans were killed, heroes all in a war that was mismanaged from the top, to say the least.

Back to a land of ghosts.

They were gone less than two hours later.

All nine C-5s rose into the air, formed up and as one headed west, leaving the Canadians and several ferry pilots behind. The Galaxys would refuel twice enroute, both times courtesy of free-lance aerial tankers working out of Australia. Then it would be on to Vietnam, specifically the base at Da Nang, which according to the Blackbird's recon photos appeared to be in the hands of the country's defenders.

After that, it would be a matter of improvising.

PART TWO

Chapter Twelve

Over the South China Sea

It was about an hour after their second aerial refueling when they began getting the strange radio signals.

Hunter was at the controls of *Bozo* as usual; Ben was in the copilot's seat. They were about ninety minutes out from the coast of South Vietnam, two hours from Da Nang. They could see an enormous storm forming way off on the southern horizon, its dark clouds and swirling winds indicating it was probably part of a larger monsoon.

They were working out alternative approaches should they be unable to avoid the storm when the gunship's radio officer came up and tapped Hunter on the shoulder.

"Just picked up some very weird transmissions, Hawk," he told him.

"Weird like how?"

The radio officer screwed up his face. "Better come and listen for yourself."

Hunter turned control of *Bozo* over to Ben and made his way back to the mid-flight deck where the long-range radio gear was kept.

He put on one of the many sets of headphones and settled down to listen. It didn't take long for him to hear what the radio officer was talking about.

The airwaves were absolutely jammed with radio trans-

93

missions. There were voices of men, women, even children. Some were shouting, some screaming, some even crying. Some were live, some were obviously recorded. There were even some in morse code.

But they were all saying the same thing: "Save us . . ."

"They're on every frequency, every band," the radio officer told Hunter. "All across the dial. Some are shortwave, some long, some are coming over AM radio; others FM. Some are bursts. Some are clean. Some are scrambled. I'm sure we'd pick up sat-coms too if we could."

"But it's the same message over and over?" Hunter asked.

The radioman nodded. "Same thing."

"And the points of origin?"

The radioman grimaced slightly. "As far as we can tell, they're all being broadcast from along the coast of South Vietnam."

The words reverberated around Hunter's ears for a few seconds.

"I'll be damned. Are you sure?"

The man nodded. "Checked it up and down, four times . . ."

Hunter thought it over for a moment. First, the tens of thousands of disturbing satellite-bounce messages, along with the hidden "Victor is Alive" addition. And now this.

"What the hell do you make of it?" he asked the radio officer.

The man just shrugged. "I think a lot of people are in a lot of trouble."

They seemed to have come out of nowhere.

It was an hour after the cacophony of SOS messages were first heard. Hunter was back in the pilot's seat, catching a rare nap while Ben watched things from the copilot slot.

Suddenly Hunter was wide awake, his body vibrating from head to toe.

"What's our position?" he asked Ben urgently.

"We're about a half hour out from the coastline," Ben quickly reported.

Hunter was up and looking out the side window. Below him was the *JAWS* plane, beside them was *NJ104*. Way out to the south he could see Crunch's three-ship group. Directly below him, were the Football City troop ships.

About thirty-five miles dead ahead was the nasty storm roaring up from the southwest.

Hunter was on the fleet general radio in an instant.

"Close up! *Close up!*" he was yelling, all radio protocol forgotten. "Close up the formation . . ."

Ben was unquestioningly following Hunter's urgent request. He put the big gunship into a left side bank, following *JAWS* and *NJ104* as they too moved towards Crunch's center group.

"Put air defense radars on high!" Hunter was yelling into the radio. "Lock down for evasive action . . ."

"What have you got, Hawk?" he heard Crunch's voice ask through the increasing radio static.

"I don't know," Hunter replied honestly. His highly developed sixth sense was literally shaking him up and down. He'd come to know that feeling as meaning very bad news.

The nine C-5s were formed up in their mutual defense formation within a half minute of Hunter's original warning.

The MiGs attacked about twenty seconds later.

Hunter saw them before the radar did—they came out of the northwest, flying so fast and so high, the C-5s' air defense systems had barely picked up the blips.

There were four of them. They were MiG-25 Foxbats, super-duper-sonic interceptors built in the old Soviet Union years before, and now fairly prolific on the world's high-priced weapons black market. Hunter was surprised the MiGs were flying this far out to sea. They wore no markings; no ID numbers. This told him they were probably free-lancers hired to patrol the coast of Vietnam.

Aerial attack was always a concern for the large airfleet. Hunter *did* notice as the Foxbats roared by that they were armed with cannon only, and this was some small measure of relief. If they had been carrying air-to-air missiles, the C-5s would have made very fat, very tempting long-range targets.

The MiGs passed over the C-5 formation and went into a flare attack formation. They turned back and their leader and his wingman opened up. Football City troop transport Number Two got it first, the two MiGs tearing cannon barrages across the C-5's wing and tailplane. The third and fourth MiGs mimicked the leaders' attack profile, strafing *Number Two* with a spray of deadly shells. Then the four interceptors streaked high above them, formed up again, and began another dive.

Hunter quickly identified the MiGs strategy. "They're chicken bastards," he yelled over to Ben. "They wouldn't know a fair fight if they fell into it."

In an instant he was back on the radio, screaming for the C-5 formation to get as tight as possible: the less room the MiGs had for maneuver, the less accurate their shots would be. But he also had another reason in mind. With the nine C-5s flying just about wing to wing, Hunter suddenly decreased *Bozo*'s power and began dropping behind the others.

The MiGs went by again, lacing the *JAWS* plane with a quartet of cannon barrages. Instantly the big, sharkmouth-adorned plane began smoking. The Foxbats started their turn back when the flight leader spotted *Bozo* falling behind the rest of the formation. He immediately identified it as the weak sister, the easy prey. That was obviously the MiGs MO—pick on the weakling. Predictably, they turned back south and then east again, passing up the rest of the formation to come at *Bozo* from its exposed left side.

And that, of course, was exactly what Hunter wanted.

"All weapons bays . . . activate!" he yelled back to the gun crew.

Instantly the airplane gave a little shudder as the twenty-one gun port slats snapped open at once.

"All weapons to On . . ." Hunter yelled.

At that moment the lights inside the cockpit dimmed slightly as the gaggle of weapons in the back went on primary power.

The first MiG came in tight, laying a string of cannon shells across *Bozo*'s tail. The airplane bucked once, but regained itself quickly. The second MiG also came in tight, lining a fiery barrage along *Bozo*'s left wing, perilously close to the inner engine. Once again the airplane shuddered; once again Hunter quickly brought it under control.

The next two MiGs came into together, very flat, their sights lined up on the fat part of *Bozo*'s left side fuselage.

And that was the whole idea.

Hunter counted to three, then yelled: "All engagement weapons . . . *fire!*"

Instantly the left side of the huge Galaxy erupted in a sheet of flame as all of the Gatlings, all of the AA-guns, all of the field artillery pieces fired at once.

The MiG pilots never knew what hit them. Both of the speedy interceptors flew right into the fusillade and were simply vaporized. There was nothing left of them but a cloud of microsized pieces of wreckage, hurtling through the air at 350 knots.

Seeing their companions' destruction, the two remaining MiGs immediately went into a steep climb, circled once and then quickly roared off to the northwest from whence they came.

There was a round of cheers from the other C-5s as the MiGs exited the area; the threat for the moment seemed to be over.

But Hunter knew better. No sooner had the pair of MiGs disappeared from sight when his sixth sense began vibrating again.

"Damn!" he yelled. "I don't believe this."

Ben stared at him and then straight ahead of C-5 formation. That's when he saw the swarm of MiGs streaking right towards them.

"Jessuz, there's a hundred of them!" Ben cried.

He wasn't too far off. In an instant Hunter counted as many as 50 MiGs of all types, shapes and sizes. They were rising up from the lower altitude, where they'd obviously been hiding while the first four MiGs probed the C-5 fleet's air defenses.

"We've got to get into that weather now!" Hunter yelled in his lip mic, eyeing the huge storm which was now about a half minute off their left wing.

The nine C-5s instantly turned south, their engines on full power, desperately racing into the heart of the violent storm. They reached it in record time.

The MiGs followed them in.

In all his years of flying, Hunter had never seen anything like it. The nine huge C-5s were suddenly in the middle of a storm of typhoon-proportions—with a swarm of MiGs streaking all around them, firing barrage after barrage at the near-defenseless Galaxys.

Hunter had the guns in *Bozo* firing almost nonstop. Any MiG that came anywhere near the gunship received a broadside unlike anything in aerial warfare. In the confusion of the storm and the air attack the gunners on *Bozo* destroyed seven MiGs in little more than a minute. Meanwhile Hunter and Ben were wrestling with the huge C-5's flight controls. In the near zero visibility they could see MiGs flashing by, followed by parts of C-5s, then more MiGs, then more C-5s. It was total, frightening confusion. The flight panel was lit up like a Christmas tree, and every few seconds or so they could feel the big airplane shudder after receiving a barrage of MiG cannon shells somewhere on its fuselage or wings.

The battle went on like this for what seemed like forever—some of the MiGs apparently figured out that

Bozo was defenseless when attacked from the right side, and they poured it into the huge airplane, even as the tremendous storm roared on around them.

At some point *Bozo* crossed over land itself, where the storm actually grew worse. The weather was so bad, it took them a few minutes to realize the battle was over. The MiGs had disappeared; all the firing had stopped. They'd also lost sight of the rest of the C-5s.

Now the C-5 was lurching blindly through the thundering sky.

"I can't see a damned thing, Hawk!" Ben shouted over the intercom.

Hunter clenched his teeth and tried with all his might to keep his control column steady. He'd been in tight spots before—but this was the worse by far.

The sky was dark as night even though it was the middle of the day. Sheets of rain totally blocked out any hint of guiding light, either from the ground or from the sun. The C-5's wipers raced back and forth across the windscreen, trying vainly to clear away the pounding rain. Every warning bell, buzzer, and beeper on the airplanc's control panel was going off at once—all adding to the chaos inside the dimly lit cockpit.

Bozo had given the MiGs a hell of a surprise with its massive, aerial broadsides—but the C-5 hadn't escaped unharmed. The damage report was grim. Hundreds of MiG cannon rounds had ripped across the fuselage and wings during the air battle, severing hydraulic hoses, electrical wires, and fuel lines. Most critically, the right wing's stabilizers were shot to pieces, causing the already-unbalanced airship to list even more horribly to the left.

The flight controls were shaking so violently now that both Hunter and Ben had to struggle just to hang on. An earsplitting vibration was rattling through the entire airplane—it seemed that all the rivets holding the Galaxy together were going to pop at any second. Loud banging and screeches of steel on steel were echoing through the cavernous hold behind them. Shouts of concern and out-right fear were coming from the gun crews below.

The dials, gauges, and hydraulic pressure LEDs on the airplane's shattered control panel all told the same story—the big transport-turned-gunship was in serious trouble.

And things were quickly getting worse: because of their shot-up wing tanks, they were now running out of gas.

Hunter rapped on the fuel gauge with his knuckle. "We've got about two minutes to put this baby down," he yelled to Ben. "Maybe less . . ."

"Easier said than done, Hawk . . ." Ben yelled back. "We need something long and flat, very quick!"

They put the giant lumbering plane into a wide descending circle, trying to eyeball the jungle below through the horrible blackness of the storm. They were searching for anything clear enough to land the Galaxy, but no matter where they looked, nothing—no landmark, terrain, or landscape feature—could be made out. It was an eerie feeling, flying completely blind—if it wasn't for quick glances at the gyro, they could have easily been flying sideways or even upside down.

"We're down to a minute-twenty of gas, Hawk," Ben yelled, his voice filling with resignation. "This might be it, old buddy."

Hunter had no reason to disagree with him. Then, suddenly, he felt a tingling in the back of his neck. It was *the feeling*, his incredibly developed ESP, breaking through to his conscious state. He steadied himself, reacting purely on instinct as well as his learned acceptance of this lifelong unexplained phenomenon. For an instant, everything seemed calm inside the battered cockpit.

"Southwest," he told Ben. "About twelve miles . . ."

Ben didn't hesitate a beat. Together, they fought the murderous headwind and slowly turned the big plane to the southwest. As they did so, *the feeling* got stronger, telling Hunter that he was heading in the right direction.

But it was also telling him something else. . . .

They continued to wrestle with the flight yokes, nearly out of control in the brunt of the howling wind and rain storm. The Galaxy shook under the strain of the turn and Hunter, Ben, and the gun crew in the hold were bounced around mercilessly as the plane was battered by powerful hurricane-strength airstreams.

Then suddenly, Hunter spotted a flash of light below.

"Do you see that?" he yelled to Ben. "About ten miles dead ahead . . ."

Ben did. There was a bright glow cutting through the clouds.

"What the hell is it?" Ben yelled back. "Searchlights? A fire? Explosions?"

Hunter didn't know—but it was all they had to go on. They brought the bucking C-5 down to 1500 feet—finally breaking through the overcast. In that instant, they found what they were looking for—a long strip of black asphalt cutting through the rain and haze on a north-south position. Once again, *the feeling* had not failed; they were approaching a landing strip.

They eased the C-5 down to 1000 feet and reduced their airspeed to just 150 knots. They were over a very mountainous area, mostly covered with thick jungle and foliage. The glow up ahead got brighter and gradually, they could see what was causing it. Flashes of lights, balls of flame, a long column of black smoke rising into the sky; Hunter and Ben were startled. They'd seen such things before. There was a battle going on down below. A big one.

"Jesuzz—are we really going to land in the middle of a firefight?" Ben yelled.

"We've got no choice," Hunter yelled back. A second later, the left side outer engine kicked once—then died. The right outer one instantly followed suit. Both were out of gas. "We've got to go in. . . ."

The C-5 was down to 800 feet when a flare round went up from the treeline to their left, bursting right in front of them. Despite the torrential downpour, the magnesium round brilliantly illuminated the area for a brief moment. Hunter and Ben were astounded at what they saw below.

Thousands of soldiers were charging from the treeline across an open marsh towards a haphazard collection of bunkers, foxholes, and shallow trenches that stood between them and the airstrip. The airstrip itself was littered with dozens of crashed airplanes—not a very good omen. Even worse, it didn't look like a single round was being fired in defense from the airbase's fortifications.

In the blink of an eye, Hunter knew he had to make a tough decision. He had no idea who was fighting who on the ground, or who was on who's side. But he *did* know from the hundreds of Mayday calls they'd received that the people of Vietnam were under attack. His gut then was telling him the thousands of attacking soldiers below were the bad guys.

And he was about to land right in the middle of them.

"I think we're about to join the underdogs," he yelled over to Ben.

Ben took a quick glance out the window as the human wave attack was drawing closer to the weakly defended fortifications.

"I don't think you'll get any argument from anyone on board," he yelled back.

Hunter brought the C-5 down even further as Ben patched into the plane's intercom system to the gun crews in the back. At that moment, tracer fire came up from the ground directly at the plane, pinging off the huge nose, and left wing. That was it—they had just made an enemy.

Holding the huge plane fifty feet above the treeline, Hunter twisted it into a wide arc, giving the guns on weapon engagement side just enough angle to be used effectively. Then he took a deep breath and called back for the half dozen GE Gatling guns to open fire on the massive human wave assault.

Instantly, the six guns, each firing at a rate of 4,000 rounds per minute, tore into the mass of charging soldiers.

Through the blaze of gunfire flaming from the port side of the C-5, Hunter could see the deadly Gatlings chew up the ranks of the attackers.

But in the dimming glow, he saw something else that made his heart freeze. A second and even larger wave of attackers was emerging from the treeline on the heels of the first, charging over their fallen comrades, some even using the blasted and bleeding bodies as stepping stones to cross the foot deep water of the marsh.

With only enough altitude for one try, and no fuel to pull her up again, Hunter and Ben put the transport into another steep bank to the left which took them over a small mountain at the south end of the runway. It was near here that most of the base's inhabitants seemed to be positioned.

As the C-5 turned toward the head of the runway, for what they knew would be it's final descent, Hunter saw that the second wave of attackers was closing in on the airfield.

"Ben, call back to the crew," he said evenly, "Get ready to open fire again. . . ."

Ben did as requested as Hunter calmly dropped the wing flaps to increase drag. In the hold, the rest of the portholes on the plane's left side—the "killing side"—snapped open.

Hunter continued to decrease his throttle while keeping the enormous plane steady through the crosswinds and the blinding rain. Behind him, the gun crews of *Bozo* were chambering rounds, cranking down elevation, adjusting ranges, all while being bounced around in an airplane that was practically coming apart at the seams.

"Get ready . . ." Hunter called back to the gun crew.

An instant later, he dropped the landing gear, applied the air brakes, and then he and Ben pulled back hard on the controls to lift up the nose.

To the attackers, the C-5 looked for a moment to be suspended in midair. Confusion overtook them as many halted in midcharge and stood with their mouths agape, staring in confusion at this big plane inexplicably adorned in circus colors and scrolling details.

For most of them, though, it was the last thing that they would ever see.

"Fire!" Hunter yelled into the intercom.

A heartbeat later, all of *Bozo's* weapons opened up at once.

The darkened sky was instantly lit up—the thunderous fusillade was deafening. Explosions erupted across the entire front of the attackers, carving deep within their ranks. A tremendous white hot flame, erupting from the right and rear side of the C-5's specially-rigged rear-end blaster, deflecting the propulsion of the thirty-six rockets fired from the LARS II, added to the bizarre light show. Shattered bodies rose high into the air, obliterated by the forceful barrage. Hundreds were killed in a matter of seconds.

But those that survived this lethal outpouring just kept coming—through the wire, past the defensive positions and straight for the airstrip where the C-5 was about to touch down.

"At least now we know which side we're on," Ben yelled as the number 3 engine died. But he and Hunter had a more immediate concern. They still had to put the plane into a steep bank and to turn it over the runway. The ground was coming up fast towards them. Ben called back to the hold for everyone to brace themselves.

Hunter clenched his teeth. *"Here we go. . . ."*

He slammed the control column hard to the left. The C-5's wing dropped and the giant airplane seemed to turn on its tip in midair. The instant Hunter saw the nose of the plane line up with the runway, he pushed the column hard to the right, yanked back, then dropped her down.

The C-5 hit the edge of the tarmac with a resounding thud, its remaining engine screaming for life. The plane bounced—fifteen feet or higher—then came crashing back down on the battered runway. Ben immediately deployed the drag chutes and Hunter locked up the main landing gear brakes—in seconds they were a screeching mass of burning rubber. But it was not enough. They were going too fast and running out of runway very quickly. Aided by the blazing fires burning out of control from the attack, they could see the rapidly approaching far end of the airstrip. And beyond that was the base of the small mountain.

They had to slow down—*fast*.

"Every weapon that's loaded, fire *right now!*" Hunter yelled back to the gun crew.

An instant later, a huge eruption of flame burst from the plane, its blast deflecting out and down. The C-5 shuddered to its rivets, lifting off the ground once again and slamming back to earth—the pure violence of the maneuver effectively cutting down the speed of the plane.

"Hang on!" Hunter yelled.

In the next instant, he disengaged the brakes on the left side, then pulled back hard on the stick. In a blur of movement, Hunter then yanked the controls hard to the right, jammed down with all his weight on the right rudder pedal, and gunned the last port engine with the remaining drops of fuel. The great plane lifted with a hellish scream, and in what seemed like one giant ballet movement, pirouetted on the locked right landing wheel until it did a complete one hundred and eighty degree turn. Dropping hard onto the side of the runway, the plane screeched backwards for several hundred feet until it skidded sideways off into the soft earth alongside the airstrip. Finally, it lurched to a sudden halt, its front gear collapsed, its right wing lodged in the mud.

"Jesuzz!" Ben yelled as he tried to shake out the stars. "Did we really make it?"

"We did." Hunter yelled back—"But maybe not for long . . ."

They were both astonished to see out the port window another human wave of attackers, bigger than the first two combined, racing right towards them.

Hunter didn't have time to think about it.

"All weapons—fire at will!" he called over the intercom to the gun crews in the back.

The big guns behind them began to blast away, violently shaking the airplane once again. Hunter and Ben quickly unclipped themselves from their harnesses. Hunter grabbed his M-16 and a bandolier of tracer clips from the cockpit rack.

"Cover up!" Ben yelled as he unholstered his 9-mm Berretta. He fired off six quick rounds, blowing out most of the C-5's windscreen. A blast of glass shards and pounding rain blew back on them and into the cockpit. But they were now able to see the first line of attackers just as it reached the left side of the plane.

Hunter took an instant to get a good hard look at these soldiers. They were dressed in black "combat pajamas," wearing canvas hats and pith helmets. They looked exactly like an enemy of years ago. But who these men were or for what cause they were fighting, Hunter hadn't a clue.

The Gatling guns were cranking furiously in the back, their muzzle flashes silhouetting the dozens of attackers racing along the tarmac right at the front of the plane. Hunter slapped a 30-round clip into his M-16 and yanked back the bolt to chamber the first round. Then he laid the forearm stock across the shattered windshield's frame and squeezed the trigger.

His tracer rounds found their marks as if they were laser guided. One small line of attackers fell—but more kept coming.

Hunter slapped in another clip as Ben tossed out two hand grenades. Hunter snapped his M-16 to auto and opened up again, trying desperately to cut down the stunned attackers.

Round after round of incoming 7.62-mm ammo zipped and pinged, slamming into the cockpit all around him. Hot shrapnel from detonated grenades sizzled through the air, and the sounds of concussions, explosions, gunshots, mortar blasts, and screams blended into the one long, inexhaustible, blood-curdling roar of all of *Bozo*'s weapons going off at once.

Suddenly a tremendous *baaaaang* rocked the entire airplane. It came from the right rear side.

"I'm going back!" Hunter yelled to Ben. "Do your best up here!"

Ben continued to blast away with his pistol as Hunter scrambled over the tangled masses of hoses, wires, oil lines, and ammo belts, and down the ladder into the weapons hold to investigate.

It was a madhouse.

The gun crews were frantically reloading and firing their weapons as fast as they could. Empty casings were flying everywhere as the crews laid in volley after volley of concentrated firepower.

But outside, the attackers just kept coming.

Orders were shouted, and the hurried sounds of gears clicking could be heard as the muzzles of the guns were depressed as far down as they could go to meet the charge head on. Proximity fuses for the AA guns were set for detonation almost immediately upon leaving the barrels. Shouts of "Ready!" echoed up and down the firing line.

"Fire . . . !" came the screams, over and over.

And each time, the guns opened up once again into the swarming mass of aggressors.

To Hunter, *Bozo* seemed like a three-masted man o' war, unleashing broadside after broadside in a great naval battle on the high seas.

But now the blasts themselves were beginning to rupture the side of the plane. And the attackers kept coming.

In between fusillades, cases of hand grenades were being dispensed in the hold. Now each member of the gun crew put their personal weapon near at hand—the situation was so chaotic and the attackers getting so close that hand-to-hand fighting was looming as a grim possibility.

More explosions rocked the C-5 as Hunter made his

way to the rear. He dashed to a port hole on the other side, keeping low to avoid the armor-piercing rounds that zipped back and forth through the skin of the plane's hull. Peering out he saw the entire outside of the plane was covered with enemy troops trying to blast their way inside.

The situation was beyond critical. The big guns aboard were now ineffective. With their elevations cranked all the way down they could now only fire above the attackers heads—not down at them. The gun crews began to drop hand grenades out the portholes on the left side and through ragged-edged holes on the right side in attempt to blast off the attackers just twenty feet below. Others were firing their small arms at the ceiling of the plane, trying to kill the attackers who were racing back and forth along the top of the fuselage. By now, the Galaxy was peppered with so many bullet holes and shrapnel punctures that the rain was coming down as hard inside some sections of the plane as it was outside.

Three explosions rocked the rear blind spot of the plane. Hunter bolted to the back of the weapons hold, fired a burst through a jagged shell hole in the cargo bay doors to the ground below, and then once again took a look out.

A sizable force, unseen by the gunners on *Bozo*, had amassed underneath the back of the plane. They appeared to be laying explosives under the C-5's huge rear cargo doors, hoping the resulting explosion would split the plane wide enough for them to get in. Hunter passed down the word: this threat had to be dealt with immediately—and preemptively.

Those inside the gun hold that had bayonets attached them to their M-16s; those that didn't grabbed wrenches, pipes, any heavy tool they could use as a club. They all now knew that it was going to come down to a primitive fight for survival.

Thirty seconds went by as the *Bozo* crew got ready. On a nod from Hunter, the gun crew chief finally yelled: "Open the doors!"

With an earsplitting screech, the two heavy rear doors swung open wide, revealing the hundreds of stunned attackers below.

What the attackers saw was a haphazard collection of gun crews and flight mechanics; some kneeling in classic forward-fire-stance, others standing behind them—their M-16's level and ready. . . .

Standing in the middle was a man in a pilot's suit and a helmet.

"Fire!" someone screamed.

Instantly, Hunter and the *Bozo* crewmen opened up. A great roar of gunfire erupted. The first line of astonished attackers were blasted back, another wave took their place and they too were mowed down by the concentrated volley. A third line met the same deadly result. But the attackers were determined, fanatically so. Those surviving the fusillades streamed inside the hold of the plane. There they were met by more gunfire, the razor sharp points of the bayonets, and blunt pieces of steel.

Slashing and stabbing and butting, the fight inside the enormous hold escalated instantly into furious hand-to-hand combat. The screams of the dying were overpowering, and the deck was quickly slippery with blood. But no matter how many attackers were stabbed, bludgeoned, shot, or killed, more charged into the hold of the plane.

Hunter was up front, fighting madly—it had been years since he'd been in a battle like this. But this time the hand-to-hand struggle was so severe and so close that he was reduced to using his M-16 as a club. *It was strange,* he thought in a heartbeat. He had survived hundreds of hours of intense aerial combat—dogfighting against the most sophisticated fighters in the world. He never thought it would end this way—in the mud and the blood, out in the middle of nowhere.

But then a very odd thing happened.

The monsoon downpour suddenly stopped. And just as suddenly, a dozen bugles sounded out. The fury of the attackers instantly dissipated. In a semicontrolled retreat, the enemy soldiers quickly fought their way backward out of the hold of the airplane and jumped down to the tarmac below. Then they all turned tail and ran back across the open ground, eventually melting into the treeline in the distance. The carnage was suddenly over.

An unearthly silence finally descended upon the hold of the transport plane. It was as if everyone inside had been delivered from death by some unseen force.

A weary voice from amidst the astonished crew said it all.

"What the hell happened?" it asked.

Chapter Thirteen

It took almost an hour to wash the blood from the C-5's cargo hold.

It was a disgusting job. Water from the plane's engine cooling apparatus was rerouted into its fire extinguishing systems and sprayed on top of industrial strength disinfectant. The sudsy mixture turned a sickly bright pink as it mixed with the blood of the attackers on the floor and walls of the plane.

Removing the dead bodies of the attackers was even more stomach-churning. There were 74 of them alone inside the plane, another 122 blocking the rear cargo doors. The crew used lengths of pipe and ropes to push and drag the corpses off the airplane and away from the cargo doors. Miraculously, the Americans had suffered only twenty wounded.

Only when the hold was clean and the rear doors closed again did the crew collapse from sheer exhaustion.

All except Hunter. He was up on the C-5's flight deck, frantically trying to get one of its radios working. Both primary radios and the two backups had been shot up either in the MiG attack or the ground battle. He tried every electronics trick he knew, but it was to no avail. All four were beyond repair.

It took a little doing, but he was able to get his long-range NightScope binoculars working. Hanging half way out of the busted front windshield, he scanned the immediate area around the crashed C-5. It was getting to be dusk, and everything was turning to shadow. There were no enemy soldiers in sight, but he could clearly see campfires burning in the hills which bordered the battered airbase on three sides.

Hunter turned towards the embattled fortifications which were about 100 yards off the end of the mud-stuck left wing. He wasn't sure whether anyone was still left alive inside the pathetically ragged set of bunkers. He saw no flags, no manned defensive positions, no attempts to put out the fires still burning all around the fortifications.

The sudden appearance of *Bozo* had definitely diverted the main attack on the base away from the bunkers—if there were any living souls in the fortifications, they at least owed the plane's crew a vote of thanks. Yet no welcome wagon had appeared.

While there was always the chance of another attack, Hunter's gut was telling him one was not imminent. The enemy's sudden retreat still puzzled him; the only causal effect was the end of the monsoon rainstorm. Perhaps the attackers were using the downpour as a shield, or for some other reason—he didn't know. In any case, their brutally crude method of human wave attacks didn't lend itself to night operations.

Still, the gun commanders had already organized a well-armed sentry force, which would be dispersing to positions around the wrecked jet within the hour.

But Hunter couldn't wait that long to find out what was going on, or where the hell they were.

He had to get some answers—quick.

Ten minutes later, Hunter and Ben dropped to the tarmac from *Bozo*'s port side hatch and quickly scrambled behind what was left of the crushed forward landing gear.

To their dismay, the massive airplane looked as bad outside as it did inside. The wounds suffered from the MiG attack had been bad enough. The tremendously severe damage inflicted upon the Galaxy by the massive human wave assault was beyond repair. There was no longer any question about it—the big C-5 would never fly again. They were stuck here—wherever "here" was.

In the drizzle that continued after the monsoon downpour, they could barely make out the large, fortified bunker, a hundred yards away. It looked like the most likely headquarters for this battered, lonely outpost and appeared to be the main target of the fanatical attackers before the C-5 arrived.

"We've got to start looking for some answers over there," Hunter said to Ben, surveying the torn-up, muddy ground that separated them from the bunker. "You up for a little foot race?"

"Loser buys the first round," Ben replied grimly.

They both tightened their gear belts and checked their weapon's ammo loads.

"OK!" Hunter yelled, *"Let's go . . ."*

They were both up and running a second later. But no sooner had they stepped out into the open, when Hunter's sixth sense began to vibrate.

"Damn!" he yelled. *"Incoming . . ."*

In an instant, he yanked Ben down into a shallow trench next to the runway, covering both of them with thick mud in the process. In the distance up in the hills, he'd heard the distinctive *boomp* of heavy-mortar tubes being popped. Five seconds later, a trio of mortar shells came crashing down near the spot where they'd been before Hunter's warning. The explosions rocked the earth all around them.

"Boy, these guys really don't like us," Ben said, wiping the mud from his face. "What'll we do now?"

"We've got to keep going," Hunter replied grimly. "Before they pop again."

Once more, they jumped up and ran like hell towards the bunker. But just as suddenly, the muddy ground in front began to erupt in small geysers of wet dirt. They dove head first into a crater hole, the *CRACK-ziiiingggs!!!* of heavy-caliber rifle rounds zipping all around them. It didn't take long to determine they were being fired on by high performance rifles located in the treetops 300 yards away.

"Snipers, too?" Ben wailed in disgust. "Man, I *hate* snipers."

Hunter could only agree. "This is going to be a real pain in the ass," he said.

They had no choice but to keep moving. For the third time they jumped up and started running. Once again all hell broke loose as sniper fire zipped by them and mortar shells began exploding all around them. But running in a crouch, Hunter and Ben zigged and zagged to the other side of the pockmarked runway—just barely managing to dodge everything that was thrown at them. Skidding down into deep trench, they were finally out of sight and safe—for the moment anyway.

Quickly studying their surroundings, they realized that the ditch was actually part of a series of interconnecting trenches which served smaller fortifications leading up to the larger pockmarked bunker. But all of these smaller positions—gun nests surrounded by sandbags or earthworks—appeared to be abandoned. Crouching low under the streams of sniper bullets whizzing by overhead, Hunter and Ben followed the twists and turns through the defense line and made their way toward the large bunker.

As they moved along the trenches, it was obvious the gunposts had been poorly maintained. Gaps in the sandbagged walls from previous attacks had not been shored up. Discarded weapons, shell casings, and personal equipment were scattered everywhere. Six inches of stagnant water at the bottom of some of these trenches attested to the fact that no system of drainage had been initiated or maintained.

Then there were the skeletons.

The trenches were littered with them; they made for a ghastly sight. Apparently the fighting had been going on here for quite some time, and some of these soldiers had been killed and then buried where they fell. But the constant barrage had gruesomely unearthed them, again and again. At some point, Hunter figured, those who survived must have just given up on the burial details altogether. Outside the trenches was even worse. There were hundreds of skeletons of enemy soldiers snagged on the wire. No attempt had been made by the other side to bury their dead either.

They continued moving through the trenches. Suddenly Hunter stopped dead in his tracks.

"Wait," he whispered urgently. "Listen."

Ben froze.

"Do you hear that?" Hunter whispered.

Ben heard it a moment later. It sounded like voices. Muffled voices.

"Over there," Hunter whispered, pointing his M-16 towards a crude hole dug into the side of the trench, the opening covered only by a tattered blanket.

He motioned for Ben to cover him. Then he silently moved over next to the opening and slipped out his K-Bar knife. Holding his M-16 level in his right hand, he drew back the blanket with the edge of his knife and poked the barrel through the opening.

Ben saw the astonishment on Hunter's face, and soon learned why. Inside were three ragged soldiers, huddled in fear. They were not Asian like the attackers. In fact, they seemed to be European. And though their clothing was threadbare, filthy, and ragged, enough was left for Hunter and Ben to see that they were wearing a variation of the uniform of the legendary French Foreign Legion. These men were emaciated and pale, their faces utterly devoid of expression. Except for their eyes. They had that classic "1,000 yard stare," the frightening gaze that comes with being faced with death every minute of the day.

"Americans," Hunter told them, "We're Americans."

Each, in turn, slowly gave a weak smile. "Are you here to save us?" one asked wearily.

Hunter and Ben stared into the men's faces. At one time, the Foreign Legion had been among the most-respected units in the French Army and indeed, the world. But these soldiers had been reduced to animals, living in holes, apparently unfed, barely armed, surviving moment to moment.

"*Are* you here . . . to save us?" the soldier asked again.

"Maybe," Hunter finally answered.

He and Ben continued their journey through the trenches, passing many similar holes sheltering even more shattered soldiers. Not all of them were Legionnaires. Some wore tattered uniforms of black and orange camouflage, some green camos. There were some dressed in Belgian combat issue, others in the uniform of the Royal Peruvian army. There were even some in the uniform of the army of Morocco. It was quite a mix—obviously many were mercenaries. But they all had one thing in common: extreme combat fatigue.

The enemy gunners up on the ridges and in the jungle around the base continued to pepper the air with lead. It was obvious now that the attackers had the airfield covered on at least three sides. The constant crack of gunfire dictated they keep their heads down. But finally, Hunter and Ben made it to the main fortification.

Crouched on either side of the door frame, they could hear voices inside.

But these were not the weak haggard voices of emaciated soldiers. Rather, their tone sounded strong, forceful, determined.

They also sounded organized—another hopeful sign.

"It sounds like a briefing's going on in there," Ben whispered to Hunter.

"Let's crash the party," Hunter whispered back.

They slipped inside through the double layer of blackout material that hung in the doorway.

They were amazed at what they saw.

There *was* a briefing going on. And the contrast between the conditions of the trenches and the level of military professionalism inside this bunker was as different as night and day.

"Shhhhh . . ."

Startled, Hunter and Ben looked to their right to see a French Foreign Legion officer positioned by the door.

"The commander is speaking," he said in a heavily accented whisper. "Please sit down and be quiet. He must not be disturbed."

Hunter shrugged to Ben, and the two found seats at the back of the bunker.

Before them a dozen lower-ranking officers were seated in rapt attention. At the front of the room was the apparent commander of the base. He was a thin, elderly man, dressed from head to toe in tiger camouflage with a red beret set at a jaunty angle. This was at one time the standard jungle issue for the French Foreign Legion.

This commander, a colonel, was in the middle of a detailed strategy session. A large, ancient-looking map stood on an easel behind him, and just out of sight from Hunter and Ben.

"Our position is here," he said as he swung his pointer at a place on the map. "The Viet Minh is dug in along here." He indicated a wide arc to the west. "Overall, the plan is to constrict our position to a point where it will be impenetrable. Several important steps must be taken to achieve that goal—and in a minimum amount of time. Now, my first order is for you, sir." The colonel nodded his head towards an officer with a long scar running down the side of his face. "You are to reconfigure the heavy guns to these northwest and southwest points on our perimeter for maximum counterfire." He indicated several precise positions on the map. "This has to be done by 0800 hours," he went on. "Do you have any questions?"

"No, sir," the scarred officer crisply replied.

The colonel continued on, using his pointer to indicate how, where, and when other defensive positions were to be shored up on the map. He gave orders for the airstrip to be cleared and repaired, to organize patrols to probe the enemy defenses, to establish ambush points, and to forage for potable water.

Sitting in the shadows in the back of the bunker, Hunter and Ben listened and observed as this colonel went down the line, giving detailed instruction to each of the officers before him. They were surprised by the thoroughness of the briefing and with the spirited elan of the presentation. For the first time since their arrival, their spirits began to rise.

But Hunter edged a little closer. Something wasn't right here and he felt uneasy.

Then he saw why.

The chart the colonel was outlining his strategy on was a map of France. According to him, they were defending the city of Lyons.

Hunter and Ben just stared at each other.

"What the fuck is going on here?" Ben gasped.

Hunter could only shake his head. "It's a cuckoo's nest," he replied bitterly. "These guys are just as nuts as the ones in the trenches. They're just better dressed."

They'd seen enough. With little regard for courtesy, they got up and hastily left the bunker.

They stepped outside and immediately a barrage of shots was fired at them from the treeline three football-field-lengths away. Hunter yanked Ben into an adjacent slit trench, the stream of bullets striking exactly where they had been standing.

"These guys are really fucking bugging me," Ben said through a mouthful of dirt.

Hunter could only agree. But his thoughts were on the

C-5 and the men of *Bozo*. It was becoming painfully obvious that to get out of this dire situation, whatever they had to do—whatever *that* could be—they would have to do on their own.

They inched their way out of the trench and scrambled to a bigger, deeper ditch.

"So where the hell are we, Hawk?" Ben asked wryly. "Dien Bien Phu?"

Hunter quietly scanned the surrounding ridges and mountains that poked out through the heavy mist. And then at the acres of ground up earth, discarded weapons and broken bodies. He just shook his head.

"We're not at Dien Bien Phu, Ben," he said grimly. "I think we're at a place they once called Khe Sanh."

It took them almost an hour to get back to *Bozo*—sniper bullets and mortar rounds following them the entire way.

Night and an even thicker fog had settled around the plane by this time. They found sentries posted in a defensive perimeter upon their return. And not surprisingly, the *Bozo* crew had already begun to fortify their position.

As usual, Hunter threw himself into the work and seemed to be everywhere. He reconfigured the positions of some of the big guns to provide firepower on both sides of the battered airplane. Then he handled an on-board acetylene torch in cutting some of the gunports on the starboard side of the plane. Once all the holes were cut, Hunter and the crews pushed and strained, moving several of the Gatlings and AA guns into position at their new placements and securing them to the main frame structures of the plane. Then began the arduous task of re-arming the weapons.

And the work continued.

With Hunter's help, the flight engineers rigged auxiliary electrical power, splicing wires and patching hoses, repairing what damage they could. With the mechanics, Hunter helped plug the larger holes that perforated the deck and ceiling of the plane. After everything was done to give them at least a fighting chance should another attack come, many of the crew members collapsed, some even falling into a fitful sleep.

But not Hunter.

He'd spent another hour trying to get the flight deck radios to work—but again, it was no use. Now he sat alone in the C-5's cockpit, staring through the shattered windshield and off into the darkness. His mind was spinning too fast to sleep, pondering the dire situation. He couldn't shake the feeling that he had let everyone down.

He had landed the plane in the worse place possible, right in the middle of a desperate military situation, and right in the middle of a country that was apparently overflowing with desperate situations. And the base defenders appeared to be the worse military organization he had ever seen. Just what the Legionnaires were doing here, he had no idea. This was a place under siege and attack, yet they had no command structure, no discipline, no nothing. Judging from what they'd witnessed in the Legion's bunker, insanity ruled this place.

And now they were stuck in the asylum.

He sat there all night, mulling over every detail, fact, and piece of information he could conjure up. Right through the darkest hour before dawn, he hoped that somehow, two, or three of these details would add up to something—something tangible, something he could use to turn this whole thing around and get his men out of this trap. But nothing added up. The hills themselves prevented them from walking out, even if they weren't crawling with enemy soldiers. They had only so much ammo on board the downed plane, so much fuel for electricity, so much food and water. The enemy was obviously well-equipped. From what he'd seen during the attack, they might be two full infantry divisions strong, and not reluctant to sacrifice large numbers of men.

The situation seemed hopeless.

Dawn finally broke. Before the monsoon clouds rolled in, the sky overhead was perfectly clear. Hunter watched gloomily as the early morning sun sent shafts of sunlight across the surrounding ridges and probing through the thick fog that covered the jungle floor, the base, and the runway. As the morning mist slowly burned off, he began to make out the shapes of the dilapidated bunker and fortifications of the battered outpost. And he was reminded, once again, that he was responsible for placing the lives of his men in jeopardy, here in the middle of a muddy, battered hell.

But then through the fog, a reflective glint caught his eye. It came from the direction of the other end of the runway, about a mile away. As the fog lifted, he squinted hard, trying to make it out.

Then suddenly, he saw it very clearly. Lying belly down at the opposite end of the runway was another battered C-5. And on its crumpled wing were about twenty soldiers waving their arms.

They had seen Hunter before he had seen them.

Chapter Fourteen

It turned out that the other C-5 was the one flown by the New Jersey 104th—Frank Geraci's elite combat engineers.

As soon as he'd spotted the Galaxy at the far end of the runway, Hunter rushed back into the hold of *Bozo* to get the brightest hand-held torch in the plane. Word had traveled fast throughout the plane that another C-5 was down on the base. Now many of the crew were crowded into the *Bozo*'s cockpit, anxiously watching as Hunter conducted a morse code conversation with the other aircraft.

Flashing back and forth for more than ten minutes, the crew on *Bozo* learned that *NJ104* had come down shortly after they did, sometime during the attack. Thankfully, according to the flashing message, with no casualties.

Only by the fact that they had landed at the opposite end of the base did they avoid the brunt of the last human wave assault. But it was clear that *NJ104* was in a very vulnerable position—in a wide open area and completely exposed.

Hunter sent one last return message to the other Galaxy, telling the crew to stay put until he got there.

Then he grabbed his M-16, a bandolier of smoke grenades, and went back into the hold of the plane.

* * *

Ten minutes later, Hunter and a squad of volunteers from *Bozo*'s crew hit the tarmac and broke into a run.

Within seconds, sniper fire and mortar rounds began to rain down on them. But following Hunter's expert lead, they made it unharmed to the main forward trench. From there they followed the man-made ditches through the camp, making left and right turns through many junctions, stopping occasionally to get their bearings. Finally, they came to the end of the trenches about center field—500 yards from where the 104th's C-5 sat crumpled at the far end of the runway. There, the squad took cover in the rusted hull of a long-ago crashed C-124 Globemaster.

Hunter considered the immediate situation. From here on, it was 1,500 feet of wide open, flat, bare tarmac with not a blade of grass or a mud hole for cover. It was a virtual shooting gallery for the snipers and mortar crews hidden in the hills. He couldn't risk the lives of the other men of the patrol—from here he would have to go it alone.

He had a plan, though.

He checked the wind direction. There was a good breeze blowing towards the direction of *NJ104*—about 10 mph, he figured. Gathering his dozen smoke grenades, Hunter yanked the pin on one of them and tossed it out into the open. The grenade popped and hissed, emitting a cloud of thick white smoke that started to drift downwind. Taking a deep breath, he jumped out of the trench, into the smoke, and started his long run towards Geraci's Galaxy.

Immediately, the air rang with the cracks and zings of sniper fire. Hunter was safely hidden from view—but not for long. As soon as he outran the smoke, he dove flat out on the tarmac. The snipers and mortar crews in the hills opened up again. Hunter quickly yanked the pin to a second grenade and tossed it ahead. Then he was up again and into the white cloud, dodging and twisting the hail of hot lead probing for him through the smoke.

Now he was throwing the grenades ahead of him as he

ran, planting before him a path of hissing canisters to continue obscuring his mad dash.

But every sniper in the area quickly got wise. They immediately sighted in on the general direction of the white smoke and opened up. The mortar crews had seen what was going on, too, and cranked down to get the most distance. Realizing that this man would soon be past their limited range, they dropped their shells all over the thinning white cloud drifting along the runway.

Hundreds of pieces of lead flew past Hunter, sounding like a mass of insane mechanical bees. Explosions rocked the ground all around him, sending him sprawling several times. But as soon as he dove for cover, he was up and running again. Rifle fire continued to stab into the smoke, searching for a target, but the snipers were firing blind. On the other hand, Hunter could feel their cross hairs trying to catch him, and many times abruptly changed his course just as a round zipped by where he had been.

With only 100 yards to go, he tossed his last smoke grenade. Now it was going to be a wide open run for him.

But then a weird thing happened.

The bullets and the mortar shells stopped following him.

Hunter quickly realized that the enemy's weapons were no longer able to reach him. As they were currently positioned, he was out of their range.

Still, Hunter had to scamper the last forty yards without the benefit of his smoke covering.

It took two rolls to avoid the longest-range sniper bullets. With one last dive he made it over a ditch and into a small stream. He hit it with a spectacular splash of mud and water. When he looked up, he saw the grinning faces of Geraci and his men looking down at him.

"Nice technique, Hawk," Geraci told him. "Good follow-through. Good extension."

Hunter picked himself up and started wiping the mud off his already dirty flight suit. "I should have packed another bag."

They helped him out of the ditch, the crack of sniper fire still echoing in the distance. There were handshakes all round—Hunter just could not believe that they were actually there.

"We must have come down right after you," Geraci told him. "We saw the fires and the smoke, but we had no idea that you guys were in the middle of it."

"Don't feel bad," Hunter told him. "It was a party you were better off missing."

He quickly filled them in on the vicious attack on *Bozo*, and the discovery of the madman in the Legion bunker. He also told them that *Bozo* was wrecked beyond repair.

Geraci shook his head gloomily. "Same for us," he said pointing back to *NJ104*. "It's a miracle we all made it down in one piece."

Hunter studied the big C-5 wreck. Like *Bozo*, its wings were crumpled, its fuselage battered and laced with MiG cannon shell holes.

"Those MiGs really fucked us up in that storm," Geraci told him. "We came in just about dead-stick. I'll tell you, we were literally gliding at the end. Lucky we had a good man at the controls . . ."

That's when Hunter looked over Geraci's shoulder and saw the smiling face of Frost, his long-time friend.

They embraced warmly. "You did have the best," Hunter told Geraci. "Compared to what I did with *Bozo*, it looks like you came down on a three-pointer."

"Hardly," Frost told him. "Let's just say I did a classic pancake—with my wheels down."

They walked back to the crumpled airplane, several mortar rounds coming down out-of-range about fifty yards away.

"Well, you picked a better spot to set down than I did," Hunter said. "At least they can't shoot at you from here—not yet anyway."

Geraci had already deployed *NJ104*'s six bulldozers around the exposed end of the Galaxy, giving the crew some protection from wayward shrapnel or an incredibly lucky shot from the enemy-occupied hills. Other heavy equipment aboard the airplane had been used to break up some of the tarmac and place it around the airplane as a barrier should the Minx decide to launch what would be for them a very long-range ground attack. Several machine-gun posts were set up along this asphalt defense perimeter, with lines of concertina wire and claymore mines serving as the tripwire.

But they all knew that it was just a matter of time before the Minx moved at least some of their weapons and bring them to bear on the second C-5.

"This is quite the pickle then, isn't it?" Frost asked Hunter with classic understatement.

"We always seem to find ourselves in these kinds of predicaments, don't we?" Hunter replied wryly. "Maybe we should get a different agent."

"I think we need a meeting of the minds," Geraci said. "And we should combine our forces. The question is: our place or yours?"

Hunter thought for a moment. "Well, the accommodations aren't as good," he replied. "But we've got more firepower on *Bozo*, therefore better defense. If these guys ever attack you way out here . . ."

He didn't have to say anymore. Both Geraci and Frost were nodding in agreement.

"We'll go back with you now," Geraci said, retrieving a bag of smoke grenades. "Then we'll work out a plan to bring my guys over."

"Sounds good to me," Hunter said, checking the wind and finding it had shifted and was blowing in their direction. "You guys bring your jogging shoes?"

Chapter Fifteen

Behind Enemy Lines

His name was Long Dong Tru.

He was commander of all "liberating" forces in-country between the forty-sixth and forty-seventh parallel, a territory which gave him several hundred square miles in which to operate, with approximately 33,000 front-line troops to do it with.

His forces weren't part of a larger national army, per se. Rather they were "affiliated partners" in a collection of other armed units, contracted to conquer to the southern part of Vietnam. Their employers were the board members of Capitalistic Communism, Incorporated—CapCom, for short. The conglomeration of CapCom's hired military units was known as the Vietminx.

At the moment, most of Dong's forces were in position around an old U.S. Marine fire base known as Khe Sanh. They were, at last report, finally about to annihilate the most recent defenders of this cursed position, and then move on to take the strategic highway beyond. This road led to the poorly defended cities of the south, which were Dong's actual goals. They offered vast opportunities for plunder, valuable resources and taxable populations.

But his troops had to get by Khe Sanh first.

The campaign to do so had been going very slowly. The

enemy at Khe Sanh, a mishmash of Caucasian defenders, led by a cadre of romantic French fools, had certainly been stubborn. They were heavily armed and had a wide field of fire. But with each attack by Dong's forces, the enemy base came that much closer to being overwhelmed, and this brightened his spirits immensely. The sooner they were able to roll over Khe Sanh, the sooner they could reach the highway and be in position to sack the cities beyond.

Dong sat back in his custom-made chair, momentarily looking up from the most recent battle reports from the front, which was about fifteen miles to the southeast. His rather palatial headquarters looked especially pleasing to him today. It was a mixture of communications gear and artwork, war maps and fine threaded rugs, a beautiful marble conference table holding no less than twelve radio-telephones. Best of all, the HQ was mobile: it was actually built into the back of a large trailer truck which was pulled by a heavy-duty, high-performance Mercedes-Benz armored truck. This way, Dong could live in the splendor he thought he deserved, and still stay close to his line units, and thus keep them on a very tight leash.

He was very new to this commander business—up until a few months before he'd been a lowly corporal in a truck supply unit, lugging water and food to Minx expeditionary forces operating inside what used to be called Laos. Despite his middle age, he'd been conscripted into the Minx forces a year earlier. Given the most basic of training, he was handed the keys to a supply truck and told he was now a driver.

He'd never fired a gun, never faced an enemy. The extent of his military service had been driving the old Route 7 between Hanoi and the Pathet town of Qientienne and back again. A chronically stiff back, and modern version of saddle sores were his only rewards.

Then Dong got lucky. *Very* lucky.

One night, while returning from Qientienne, he came upon what he first thought was a traffic accident. There were three vehicles, two ancient Jeeps and a supply truck like his own, fused into one big pile of smashed metal and busted glass. There were a total of thirteen bodies lying about, some mangled and crushed, others bleeding, but relatively undisturbed. There was no one else around.

It took Dong a few minutes to figure out that what he'd come upon was not a traffic accident, but an ambush, one in which both sides seemed to have got the last shot in. His main clue was that seven of the dead were dressed in black pajamas and ski masks, the garb of choice for Chinese highwaymen who were known to operate in the general area. The others were apparently civilians. Closer inspection revealed that many of the dead had been shot and *then* run over by vehicles. Others had been stabbed to death. Two figures were still locked in a death embrace, their respective daggers plunged into one another's chests. In any case, there were no survivors.

Dong was two seconds away from calling in a report to the nearest Minx headquarters, when something stopped him. He would never really know what it was—an unseen force, almost physically removing his fingers from the radio button, and then leading him to the back of the heavily-damaged truck. It was here that he discovered what the ambushers had been gunning for: seventeen large boxes filled with gold bars.

By new world monetary standards, Dong had stumbled upon more than $50 million in gold. What it was doing out there, under limited guard, he would never know. Or care.

Before that time, Dong had not considered himself an insubordinant man. He had respected his father and his elders while growing up, and he respected his superior officers now. Nor did he consider himself a dishonest man. He'd been kettle-maker for most of his adult years, and had charged his customers fair value for his work. And neither did he consider himself a greedy man; he'd plied his wares in a small village near the Chinese border and he had not seen a great deal of money in that time. He never thought he needed it that much.

It went without saying that his duty was to report what he had found and stand guard over it until someone in authority arrived.

But Dong stole the gold anyway.

He barely remembered doing it to this day. It was as if a supernatural force manipulated his hands to lift the heavy boxes out of the demolished truck and put them in his own. The same ghostly force then made him start his truck, put it in gear and hastily drive away.

And it was a spirit that showed him exactly where to bury the fortune in the field near his unit barracks. And the same ethereal presence gave him the balls to march right into CapCom's main office in Hanoi and announce that he wanted to buy an army and offer its services as part of the Viet Minx.

That's how things were done in Hanoi these days. No more bullshit about "the endless revolution," or "the People," or "socialism." No—these days CapCom, Inc., would literally sell you an army, and everything needed to go with it: equipment, ammunition, weapons, food, fuel, water, and, of course, troops. And with that army, you went out and did CapCom's fighting for them.

To those who could afford it, immense power and prestige came with that army. For an army could gain conquests, and conquests meant the spoils of war, and captured territory, which meant taxes, tolls, and whatever valuables came with the land. If the product was right, the operational arm of CapCom, the Minx High Command, would even reimburse you for some especially valuable piece of conquered territory, including expenses. When the campaign was over, you simply wrote them a bill. Depending on the breaks, $50 million dollars could double or even triple very quickly. Dong had seen it with his own unit's money-hungry officers.

And now he wanted it very much for himself.

He poured himself another cup of tea, and took a sweet biscuit from his breakfast tin. Soon it would be time for him to write up a bill for the conquest of Khe Sanh and present it to the Minx High Command. He'd already added up the figures in his head. The operation had cost him 4,100 troops so far. High casualties were not unexpected in human wave attacks—he was due then a rebate the equivalent of $500 per man. Equipment losses equaled about half the dead-troop fee, and he figured he could charge off at least half his ammunition expenditures as expenses to the High Command. Extra food and water he had to pay himself.

The whole one attack-a-day operation was in the black so far—and he had to do everything in his power to keep it that way. This was why he was trying to take Khe Sanh a little bit at a time, using only light infantry troops, without long-range artillery or air support. Those luxury items were available, but expensive, and the bottom line was what was important in this war. CapCom was a demanding employer, and the competition for lucrative conquests among the other independently-run Minx units was fierce, so holding the line on costs was the only way to go if a commander wanted to turn a profit.

Dong slowly sipped his tea and then turned back to the latest front line reports.

It was time to get back to work.

Bad news walked in the door five minutes later.

It was one of his command staff aides, and the man was visibly trembling. Dong asked him what he wanted and the man let loose with a burst of apologies. Then he got to the doom and gloom: Not only had their most recent attack on Khe Sanh failed to finally overrun the base, there were reports that two large cargo planes had crash-landed on the airstrip, and they had brought some measure of reenforcement to the embattled defenders.

Dong dropped his tea cup onto his lap. He couldn't believe what he was hearing. He began ranting. *Who the hell would be flying reenforcements into Khe Sanh? Who the hell cared about the people dying there?*

The aide was frozen with fear. "There are unconfirmed reports, sir," he gulped, "that they might be Americans."

Dong felt his eyes go wide with fear and befuddlement. *"Americans?"*

The aide could barely speak at this point. "Our intelligence people say the airplanes are of American manufacture," he said, his voice barely a whisper. "They are painted in strange, garish ways, typical of aircraft flown by the Americans these days."

Dong was simply astonished. "Why would the Americans come here?" he asked, more to himself than the aide. "For what reason would they want to become entangled in this?"

The aide didn't know what to do, so he just shrugged. He was certain that Dong would execute him on the spot. This was the usual response of Minx commanders when they were given bad news.

But Dong surprised him.

"Americans are always trouble," he said, pulling on his chin in gloomy thought. "And bad for business. Maybe they want to take over the place themselves, and then the highway beyond. Maybe they want a cut of our action, or maybe make a separate deal with High Command . . ."

The aide just shrugged again. "We should wipe them out quickly, sir," he offered.

"We must ascertain their intentions first," Dong said. *"That* makes the most business sense. We must learn if they are here to stay. And more importantly, whether more are coming."

"What shall I do, sir?" the aide asked.

Dong was quiet for a long moment. "Bring me the fastest, most intelligent, most decorated soldier in our corps," he said finally. "He will volunteer to get very close to the enemy base and be my eyes and ears. I must learn more about these Americans even as we are destroying them."

Relieved, the aide heartily agreed. "I can process the new orders, sir . . ."

"Do that," Dong replied, unsteadily returning to his tea cup, "and then report to the front line. You will take your place in the next human wave attack."

Chapter Sixteen

Khe Sanh

It had been a hell of a run.

Hunter, Geraci, and Frost had made their way back across the open 500 yards to the perimeter of the trench works by using the favorable shift in the wind and Hunter's smoke grenade technique.

Once they were back within range, the enemy sniper and mortar crews opened up on them every time they could be seen through the thinning smoke. It had been another crouch, run, and dive exercise, with each explosive thud hammering home the extremely dangerous situation in which they now found themselves. More than once, Hunter's finely tuned sixth sense saved them from being hit by incoming mortar rounds.

Finally, they made it to the rotting hull of the Globemaster. Hooking up with the waiting rifle squad, they dashed into the deeper trenches. Weaving their way back through the web of defensive positions, they soon reached the shattered hulk of *Bozo*.

It was now the most heavily fortified position on the base. Weapons were poking out of every conceivable orifice; so many, it was almost comical, especially with *Bozo*'s wild circus color scheme and scrolling designs.

Inside the wrecked plane's great hold, though, it was all

business. The crew was working at a feverish pace, as always. Some were adjusting the new gun positions and running ammo or powder or both to the weapons' systems. Others were posted on the portholes that now lined both sides of the fuselage, machine guns and M-16s at the ready. It was obvious that the *Bozo* crew was ready for whatever the foreseeable future held for them.

After a brief reunion with the *Bozo* gun crew, Hunter, Geraci, Ben, and Frost climbed up to the shattered flight deck and quickly got down to work.

Ben started off, flipping through the pages of his flight notebook, and gave a grim update of the situation aboard *Bozo*. About 50 percent of the electricity and hydraulic power had been restored, and all the heavy weapons would be working or will be working within two hours. Cutting out the new gun ports and the reconfiguration of the weapons around the interior of the hold was finished. Some measure of 360 degree firepower was now available. There was 65 percent of the on board ammunition left. And despite the hellish battle on the runway the previous day, all thirty-six men of the gun and flight crews were in fairly good fighting shape.

It was now Geraci's turn.

"I've got a total of 100 men," the combat engineer began. "We've got six bulldozers, a backhoe, two front-end loaders, and two medium-size cranes. As far as weapons, besides our small arms, we've got five TOW launchers, a half dozen 105-mm field howitzers, and about thirty heavy- and light-machine guns. We're at 100 percent ammo for all of them at the moment. We've also got a half ton of TNT, Semtex, and C4."

Hunter was next.

"What can I say?" he asked with no small irony. "We're totally pinned down by those fuckers that attacked us yesterday. They hold the hills on three sides and we'd never make it over that mountain behind us—not all of us, anyway. We are, in a word, trapped: there's really no way out."

The other men on the flight deck could only shake their heads in agreement.

"And the guys running the show here are really *that* nuts?" Geraci asked after a long pause.

Both Hunter and Ben gave a grim laugh.

"Worse," Hunter replied. "It's really looney tunes."

He quickly repeated some of the unintentionally humorous events they'd witnessed inside the Legion bunker—but stopped in midsentence.

"Something's up . . ." he said enigmatically.

At that moment, they heard a low whistle from below. Hunter went to the cockpit and stuck his head out of the smashed window. Below were two of the sentries posted forward of the C-5's nose. Between them was a French Foreign Legion officer. Hunter immediately recognized him. It was the officer with the long scar on his face that they had seen inside the Legion bunker.

"We caught him poking around our perimeter," one guard reported.

"I am Captain Jacques Zouvette," the Frenchman called up to Hunter. "I must talk with you."

Hunter thought it over for a moment, then gave the sentries the high sign.

"OK, bring him up."

Five minutes later, the Legionnaire officer was standing before them. His uniform was in slightly better shape than the Legion soldiers in the line trenches, but he was just as thin and haggard. He was sweating profusely—it was getting hot outside as the blazing sun rose higher in the sky.

"My apologies to you all," he began in thick English. "I don't think you saw a true representation of the defensive forces here. I would like to correct that if I may."

Hunter eyed him closely. The haunted eyes and the scar

running the length of his left cheek spoke volumes of this man's combat experience. There was something honest-looking about him.

"Can you tell us exactly what is going on here?" Hunter asked him.

The Legion officer gratefully sat down.

"I can try," he said.

As they listened to his story for the next ninety minutes, there was no disagreement among them—they had landed in one of the most indefensible positions imaginable. The ridges to the west and the jungle-covered hills to the north and east were held, not by the Viet Minh, as the colonel in the bunker had called them, but by "liberation" forces, nicknamed the "Viet Minx." The Minx were a collection of well-equipped fanatical armies, subcontracted by a part-nership of ruthless Asian warlords called "CapCom." These warlords stopped at nothing in their quest to con-quer the entire country—and, ironically, in the face of their Marxist predecessors, make a profit doing so. Many of the long-rumored offshore oil and gas deposits in and around Vietnam had been found in the past five years—now the country had the potential to be the Kuwait of Southeast Asia. And even in the unstable conditions around the world, oil was still king.

As Zouvette told it, the base here stood in the way of the Minx's attempt to secure this part of the valley and a sec-tion of a battered highway beyond called Route 9. That is what the Minx and, ultimately, CapCom wished to own, for it would expedite the conquest of the prosperous cities to the south. When those objectives were taken, the Viet Minx would control the top third of the country. This, coupled with the impending large attacks in the Middle Highlands and the southern Mekong Delta area, was ex-pected to lead to the fall of the entire country. Only the stubborn resistance by the Legion for the last six weeks had prevented the Minx from rolling over the base and moving on.

As Zouvette explained it, it had been six weeks of hell.

From an original force of 12,000 paratroops—a multinational force of Legionnaires and mercenaries airlifted from what was once called India—all that remained after the nonstop brutal onslaught were about 150 men. And now they were all in a state of shell shock, barely capable of concerning themselves with anything but basic survival.

But that was not all.

"The entire medical staff is dead," Zouvette went on. "The direct result of a complete lack of respect by the Viet Minx for the big red cross. We have no medical facilities. The distribution of supplies is nonexistent.

"Though it rains buckets everyday, the drinkable water supply is drying up very quickly. Just two days before your arrival, a nearby spring that we drew water from was poisoned by the Viet Minx. My men also do not have much in the way of food. Most of them have been hanging on by sheer willpower alone."

There was no doubt that these defenders were fortunate that *Bozo* had come when it did, Hunter thought. Otherwise, the last assault would probably have turned into a complete slaughter, and the base finally overrun.

But the unspoken grim conclusion by everyone in the meeting was that the American's sudden arrival had simply forestalled that outcome—by only a few days at the most.

Zouvette took a deep breath and went on. "We are surrounded by a seemingly bottomless reserve of attackers. Though they lack air power and heavy guns, the base is constantly pounded night and day by mortar and covered by sniper fire, as you have probably noticed. As soon as the monsoon season started, we were faced with human wave assaults—exactly like the one you landed in the midst of. Every time the heavens open up and the rains pour down, they attack. Whenever the downpour stops, so does the attack."

Hunter just shook his head.

"But that seems ass-backwards," Ben said. "Why attack

constantly and then withdraw completely? If they continued, they could at least hold some territory—there seems to be plenty of them."

"They do many strange things," Zouvette agreed. "Each assault succeeds in overrunning one or two forward positions. Before they withdraw, they fill it with mines, poison, or even toxic waste to make it completely unusable for us again. It's actually very clever, the little bastards. With each attack the perimeter shrinks, as does our force total. We will soon have our backs against the wall," Zouvette said, indicating the small mountain about 100 yards behind *Bozo*. "This base was once three times as big, covering almost a hundred acres. Now, all that is left is this area here, a battered collection of bunkers, foxholes and trenches, most of which are over thirty years old. And I am sad to say that all of them are in shambles. Unfortunately, our resources are so depleted that nothing can be done to strengthen them or build new ones."

And Zouvette confirmed one more thing for them. There was absolutely no command structure at the base. The commander, Colonel LaFeete, was quite insane.

"His orders have no ground in reality, either in a military sense or in his regard for the welfare of his troops," Zouvette said quietly. "For this last assault, we only had just enough strength left to wait for them to walk into our bunkers. After that . . ." His voice trailed off and his eyes misted over as he thought of what might have happened. He tried to apologize for not having the ability to come to the rescue of the besieged C-5.

But Hunter would hear nothing of it.

"You've already gone above and beyond the call of duty, my friend," Hunter told him.

"My thanks to you, sir," Zouvette said. "To all of you. Your timely arrival has saved us from being completely overrun. We are most grateful."

Ben mixed up a pot of hot coffee; its aroma quickly

filled the small space. Now close to noon, it was getting hot outside and in.

Zouvette took a long deep sip. Then his face brightened slightly. "Can your planes be fixed?" he asked hopefully.

It was up to Hunter to deliver the bad news.

"While the runway is basically in usable shape, it is a moot point." He paused and looked at Zouvette. "Neither of our C-5s are going anywhere—they are not in flying condition. Nor could they be made so—we just don't have the gear, the spare parts, or the capability."

Zouvette's expression instantly changed from hope to despair.

"Then we die here," he said gloomily, staring into his coffee cup. "As will you, my friends."

No one could disagree.

All in all, it was a bad state of affairs. Hunter knew from the radio transmissions picked up on the way in that they were not the only ones in desperate straits. The whole country of Vietnam was in big trouble, and the likelihood of someone coming to their rescue was practically nonexistent. As far as he knew, the people back at Edwards had no idea where any of them were. And even if they did, there was little they could do about it.

"The way I see it, we have two very clear objectives," Hunter slowly began, using a real map of the area brought by Zouvette. "First, we have to defend ourselves. We have to secure the area. We can rebuild the bunkers and shore up the trenches with the heavy machinery on *NJ104*. We should also repair the wire, and contract our defensive area into a triangular formation. This way we can use the guns from *Bozo* for interlocking fire to the three main bunkers at the points of the triangle. We need to maintain these close-in positions as well as monitor the status of the entire outer perimeter. If the Minx continue to attack and make useless any forward positions, as Captain Zouvette has told us, we need to be updated constantly on the situation.

"Water supplies should be put on strict rationing," Hunter went on. "Luckily, though, food isn't a problem right now, as both *Bozo* and *NJ104* are loaded with MRE packs—we will supply the Legion with our surplus immediately."

Hunter looked at each of the officers as they passed the coffee pot around the flight deck. Despite the dire situation, not one of these men showed the slightest hint of resignation. Instead, Hunter saw what might be considered as a contradictory vibe: a grim "can do" attitude. He'd been through a lot with them—especially Ben and Frost. But their demeanor never changed. He was proud of them, and proud that he could call them friends. And he knew that because of these men, and the men that served under them, ideas like freedom and democracy would prevail, no matter what the odds.

"Then," Hunter continued, "The second thing we have to do is start thinking of ways to get out of here."

Each man stared up at him, the expressions a mix of surprise and concern.

"How will we do that?" Frost asked.

Hunter just shrugged; he really had no idea. Yet.

Suddenly, they all heard the spatter of raindrops begin to splash onto the hull of the C-5. Now understanding what it signaled, they all froze—but just for a second. The Minx were about to attack again. They quickly grabbed their weapons.

"It's time to take a closer look at who we're fighting," Hunter called over his shoulder as he climbed down into the hold.

Then he leapt from the port-side hatch and ran out into the intense downpour.

Not five seconds later, more than a thousand screaming, bugle-blowing, flag-waving Viet Minx emerged from the treeline 300 yards away and began a charge towards the base. This human wave was more than 200 yards wide and half as deep. Its obvious target was *Bozo*.

Hunter looked back towards the battered airplane and saw the gun crews inside were scrambling to their positions. Off to the left, a small stream of tattered Legionnaires and their mercenaries were running through the trenchworks near the main bunker, manning what was left of their meager defense line. The arrival of *Bozo* seemed to have infused some hope into these desperate defenders.

Suddenly Ben was beside him.

"Our center and left flank are covered," Ben yelled over the racket of bugles, screams, and pouring rain.

"Yeah, but our asses are hanging out on the right," Hunter yelled back.

It was true. While there were some Legion positions to the right of *Bozo*, they were unmanned.

"Help the guys inside," Hunter told Ben "I'll see what I can do over here."

With that, he was off into the torrential downpour.

Mortar rounds exploding all around him, Hunter ran about fifty feet before he spotted an abandoned M-60 machine-gun post at the edge of the wire. He dove in, head first, landing in a pool of thick mud. Wiping the sludge from his eyes, he saw the position was unmanned; the gunner and ammo feeder were lying in a crumpled heap at the back of the hole, cut to pieces by shell fragments. Judging by their skeletal appearance, they had been dead for quite some time.

Then he heard the screams. The attackers had reached the wire. To his far left, the front-line Legionnaires were meeting the onslaught head-on. To his near left, the gunners on *Bozo* were wisely holding their fire.

Leaping to the front of the post, Hunter cracked open two boxes of ammo, quickly loaded one belt into the big M-60, found its end, and with expended links that littered the hole, clipped it to the lead of the ammo in the second box. Then he quickly rolled over, jammed the butt of the gun against his right shoulder, and steadied himself against what was left of the sandbag wall.

The front of the first human wave was now less than fifty feet away from *Bozo*. For the first time he could see the faces of the enemy. To a man, they had that glazed look of a fanatic, one who was not only unafraid of dying but who seemed eager to embrace death in combat.

But there was something else that startled Hunter. The enemy soldiers were outfitted in exact replicas of the old field uniform of the Communist North Vietnamese army— the dreaded NVA. They were carrying AK-47s, wearing pith helmets and rubber-soled sandals. Hunter felt like he'd been suddenly transported back in time—to 1968, to the original battle of Khe Sanh.

It was very strange.

The front element of the human wave was now only thirty feet away. Their screaming got louder, their bugles were echoing, and the rain was coming down even harder.

Hunter waited a few more seconds—then he pulled the trigger.

His first burst laced across the center of the enemy charge now just twenty feet from his position. A dozen Minx dropped in their tracks. But more raced over their fallen comrades, screaming so madly Hunter thought he could see foam running from their mouths. He continued to fire, waving the smoking barrel back and forth, cutting down anything immediately in front of him. To his left, he could hear the roar of the guns on *Bozo* open up, the multitude of weapons blasting away at the main force of attackers. The rain was coming down incredibly hard now, totally blotting out the sun and making it as dark as midnight. Even the muzzle flash of Hunter's big gun barely cut through the torrential downpour. He was firing blind—but he knew his bullets were finding their marks, simply from the screams of agony he heard between bursts.

But a big problem was looming. He was already through the first box of ammo and was now deep into the second. There were at least ten more boxes of ammo at the far edge of the gun post, but how was he going to get to them?

The vanguard of the attackers were less than twenty feet away, with at least three more waves behind it.

Just then, Hunter sensed someone was in the hole beside him. Whirling around, he was startled to find a soldier, dressed in U.S. Marine combat fatigues and carrying no weapon, had apparently jumped into the gun position with him. Even though there was a serious puncture in his helmet, the Marine didn't appear to be hurt. Nor did he seem to be concerned with the human wave assault that was almost right on top of them.

Hunter yelled to him, indicating the other boxes of ammo lying nearby. Then he turned, pointed the big M-60 back in the direction of the attackers, and began firing again.

But the man just smiled—and didn't move.

Hunter ran out of ammo just as the first Viet Minx soldier reached the lip of the foxhole. Swinging the big gun around, The Wingman smashed the barrel into the enemy soldier's face, sending him sprawling backwards. Another Minx leaped on top of Hunter—but Hunter rolled hard, kicking the man away. Rolling again, he slid up against the ammo boxes, and quickly broke one open with the gun butt. Another Minx was dispatched with a hard kick to the groin. Then Hunter jacked the lead round of the new belt into the M-60 and began firing once more.

One long burst took care of the seven other Minx who had overrun the gun post. Hunter ran back to his original position, dragging two more boxes of ammo with him. The man in the Marine uniform was still there, sitting as calmly as if it were a summer's day at the beach.

"Thanks for the freaking help," Hunter yelled at him angrily.

"You're doing OK by yourself," the Marine calmly replied.

"No thanks to you," Hunter barked back over the chatter of the gunfire.

"I just want to offer a little advice," the Marine told him.

A smoking hand grenade landed with a thud in the center of the gun post. In a flash, Hunter picked it up, hurled back at the charging Viet Minx, covering himself just as it went off in midflight.

"Are you crazy?" Hunter screamed at the Marine over the roar of the battle. "You're going to get your ass killed!"

The Marine just laughed.

"Either help me or get the hell out of here!" Hunter yelled at him, pulling the M-60's trigger once again.

But then in a voice that seemed to cut through the raging battle, Hunter heard the Marine clearly and forcefully say, "Don't let what happened to us happen to you."

Hunter hastily fed yet another ammo belt into the big M-60. "Yeah? What the hell happened to you?"

"They made us go about this thing the wrong way," the Marine answered evenly. "They never let us ever get to the heart of the matter. Never let us fight it on our own. Just don't make that same mistake again."

Hunter stopped for a moment and stared into the man's eyes. They were almost entirely white.

"What the hell outfit you with, anyway?" he asked him. "I haven't seen anyone in Marine uniforms around here."

"Charlie Company, First Battalion, Twenty-sixth Marines," the man answered. "Oh, and another thing, get your head down."

Hunter had already ducked on his own. An instant later, an RPG round exploded not five feet behind him. Hunter never heard the sound, he only saw the flash. If he hadn't ducked, he would have been decapitated. Still, the concussion had been powerful. A heavy blackness enveloped him. He was floating . . . floating . . . floating away. . . .

The next thing he knew, Ben was shaking him violently.

"Hawk, Hawk!" he was yelling into Hunter's face. *"Wake up,* buddy . . ."

"I'm all right," Hunter groaned slowly. He reached up

to his throbbing head and found that it was sticky with blood. He had been wounded.

"It's OK," Ben told him, "looks a lot worse than it really is."

Hunter glanced around. He didn't know how long he'd been out. Could have been seconds—maybe minutes—maybe longer. But the rain had stopped and the attack was over. Hundreds of enemy bodies littered the ground around the gun post and up and down the entire base perimeter. He heard a sizzling sound and looked down to see that the barrel of the M-60 he had been using was still red hot and evaporating the mist hanging in the air around it. Only then did he remember exactly what had happened. The gun, the ammo boxes . . . the Marine. His blood suddenly went cold. He looked up at Ben, his face as white as a sheet.

"Jeeez, Hawk, you look like you've just seen a ghost."

Hunter froze for a second.

"I think I just did," he replied.

Chapter Seventeen

Lieutenant Twang was wet, angry, and more than a little depressed.

This was not the kind of mission he usually pulled. After all, he was a highly decorated soldier of the Third Squad, Second Cadre, of the elite Minx Peasta Corps. He had seen combat all around Vietnam in the past two years and had received CapCom's highest decoration—the gold-planted Leaf of Glory—three times for valor under fire. But now, by direct orders from Commander Dong himself, he was performing a different mission.

Twang had used that morning's human wave assault as a cover to get to the small underground observation post located not twenty-five yards from the southeastern perimeter of the enemy base at Khe Sanh. And now he was stuck in this stinking pit—appropriately nicknamed a "spider hole"—with water up to his ass and bugs eating his extremities. His orders: to report any and all unusual activity inside the enemy base and especially around the two crashed airplanes directly to the High Command itself, via his radio. In other words, he, the three-time recipient of the highest honor possible, had been reduced to the lowly position of being a spy.

But maybe it wasn't so bad after all.

He was, at last, away from the Minx High Command, an institution that, medals aside, treated their soldiers as little more than disposable products. The trip out to the hole, through the bloody carnage all around, had opened his eyes to that.

Because he was an officer, Twang had been spared duty in the body-churning human wave assaults; coordinating sniper squads had been his previous mission. That morning had been the first time he'd seen one of the suicidal attacks up close. He was astounded not only by the ferociousness of the assault and the crazed intensity of his fellow Viet Minx, but also by the resoluteness of the defenders. Hundreds of his comrades had charged right by his little spider hole and into the guns of the Caucasian enemy. And now most of them were dead. Their bodies lay all around him, twisted in bloody grotesque poses. He could still hear the screams of the wounded and dying, but he dared not risk his hiding place to go to their assistance. It was against his orders, and besides, there wasn't anything he could do for them.

So between the cries and the blood and the mud and the water in his hole, Lieutenant Twang was very uncomfortable. And tired. And scared.

But at least he was still alive.

Chapter Eighteen

Hunter gingerly touched the wound on his right forehead and winced slightly.

Night had fallen, and he was sitting in the pilot's seat of *Bozo*, amid the remains of the smashed cockpit. Frayed wires hung like vines all around him. The glass from busted readout screens and the shattered windshield littered the flight deck floor. The wind was whistling through the hundreds of perforations in the skin of the C-5, the smaller ones caused by the MiG attack over the Gulf of Tonkin, the larger ones from the two battles they'd fought since dropping into this little piece of hell.

He rubbed the wound again; the swelling had gone down considerably and his self-diagnosis techniques confirmed that he didn't have a concussion. Only his crash helmet had prevented a serious head injury.

But the fact he was on the mend didn't raise his spirits a notch. Just the opposite. He couldn't remember ever feeling so low. Where was his vaunted luck now? Where the hell did this whole pipe dream come from? A great air fleet to free the oppressed on the opposite side of the globe? Some idea. Some great thinking. What they've got for their troubles was the near-tragic encounter with the pack of MiGs, the scattering of the air fleet, a crash landing in the middle of a very one-sided battle, and a close call in the next. There was no chance for rescue; no chance to even send out a SOS. And the only thing they had to look forward to was another murderous assault from the fanatical enemy hidden in the hills.

He leaned back on the ripped and tattered pilot's seat, knowing it would be impossible to even relax for one second. Geraci's men had begun their nocturnal relocation just an hour before, and now much of their equipment was locked inside *Bozo*. It made for a stronger defense, but also tighter quarters. Everyone on the crowded gunship had carved out a space for themselves, and Hunter had chosen this place, the battered flight deck. Now the irony of it was slugging him in the stomach.

What cruel fate would sentence him to sit in the pilot's seat of an airplane that would never fly again?

But there was something more. Something that was gnawing at him even more deeply than the present dire situation. Something that challenged his very sanity. If the cosmos was going to dictate that he was to die, here and now, in the muck and mud and blood of a foreign land, then he deserved from them the answer to one last big question.

And the only one who could provide that answer was a crazy man.

He stood up, and had to steady himself for a moment. He was off-balance, a state that terrified him. He slipped his crash helmet gently over his head wound and strapped it loosely around his neck. Then he picked up his M-16, checked its full clip and slid down the access ladder and out into the steamy jungle night.

There were mortar rounds dropping all over the encampment, but there was little doubt that they were being fired randomly, more for harassment purposes than against any one target. There was also the constant *zip*-zinging of sniper's bullets, but the old battlefield maxim of "if you hear it, it ain't going to hit you" usually held true.

Still, he leaped from one of *Bozo*'s battered landing gear struts directly into a nearby ditch, just as a hail of enemy

150

bullets zipped overhead. Running in a low crouch, he made the length of the ditch, and then scrambled over to one of the Legionnaires' near trenches, diving in headfirst just as a pair of mortar rounds came crashing down twenty-five feet away.

He picked himself up and brushed some mud from his eyes. When his vision cleared he found himself staring right into the empty eye sockets of two skeletal faces, Legionnaires who had died weeks ago. Both still clutched their weapons in hand, their mouths were wide open as if caught in a scream.

Hunter moved on.

He ran through two trench intersections, once coming upon a mercenary machine-gun crew who were firing tracer rounds randomly into the nearby hills. Their gun pit was littered with piles of empty shell casings and five skeletons, all in some state of dismemberment. They did not acknowledge his presence in any way as he passed by—he could have been a Minx sapper for all they knew. They simply kept firing, one on the trigger of the big .50 caliber, one feeding the belt, eyes staring straight ahead, partners in a combined madness.

A particularly intense mortar barrage held him up near another trench crossover; sheer frustration caused him to unleash a stream of tracer rounds back towards the general area where he calculated the enemy rounds were coming from. The barrage stopped—temporarily. But it was just long enough to allow him to continue his journey.

He finally reached the main entrance to the Legion's headquarters bunker. As before, there were no guards posted outside, no security measures in place at all. Out of habit, he checked his gun clip and found it three quarters full. Then he paused for a breath and made the last dash to the bunker entrance.

This time he had no idea what he'd find inside.

What he did see chilled him to the bone.

There was the crazed Colonel LaFeete, in his dress uniform, standing on a chair placed in the middle of the otherwise empty bunker. One end of a rope was tied around the center roof beam. The other end was fashioned into a hangman's noose and wrapped around LaFeete's neck.

"Stay where you are, American!" LaFeete shouted to Hunter in his raspy, heavy accent. "Do not come a step closer."

Hunter froze.

Just then a mortar round dropped outside the bunker and the entire place shook. The chair rocked back and forth beneath LaFeete's feet, but he managed to stay upright.

"It's all over for me, my career is finished," LaFeete declared in a maddeningly matter-of-fact voice. "I have failed my men. I have failed France." He reached up and gently tightened the noose around his neck.

Hunter began to slowly edge towards the deranged officer.

"Colonel," he began, "I think you ought to reconsider. You're needed here. Your men need you."

"Nonsense!" LaFeete shouted back with steely determination. "When I first came here, things were much clearer. We knew who the enemy was, and for the most part, we knew *where* he was. We came here to free these poor people. To do the job we failed to do in 1954. We came here to be heroes—finally. But it is different now. Now the enemy is everywhere. I hear them inside the wire, inside my bunker, and sometimes, I hear them inside my head."

"We all do, at sometime or other, Colonel," Hunter replied, moving even closer to the distraught officer. "What you've been through would take a toll on anyone. But it's not over, sir—not yet. There's still time. . . ."

"Yes, time," LaFeete sighed, once again nearly losing his balance. "Time is something we all have—some just more than others."

A burst of 7.62-mm bullets raked across the front of the bunker, thudding into the sandbags outside.

But LaFeete didn't hear them. Instead, he began to stroke the noose around his neck. "I am, in the end, a grand failure."

Hunter took a deep breath. For a brief moment he wondered if it was just as better to let this man go. For such a tortured soul, death might seem a reprieve. But in the next moment, he knew he couldn't. It was a human life hanging in the balance here. Nothing on Earth was so precious— crazy or not. Besides, he needed to know something from the man.

He took another deep breath.

"Sir," Hunter began. "Are there any U.S. Marines stationed here? Or soldiers in your command wearing old U.S. Marine uniforms?"

"Marines?" LaFeete laughed, nearly losing his balance a third time. "The only American Marines I saw here, my friend, were dead. And they had been dead for a long, long time."

At that moment the mad Legionnaire officer looked sharply into Hunter's eyes. And then he chuckled. Suddenly the color returned to his face. His eyes took on a more rational look. His whole body seemed to relax.

"I'm really just a foolish old man," he told Hunter with a grin. "I really should have retired years ago. These little episodes are simply cries for help. But I'm feeling much better now."

The tension in the bunker eased with LaFeete's sudden lucidity. Hunter let out a long breath in relief. LaFeete looked at him and somehow managed to combine a smile and a frown.

"Well, then, help me down from here," he said. "We both have a lot of work to do." He started to bend over to grab the back of the chair.

But then he suddenly lost his balance for real.

Hunter watched in horror as the chair accidently kicked out from underneath the Colonel. He dove towards the officer, but it was too late. LaFeete dropped the three feet to the floor and the noose cleanly snapped his neck.

He was dead an instant later.

Midnight

The officers and men of the battered Legion outpost gathered together just three hours after Colonel LaFeete's untimely death.

They had come to pay their respects to the man who had been their leader. And though emaciated and in tatters, they managed to present an image of proper military pomp.

Hunter, Frost and Geraci were in attendance as well—but more out of respect for all those Legionnaires and mercenaries who had died as well as a courtesy to those who were still alive.

Wrapped in a French flag—hastily sewn together from scraps of filthy red, blue, and white cloth—LaFeete's body rested on top of a pile of shattered timbers soaked in oil and gasoline. It was a funeral pyre—the classic send-off for a warrior of greatness. But the method of LaFeete's bodily departure from the world of the living had been chosen for less heroic reasons. Simply put, cremation was much more efficient than an interment into the ground at Khe Sanh these days.

Although an occasional sniper round forced the mourners to take cover several times, Captain Zouvette persevered in conducting the abbreviated service. A short prayer was recited in French. Zouvette then read a hastily composed eulogy. Appropriately, nothing was said about the Colonel's recent failures as a commander. Only his victories were cited.

When Zouvette was done, a very scratchy rendition of the French national anthem played out from a hand-cranked Victrola. Those gathered stood at attention in silence, heads straight, salutes in place, despite the crump of mortar shells exploding in the distance. When the anthem was over, seven Legionnaires, lined up off to the side, fired their rifles three times into the air.

Then the pyre was lit.

With a roar, the pile of lumber burst into flame, lighting up the dark night. In an instant, enemy snipers and mortar crews in the hills took advantage of the glow of the fire and opened up. The mourners scattered, throwing themselves into whatever hole, ditch, or trench they could find.

For Hunter—taking cover in a shell hole filled with stagnant water—it was an appropriate ending to a service for a man he considered a sad but dangerous soul. For the scar-faced Captain Zouvette, who had taken shelter in the same hole, it was also a big relief.

"Well, we are finally rid of the magnificent madman," he said, in between crashing of nearby explosions. "And now that he is dead, I can at last tell you something something that fool had ordered us all to keep in secrecy."

Hunter looked at Zouvette, waiting for him to continue.

"There is a place, a very secret place that LaFeete had forbid all of us to enter," Zouvette cryptically told him.

"What place is that?" Hunter asked.

"A place you should know about—before we all die here," Zouvette replied. "I will take you there—now."

Chapter Nineteen

Two hours later

There are really no such things as illusions.

People see what they want to see—any misinterpretation is simply the result of lack of information. This proved, to Hunter's way of thinking, that everyone, and everything, big and small, held at least one secret.

But still, Hunter had ever seen anything like this.

It was the small mountain located at the far end of the runway, about 150 yards from where *Bozo* had come to a muddy stop—the one which Hunter had slammed on the brakes to avoid smashing into during the breakneck crash landing.

On closer inspection, it *did* look odd. The side facing the base was unusually pristine when compared to the bomb-blasted, torn-up terrain all around it. It was covered with vines and shallow vegetation, all of it a slightly brighter emerald than the dull, dirty green everywhere else.

Also unusual was that while the Minx always launched their attacks from the same direction—out of the jungle to the north and west—they always avoided the small mountain, giving it a rather wide berth. And tactically, this was the incorrect thing to do. Had the Minx chose to take this high ground, they would have had an ideal location from which to launch their mortar attacks, one which would have increased their accuracy at least five-fold.

So it would come as no surprise to Hunter then when he learned later on that the small mountain was considered by the Minx to be haunted.

It was about 0400 when Hunter, Zouvette, Ben, and Geraci reached the foot of the mountain, which the Legionnaires had named "Magic."

Close up, it was obvious why the vegetation on the mountain was of a different color: much of it was fake. Similar to the ersatz foliage used by the Asian Mercenary Cult to camouflage targets on the Japanese Home Islands, this stuff looked real, felt real, and even smelled real. But it was all very artificial—and its purpose was to hide something very important underneath.

Zouvette consulted a map which had been drawn up by the late Commander LaFeete himself. It took several minutes to hack through the plastic vegetation, but finally the Legionnaire found what he was looking for. It was a small fuse box, located next to a black electrical panel which held twelve On-Off switches.

Zouvette carefully brushed away several months of dirt, dust, and cobwebs from the fuse box, and then gingerly screwed in four 5-amp fuses into the four empty sockets.

"This equipment is originally French-made," he whispered as he worked. "It's been here for years. I hope it still works."

Once the fuses were in place, Zouvette snapped all of On-Off switches to on. Within seconds, they heard a faint humming noise.

"I think it's working," the French officer whispered, the glee evident in his voice. "Definitely well-made equipment."

Hunter and Geraci looked at each other and shrugged. They really had no idea what the hell was going on.

Zouvette consulted the map again, and then suggested they all step back a few paces. It turned out to be good advice. Suddenly the ground beneath them began to tremble; then the side of the mountain began to open up—literally.

Even Hunter was surprised—and more than a little impressed. Zouvette had activated a years-old hydraulic generator, which in turn locked into a mechanism which was now parting two huge heavy metal doors. It took them about ten seconds to creak open about halfway, but when they did, they revealed the secret of Magic Mountain: Buried deep inside was an artificial cave, at least the size of the biggest hangar at Edwards.

Geraci looked over at Hunter and shook his head.

"This is getting interesting," he said dryly.

Hunter nodded. "To say the least."

They quickly slipped inside the artificial chamber, and Zouvette, upon finding a similar electrical box on the inside, activated the doors to close again.

Again Geraci got Hunter's attention. "I hope this great French machinery stays together long enough to open those doors again."

Hunter could only nod in agreement. What was worse? Going down in a massive enemy attack, like Davy Crockett at the Alamo, or being buried alive?

The ever-industrious Zouvette next located another control box which held a light switch. He flipped it on triumphantly, only to hear at least a dozen light bulbs in outlets on the cave's ceiling pop and die as their decades-old filaments burst with the sudden surge of electrical power.

But about a half-dozen bulbs stayed on—and they provided enough light to reveal what the cave contained.

At first look, it didn't seem like much. There were several dozen fuel barrels, some empty, some slowly leaking. Against one wall there was a large tool cage containing instruments Hunter instantly recognized as those used by aircraft mechanics. Scattered about were pieces of sheet metal, copper tubing, and lengths of rubber hose. The floor was also littered with coffee cups, sandwich wrappers, and newspapers, some in English, others in Vietnamese, Chinese, and even Russian. Hunter picked one up. It was a copy of *Stars & Stripes*, the U.S. military's old in-house newspaper. He read the date: "July 15, 1968."

"They've got to get another paperboy," he said, handing the paper to Geraci. "This one's been here a while."

It was becoming quite clear that the place was not only large enough to be an aircraft hangar, it *was* an aircraft hangar—or more accurately, an aircraft maintenance barn.

But who built it?

Zouvette didn't know—no one in the Legion did. They found the man-made cave when they decided to defend Khe Sanh against the Minx. In some ways it appeared to have been built during American involvement in Vietnam; all of the tools were American-made and stamped with Marine ID numbers. But in other instances, especially the gears and works for the doors, there was obviously French influence, possibly dating back to the 1950s. Yet the Chinese and Russian newspapers pointed to activity after the U.S. pullout in 1975. But then again, it was obvious that the area's current oppressors—the Minx themselves—didn't know of the cave's existence.

Hunter was sure they'd probably never figure out just who built the cave, or why.

But its existence *did* beg several other questions, one of which Geraci hit upon right away.

"I don't get it," he said as they wandered around the deep cavernous space. "Mr. Dien Bien Phu allows his men to get torn up out there, when they could have been all safe and cozy in here—at least for a while."

"The commandant would never have allowed it," Zouvette replied. "That's why he kept this place secret from all but his officers. It may be hard for you to understand, but the commandant believed that to fight meant doing so on equal terms with the enemy. He would have considered using this place as a haven as simply running away, avoiding the fight. It was a matter of honor, for him and the Legion."

Geraci almost burst out laughing at the man. "Sorry, compadre," he said, "But that's the lamest excuse I've ever heard."

He turned to Hunter. "No wonder they've been getting their ass kicked."

Hunter just shrugged. "LaFeete really went by his own book."

Zouvette's face sagged, but then his eyes lit up again.

"This is true," he said. "But there is something in here that might surprise you even more about him."

They walked into the darkest recesses of the cave, into an area that was lit by one very dim bulb. There they came upon a large object wrapped in an old oily tarp.

"Did you know the commandant was also a pilot?" Zouvette asked them.

Both Hunter and Geraci shook their heads no.

"Well, he was," Zouvette continued. "And a great one. He could fly anything—even did some test piloting in his earlier days. And I have to believe because of this fact, he thought about this place, this thing here, every day."

With dramatic fashion, Zouvette yanked the dirty tarp off to reveal a very old airplane.

"You see," Zouvette said, pointing to the aircraft. "He could have left here any time he wanted."

Hunter barely heard Zouvette; he was too busy staring at the old airplane.

"Goddamn," he whispered. "Is that a Skyraider?"

It *was* a Skyraider—an AD-1J to be exact. And after his initial surprise died away, Hunter realized it wasn't too out of the ordinary that this particular airplane was here.

The Skyraider was a flying warhorse. Designed at the end of World War II by the Navy as a torpedo-carrying dive bomber, the single-propeller airplane first saw action in Korea and then in Vietnam. Used as a bomber and ground support aircraft for the Air Force, Navy, and Marines, it was a huge aircraft for its day, famous for its thick, heavily armored design, built to withstand carrier takeoffs and landings.

It possessed a bulky 3050-horsepower engine, but its weight and lifting capacity saddled it with a top speed of only about 315 mph. But this was OK, as it meant the Skyraiders could lug around a lot of fuel and a lot of bombs, and stay in the air long after newer, higher-performance jet aircraft had to go home and gas up. No surprise it was a favorite among the ground troops during the Vietnam War.

This particular airplane was sporting U.S. Marine markings, but just how it got inside the cave was a mystery. It probably wasn't any great leap to deduce that the Skyraider could have put down at Khe Sanh sometime during the famous siege and was unable to take off again. But did they build this huge cave around it? No way. Not with the depleted resources the Americans were forced to live with here. Besides, when the Marines finally abandoned the fire base, they were supposed to have destroyed everything they left behind. Whoever moved in after the fall of Saigon, and what they did here at Khe Sanh, was anybody's guess.

The aircraft itself looked like it was in relatively good shape. Its fuselage was patched in several places, and its engine had long since leaked all its oil and hydraulics. But other than that, it appeared very flyable.

"Well, the commandant really knew how to keep a secret, didn't he?" Geraci commented. "I don't know whether this proves he was more nuts or less—I mean, this was his ticket to freedom right here."

"Nuts or not, he would never leave his men behind," Hunter replied, running his hand along the venerable fuselage. "Not his style."

They walked back into the more lighted main area of

161

the cave, where Geraci took a closer look at the tools on hand.

"This stuff is old, but it's in working condition," he said, studying an ancient hydraulic jacksaw covered with Marine serial numbers. "These bastards were getting rocketed and mortared every day, and they still kept their tools cleaned and oiled."

"That's the jarheads for you," Hunter said.

He checked the time—it was almost 0500 hours. The sun would be coming up soon, and with it the waiting game for the next big Minx attack.

It was time to go.

Zouvette dutifully shut off the cave lights and they carefully exited the way they came in, taking pains not to create any disturbance that would attract the attention of the Minx gunners.

Then they set out over the battered torn-up ground again, past the dozens of rusting crashed airplanes, into the first line of muddy trenches and toward the relative safety of *Bozo*.

By the time they were halfway home, Hunter had already conjured up the beginnings of a bold plan to escape from the hell of Khe Sanh.

Chapter Twenty

The next day passed in almost surreal fashion.

The rest of the New Jersey 104th Engineers had repositioned to *Bozo*, where they would share in the common defense of the Americans' untenable position. They'd wired their C-5 with dozens of makeshift booby traps, enough to discourage any Minx from snooping around the giant abandoned cargo plane.

More defensive positions had been established around *Bozo;* all day long everyone's eyes were fixed on the sky overhead, looking for any sign of clouds gathering. The Legionnaires knew all too well that the Minx only attacked during the daily downpour, so even the slightest bit of wind was enough to send an alarm through the beleaguered camp.

But this day was different. This day, the rains did not come. The sky stayed clear; it was unbearably hot, unbearably humid. But it did not rain. And everyone in the base thanked the stars for giving them another day of life.

The officers aboard *Bozo* found different ways of busying themselves. Frost took a complete inventory of food and medical stocks from both C-5s; they had about a two-week supply, and then some left over to give to the beleaguered Legionnaires. Ben did the same for ammunition; based on one major attack per day, they had enough for about ten days, with some left over for Legion defenders. Geraci had his men surveying the most vulnerable spots on *Bozo*'s hull and covering them as best as they could.

Zouvette assigned a squad of his healthier troopers to fill sandbags for placement around the downed cargo jet. They stopped only at noon to pay a short, but emotional visit to the grave of their fallen commandant.

No one had seen Hunter for most of the day. He'd been up on the *Bozo*'s flight deck for hours, the specific reason being unknown to the others. But they all had a good idea. Many had been in tight fixes with The Wingman before— though not many tighter than this. It always fell to Hunter to come up with a plan, a strategy, a way to give them at least a fighting chance to escape their dire straits.

And they needed him to do so now more than ever.

As soon as dusk came, the Americans began to relax a little. The Minx never attacked after sundown—they were way too superstitious for night ops. The guard was doubled outside nevertheless, and a makeshift radio link established with the Legionnaires' main bunker, 100 yards away. Then, those who could be spared settled down inside the hulk of the *Bozo* and either caught some sleep or dined on MREs.

Ben, Frost, and Geraci gathered near the battered nose of the huge plane and prepared a meal of MRE-style chicken à la king, applesauce pie, and coffee.

"How long has he been up there?" Geraci asked once the meal was ready.

Ben checked his watch. "Going on fourteen hours now."

"No coffee? Nothing to eat?" the engineer asked.

Ben shook his head. "You know what happens when he gets in these modes," he said. "I've seen him go for five days without a meal, a drink, or even a nap. It's scary."

Frost took a spoonful of chicken and washed it down with a swig of coffee. "He feels responsible," he said quietly chewing. "He's blaming himself for us being here."

"That's ironic," Ben said. "None of us on *Bozo* would be

alive now if it wasn't for him. I've never seen anyone put a plane down like he did this one."

Geraci finished his chicken and then tore into a piece of pie. "Well, he'll have to pull a real rabbit out of his hat to get us out of this fix."

"That's why we've got to start right away . . ."

All three men looked up to find Hunter standing before him. Despite the conditions aboard the crashed jet, he looked well-rested and refreshed. His flight suit was neat and seemingly pressed, and not a hair on his head was out of place.

He was even smiling slightly.

All three men quickly got to their feet. "You come up with something, Hawk?" Ben asked. "Something to get us out of here?"

Hunter gave a kind of noncommittal shrug. "Maybe," he answered. "But we've three big hurtles to get over—and like I said, we've got to get to work right now."

Their spirits instantly revitalized, the three men began to discard the rest of their meals. But Hunter spotted one last MRE that was already heated. He very nonchalantly sat down on the twisted floor and began to dig in.

His three comrades looked down at him in mild wonder.

"I thought we were in a hurry," Ben asked him.

Hunter just shrugged again.

"Hey, a guy's got to eat," he said.

Early the next morning

For Lieutenant Twang, it began with a rumble.

It was so violent, he was literally shaken awake. He blinked his eyes rapidly, suddenly short of breath. *What was happening?* He looked at his watch and saw that there was about one hour of darkness left before the sunrise. A sudden sickening feeling overcame him—he had fallen asleep on watch, the worst thing a soldier of his caliber could do.

But what had woke him? Had the unearthly shaking simply been the end of a bad dream? But then he felt the rumbling again, this time even harder, even more frighteningly. He froze with fear once again. It had not been a dream.

But what was it?

He slowly lifted his head up over the edge of the spider hole and peered out into the inky black darkness of the moonless night. The enemy base looked no different—ragged shacks, broken sandbag walls, the fires burning here and there—all under an occasional stream of tracers zinging back and forth or mortar rounds landing sporadically every ten seconds or so. At first, the darkness, smoke, and fog, prevented him from seeing what was making such a horrific noise and causing the earth to shake. But then a slight breeze picked up and cleared his view.

His jaw dropped in astonishment at what he saw.

The rumbling was coming from six bulldozers spread out, fanlike, in front of the second huge airplane which had crashed at the far end of the runway. Twang quickly picked up his binoculars. Aided by the dim glow of the fires, he saw that all the bulldozers had large slabs of metal welded to their right sides—as bullet-shields. Trailing behind each earthmover were three heavy duty chains, braided together. It appeared to Twang that the other ends of these chains were attached to various points underneath the enormous wrecked airplane, but he couldn't be sure.

As he watched through the spyglasses dumbfounded, Twang saw a small light flash three times from the plane's cockpit. At that moment the bulldozers dropped their transmissions into low gear and slowly began to move forward. Twang watched as the six lengths of braided cables rose from the ground. They *were* attached to the airplane. The cables instantly tightened from the straining bulldozers and their giant steel treads began to bite into the soft blacktop of the tarmac.

But the plane didn't budge.

A moment later, a burst of flame shot out of the airplane's right inside engine. Suddenly it popped and screamed to life. In the light of the engine flare, Twang saw a man in fighter pilot overalls, a white flight helmet barely covering his long hair, sitting inside the plane's shattered cockpit furiously working the controls. Who this man was, Twang had no idea.

Suddenly he heard the engine wind higher and higher. The plane began vibrating so much that Twang thought the whole damn thing was going to fall apart.

But instead, the huge plane began to move.

Twang reached for his radio—but at the same moment he realized that his call would make no difference: the combined noise of the bulldozers and of the jet engine was so ungodly, he was sure his comrades in the hills would hear it too.

He was right.

Five seconds later, a flare went up from the far treeline and burst over the runway. At once, the night-duty mortar crews and snipers saw the source of the tremendous racket and immediately stepped up their firings. Then more flares went up. Suddenly it was as bright as day. By this time, Twang understood exactly what this enemy was doing— they were moving the huge airplane down the runway. But why? He thought for a moment that they were trying to escape—but how could they hope to take off in such a battered airplane?

Twang watched as the plane slowly moved toward the edge of the Minx's effective mortar range. Then he heard the tubes in the hills begin to pop with a vengeance.

A half dozen shells immediately exploded right in front of the lead bulldozer. Suddenly, heavy machine guns mounted on the back of the bulldozers opened up, spraying the treeline with hundreds of rounds of tracer rounds.

But the machine-gun fire was answered by dozens more mortar rounds that began to rain down all around the airplane and the bulldozers. The air was instantly thick with red hot shrapnel and torn up pieces of tarmac. Each illuminating flash of a mortar round lit up the area like a strobe light, revealing images of the base soldiers furiously returning fire into the hills while trying to keep their heavy equipment operating.

Through it all, the giant airplane crawled forward, inches, feet, yards, its progress somehow unimpeded by the barrage.

Another set of flares went up, giving the snipers more light to get their range. Bullets ripped through the air, striking all around the fuselage of the big airplane. More mortar shells dropped. Twang saw chunks of the aircraft blown off, its wings peppered and perforated by tracer bullets. But the enemy kept firing back from the bulldozers, somehow still avoiding major mortar hits.

And the plane kept moving.

Just as the towed airplane reached the halfway point on the mile-long runway, Twang heard the other big plane at the base end of the runway open up its large machine guns. Instantly, thousands of rounds of ammunition were dispensed through treeline and into the hills beyond. A few seconds later, grenade launchers and rockets were added into the mix. Twang was petrified. The sudden and brutal firepower was just what the enemy needed to keep the Minx gunners from zeroing in on the slow-moving airplane.

The towed plane continued to lurch from bursts of power of the single jet engine and the earthmovers. Incredibly it was now only 200 yards away from the opposite end of the runway, and the other crashed jet.

Mortar rounds, bullets, and RPG shells kept coming in, and a fierce stream of automated fire was going out. Twang had never seen anything like it. Shrapnel blasted more holes in the sides and the wings, but somehow the plane managed to avoid any direct hits.

And it kept moving—moving until at last it reached its apparent destination, the base end of the runway, next to the other great airplane. And then suddenly, all the firing stopped.

As the dawn's early light broke, Twang shook his head in wonder. Why the hell did the enemy go through all this? What was the point?

Chapter Twenty-one

It was pandemonium inside Commander Dong's palatial mobile HQ.

Report after report streamed in by radio or by courier, and none of the news was good. Casualties among his troops had soared in the past forty-eight hours. Weapons expenditures had also gone through the roof. In a panic, the aides inside this air-conditioned trailer desperately tried to piece together the fragments of information coming in from the front to get a clearer picture of the situation for presentation to their leader. But it was nearly impossible.

It had all started with the dozens of reports on the landing of one huge plane at the encircled base at Khe Sanh; more reports on how it had repulsed the last large-scale Minx attack with unheard-of firepower. Then, later on, it was confirmed that something else landed at Khe Sanh, an aircraft that differed from the first. After much debate, it was finally concluded that *two* planes had actually arrived at the embattled enemy camp. This was finally confirmed by a report from a slightly hysterical Lieutenant Twang, who just within the past hour also described a bizarre, gigantic towing operation successfully completed by the enemy right before dawn that day.

Commander Dong gloomily scanned each updated report. While incomplete, these bits of information told him one thing: time was running out on his campaign of conquest. His troop strength was ebbing—especially after the losses incurred the day before against the mysterious armed airplane. His ammunition was getting low, as was food and water. Suddenly he felt like a house of cards was collapsing on him. He had tried to cheap out and wound up stretching his resources way too thin. Now, his chance of getting a big slice of Vietnam once the war was over were growing slimmer by the hour. Now *he* was beginning to feel backed up to the wall.

And all because some Americans had decided to stick their noses into something that was none of their business.

There was only one option left open to him—a very expensive option. It was a step he dreaded, but, nonetheless, one he had to take. He would be forced to personally pay a visit to his employers—the chairman and the members of the board of CapCom, the people who were the brains—and the bankrollers—behind this latest Vietnam war.

Dong reluctantly wrote out a short order which commanded all his officers to cease all but sniper and mortar harassment operations until further notice. Then he ordered his command helicopter readied.

Retiring to his dressing quarters, his valet gloomily helped him into his full dress uniform, complete with all the necessary accoutrements—battle citations, medals, spit shined black leather riding boots, and ceremonial sword. A distinctive *whop whop whopping* sound signaled the arrival of his chopper several minutes later. After a last glance in the full length mirror to make sure everything was in place, Dong glumly shuffled out to the concrete landing pad. Accompanying him were two aides straining to carry a heavy iron chest between them.

The jet-black Soviet-built Mil Mi-8 Hip-C touched down lightly—just long enough for Dong and the two aides to climb aboard with their precious load. The two 1268-Kw Isotov TV2-117a turboshafts powered up, and the heavily armored helicopter roared into the sky, quickly turning due north.

While the jungle below sped by, Dong pondered his dire situation. Here he was, a proud Mandarin with a large army bought for his disposal, reduced now to playing the role of a pleading subcontractor for CapCom. His experience with the people who sold him his army told him that they knew very little about military operations. Rather, the members of CapCom were ranting commercialists, driven by an ironically twisted sense of Communistic capitalism and an insatiable greed for money and power. They were very adept at using their purse strings to yank a man by his balls and squeeze them until something gave. And now Dong found himself at the full mercy of their royal scam. He'd gotten in way too deep—and now he had to pay dearly. At times like this, Dong hated Cap Com more than he hated the enemy at Khe Sanh. At least the enemy fought and died for what they believed in. His employers at CapCom preferred to buy off people to do their dying for them.

Two hours later, Dong's chopper was nearing the outskirts of Hanoi.

The dense jungle below ended and the helicopter came upon an incredibly beautiful country estate, far different than the front line battle command area Dong had left behind. The chopper passed over acres and acres of rolling manicured lawns, rock gardens, with waterfalls, stables of thoroughbred horses, polo fields, swimming pools, and an eighteen-hole golf course. The Mil Mi-8 Hip-C finally touched down before a French-Colonial-style mansion that covered more than fifteen acres. Inside were hundreds of rooms, including two ballrooms, a dining room that sat fifty, three kitchens, a bowling alley, a rifle range, an indoor pool, a fully equipped gymnasium, many saunas, geisha rooms, hot tub halls, and one, enormous well-appointed boardroom. There was also a large and elaborate torture chamber. Thankfully, it was the boardroom where Dong was scheduled to meet his employers.

He strode through the great entrance hall and down the long corridors as guard after guard snapped to attention. But Dong was not thinking about the impressive array of crack troops that secured this place. Rather he was contemplating how he would have to first endure a demeaning harangue from the chairman of CapCom about his lack of success in conquering the enemy's base at Khe Sanh, before he got down to the real purpose of his visit.

Dong wondered if he had the stomach for it.

He reached the board room's outer offices and was ushered to a small waiting area lined with uncomfortable seats. For twenty minutes he cooled his heels, knowing that this too was all part of the board's little game. Finally, an officer entered and announced that they were ready to see him.

Two great oaken doors were swung open and Dong was led inside.

The room reeked of cheap cologne and cigarette smoke. Curtains blocked the sunlight from streaming in through the floor-to-ceiling windows, and the room's half dozen giant, crystal chandeliers were dark. Instead, the chamber was lit by an impressive array of audiovisual equipment, which were continually projecting charts and graphs of annual growth percentages, operating costs, and profit margins onto more than a dozen huge TV wall screens.

Dong crossed the heavily carpeted floor and stood before the chairman and the twelve members of the board. Sitting behind a highly polished mahogany table lined with bottles of imported scotch and American whiskey, these men were all in their late fifties, all of oriental descent. Their oily hair glistened and their hands sparkled with jeweled pinky rings. Each was bursting out of his custom-made Italian suit. Dong considered them all disgusting. He was certain that not one of them had ever seen a day of combat.

Dong was not offered a chair. Rather, he had to stand as the chairman commenced to humiliate him.

"I don't understand why you have not yet captured this tiny insignificant *nothing* of an enemy base!" the Chairman suddenly erupted. "A base that has been standing in the way of our entire northern campaign! Why have you not used the resources at your disposal effectively? We were under the impression that you were a great warrior, a professional, a military man. But now we see you are still the lowly truck driver you were when you first came to us. You are worse than a corporal, even worse than a civilian!"

The other twelve members of the board burst out laughing, but the chairman silenced them with a quick wave of his hand.

"Why have you not succeeded in your duty?" the chairman continued, his voice echoing in the large room. "Why have you shamed us, your family, and yourself with this failure?"

Dong opened his mouth to reply, but was instantly cut off.

"How dare you try to contradict your superiors!" the Chairman screamed.

Dong could feel the anger begin to boil inside him. But he had no choice but to endure this tirade—and not just to save face.

Two full minutes of absolute silence passed. Finally the Chairman spoke again.

"Well?" he asked. "What do you have to say for yourself?"

Dong cleared his throat. "I wish to make another major purchase."

The chairman's demeanor changed instantly.

"Really?" he asked, his eyes suddenly growing wide. "How much?"

"About double my most previous purchase," Dong replied.

"Excellent!" the Chairman said, laughing. The twelve

174

board members nodded in gleeful agreement. Dong saw nothing now but smiles. The magic word of money had been spoken. An aide appeared out of nowhere and handed the chairman an inventory printout and price list. They got right down to business.

"OK, my friend, what do you need?" the chairman asked.

He and the members of the board were now absolutely silent in rapt anticipation. Dong paused for a long moment, then began to tick off his shopping list.

"Two hundred magnesium flares, ten thousand AK-47s and fifteen thousand rounds of ammo, two hundred .81-mm mortars and three thousand mortar rounds, fifty crates of rocket-propelled grenades . . ."

The chairman was making notes and working his calculator as fast as Dong could mention the items.

"And five thousand more troops," Dong added.

The chairman looked up. *"Five thousand troops?"*

"That's correct," Dong answered. The Chairman's shock turned to absolute delight when he realized that Dong was serious. He had reason to be happy—everyone knew that CapCom's profit margin was far greater for human flesh than equipment.

"Exactly what are you proposing to do?" the Chairman quietly asked after he regained his composure.

"I am planning a final push—a large bombardment followed by a huge ground attack. It should solve all our problems," Dong replied.

After a flurry of additional calculations, the chairman arrived at a price.

"Five hundred bags of gold."

Dong just stared back at him. "Too much," he said.

The Chairman looked Dong squarely in the eye. "Then why don't you go somewhere else."

Capitalist pigs! Dong thought to himself. But now it was time to play the game—a game that he despised. He sent word to summon for his two aides who had been waiting

175

outside. Within seconds, they entered the huge room, carrying the iron chest.

Dong opened up the chest and quickly counted out four hundred bags of gold, just about all that was left of his magnificent gold find on the Pathet road just a few months before. He laid the pile of precious ore on the table in front of the Chairman. He could see the man's mouth literally begin to water.

"This is my final offer, gentlemen." Dong said, then added, "And I expect delivery of the weapons this very afternoon. The soldiers over the next twenty-four hours—their transportation at no extra charge."

There was a burst of grumbling from the board, but it was obvious that Dong was standing fast. Finally, the men began nodding their heads. Then the thirteen smiles reappeared.

They had a deal.

The chairman himself walked Dong back to his helicopter, presenting him with a small gift for being such a valued customer.

The chopper lifted off. From the air, Dong could see a convoy of supply trucks already on their way from the estate's underground supply depots to the dozen cargo helicopters parked on the tarmac below. But Dong was far from happy with the situation.

"Bastards," he whispered once they had turned south and started back to his base. "Rob me blind with your prices, and *then* you ask me why I have failed?"

An hour later, when the helicopter was passing over a boulder strewn ravine, Dong took the Chairman's "small gift" and tossed it out the open door. With great joy, he watched the toaster oven drop five thousand feet and smash to pieces on the rocks below.

Chapter Twenty-two

Except for the continuous sniper fire and mortar shelling, the next day passed in relative peace at Khe Sanh. The rains came, but there was no attack. No one knew why. But many had already given up trying to figure out the very unorthodox enemy in the hills.

Geraci's engineers took advantage of the situation and worked furiously on the two Galaxy transports. Using hundreds of sandbags and as many corrugated sheets of tin they could scavenge from the dozens of battered and useless Legion bunkers, fifty of Geraci's men began work on erecting a giant wall encircling *NJ104*.

The other half of the 104th's engineers concentrated on *Bozo*. Using jury-rigged jacks and counterweights, the wrecked C-5's right wing was lifted out of the mud. Then the entire plane was righted on the runway.

Bozo was then shored up on all sides. Pieces of corrugated tin were welded together and erected over key areas of the once great airship. Several shoulder-high walls of sandbags—the first barriers of defense—were built all around the perimeter at distances from ten to thirty yards out.

Now jokingly rechristened "Fort Bozo," serious work had been undertaken inside the C-5 as well. A number of defensive plans against the human wave assaults were worked out. The gun crews practiced in the spacious hold of the huge cargo plane to make the directing, loading, and firing the big guns more efficient, more accurate. They also drilled extensively on swinging the guns from one side of the plane to the other, using newly installed makeshift rails designed for that purpose. Additional ladders were rigged to the upper gun port stations and to the flight deck for quicker access. Any extra time was spent diligently cleaning and oiling personal weapons as well as the big guns of the ship. The crew took their MRE chow once every twelve hours, and slept in shifts—those that could sleep. Soon, like anything else, the little things became routine.

Trapped as they were, the crew of *Bozo* had become well-oiled cogs within a well-oiled, if improvised, killing machine.

Hunter and Ben arrived at No. 6 gunpost ten minutes after getting the urgent call.

Located about 75 yards off the tail of *NJ104*, the reconstructed mortar pit was now the furthermost American position facing the enemy held hills. The One Hundred and Fourth's General Tom McCaffrey, a man who had come out of retirement to join the great airfleet mission, greeted them. Behind him was the reason for his request that Hunter and Ben come up immediately.

Held at gunpoint by three other engineers was an elderly man, wearing nothing but a ragged loincloth and a tooth-gaped smile.

"This guy just showed up out of nowhere," McCaffrey explained. "One minute, everything was clear, the next minute—there he was."

Hunter and Ben looked at each other, then back at the intruder.

Hunter recognized the man right away as a member of the famous Montagnards.

The Montagnards were the tribal people who once lived

in the mountainous region of the Central Highlands, an area that straddled the political boundaries of three countries: Vietnam, Cambodia, and Laos. As part of the "Hearts and Minds" program during the last Vietnam war, the Montagnards joined forces with the U. S. Army's Green Berets, trading jungle survival knowledge and local support for military protection against the hated Viet Cong. But when the war ended, and they found themselves on the losing side, the tribe had to scatter far and wide to escape certain extermination by the Communists.

"I have no idea how he did it," McCaffrey went on. "We've got this whole area covered with razor wire, claymores—even old hydro-fluid cans hanging from string. Anybody out there would have been blown to bits. Or at least made *some* kind of noise. But this guy got through in one piece—and without a peep, in broad daylight."

Certain that Hunter was this odd white tribe's Chief, the old Montagnard increased his near-toothless smile even wider.

"Do you speak English?" Hunter asked him.

The old native continued to grin. Then he pointed at McCaffrey, uttered a few words that were unintelligible, and indicated with his hands that something had been taken away from him.

"He means this, Hawk," McCaffrey said. He handed Hunter a walking stick.

The Montagnard shook his head in agreement and pointed to the top end of the shaft.

Hunter looked and saw it was a carving of an airplane.

"Hey, not bad," Hunter said, studying the workmanship. "Looks like a Phantom."

"That's when the old man indicated to Hunter that he wanted to take him somewhere—somewhere far out into the dark jungle.

And that it had something to do with the carved image.

Hunter knew that many years ago, when this native was younger, the Montagnards had been a great ally to the

U. S. forces in Vietnam. He wondered if that was still the case. His gut feeling was telling him that this old man—or whoever sent him—were still sympathetic. He decided to take a chance.

Hunter handed the intricately carved walking stick back to the old Montagnard.

"We will go," Hunter said, indicating with his hands that he would follow. The Montagnard smiled even wider, turned, and started to make his way back through the perimeter.

Ben grabbed Hunter's arm. "You're not going alone, are you, Hawk?"

"Nope," Hunter replied, "You're coming with me."

With that, the two of them climbed out of the gunpost and caught up with the willing guide.

McCaffrey watched as they stealthily zigged and zagged through the trip wires of the base's defense, following the old man's lead.

"Either they're very brave or very crazy," McCaffrey said to the other engineers. "Or both."

It took them almost three hours to reach the cave.

Getting past the Minx lines proved easier than Hunter thought. There were dozens of enemy positions just inside the extended treeline from which they launched the vicious assaults, with hundreds of Minx snipers and mortar men manning them. But the spry Montagnard had led them to a dry stream bed which cut right through the Minx lines. Using the bank overhang as cover, they were able to slip past several lightly manned sniper positions, finally coming to a large river on which they floated away from the Minx forward positions and into a small mountain river valley, a place even more isolated than Khe Sanh. Though still controlled by the Viet Minx, the area was lightly occupied. At a turn in the river, right before a series of cascading falls, they crawled up onto the bank and, without a rest, started up a steep ravine. Thirty minutes of nonstop climbing led them to the mouth of a cave. At this point, the Montagnard bid them a silent, smiling farewell.

Correctly guessing this is where they were supposed to go, Hunter and Ben slipped into the cool, dark cave.

It smelled musty and damp, but oddly, they also detected the distinct odor of electrical gear, a burnt rubber scent. Hunter spotted a wiring conduit, running along the cave's inner wall. They followed it through several winding passages, finally coming to a small chamber packed to the ceiling with various electronic devices, acoustical gear, and oscilloscopes. A small generator was humming in the corner, keeping the gear up and running and providing the telltale electrical smell.

"What the hell is this?" Ben asked. "The local phone company?"

"Talk about reaching out and touching someone." Hunter replied.

At that moment, they heard a stirring noise. Then, in the dim light thrown by a single kerosene lamp, they saw an old army cot against the far wall.

And on that cot was a very, very old man.

Hunter quietly approached the cot. He found the man barely breathing.

The old man looked up and saw Hunter leaning over him. His eyes went wide with amazement.

"You've . . . you've finally come?" he gasped in a mixture of relief and disbelief. Hunter nodded slowly.

"You're here?" the old man cried, this time with more energy. A wide, creaky smile spread across his creased, tired face.

"I'll be goddamned, you've finally come," the old man went on, propping himself up on one elbow and shaking his head. Then he offered his bony hand.

"My name is Willy Rucker, *Colonel* Willy Rucker, Special Forces."

Hunter shook the old man's hand. "Hawk Hunter, Major, United American Forces. This is Captain Ben Wa."

"I see my Montagnard friend was able to convince you to follow him," Rucker said with a smile. "If it weren't for him and his tribe, I would have perished long ago. They've looked after me all these years, especially now that I don't get around too much anymore." The colonel painfully shifted his position. "When he told me of 'great wounded birds no longer able to fly' battling the Viet Minx at Khe Sanh, my curiosity got the best of me. What's the hell is going on down there?"

Starting with the buildup of the great airfleet, Hunter explained what brought them here. He described the MiG air battle, how they ended up at Khe Sanh, the dire circumstances of the beleaguered base, the condition of their two C-5s, the constant barrages and sniper fire. And the daily human wave assaults.

The old man nodded throughout—obviously he was in frequent contact with the Montagnards who apparently hated the Minx as much as they hated the Viet Cong. And Hunter's story confirmed everything they had told him.

"But how did *you* get here, Colonel?" Ben asked.

The man cleared his raspy throat and began his story. He was a Green Beret—maybe the last one ever. At the height of the last Vietnam War, he had been attached as an observer to a secret governmental organization known as the Jason Group. Their mission was to develop high-tech sensing devices used to detect the movement of Viet Cong and North Vietnamese regulars crossing the so-called Demilitarized Zone which separated North and South Vietnam.

Some of these devices were quite bizarre, Rucker explained. One was called a "people sniffer." It was capable of detecting the presence of humans by taking samples of the air and analyzing it for the elements of ammonia prevalent in human urine or sweat. Another device was aptly labeled "ROCKSID." These were seismic devices made to look like small rocks that were dropped from helicopters or slow moving aircraft. When disturbed, they sent out a

182

short, low-end radio signal, indicating some kind of troop or equipment movement. Other devices were more conventional: some could either sense ground vibrations or actually hear the enemy moving. Still others were camouflaged to look like small indigenous trees, branches, or even leaves.

As Colonel Rucker relayed all this information, Hunter saw a metamorphosis come over the old soldier. Instead of this effort draining the life from him, the elderly officer appeared to get stronger. As his story unfolded, the years of age seemed to amazingly shed rapidly from his face.

He continued his tale. At the height of the Vietnam war, he was part of the primary Jason group airdropped to place some of the far-out listening devices near what was considered at the time to be key NVA traffic points. As they made their way to the pickup point during one of these missions, they were ambushed. Most of Rucker's unit was brutally wiped out by the Vietnamese Communists. Those that lived through the attack were taken prisoner—himself included. They were marched deep into what was then called Laos, and held at a prisoner of war camp.

The camp was basically self sufficient—the guards ate meat culled from hunting; the prisoners had to subsist on what they could grow in scratch gardens. Years passed. Some of the other prisoners died off. More years passed, and more prisoners died. And then the guards began to die off too. Rucker outlasted them all.

"I guess they forgot about their own people, too," the old man said.

But his story was not over.

By the time the last guard died and he walked out of that camp, the Big Global War had already happened. The whole world had been turned upside down. Rucker no longer had a country to go home to. So he made his way here, to this cave, and single handedly rewired it so that he could monitor many of the decades-old listening

183

systems, which were spread out all over the northern part of South Vietnam.

"I had to do something, just to stay sane," Rucker told them. "For years I took notes of the activity all around—troop movements mostly. I figured out what they had, which direction they were headed. I knew that there was no one I could relay it to—no one was interested anymore. But it was my duty, and until I was told otherwise, I did my job. I had to . . ."

"We know that feeling," Hunter said.

"But then all the activity stopped," Rucker continued. "For years there was nothing. Maybe some peasants here or there, but as far as any troop movements, I was getting a big blank." Excitedly, the old man got up from the cot and began pacing back and forth. He was now full of energy.

"Then, about a year or so ago, I suddenly started to pick up heavy activity again. I'm talking major duty—tanks, supply columns, thousands of troops—all sneaking south, just like before. I even went down and took a look for myself. The odd thing was, after all those years, they looked like old *NVA*."

"They're called the Viet Minx," Hunter told him. "Different name, but same screwy expansionist ideas."

"Tell me about it," the Green Beret replied with a nod. He shuffled over to a small chest, opened it, took out a large knapsack. This contained a device which looked like a combination all-band radio and radar screen.

"This is the Jason Transcoder Module." Rucker explained. "With it you can monitor just about all of our old listening devices." He looked up at them. "You look like smart boys," he said with a crinkly smile. "You should be able to figure out how to use it."

He then retrieved a stack of hand drawn maps. He selected a couple dozen and handed them to Hunter.

"And if you're stuck at Khe Sanh, then you better have

these," the old man said. "I've noticed an increase in activity near there."

Hunter studied the maps. One indicated precisely where a particular field of listening devices had been planted; another detailed the trails to take to get there.

"I hope all this helps," the old man said.

Ben looked at the elderly soldier. He might have been 100 years old or even older. "But won't you need this stuff, to continue your mission?" he asked.

The old man smiled. "Don't you think it's time I started to collect my pension?"

Suddenly he exhaled violently, as if he'd been kicked in the stomach. His body began to shake from a horrible coughing spasm. He couldn't speak—he could hardly breathe. Hunter and Ben carefully led him back to the cot.

The old man tried to regain his breathing—but couldn't. He looked up at Hunter, the years of solitude and depravation instantly returning.

"I'm glad . . . someone finally . . . came for me," he managed to gasp. "I knew they wouldn't forget me. . . . Tell them I stayed with the mission." With that he closed his eyes.

Hunter was stunned. He shook the old man, and then checked his breathing, but it was too late. Ben quickly began CPR but to no avail. The man was dead.

"Well, I'll be damned," Ben said. "Talk about flaming out. No wonder the native wanted us to get up here so quick. He knew he was close to checking out."

Hunter nodded sadly and pulled the blanket up over the man's face.

"Another ghost," he said quietly.

It was unforgiving, primitive terrain. Impenetrable jungle, vertical cliffs, swamps. Quicksand. If you got lost, you stayed lost.

And then you died.

But using one of the dog-eared, hand-drawn maps given to them by the old man, Hunter and Ben were able to follow the slightest of trails through the thick forest, paths that led them around insurmountable rock formations and brought them to shallow crossings of otherwise unfordable rivers, all the while taking turns carrying the heavy sack containing the Jason Group's transcoder module. They were grateful for the map's accuracy and appreciated the care the old man had taken to create it. The scale was perfect, and the landmarks were clearly and exactly noted. As was their destination—just six miles north of Khe Sanh.

But the going was tough. Often they had to deftly skirt Minx positions or stop and sit tight as a Minx convoy passed by. But two hours after leaving the old man to be buried by the Montagnards, they finally reached their destination.

They silently crept forward until they came to the edge of a clearing.

That's when Hunter and Ben saw the airfield.

It was a single runway job, 5,000 feet of asphalt cutting through a cleared field of about 100 acres and surrounded by dense jungle forest. There were three Quonset-style buildings by the runway and a modest wooden tower which functioned as the air traffic control center. Two small fuel tanks anchored the southern end of the base; a water tower stood nearby. At the far end, there was a large erection of some kind, covered by camouflaged netting. Undoubtably, this was where the small base's aircraft were kept.

But Hunter noticed right away that something was wrong with this picture. The base was about six miles due north of Khe Sanh—this placed it in a fairly volatile area. Yet the personnel here were anything but combat ready. They could clearly see ground support people lounging around the base's grassy infield. Some were playing Ping-Pong on one of the several tables set up near the control tower. Others appeared to be playing cards or maybe dice.

And even though the base was obviously well-stocked with fuel and ammunition, they could see no guards on duty, no defense positions manned or weapons ready. Not even a perimeter wire surrounding the place.

Hunter slipped out his binoculars and focused on the edge of the field that was covered by a maze of camouflage netting.

That's when he saw them.

There were four of them, all the same model; all MiG-25 Foxbats.

These were the same kind of MiGs they'd encountered first over the Gulf of Tonkin. Built in the mid-sixties, the MiG-25 was designed as a high-altitude interceptor. With a speed approaching Mach 3.2, it was able to reach heights of more than 80,000 feet. Hunter flipped up the power of the binoculars to take a closer look at what they were carrying under their wings. His worst fears were confirmed.

Instead of being armed with its usual complement of air-to-air missiles, these particular fighters had been converted to a ground attack role. The armaments bolted underwing of each of them attested to that gloomy fact—three 550 lb. GP bombs, two 1,100 lb FAB-500 GP bombs, and an array of AS-7 Kerry air-to-surface missiles. He handed the glasses to Ben.

"Fucktheduck," Ben whispered as he scanned the jets parked under the netting. "This is the first time I've seen Foxes rigged for ground attack. You'd think they'd be too damned fast."

"They are," Hunter replied. "But let's face it, these Minx guys are nothing if not unpredictable."

Ben handed the glasses back to Hunter. "I just don't get it," he said. "These guys have four kick-ass airplanes, no more than ten klicks away from us—and they don't use them? How come?"

Hunter could only shake his head. "The same reason they do *all* the screwy things they do, I guess . . ."

But deep down, Hunter's psyche was telling him it was only a matter of time before the four jet fighters came into play. And he knew he'd better be prepared when they did.

He nudged Ben and they began inching their way from the edge of the clearing and into the bush.

They had to get back to the base.

Chapter Twenty-three

Khe Sanh

Frost's hands were bleeding.

His fingernails were split and ragged, his knuckles gashed and stiff. He'd lifted so many sandbags that he'd developed dozens of water blisters, especially on his thumbs and forefingers. With each sandbag, a blister would break and start bleeding, only to be covered up by an even larger blister.

It was getting close to midnight. Frost and the ten men in his group had been busting ass for almost five hours now, building the northwest corner of the fifteen-foot high, six-sandbag-deep wall which was slowly growing around the outside of *NJ104*.

More than eighty men were at work on this massive project now. Once completed, the wall would shield the battered C-5's fuselage and engines from most mortar blasts; a roof being constructed with corrugated tin and planking copped from destroyed Legion bunkers would help protect it from direct hits.

To the casual observer, it might have appeared that the enormous sandbag and tin cocoon was being built too late. *NJ104* was literally a wreck. It had been three times battered; first, in the MiG battle, then in its subsequent pancake crash, and finally in its painful, asphalt-scraping, wing-twisting towing from one end of the runway to the other. Now, its right wing was hanging by less than a dozen bolts. Its tail section was on the verge of collapse, and its cockpit and flight deck were absolutely riddled with cannon holes. Its two outer engines had already fallen off; a third—the inner right engine—was drooping very low. So in many ways, *NJ104* looked to be in worse shape than *Bozo*.

But in many ways, *NJ104* was more important than *Bozo*, despite that airship's massive weaponry. For the wrecked Galaxy once flown by the New Jersey combat engineers held the key to survival for the base defenders. Without it, they were surely doomed to die here in the mud of Khe Sanh.

It was ironic, then, that there were no weapons anywhere on *NJ104*'s sandbag barrier, nor on its protective roof. In fact, there were no weapons at all on the enclosed airplane. The idea was not to have any gunfire coming from the sheltered C-5. This way it was hoped the Minx would bypass it when they attacked.

It was straight-up midnight when Geraci himself arrived, bearing a pot of coffee and some barely cooked MREs.

Frost's sandbag crew was granted a well-deserved five-minute break. As the rest of the workers sat down for what would be a quick respite from the back-breaking labor, Frost and Geraci walked a hundred feet away from the airplane and settled under the splintered wooden roof of a half-collapsed Legion gun position.

Geraci passed the Canadian a cup of coffee.

"What do you think the chances are of finishing the whole wall by 0300?" he asked.

Frost wiped his bleeding hands on his coveralls and took a long sip of the hot java. "We'll need more guys," he replied. "With the crew we have now, I can't say we'll have it finished even by sunup."

Geraci shook his head slowly. "We might be able to spare two or three guys at the most in about an hour," he said. "But I don't have to tell you that manpower is our biggest problem right now."

Frost could only shrug in grim agreement. There were about 150 Americans and 100 Legionnaries and mercenaries left stranded at the airstrip, and every one of them was involved in some sort of labor essential to what had come to be called simply, "The Big Plan." Even the normal complement of sentries around the shrinking perimeter—made up mostly of the *Bozo* gun crew—had been cut in half, a dangerous yet necessary circumstance. At the moment, their muscles were more important than their sharp eyes and quick trigger fingers.

Even more hazardous was the fact that more than half of the base defenders—just about all of them belonging to Geraci engineers—weren't outside at all. They were now locked inside Magic Mountain, working feverishly under dim lights and little air circulation. An enormous amount of pressure weighed down on these men, much of the Big Plan depended on their endurance and skill. And though protected by the mountain walls themselves, these men were also in the most dangerous spot in a place filled with dangerous spots. Should one rogue mortar round fired from the Minx in the hills hit the mountain's ancient mechanical doors, these men would be entombed forever, and with them, the hopes for the rest of the defenders' survival.

Frost took another long swig of his coffee and then wiped his weary brow. He looked back towards the rear end of *NJ104*'s sandbag shelter, contemplating the hours of hard work that still lay ahead.

"If I get out of this," he said, only half-joking, "I'm retiring from this hero business. I'll leave it to you Yanks. You do it better anyway."

"I'm no hero," Geraci replied. "I just seem to get stuck hanging around with heroes."

Frost laughed. "Hang around long enough," he said. "It starts to rub off."

Geraci checked the time. It was 0005 hours.

"I'd just feel a whole lot better if Hawk and Ben were here," he said.

"They'll be back," Frost said, finishing the last drops of his coffee. "They always come back."

No sooner were the words out of his mouth when suddenly there was a bright flash above the base.

It was so intense both Geraci and Frost immediately hit the ground. Instinctively they put their hands over their ears—but there was no accompanying explosion. Rather the flash was caused by a magnesium flare, launched from up the hills and slowly floating down towards the base on a time-delayed drag chute.

Geraci and Frost froze. Usually a flare of this size was a harbinger of a Minx attack, providing light for their soldiers in the dark of the midday monsoon rain.

But it was now the dead of night; the enemy never attacked after dark.

At least, they hadn't so far.

An instant later, they heard the telltale sound of mortars going off in the hills. But this was not just the usual, sporadic popping—this sounded more like a string of huge firecrackers exploding in the distance.

"Jesuzz, *what's happening here?*" Frost yelled.

"Damn if I know," Geraci yelled back.

That's when the mortar shells started coming down.

Boom! Boom! Boom! Boom! Boom! Boom! Boom! Boom!

In a second, there were so many enemy shells exploding, it sounded like one, long horrendous roar. Dozens of mortar trails lit up the sky brighter than the flares. In seconds, .81-mm high-impact shells were crashing down all over the base. It was so loud neither Frost or Geraci could hear each other yelling.

Frost dared to look up from his cover-up position. He couldn't believe the intensity of the enemy barrage. The sky itself looked like it was on fire.

"Looks like these guys got resupplied," he yelled.

"We've got to get better cover," Geraci finally managed to scream over the tremendous roar.

Instantly, both men were up and running, heading at full sprint for the sandbag cocoon surrounding *NJ104*. Many of the defenders were scrambling to the same location as it afforded the most protection from the thousands of mortar fragments that were suddenly zinging through the air like snow in a blizzard.

The two officers somehow made the short dash in one piece, joining the crowd of engineers, Legionnaires and mercenaries already hunkered down behind the opening on northwest wall of sandbags. Though pressed tight up against the half-finished barrier, Frost and Geraci could clearly see the gun crews of *Bozo* running into the back of their airplane, the screech of weapons' generators powering-up barely audible over the roar of the incredible mortar barrage.

"We don't have to worry about those guys," Geraci yelled in Frost's ear, pointing to *Bozo*. "It's the people inside the mountain."

In seconds, they both had their NightScopes out and trained on the camouflaged entranceway to Magic. Some of the enemy shells were coming down perilously close to the hidden portal.

"If we lost them," Geraci said, "that's the ball game."

But oddly, Frost wasn't listening. Instead he had his NightScope trained in the other direction, towards the northern edge of the base, out beyond the last line of Legion trenches.

"I don't believe this," he said, his voice rising above the rain of crashing mortal shells.

Geraci heard him, and immediately turned his scope in that direction.

That's when he saw them too.

Illuminated by the horrible explosions out on the edge of the base were two figures, running full-tilt over the churned-up, muddy ground, heading right for them.

"Jessuzz . . ." was all Geraci could say. "They *are* crazy."

It was Hunter and Ben. They were darting and dodging around the mortal explosions, sometimes running in a low crouch, sometimes as straight up as sprinters finishing a 50-yard dash. Every few seconds they would disappear from sight completely—usually Hunter yanking Ben to the ground in anticipation of a particularly close explosion. After several frightening seconds, the pair would invariably pop up again, running at full-speed through a haze of fire. They were carrying something with them—it was a knapsack. And even in the confusion of the mortar shells going off, the flares above, and the noise, it was obvious they were taking special care with the package.

Suddenly there was an even more frightening noise—it was so intense it startled Frost and Geraci into temporarily losing sight of Hunter and Ben. On someone's call, just about every weapon on *Bozo* had opened up at once. Instantly one long streak of flame erupted from the left side of the downed gunship, shooting into the enemy-held hills about a half mile away.

Suddenly the noise, the flame, the smoke and the utter confusion of battle around Khe Sanh had doubled in intensity.

"This is crazy!" Frost heard himself yelling.

The sky was absolutely filled with tracer streaks now, mortal shells coming down, explosions going off, flames, billowing smoke everywhere—all lit beneath the continuously falling magnesium flares. It was not just a vision of hell—but hell itself.

By the time Geraci and Frost turned their scopes back to where Hunter and Ben were last spotted, they could see nothing but flames, rising high into the air. One of the enemy shells had made a direct hit on the Legionnaires' modest ammunition bunker, and now the entire area was being wracked by secondary explosions.

Both officers felt their hearts sink. The violence of the ammo going up along with the mind-boggling exchange of weapons fire made it impossible for anyone not under cover to survive.

Almost impossible, that is.

The next thing they knew, here came Hunter and Ben literally running out of a ball of flame, explosions going on all around them, heading right for the bunker.

"Jessuz, make some room!" Geraci yelled. But before the words were out of his mouth, Ben was already diving over the wall of sandbags, Hunter was right behind him.

They both rolled once and then were suddenly on the feet again. No one in the bunker could believe it. They had never seen anyone run so fast, amidst so much incoming ordnance. It seemed almost impossible they'd had made it unscathed—their uniforms were smoking. But here they were—out of breath, but alive.

"Welcome to the party, guys," Geraci told them, ducking back down beside the sandbag wall. "Our friends in the hills are a little restless tonight."

Hunter and Ben were soon hugging the sandbag wall, too.

"And we thought they were heavy sleepers," Hunter replied.

The battle raged all through the night.

The Minx mortar barrage did not let up one iota, nor had the return fire from *Bozo*.

Still huddled against the *NJ104* sandbag wall, Hunter and Ben had long ago given up trying to wolf down some cold MREs; it was almost impossible to swallow in between mortar blasts.

They had already recounted their trip to Frost and Geraci, first detailing the climb to the Green Beret's cave and subsequent journey to the nearby MiG base. The others listened with growing anxiety. The presence of the MiGs so close by was as disturbing as it was baffling. As heavily armed as they were, the base defenders had little in the way of antiaircraft weapons. One or two attacks by the speedy, bombed-up MiGs and the party at Khe Sanh would *really be* over.

The enemy shells continued to fall for hours. The incredible nonstop barrage underscored just how desperate the situation at Khe Sanh was getting—the already-tight timetable for the Big Plan was shrinking further and further even as the Minx attack seemed to grow stronger and stronger.

And Hunter was certain that it was just a matter of time before the MiGs based over the hill came into play, too.

There was only one bright spot in the whole dark mess—and they had Willy Rucker, the last Green Beret, to thank for that.

It was the Jason Transponder Module—the JTM. Hunter had spent the time huddled against the sandbag wall studying the bulky, 50-pound device. He was astounded at its sophistication. On the surface, it looked like something out of a bad spy movie. Dials, switches, levers, and a handful of multicolored wires running out of a multitude of holes, and into the ancient nickel-cadium battery at its base.

In the JTM's center was a circular radar-screen type window with a fading grid scratched into its orange-tinted glass covering. This looked like the hokiest item of all. But as soon as the device was turned on, all of the tinsel seemed to fade away. The light behind the orange window was bright and deep, the noise coming from it sounded authoritative. It was actually a series of continual beeps and tones; their frequency and pitch levels Hunter had yet to decipher.

But what he *did* know about the JTM was that when the proper grid was set inside the orange window, and the device tuned to the correct frequency of the built-to-last Jason noise and motion detectors, then it would be able to provide them with extraordinary information on the movements of enemy troops in the immediate area as well as all over the northern part of South Vietnam.

But they had to survive to have the JTM do them any good. And as if to underscore that fact, a particularly brutal barrage of mortal shells came crashing down not five feet from the sand bag wall where Hunter and the others were huddled.

It was now 0530 hours. The sun would be up soon and with it the grim unpredictability of another day. Luckily most of the work had been completed in the NJ104 wall, and similarly protected *Bozo* was somehow weathering the long attack.

But, still, Hunter knew it was time for some hard questions.

"What will happen if we move the deadline up by twenty-four hours?" he asked Geraci.

The top engineer just shook his head. "I can't really say," he replied, gesturing towards Magic Mountain where more than half his corps had been working nonstop for what seemed like days. "My guys are at the end of their rope now—and we haven't even got to the major stuff, if you know what I mean."

"How about if we leave out all the bells and whistles?" Hunter asked. "Just do the primary work and see what happens?"

Again, Geraci could only shake his head. "My guys are good," he said. "Miracles might be a little out of our league, though."

"But that's exactly what we need," Ben said. "Divine intervention. A lot of it. And quick."

Another massive barrage came down at that moment, this one even closer than the one a half minute before.

All eyes were on Geraci now. He just shrugged. "We really don't have much choice, I guess," he said wearily. "OK, I'll pass the orders down. If we survive the ground attack tomorrow, we go all out on Phase Two of the Big Plan tomorrow night."

It wasn't until dawn cracked the sky that the massive shelling finally stopped.

Looking out over the airstrip, the survivors beheld a scene of utter destruction. Plumes of black smoke rose high above the base. Dozens of fires were burning out of control throughout the Legion fortifications. Shattered gear, ripped sandbags, chunks of timbers, pieces of corrugated tin, and lengths of barbed wire were scattered everywhere, all mixed up in the mud that had been churned up over and over again. Many bunkers had collapsed, others were just gone, obliterated. Everywhere, there were bodies—recently killed or long dead, their graves turned up once again by the shelling.

It was a moonscape, apparently devoid of any kind of life.

But slowly, those defenders who had survived dug themselves out of the rubble. And once again, they struggled to rebuilt their defense lines and try to bury some of their dead, just as they had done so many times in the past.

But no sooner did the sun come up when the clouds of another monsoon began forming over the base.

Hunter, Ben, Geraci and Frost quickly made the dash back over to *Bozo*.

They were certain the hours-long mortar barrage was actually a warm-up for a huge Minx ground attack.

As it turned out, they were right.

One hour later

The innocent splattering of the raindrops upon the fuse-lage of *Bozo* gave the crew just enough warning. They knew by now what the coming of the rains signified.

With well-rehearsed precision, positions inside the forti-fied aircraft were manned and weapons were loaded. The outside guards scrambled up the cargo door, which was then closed and locked. All lights were turned off. Loose ammunition was secured. Sandbag walls next to the bigger holes in the fuselage were checked and quickly reinforced where needed. Helmets and flak jackets were distributed, small arms loaded.

Then as the clouds opened up and the rain came down in earnest, the Americans waited for what they knew would soon come.

The sky became darker and darker. The visibility rap-idly diminished with the increasing intensity of the rain. Within minutes, the clatter of the downpour was the only thing that could be heard inside their battered fortress.

The tension mounted. Each weapons' commander had his finger on his activation button, each ammo feeder cra-dled the next rocket, shell, or bullet he would slam into the chamber. And they waited—ready for the another murder-ous onslaught. Ready for the command to fire.

Minutes went by, and still no attack. The anxiety level inside *Bozo* rose dramatically with each passing second. Where the hell are they, each man silently asked, *what the hell are they waiting for?*

Suddenly, twenty-five magnesium flares burst overhead, lighting up the entire base in spite of the torrential down-pour. Then came the screams. Then the bugles. Then hundreds of Viet Minx, charging from the treeline, bellow-ing at the top of their lungs, began to cross the 150 yards of the open marsh—heading right toward *Bozo*.

A flurry of activity erupted inside the plane as heavy

weapons were quickly rotated along the makeshift tracks to the port side—to fully meet the charge head-on.

"Get ready to fire!" called out the various gun commanders. "Eyes sharp. Weapons to on."

The charging Viet Minx were getting closer and closer by the second—they were now just 100 yards away.

"Power up!" the gun commanders cried.

"Deflectors up!"

"Chamber rounds. Set fuses . . ."

"Seventy five yards."

"Ready . . . FIRE!"

The six GE Gatling guns roared to life first, delivering a stream of 30-mm shells into the brunt of the attack, chewing through the mass of attacking Viet Minx with brutal mechanical horror. As the Gatlings raked back and forth across the front of the human wave, the five Mk-19 automatic grenade launchers, cranked down to their minimum elevation, were fired, blasting furiously into the enemy's ranks just behind the first line. Five seconds later, the 120-mm Soltam and the two 105-mm Royal Ordnance field artillery pieces, now loaded with antipersonnel shells, opened up in tandem, their shells ripping through the third line of tightly-packed enemy soldiers, sending thousands of pieces of hot, screaming steel into the attackers.

But the Minx kept coming.

The sound inside *Bozo* quickly grew to a deafening roar. The disabled plane shuddered with each massive volley. The sandbag walls protecting the fuselage were being ripped to shreds by the hundreds of enemy AK-47 rounds, and within seconds, the bullets began to find their way through the C-5's already perforated hull. Hails of them were now zinging around inside like deadly high-speed sparks.

The three 20-mm AA Guns then erupted, the fuses of their explosive shells set to go off five seconds after they left the muzzles. Their impact along the first Minx line added to the murderous slaughterhouse effect. Like before, it had become a battle of high technology versus sheer numbers and brute force.

But still, the Viet Minx kept coming.

Stationed at a gun post near the front of the battered plane, Hunter kept jamming clip after thirty-round clip into his M-16, knocking down scores of enemy attackers. But it was like trying to empty the ocean with a leaky bucket. As quickly as they were shot down, more Viet Minx replaced those who had fallen.

And beyond them, three more waves of Minx emerged from the treeline.

It was the biggest, most intense attack yet, Hunter quickly realized. The Minx were throwing everything at them *including* the kitchen sink. It was apparent that the thousands of bloodthirsty Minx coming right at *Bozo* had but one objective—to conquer and destroy this last stronghold.

And if they succeeded . . .

Hunter scrambled down from the flight deck, dodging a hail of enemy bullets coming through one of the fuselage's bigger holes. He was headed for the LARS II.

Geraci was in charge of the Gatlings. He had to quickly split his command, ordering three of the guns to the opposite side of the hull to fight the Minx that had managed to get around to that side. Manpower was needed to move the guns, so Hunter pitched in. He and the crews went immediately into action, unhinging stress bolts, unlocking recoil brackets, pivoting the guns on their swivel pedestals. Rounds of enemy rifle and machine-pistol bullets were flying all around them. Suddenly there was an ear-splitting scream. Then another. Then another. Three of Geraci's men were hit and hit bad. The wounded were taken from harm's way as quickly as possible as Hunter and the rest of the crew continued to slide the guns across the wide belly of the plane on the makeshift rails to the opposite posts. Then, just efficiently, they secured the guns and redirected the overhead racks of belted ammo. The hours of endless drilling was paying off.

At once, the three repositioned Gatlings opened up, slicing through the ranks of the Minx that had circled around that side. More attackers rushed up to take the places of their fallen comrades and the fierce assault on the beleaguered C-5 continued unabated—but now on all sides. As Hunter resumed his arduous trek back toward the rocket launcher, he glanced over his shoulder and saw that Geraci was firing one of the Gatlings practically single-handedly.

Round after round of .81-mm mortar shells began to rain down on and along the sides of *Bozo*, sending chunks of shrapnel ripping through the hull. More men were wounded. More mortar shells dropped and exploded. They had never undergone a combined attack this intense, this concentrated. Even the barrage all night paled by comparison. The plane was now shaking nonstop from the blasts and concussions. And the attack only increased in ferocity.

Hunter had to get to the LARS II—and fast.

He reached midfuselage when six mortar shells exploded at once, rocking the plane so violently that he was thrown to the deck. Hunter picked himself up and started on his way again, but then something made him stop short. Right in front of him, there was a man lying in a pool of blood. He turned him over. It was Frost.

"Hawk, old man." The Canadian's whisper was barely audible with the raging sound of guns firing and the screaming all around them. "Did they get the family jewels?"

Hunter studied his friend's wounds. Frost's right leg was a bloody mess; his left hand was also seriously torn up. Hunter unsheathed his K-bar knife and hurriedly slit open Frost's trouser leg. A piece of shrapnel had ripped through the skin a few inches above the knee. But luckily it hadn't severed the artery, and was too low to affect Frost's equipment.

"Take it easy, Frostman," Hunter told him. "You'll be able to climb in the saddle again. Just stay put."

"Got no choice, have I?" Frost replied through a tight smile.

More determined than ever to end this nightmare, Hunter scrambled down through the fuselage until he finally came to the LARS II.

The massive long-range rocket launcher was powered up and its crew ready for the command to fire. But on Hunter's orders, the gunners quickly elevated its rocket tubes to an extremely high angle. Instead of having been depressed to ground level, the tubes were now pointing three degrees shy of straight up.

Hunter crouched next to the LARS control panel. Through a recently cut port hole on the right side, he saw that despite the enormous fusillade that continued to pour from the heavy guns, a main force of Minx was now swarming over *Bozo*'s first line of sandbag barriers—no more than thirty-five yards away. Like an army of crazed fire ants, they were coming from everywhere, heading for the airplane to devour it. And nothing was stopping them—not the Gatlings, not the grenade launchers, not the AA-guns, and not even the field artillery. During the Vietnam war, desperate commanders in similar situations had called in air strikes on themselves.

Now Hunter was about to do the same.

He knew the risk he was about to take. It was indeed a drastic measure. But he also knew that it was absolutely necessary. He took a deep breath and then checked the LARS firing mechanism again.

Then he pushed the activator button.

Thirty six rockets streaked up into the darkness of the monsoon rain. Quickly reaching the apex of their arc, they slowly turned and then began falling back to earth.

Suddenly, a stunned silence fell over the battlefield as

the attacking Minx froze in their tracks, watching with awe as the giant rockets lit up the sky and then began to streak back toward them.

One gigantic scream of sheer panic rose up as the Minx realized the rockets were coming right at them. Many tried to run, but it was no use. They were too tightly packed together, and there was no place they could go.

Then the rockets hit.

One after the other, the 110-mm high explosive warheads came crashing down—right into the clamoring mass of Viet Minx attackers. And not thirty yards away from *Bozo*.

The effect of the monstrous rocket barrage was devastating. The tremendous series of powerful explosions went right through the thousands of the attackers. Immense geysers of earth, water, debris, and Minx soldiers were thrown high into the air. Chunks of screaming, hot shrapnel tore through the flesh of the attackers, concussions sucked the air from their lungs. The killing field turned into a bloody charnel house as hundreds of the enemy were obliterated and many more were severely wounded.

But the explosions also took a great toll on the C-5. The entire length of the fuselage was further battered and weakened by the blasts. The hull was seriously ripped up by the shrapnel, the port-side wing shredded, and fires were raging on several areas of the fuselage, in defiance of the monsoon rains that continued to pour down.

But those inside had survived, despite having called down, in effect, a massive missile strike on themselves.

The Gatlings managed to continue to fire, as did the artillery and the AA guns. But the back of the enemy charge was broken. Some of the Viet Minx field commanders tried to rally their men to continue to the attack, but there wasn't enough of them left that could carry the charge effectively. Now the brutal assault turned into a panicked, all-out retreat. Many enemy soldiers were cut down as they ran away. Others simply threw down their arms and fled.

Within two minutes of the LARS barrage, the shooting had stopped.

Five minutes after that, the rain began to let up.

Chapter Twenty-four

Hours Later

Lieutenant Twang couldn't breathe.

He was sucking in dirt and debris even as he was digging furiously outward. As a warrior, he wasn't supposed to be afraid to die—but that applied only to battles. Not being buried alive.

Twang had watched the entire attack on the heavily armed airplane from his spider hole.

Only twenty-five yards from the perimeter of the base and 125 yards away from the plane itself, he had practically been in the thick of the battle. The concussions from the explosions all around him had been horrific. Dozens of his Minx comrades had unknowingly charged over his camouflaged hole. But as the battle raged all around, it was only the dead ones that fell in upon him. He'd been forced to push out as many as seven mangled corpses, men who had been in the rear lines and sliced up by the short-fused AA fire. Throughout the entire battle, Twang knew that if just one shell out of the thousands expended had landed on top of him, he would have disappeared in a bloody mist. But he had been lucky. He'd watched in horror as the rockets roared out of the airplane and soared straight up into the sky. Then they came back down. Right at him. And that's when everything went black.

He never knew what hit him—only that it knocked him cold, and raised a bump the size of a small fist on the top of his head. When he finally came to, he thought he'd been killed and was waking up inside his own coffin.

But then he came to his senses.

He'd spent the past half hour madly pushing his way through the dirt and debris that had collapsed on top of his hole. His stomach was twisted with the fear of being entombed alive; his brain was reeling from the concussion on the top of his skull. But somehow, someway, he finally broke through to the top.

He gasped for air. It tasted of cordite and the stench of burned, dead bodies. But he sucked it in greedily, still shaking. Still alive.

Now self-exhumed. Twang peered over the edge of his hole. He couldn't believe it—it was already nighttime. He'd been unconscious for hours! Several small fires were still burning from the attack and they illuminated the immediate area. It was a grisly landscape. Bodies were sprawled everywhere. Even worse, parts of bodies were also strewn about. Smoke was still rising from the hundreds of shell hole craters, and an eerie, low fog covered the entire battlefield. And in the glow, he saw, flying over the center of the fuselage of the battered plane that repulsed the attack, a tattered, yet furling American flag.

"So they *are* Americans . . ." he thought.

Suddenly, a bright burst of white light temporarily blinded him. Dropping back into his hole, he rubbed his eyes until the spots dancing on his retinas disappeared. Then he looked out again.

This time, he saw several bursts of the white light along the runway far out in the distance. But these were not muzzle flashes—rather, he quickly realized, they were acetylene torches. Twang estimated that there had to be at least twenty torches in all, telltale streams of sparks showered around each of the places where they were cutting.

Those twinkling on and off in the distance looked like fire-flies.

Twang studied the torching activity for a few moments, wondering what the defenders were up to. He considered calling back to his base. But the popping of mortars going off from the jungle behind him told him it would be unnecessary. His comrades in the hills had also spotted the torches.

But then an odd thing happened. All of the torches suddenly shut off.

Twang quickly took cover just as the .81-mm shells, dropping close to where the torches were being used nearest the runway, exploded. When he looked up, it was pitch black again. Twang felt a burst of pride for the Minx mortar crews. For once, they had been accurate as hell—their rounds had come down exactly on their targets.

Or so it appeared.

He found himself smiling for the first time in months. He'd been nearly killed and then entombed alive, due to the enemy's fire—now they were getting it in return. But suddenly his vengeful grin turned to a look of amazement. One by one, all the acetylene torches began to flare up again.

Through the throbbing pain of his head wound, Twang watched as the enemy soldiers resumed their cutting. The mortar fire resumed as well, but this time the crews in the hills were aiming for separate torchlights. Their lack of success, however, didn't change. All along the runway, the torches flared off just seconds after the mortars popped. The shells would land and explode. And after the echoes of the explosions faded, the same number of torches flared up again—sometimes at the same locations, sometimes elsewhere. This pattern repeated itself over and over for the next ten minutes.

These defenders are a cunning lot, Twang thought, his head wound now making him very dizzy. By cutting the torches off and moving to other sites, they thwarted the mortar crews from zeroing in. Thus, they not only avoided being killed, they were able to continue their work.

But what they were working on, and exactly what they were cutting, he had no idea.

His head spinning, Twang slumped back into his hole, for the first time feeling the twin streams of blood running down his face from his wound. Suddenly, he felt very tired, as if he hadn't slept in weeks. He knew it was against orders—but he couldn't help himself. He closed his eyes— and was soon fast asleep, again.

Geraci, too, was exhausted.

He hadn't slept going on thirty-six hours. Between the moving and then sandbagging of *NJ104*, the uprighting of *Bozo*, the massive nighttime barrage and the recent attack, he had burned up his reserve long ago. But he kept going, if only to keep up with Hunter, who if anything was working harder and longer.

Geraci was manning one of the acetylene torches while overseeing eight other torching crews scattered in the darkness around him. His second-in-command, Captain Don Matus was directly supervising the work of four of the crews about a half mile away. Another one of his officers, Captain Ray Palmi, was looking after the other four closer to the end of the runway. Each crew consisted of five engineers: two torchers, two others to help carry the tanks and gear—and one to keep a watch out for the telltale flare of mortar tubes going off in the hills.

With a map, a "shopping list" provided by Hunter, and a set of steel balls, Geraci and each of the other torchers were cutting away in the dark on the scattered hulks of the wrecked planes that littered the length of the Khe Sanh runway. They were on a treacherous and deadly scavenger hunt for parts—parts that they needed, parts that all their lives would depend on.

It was a nerve-wracking job. Working at night with all

this equipment would have been a dangerous proposition, even under the most ideal circumstances. But these conditions were far from idea. In fact, they were almost impossible.

Still, he and his crews in the field were making headway. Personally, he had already managed to cut free six separate parts on his list: a leading edge panel from the tail of a Lockheed P-3C Orion, a starboard aileron from a Fairchild C-119G Boxcar, and four propeller blades from an old, C-130 Hercules.

Each of the cannibalized parts was carefully lugged to the entrance of Magic Mountain by a squad headed by another of Geraci's officers, Captain Roy Cerbasi. Once there, the parts were whisked inside where eighty of Geraci's engineers, taut, tired and hungry, began work on them, painstakingly assembling the building blocks to Hunter's Big Plan.

All of the torch crews in the field were having success getting their assigned parts, so they kept Cerbasi's men hopping between the runway and the front of Magic.

But there were many more parts to get. And the constant stopping to haul ass and take cover from the mortar explosions, and the hot shrapnel whizzing around only added to the madness.

And even as their ardous task continued in the field, Geraci was well aware that a third team of base defenders was hard at work inside the sandbag cocoon surrounding *NJ104*. They too were using acetylene torches to cut through bent and twisted pieces of metal. They too were sending a stream of parts, both useable and not, back to the men inside Magic Mountain.

And they too knew that the work done by all on this endless night would go a long way in determining their chances for survival.

Chapter Twenty-five

The next morning

The sun's early morning rays cut through the thick morning fog and somehow reached Lieutenant Twang's closed eyelids.

Still asleep, Twang smiled at their warmth. He was dreaming about a tropical island, far out at sea. The ocean waters surrounding this island were so clear they were green. There was a warm, pure white beach, and nearby, a high cliff. On the cliff, there was an airplane, surrounded by candles and covered in smoke.

Oddly, the airplane was painted pink. . . .

Suddenly, Twang's eyes popped open. He instantly felt a wave of panic washover him.

Had he fallen asleep, on duty, *again?*

He was quickly up on the lip of the spider hole and was relieved to find that he was still alone and undetected. But this relief soon turned to utter revulsion. The hole was surrounded by the corpses of his comrades, killed in the titanic battle the previous day. Twang felt paralyzed just looking at them. Some were missing arms, legs, heads. Others were horribly blown apart, stomachs, intestines, bowels strewn around them like huge hideous worms. Still others seemed perfectly fine. Their bodies were intact, their eyes open, their faces pulled back in involuntary smiles. They looked as if nothing was wrong with them—except that they were dead. They seemed to be beckoning to Twang. They seemed to want him to join them.

Twang slid back down into his spider hole. *Soon enough,* he feared.

He looked at his hands and realized they were covered with dried blood. Then it came back to him—the big battle the day before, his comrades' suicide charge, the enemy's massive rocket barrage, the chunk of something that hit him on the head and knocked him out. The terror of being buried alive and his frantic efforts to get back to the surface and breathe again rose again in his throat. His lungs were still filled with those first breaths of air; his tonsils still burned of the cordite; his nostrils still seared with the smell of the dead. He felt for the wound at the top of his head, and found a clump of puss, blood, and matted hair. He was instantly sick to his stomach—he was sure he looked worse than some of his dead compatriots lying outside the spider hole.

He slumped further down into the hole, feeling as if life itself was draining out of him. He closed his eyes and was surprised that he saw many spots—like those caused by camera flash bulbs or strobes. Was this a symptom of impending death?

Or were they caused by something else?

He had to struggle to remember—his head wound had caused a severe concussion, and quite nearly a fractured skull, so his memory was working slowly. But then it came back to him: last night. In the darkness. The enemy, armed with acetylene torches. They were cutting something. . . .

He was back up on the lip of the spider hole in an instant. In the fog, past the bodies, he could just barely see the base runway. Closer to him was the carcass of a rusting airplane; it was no more than fifty yards away, and he'd been staring at it since he arrived in the stinking spider hole.

Now he strained his eyes to see that one of this dead airplane's wings was missing parts of its wrecked propeller and engine, as well as the tip of the wing itself. Actually he could clearly see dozens of burn marks all over the airplane's rusting silver skin.

Next to this airplane was a smaller one—an old jet fighter, he thought. He could see that pieces of this wreck were missing too; the burn marks around its engine cowlings were very evident, and apparently its clear glass canopy had also been taken.

It was all coming back to him now, in a rush so fast, it was actually painful.

He had come to briefly during the night; long enough to see the enemy soldiers running around in the darkness, cutting up the dead airplanes with their torches, and dodging the barrages of mortar shells fired from his comrades in the hills.

He had watched them—but for how long? Ten minutes? An hour? Two hours? He didn't know.

But now, he imagined he could remember events from the unconsciousness that had followed. Even greater flashes of light. Sounds louder than mortar blasts. A rumbling even more earthshaking than when the enemy moved one of their wrecked airplanes the length of the runway a few nights before.

Had he dreamed all this? Dreamed it before he flew without wings to the tropical island, the one with the green waters and the pink plane on the cliffs?

Again, he didn't know. He stepped even further up the lip of the spider hole, cursing the thick morning fog, cursing his weary eyes, weakened by the knock on his skull.

The thick mist was lifting, but not quick enough for him. As it dissipated, it revealed more of the nearby wrecked airplanes—and more evidence that they had been cut up during the night. Landing struts were gone here, tailplanes were gone there. All of the old wrecked airplanes within his view looked like they'd surrendered at least one part to the torches. But oddly, there seemed to be no rationale for the enemy's nocturnal efforts, no discernable pattern. Why would the totally outgunned Caucasians choose to risk their lives and precious time cutting up old plane wrecks?

It just didn't make any sense.

Chapter Twenty-six

Behind the lines
One hour later

All it took was one look at his valet for Commander Long Dong Tru to know the small war for Khe Sanh was all but lost.

Dong stared at the man in his dressing room mirror as he arranged a set of medals on Dong's chest. He looked simply ragged. His uniform was frayed, his eyes watering, his face gaunt and etched with newly carved wrinkles. He looked like an old man, though Dong knew the valet was actually quite younger than he.

"When was the last time you had a meal?" Dong asked him.

"Two days ago, sir," was the man's barely audible answer.

Dong was authentically surprised. "Two days? I thought we had plenty of food on hand."

"We did," the valet replied, never looking his commander in the eye. "But the front-line troops stole it all three days ago."

"Stole it? *Why?*"

The valet froze for a moment. "In order to eat it all before the last battle," he replied finally.

Dong was both startled and puzzled by the words. "But why would they do that?"

The valet just shrugged as he smoothed the cuff on Dong's uniform pants. "Because they knew they were going to die," he replied simply. "They wanted to go to the hereafter with a full stomach. It's an old superstition."

That's when it hit home for Dong. For the first time he realized that his troops had recognized the futility of this adventure long before he had.

There was no way that troops with that mind-set could prevail. No wonder the battle the day before had gone so badly. Even the new weapons and troops he'd purchased from CapCom had had little effect. The tenacious base defenders had somehow held on once again.

The news from the front was so bad, Dong had refused to look at the casualty figures from the last battle—he didn't have to see numbers on a page to tell him just how miserable a defeat it was.

What had gone wrong? Dong wondered gloomily. Would he ever know? The enemy at Khe Sanh was small, weakening and desperately outnumbered. On the other hand, his troops had everything. All the ammunition they wanted, all the mortar rounds, all the weapons. And he had fed them well, too.

But for some reason, it hadn't been enough.

He quickly dismissed the valet and called for his personal aides to bring to his office the large iron chest in which he kept his gold reserves. The aides soon appeared with the large steamer trunk chest. Dong was quick to notice they no longer struggled with its weight.

They laid the chest on his desk and were dismissed. Dong himself worked the combination lock, springing it open on the third try.

One look inside only depressed him further.

He had but one hundred and twenty bags of gold left. This from the thousands he'd still owned even after purchasing his first army. The 120 bags were worth about $5 million, possibly a little more. Also inside the box was his ledger book, the one he had intended to use to bill CapCom for the overrunning of Khe Sanh and the securing of the strategic highway of Route 9 beyond.

But he could not do that now. Khe Sanh was still in enemy hands. He could not present CapCom with a bill. And that was the crux of his present problem. If he couldn't charge CapCom for the campaign, then he would not be reimbursed. No reimbursement meant that he was practically broke and out of the running when it came time to divide up the spoils of South Vietnam once the major campaigns began.

Thus, Dong felt himself in a position familiar to many a businessman through the ages. He had made two large mistakes. He had foregone direct contact with his troops, preferring to look upon them as product, and he had cut corners at crucial times, thinking that saving money during the operation would mean more money once the operation was completed.

In a word, he had been greedy. And now he was forced to pay the price.

He had but one chance left to save his sinking fortunes. It would be a one-shot effort, something he should have tried long ago. If it worked, then he still had a chance to recoup some of his fortune. If it failed, then he would be completely broke again, left with no army, no prestige, no power.

He shuddered at the thought.

Draining the last drops from his cognac snifter, he punched a button on his radio phone, spoke briefly to a Minx communications unit approximately twenty miles away, who then patched him through to his intended party.

The radiophone on the other end rang three times before it was picked up.

* * *

217

Captain Lo Ky answered the radiophone.

It was just a coincidence, of course. He happened to be passing by the base operations desk, on his way to the mess for another jug of rice wine, when he heard the device started beeping and picked it up.

The voice on the other end sounded panicky, almost as if his location was under attack. That was not unusual: the majority of people seeking help from the MiGs based at Song Ly were usually being shot at, or mortared, or bombed or shelled at the time of the call. That was, after all, the basis of the business of the MiGs at the base. They were purely damage control, called in to perform air strikes for various Minx commanders who for whatever reason found their balls in a vice and needed some untightening quick.

But this voice that Ky was listening to sounded different—it was both anxious *and* depressed. As if the battle was already over, and the caller was simply going through the motions of calling in an air strike, just so he could, in the end, know that he had expended all his options before running up the white flag.

Technically, Ky should have summoned one of the logistics officers at the base to take the call, get the coordinates of the potential customer, discuss price and method of payment. But Ky took down all the information himself—this way the logistics officer would not have to be cut in on the job, meaning more money for Ky and his three comrade pilots.

The caller was one Long Dong Tru, commander of the Minx forces fighting at nearby Khe Sanh. Ky almost burst out laughing when the man finally identified himself. He and the other pilots at Song Li had been hearing about Dong's troubles at Khe Sanh for days—it was, after all, just over the hill from them. On still nights Ky and his men could hear the massive fighting going on in the bloody mudhole just six miles away, while they lay in comfortable duck-down beds, drinking rice wine and *fricking* the local whores.

Dong in fact had become a kind of laughing stock among the various Minx military units. While they were preparing for the massive offensives in the south, Dong, reputed to be a lowly truck driver who suddenly got rich, was having trouble defeating a small bunch of white men, who had holed up at Khe Sanh with few weapons, little ammo and practically no hope of survival.

He was also reportedly running out of funds, so Ky made it quite clear to Dong that any services from him and his fellow MiG pilots would have to be paid for in advance. Dong did not put up a fight—he even admitted that he was down to his last money reserves. He agreed to dispatch a convoy to Song Li carrying the 120 bags of gold the MiG pilots required to attack the enemy at Khe Sanh. The money would arrive within five hours. Ky agreed that the air strike would take place at dawn the next day.

He hung up on Dong and proceeded to get yet another jug of rice wine from the base fridge.

"Stupid fool," he thought, laughing again over Dong's pathetic request for last-minute air cover. " 'Penny smart and pound foolish.' "

Chapter Twenty-seven

Aboard Bozo

Ben was exhausted.

He was sitting on the mid-flight deck of *Bozo*, trying to get the most out of a cold cup of instant coffee.

He'd gone so long without sleep, he had lost his sense of time. He had no idea if it was day or night. Only a glance through bleary eyes at the cracked windshield in the forward compartment told him it was indeed nighttime, probably a few hours before sunrise.

He could hear activity going on below him, the gun crews doing their best to patch up the weapons hold of *Bozo*. But it was a tall order. There wasn't much left of the airplane. After the last great battle—the one in which Hunter saved them all by literally calling in a missile strike on their position—the fuselage had more holes in it than not. The wings were just about completely severed from the body, and the tailplane had collapsed. Many of the firing positions had to be readjusted because there was so much debris scattered around the battered C-5, it interfered with weapons aiming.

But lack of firing angles weren't the only problems. *Bozo* was low on ammunition, low on fuel for the generators, and therefore low on electrical power. The crew members were simply beat. Exhaustion was showing in all the faces, and though valiant, everyone seemed to be moving at half speed, or even slower.

It was sad to say, but there was also a crisis of spirit rising among them all. Though the day had passed without a follow-up Minx assault, everyone realized they couldn't withstand another large-scale attack. And even if they did, the one after that would surely be the death blow.

Ben found himself staring out of the shattered cockpit window towards Magic Mountain. While conditions were bad on *Bozo*, he knew things were even worse inside the artificial cave. Eighty of Geraci's guys had been locked up inside the mountain for what seemed like days on end. The task before them was so enormous, even Ben had doubts they could pull it off, no matter how much guidance they received from Hunter.

The problem was time. Even the most skilled of engineers needed time in which to do their work. But it was clear that the clock was running out very quickly for them all.

He turned back to Willy Rucker's Jason Transponder Module. His present duty was monitoring the JTM, just in case it picked up any unusual activity around Khe Sanh.

Ben didn't know just how Hunter had figured it all out so quickly, but now the grid highlighted by the JTM's orange light was clearly showing the area surrounding Khe Sanh. It represented a perimeter stretching about twenty kilometers or so out from the center of the battered base.

Ben had been staring at the grid off and on for the past few hours, with absolutely nothing to report. Hunter—who was also holed up inside Magic working with Geraci and his engineers—had told him that any unusual troop movements would show up as bursts of static on the nine-inch grid; any unusual mechanical activity would appear as moving vertical lines. Should either one of those things happen, Ben could use the JTM's abundance of tuning dials to triangulate the precise location on the grid. Then by consulting the maps given to them by Willy Rucker pin-point the activity in the area surrounding them.

And then? Then, Ben thought, they would have advanced warning of what would probably be their last day.

He leaned back and tried to stretch, his muscles aching from lack of sleep. Though tired, he wished *he* was working inside Magic instead of watching the JTM's orange screen. Though the conditions were undoubtedly worse inside the mountain, he would have preferred to pitch in on the really hard work, just to keep his mind off of what he considered to be the inevitable.

But they all had their duty to do. So Ben rubbed his eyes, let them refocus, and then turned back to the screen.

And that's when he saw them.

There were four distinct vertical lines literally buzzing off the grid. Ben froze for a moment. *Does this damn thing actually work?* he wondered. Vertical lines indicated a lot of electromechanical activity—anything from tanks to troop trucks to airplanes warming their engines. He immediately began turning the tuning dials, attempting to shrink the verticals until they were just dots blinking on the grid.

After sixty seconds of frantic twisting he had successfully isolated four blinking dots on the screen's grid. He hastily pulled out Rucker's maps and began going through them, looking for the correct layout which matched the appropriate part of the grid. Suddenly he found it—it was the northern exposure map. The indications were originating about six miles north of the base.

Damn . . . Ben whispered. The activity had to be coming from the MiG base he and Hunter had discovered with the help of Rucker's maps.

He was quickly up to his feet. He had to get this news to Hunter immediately.

But at that moment, the JTM started buzzing again. Ben sat back down to find a series of static bursts beckoning from another quadrant of the orange screen. Once again, he began twirling the tuning knobs; forty-five seconds later he was stunned to realize he'd isolated a large ground force moving towards Khe Sanh from the west.

He was back up in an instant, intent on running to the front of the flight deck, sliding down the access ladder in order to summon Hunter.

But when he turned around, he was startled to see The Wingman was already there. His face was a mask of concern. His hands shaking with barely controlled rage.

"*Jessuzz, Hawk* . . . I was coming to get you," Ben said gasped.

"I know," Hunter told him.

"The transponder . . . was blinking and . . ." Ben stuttered, trying to get everything out in one hurried sentence.

"I know," Hunter repeated.

"You know?" Ben was finally able to ask him. "You know about the MiGs, the troops? You know what's coming?"

Hunter nodded grimly. "Yeah," he said, soberly. "I always do."

He leaned over and studied the JTM's grid. Quick calculation told him that Ben had calibrated the device's position finders perfectly. There were at least four MiGs warming up at the base north of them, and a large mobile force—probably troop trucks—was heading in from the highlands to the west.

Whether the two forces were acting in concert, Hunter didn't know. And it didn't really make much difference. An attack from either one would do in the defenders and end the last stand at Khe Sanh. No wonder his inner psyche had been vibrating so intensely, compelling him to leave Magic and get to the JTM device.

So it had come down to this, he thought, eyeing the JTM screen. All the fighting and work and sacrifice and death had come down to one last engagement, two at the most. And then horrible deaths for all involved.

His fists tightened and his teeth were clenched. Deep down inside his very being, he couldn't help but feel that this was exactly what Victor, or his successors, had intended it to be: a slow painful, descent into hell.

But at that moment Hunter vowed there was no way he was going to let that happen.

In a flash he was gone—out of the flight deck, down the access ladder and running back towards Magic.

Once again, a secret within held the key to their immediate survival.

Chapter Twenty-eight

The four MiG-25s lifted off cleanly from Song Li air base, quickly gained altitude, and turned south.

Each Foxbat was lugging a single 2,205-pound GP bomb, two, 1,102-pound GP bombs, and one AS-7 Kerry air-to-surface high-explosive missile. These made for quite a load for a 'Bat which was originally designed as a high flying, Mach-3 interceptor whose role it was to shoot down enemy bombers and fighters with long-range air-to-air missiles, thus avoiding dogfights.

For these airplanes to be adapted for ground attacks their wings had to be strengthened considerably, adding extra weight and drag which decreased their top-speed. Additionally, rudimentary targeting devices had to be installed on the airplanes, further reducing their performance. But still, the Foxbats could kick in at 1600 mph, fully loaded, and after all the bombs were dropped, they could easily pump it up to 2200 mph or more.

Major Ky and his associates were not anticipating any high speed flying for this job. Just the opposite. As the target was but a minute away from their base, and had no useable antiaircraft weapons according to Dong, they were not even carrying a full complement of fuel. They fully expected to come in on the target flat, do one blind pass with their big "22s," turn back, drop their 1102-pounders, turn again, deliver the Kerrys, and scoot.

In fact, they expected the attack would last but a minute, and was so elementary, Ky and his pilots didn't even bother to hold a premission briefing. They were old hands at this sort of thing—premission bullshitting was for pussies.

The four MiG-25s leveled off at 15,000 feet, overflying Khe Sanh just fifty-five seconds after takeoff. The sun was coming up, and in the early light, the MiG pilots could clearly see at least a dozen fires burning out of control at the besieged base below. In the center of these fires was their target, the gigantic, but battered American airplane which had had the misfortune of landing at Khe Sanh about a week before.

During his phone conversation with Ky, Dong had babbled something about the huge weapons load this plane was carrying, but Ky dismissed it then and now as the nonsensical ranting of a man about to lose a major campaign. The huge American airplane was obviously a cargo craft of some sort, so it was hardly armed.

Ky and the others went into a sloppy orbit above Khe Sanh and hastily worked out an attack pattern. Ky and his wingman would go in first, followed by the third Foxbat—piloted by Ky's brother-in-law, Ngyuen Ming—and finally, his wingman, Dop Soo.

Ky checked his weapons delivery computer and then took a deep breath of stale oxygen. His life had been very easy since he'd become a pilot-for-hire for the Viet Minx. In his fourteen months on the job, he'd bombed a total of fifty-two targets—everything from bridges and military barracks to churches and orphanages—all successfully, all without a single hit on his airplane from ground fire, and never from defensive fighters. He'd been highly paid for his services, and with the upcoming Viet Minx offensive in the south, the promise of more wealth was just on the horizon.

Until then, it would be profitable milk runs like this one. He signaled his wingman and nonchalantly put the

Foxbat into a screaming dive. At 3,000 feet, his weapons computer began humming. He quickly fused the big, one-ton bomb and prepared to drop it right on the nose of the battered American airplane . . . when suddenly he heard another sound inside his cockpit.

It was a high-whining noise so intense, he thought one of his engines was failing.

That's when he looked over at his wingman and saw him gyrating in his cockpit. Ky blinked for a instant, not quite believing what he was seeing. His wingman was bouncing around like a marionette being pulled madly by the strings. Then suddenly Ky could see the wingman's cockpit filling up with a red mist, coating the canopy as well as the man's face and upper body. Pieces of the wingman's canopy began to break away, and a plume of smoke burst from within the cockpit. It was all happening incredibly fast. In a heartbeat, his wingman's airplane had become perforated with flaming, smoking holes.

Only then did Ky realize that his wingman was being attacked.

Ky immediatcly yanked up on his control column, and banked hard right. All thoughts of the bombing run were abandoned as he quickly snapped off his weapons delivery computer. Twisting in his seat, he strained to look back at his wingman and was startled to see the second Foxbat was totally engulfed in flames. Ky rolled over just in time to see the MiG-25 slam into the muddy ground of the base below.

Suddenly his radio headset was filled with the panicky voice of his brother-in-law, Ming, and his wingman.

"What has happened!" they were both yelling into their microphone. *"Where is the enemy?"*

Ky didn't know. He banked again and climbed up to 8,000 feet, all the while searching the sky around him, looking for the airplane that had so quickly and suddenly dispatched his wingman.

Ky was now close to panic himself. *Where had the attack*

come from? None of the MiGs carried air defense radars or anything that elaborate; they had never had a use for them before. Nor did they carry any air-to-air missiles. And that's why Ky was now so alarmed. Bombs he could deliver; dogfights he was totally unprepared for.

He banked hard right again, pure fright rising in his stomach as he continued to search the sky around him for the mysterious attacker. But the immediate airspace was totally clear. There was nothing but a few high clouds and the rays of the morning sun. There was no place for an aerial foe to hide up here.

He looked off to his left and found the two remaining MiGs riding about 100 feet off his wing.

"What shall we do, Ky?" Ming was calling over to him. "Shall we continue?"

Ky had no idea. They already had Dong's money, and could probably steal it with no problem. But word would definitely get around that they had absconded with the funds and that would probably affect business. With the big offensive coming up soon, this would not be the prudent thing to do.

So Ky had to make a real business decision.

"We must continue," he told the others. "Ming, you lead in. I will provide cover . . ."

He could sense Ming's reluctance—but they had no choice. They couldn't afford a bad reputation—not now.

He saw Ming finally turn his nose down and begin his attack dive on the American airplane, his wingman toddling behind, apprehension quite evident in the tentative maneuver.

Ky checked his altitude. He had drifted down to 7,500 feet. Banking slightly to the right, he watched the pair of MiGs timidly descend. The sky all around him was absolutely clear—there was no where an attacker could be. Ky started calming down. Possibly the attack on his wingman had been a one-hit affair and now whoever was responsible had left the area. If this was true, and they successfully completed the easy bombing job, that would mean all the more money for them; they would only have to split the pot three ways instead of four.

His spirits thus lightened, he put his MiG into an attack dive too. The sooner they could unleash their bombs, the sooner they could get back to base and divvy up their payment.

He was now passing through 5,000 feet; Ming and his wingman were at 3,000. The crashed American airplane was looming in his sights, illuminated in the early morning haze by the fires burning around it. Ky set his big 22-bomb for computer release again; he would try to put it smack on the nose of the big airplane, if Ming or his wingman didn't hit it first.

He passed through the thin cover at 4,500 feet, and habitually tensed as his bomb run began in earnest.

Suddenly there was a flash of gray and silver off his left shoulder. Panicking once again, he jerked the Foxbat to the right and spun away. The dark form went by him with a *whoosh*, he was spinning away so fast, his eyeballs couldn't adjust quick enough to see exactly what it was. It *was* big and gray and falling like a rock. He accelerated in his turn, his vision blurring as he foolishly kicked in his afterburner. All he wanted to do at this point was get away.

The next thing he knew, his Foxbat shuddered once from front to back. Ky nearly vomited—his stomach was turned inside out. He was certain that his airplane had been hit—but he was mistaken. The violence in the air was caused by Ming's wingman's airplane exploding more than 1,500 feet away from him. Ky strained his retinas to the limit and saw nothing but a huge fireball hurtling end over end into the ground below.

He was stunned. Obviously something had set off the man's huge bombload, blowing him and his airplane to oblivion.

Suddenly Ky's radio was filled with the high-pitched

voice of his brother-in-law, screaming in panic for Ky to help him.

Ky had no intention of doing any such thing. He accelerated in his turn, twisting back up to 8,000 feet, where he had to level off or face blacking out from the high-energy acceleration. He recovered, but only after forcing some vomit that had come into his throat back down to his stomach. He turned the Foxbat over, Ming's cries searing his ears.

"Help me, Ky! He is on me! Help . . ."

Ky looked to his left and saw Ming's Foxbat, flying no more than 150 feet off the ground. He was twisting and turning, smoke pouring our of his tail pipes due to fuel overloading at low speed. Ky knew the Foxbat, a plane designed to fly fifteen miles high at three times the speed of sound, could not take the stress of such thick-air maneuvering.

"Please, Ky! For the family, please help me! He is on me!"

Ky watched Ming's Foxbat as it flew above the ground clutter of fire and smoke, and at last he saw the gray mass in pursuit of his brother-in-law. Ky was astonished. The enemy was flying not a jet, but a propellar plane that must have been fifty years old!

Astounded, he watched the old prop plane, itself belching smoke and fuel traces, mimic Ming's every panicky move, a pair of flames shooting out from its cockpit. Ky's heart began racing. What kind of a devil is this? He had taken on four of the fastest airplanes on earth and had destroyed two and was about to add a third. It really wasn't a difficult question to answer. The pilot of the prop plane had simply turned the Foxbat's advantages of high speed at high altitude into the disadvantages of low speed at ass-scraping altitudes.

Ky watched, helpless to act, as Ming's airplane, now down to 100 feet and falling, began intermittent stalling. There was no way he could get the lift needed to put the big Foxbat into an escape climb, no way he could accelerate the stalling engines to get away from his dogged pursuer. Like a cat following a helpless mouse, the chase around the thick air just above the muddy base continued with pathetic predictability.

"I cannot get away! Ky . . . help me!"

With shaking hands, Ky switched off his radio. A few seconds later, he saw the rear end of Ming's Foxbat explode. Whether it was from the pursuing airplane's fire or tailpipe overheating, he would never know. It made no difference—the big MiG-25 turned over and slammed into the ground in a huge ball of flame and smoke.

Ky turned his eyes away; his cowardice in the face of such a puny enemy was nauseating. He banked right and climbed to 10,000 feet, intent on getting back to Son Li, where he planned to steal Dong's gold and escape. With such disgrace, he knew his days as a pilot-for-hire were over.

He increased throttles and shot off towards the air base, his hands trembling so much he could barely keep them on the jarring control stick.

Over the base in a matter of seconds, he just as quickly cut back his acceleration. Foregoing all landing formalities, he put the Foxbat into a steep dive, yanking the engines back to almost stall speed. Once lined up on the long runway, he dropped his gear and deployed his drag chute. A ground crew was standing by the edge of the strip, waiting for the four planes to return, and this only deepened Ky's humiliation. He was intent on setting down, running inside the pilot ready house, taking the thirty bags of gold, getting back in the Foxbat and taking off again, for parts far away and unknown. If anyone stopped him, he'd use his sidearm to shoot them.

He was down to 120 knots and floating in at 35 feet. Suddenly he felt the rear end of the MiG buck—first once, then again, very violently. The next thing he knew, his canopy was falling apart and the wind was hitting him in the face with the force of hurricane. He twisted around in his seat and was absolutely astonished to see the strange propeller plane was right on his tail!

Ky immediately wet his pants, then he froze—there was nothing he could do. He was already committed to landing—his gear was locked, his chute was deployed. If he hit his engines now, they would explode—just like Ming's.

The bullets hit him a second later. The first barrage shattered his control panel and whatever was left of his canopy; the second penetrated the back of his skull, splitting his crash helmet in two and exiting his mouth. He slumped over onto the control stick, bloody pieces of his insides gushing out from his lips.

He tried to scream but couldn't. The plane jerked to the right, its nose now plummeting towards the pilot ready house, the same place where the bags of gold were.

The Foxbat hit the concrete structure two seconds later. In the instant before death, all Ky heard were Ming's dying screams, echoing in his ear.

Chapter Twenty-nine

It took more than five minutes for the aides to wake Dong.

There was an empty brandy flask beside the commander's bed, and this, the aide was sure, was the overwhelming factor in Dong's deep sleep.

Finally, the man stirred.

"A thousand pardons, Excellency," the aide began telling a sleepy-eyed Dong. "But there is an officer here to see you. He says it is urgent."

Dong wiped some of the sleep for his eyes. "Who is he?" he asked wearily. "What does he want?"

The aide bit his lip for a moment. "He didn't give his name," he finally replied. "But he did say that CapCom had sent him."

Dong froze. Hearing the very word "CapCom" was akin to driving a stake through his heart. And he had good reason to worry. No representative from CapCom ever called on any Minx field bearing good news.

Dong quickly climbed into his green camos and poured his swelled feet into his tight leather boots. He walked quickly from his bedroom to his office, his head aching with a brandy hangover. He had consumed more than a liter of the stuff the night before, a necessary booster after his decision to hire the MiGs. Now it felt as if his eyes were about to pop out of his skull.

He had no sooner sat down at his desk, when the main door to his mobile HQ burst open. A tall, dark man strode in, a squad of heavily armed soldiers right behind him. Dong was outraged.

"How dare you come in here and . . ." he began to protest.

But the man simply raised his large hand and shut Dong off.

"You are in no position to speak to me like that, Dong," the man said in French, their common language.

Dong studied him. He was not Asian, rather he looked Middle Eastern, maybe Arab. He was wearing an all-black combat utility uniform of a style Dong had never seen before. His soldiers, who were Asian, were similarly attired and carrying extended-fire, battlefield Uzis.

Dong was fuming now. "I am the commander here and . . ."

But once again the man simply waved Dong silent.

"Correction," the man said. "You are no longer the commander here. I am."

Dong was stunned. The man walked over to his desk, his boots squeaking on Dong's finely polished office floor. He threw a document on the desk.

"Read it at your leisure, Dong," the man said. "But I will tell you its most salient point: I am here on orders from CapCom to relieve you of this command."

Dong felt his whole world crashing in on him.

"But why?" was all he could offer by way of protest.

" 'Why?' " the man asked with a laugh. "Because your performance against a small, insignificant enemy has been dismal. Because you alone are responsible for delaying the greater offensives in the south. Because you are a disgrace to your uniform, and an embarrassment to CapCom. Shall I go on?"

Dong stared at the man for ten long seconds. While the chance of this sort of thing happening had crossed his mind more than once, Dong had one last card to play.

"Are you aware that I paid a crack fighter bomber unit to conduct an air strike against the enemy at Khe Sanh? And that I expect very positive results from this strike to reach me very soon?"

The man discourteously sat on the edge of Dong's huge desk. "That air strike has already happened," he told the ex-commander. "And it was a dismal failure."

Dong couldn't believe it. "What?" he whispered. "How . . . how do you know?"

The man retrieved a piece of yellow paper from his pocket. "All four MiGs were shot down," he said, reading from the paper. "The enemy base was unharmed."

Dong was aghast. "Shot down?" he gasped. "How? By whom?"

The man just shrugged. "Apparently, the enemy had an airplane hidden from you all this time," he said sardonically. "A small *propeller* airplane. My intelligence men witnessed the action. They said it was an A-1D Skyraider. An ancient machine. Must have been quite a pilot at the controls."

Dong was speechless. Where the hell could the enemy have hidden an airplane?

"That . . . that was the last of my money," he was finally able to blurt out. "It's all gone . . ."

"Exactly," the man told him. "And that's why I am here. You're being foreclosed, Dong. Shutdown. You're bankrupt. CapCom can no longer consider you part of the Minx Command. As of this moment, myself and my army are responsible for this sector."

Dong looked around at his palatial headquarters.

"This is all mine now too," the man said. "We're taking it against any bad debts that you may have incurred during this rather misguided campaign."

The man motioned for two of his soldiers to come forward. They did, and proceeded to strip all Minx insignia from Dong's uniform.

"Formalities," the man told him, already admiring the fine workmanship of Dong's desk.

"What do you plan to do?" Dong asked him humbly.

The man laughed. "My army had been waiting to the west of you for days," he told Dong. "Now that it is our responsibility to secure this sector, it is then our responsibility to finally eradicate the enemy at Khe Sanh, and thus remove one of the last impediments in our drive to the south."

The two soldiers then yanked Dong out of his chair, pushed him towards the office door and out into the morning sunlight.

Standing in the harsh early morning sun, he was surprised to find the vast majority of his troops were assembled and waiting for him outside his mobile headquarters.

There were about 1200 troops lined up in five ranks in the large cleared field next to the hill where his mobile HQ had been placed, beyond was the valley of the Khe Sanh itself. His men did not look like an army. They were beyond ragged, beyond shabby, beyond dishonorable. They were nothing but a rabble of the injured, the thieves and the cowards—and a barely armed rabble at that. Some were using tree stumps as crutches, others were being led by their comrades because they were either blind or shell-shocked. Still others were missing hands or entire arms. But there were also many who looked well-fed and were wearing almost new uniforms. These were the shirkers.

Dong was immediately sick to his stomach. *This* was his army?

He suddenly heard the sharp bleat of bugle. Then there was a tremendous roar of truck engines. Within seconds, a long line of black troop trucks came rumbling into the camp. Their rear compartments were filled with well-armed, apparently elite troops, all of whom were wearing the same jet black combat uniform as their mysterious commander.

The parade of trucks continued for five full minutes, the

awe-inspiring visual display intentionally reducing Dong to tears. He was being disgraced in the grandest of fashions by this officer in black.

With the last bit of dignity, he turned to the officer and asked: "Just who are you, sir?"

The man smiled, revealing a set of cracked and gaped teeth. "My name, sir, is Commander Abdul Assass."

Dong looked back out on the assembly grounds and counted more than 100 troop trucks. On a sharp order from Assass, the troops inside the trucks began jumping out and lining up in their own ranks. Once again the visual message was quite clear. Compared to Dong's pathetic ranks, the black army looked like supermen.

"What happens now?" he asked Assass.

"Your men will be fed and cared for," he told Dong. "Those that we deem recoverable will be given noncombat jobs. Those that aren't . . . well, why address any more unpleasantness on this day?"

"And I?" Dong asked. "What happens to me?"

Assass stared at him for a long moment—the combined assembly of his troops and those belonging to Dong looked on in anxious attention.

Assass smiled. "You?" he asked. "Why, you, sir, still have a role to play in the Minx conquest, of course."

Dong's eyes grew wide. His spirits suddenly soared.

"You mean, I will be allowed to stay?"

Assass never stopped smiling. "But of course," he said. "We have a special mission, just for you."

Dong straightened up to his full height. "And I will perform it to the upmost of my ability," he declared.

"Oh, that you will," Assass told him.

At that point the officer reached into his pocket and came out with a single key. He handed it to Dong and then pointed at the long line of parked troop trucks.

"Your's is number seventeen," he told Dong. "It is one of our waste disposal vehicles. And be careful, they tell me the brakes are a little worn."

Chapter Thirty

Khe Sanh

Lieutenant Twang was dead.

He was sure of it now. His legs weren't working, his head was split and still bleeding, and at times he was sure he could reach up and actually touch his brain.

Not only was Twang sure that he was dead, he was convinced that he was in hell, the place the westerners were always talking about. Why else would he be surrounded by more and more dead bodies every time he woke up?

Now they were even dropping out of the sky.

Not fifty feet from his spider hole was a wrecked Minx MiG-25, its fuselage burning, its pilot horribly impacted on its canopy, his face but a bloody smear against the shattered glass.

The airplane had come down about two hours before, falling out of the morning mist like a mighty eagle that had been killed by something bigger and more powerful on the wing. It had hit the ground so violently, it shook him out of his comalike unconsciousness. Dozens of rotting Minx bodies were thrown into Twang's spider hole as a result of the impact. Many of these corpses had landed right on top of Twang, and for ten terrifying minutes he found himself fighting them—literally *fighting* them—to push them out of his hole. During this time, he thought he might have heard the sounds of an airplane—maybe an older airplane, flying close to the ground overhead, and possibly even landing at the base. But Twang wasn't sure. So great was his terror in his battle with the dead, he wasn't interested in whether another airplane was landing at the base.

About 125 feet in the other direction, another Minx airplane had crashed. Like the first one, it had simply dropped out of the sky, its fuselage aflame, the bombs under its wings exploding as it came down. Probably 500 feet from that wreckage—out where the enemy once held many gun positions—was a third burning MiG, its wings ripped from its fuselage, the shredded body of its pilot, hanging from the cockpit by the strands of his unopened parachute.

Twang took a series of short breaths and then dropped back down into his hole. Yes, he was certain he was dead now—but amidst the horror, he realized that there were some benefits to being deceased.

Because of his demise, he no longer considered himself a soldier. Why should he? He had no more duty to fulfill. He had been sent here by Commander Dong to report on the activities of the Americans "even as we are destroying them." But the Americans were still here—and it was the Minx that were all gone. Their grotesque screaming bodies were his partners here in hell.

Because he was no longer a soldier, he had thrown away his gun and his radio. He had no use for them anymore. If he could get his legs to work, he would have climbed out of the spider hole long ago, and walked back to Go Ling, his village in the north. And once he got there, he would become a holy man, a Buddhist priest, perhaps. And he would preach nothing but peace, and love for fellow men. He was convinced that was the only real way to live—an ironic conclusion, now that he was dead.

But his legs didn't work anymore. He knew it as soon as he began fighting the corpses; he tried to move them but they didn't respond. They were cold to the touch, and it felt like his toes had fallen off.

It made little difference to him. He didn't need his legs or his toes here in the afterlife. All he needed were eyes to gaze upon the dead as they gazed back at him.

That was another good thing about hell: there didn't seem to be any war here. There were no more mortar shells falling on the base, no more sniper fire either. He could see no enemy soldiers around the battered airplane, which was now so full of holes, the sunlight was streaming through them like a thousand points of light.

In fact, he couldn't imagine it being so quiet. Only the crackling of flames from the three crashed airplanes broke the stillness in the air. That, and the fluttering of the tattered American flag flying from the top of the crashed airplane.

Twang knew now that the Americans were actually magicians. If he had found the need to report back to Commander Dong, this is what he would have said: The Americans were sorcerers, they could do unearthly things. They fight and never lose a man. They have weapons that never seem to run out of ammunition. They make Minx fighters fall out of the sky.

And soon, he would find out they could make airplanes just disappear.

He reached up and felt his brain and was surprised it was so gooey. Then he leaned back and stared at the rising sun. Someone, a long time ago, had told him that the man behind the Minx, the *real* power behind the screens, had lived for a while in Japan, the land of the rising sun. But then he moved to Siberia. Or someplace like that.

Twang wiped some slime from his eyes and leaned further back. The skies looked so peaceful this morning in hell. They were bright blue, shaded by the last reds of the sunrise. And there were still some stars visible—or at least he thought they were stars. They too were peaceful looking.

He put his hands behind his cracked head and took a long deep breath of the rotting air. If hell was this peaceful, this free of combat and killing, then he thought he might even enjoy his stay here.

The huge artillery shell came crashing down a few seconds later.

Twang felt it before he heard it. The ground was shaking—a sensation he was used to by now—and he was suddenly spitting dirt from his mouth and fighting dead bodies again. There was smoke and flame everywhere again, blotting out the rising sun and the peaceful blue skies and the twinkling stars.

Twang screamed at the top of his lungs. He had so convinced himself that he would never see war again.

Suddenly there was more crashing, five, six, seven in a row. Twang heaved out two more bodies, and balanced himself on a third in order to look out over the lip of the spider hole.

He couldn't believe what he saw.

There were soldiers running everywhere. They were coming across the muddy fields, swarming over the old enemy trenches, stepping on and over the bodies of the dead Minx. They were coming down from the hills to the south and east. They were even coming around the small mountain at the end of the runway and charging down the runway itself.

Huge explosions were going off all around them, and it was these that were shaking the very earth. They were not mortar rounds. These explosions were caused by high-explosive artillery shells being fired from the hills; he could clearly see the puffs of white discharge smoke rising into the morning sky above the long snouts of dozens of 120-mm guns that had been placed along the high ridges.

What was happening? Twang's head was spinning; the glare of fire and explosions stinging his dilating eyes. These soldiers were not from *his* Minx divisions. These men were dressed in jet-black uniforms, not combat pajamas, and they were wearing combat boots, not rubber-tire sandals. Their weapons were different too. They were not carrying AK-47s or sniper rifles, but rather a variety of weapons, including combat Uzis. Others were carrying RPG launchers, a rare item in his unit. Some even had TOW launchers, a weapon Twang had never even seen before.

Twang shook his head. It was like a dream. There were at least 15,000 soldiers charging into the base, running full tilt, firing their weapons, screaming at the top of their lungs.

And they were all heading for the same place: the crashed American jet.

Twang watched with a mixture of horror and fascination as the first wave of black uniformed soldiers reached the enormous, strangely painted and blackened airplane. They were swarming all over it instantly, like ants hungry for a meal. Some were prying open its many hatchways and doors with their bare hands. Others were hurling hand grenades directly into the battered airplane through its hundreds of shell holes.

Two more waves reached the airplane, then three more, then four. There were now thousands of soldiers covering the plane's fuselage and wings. It was so congested around the aircraft, the soldiers were elbow-to-elbow, trying to get in. All the while the huge artillery explosions were going off everywhere, some so close to the attacking soldiers they were causing casualties.

Twang could hear screaming, shouting, maybe even cries of pain coming from the American airplane, and he suddenly felt some pain, too. He had come to gain a certain respect for the Americans—they had fought so long, so hard, in a war that they apparently stumbled into by mistake. Now they were being slaughtered by a mystery army.

Or were they?

It quickly became apparent to Twang that something was amiss around the American airplane. Just about all the firing had stopped, including the artillery, and now the thousands of soldiers were milling around, apparently confused about what to do next.

He could see officers running up from the rear lines, and dozens of people pointing this way and that, mostly to the inside of the airplane and then to the hills beyond. What was happening? Twang couldn't figure it out.

Then it hit him. Was it possible that there *were* no Americans inside the airplane? Or anyone else for that matter?

Twang retrieved his battered binoculars and focused on the tail end of the airplane. He could see many soldiers and officers—but no enemy soldiers. How was this possible?

Suddenly one of the black uniformed officers pointed to the massive sandbag protector the enemy had built around the second airplane, the one they had towed down the runway what seemed like ages before. In a flash, the mass of mystery soldiers was attacking the huge structure, tossing aside its sandbags and ripping tin sheets from its roof.

Twang felt his heart sink once again. Obviously the Americans were hiding inside the sandbag bunker, and now that they were found out, they would be slaughtered.

But he found that he, like the thousands of attacking soldiers, was in for another enormous surprise.

It took but a few minutes for the soldiers to disassemble the sand and tin structure—and when they did they discovered there was nothing inside. No Americans, no Legionnaires, no mercenaries.

No airplane.

At that moment, Twang realized that his previous theory had been correct after all. The Americans must have been magicians! Not only had they and their allies simply disappeared, they were able to make the other huge airplane disappear as well!

Suddenly Twang heard the ungodliest sound ever to reach his ears. It was a tearing of metal, an ear-splitting explosion and the most frightening of screams—all mixed together. The screech was so loud, it actually stung his eyeballs. It echoed throughout the valley, bouncing off the surrounding hills and coming back again, like a huge wave.

The thousands of soldiers heard it too—and many collapsed to the knees, covering their ears in panic and fright.

Suddenly all eyes turned to the small, unopposing mountain at the southern end of the base. Twang felt his jaw drop. *It was moving.* The side of the mountain was literally opening up in a burst of smoke and fire.

Twang's mind was racing now. Was this a volcano? An explosion? *A nuclear bomb?*

That's when he saw the gleam of metal—it was reflecting perfectly off the rising sun, shining into his eyes. Suddenly it was moving—*moving* right out of the side of the mountain. Twang just shook his head. Was this real?

The gleam of metal slowly emerged from the side of the mountain and finally the glare moved out of his eyes. That's when he saw it fully for the first time.

It was an airplane—but it was unlike any airplane he'd ever seen.

It was held upright by no less than a dozen sets of thick rubber wheels under its fuselage and wings. It was small, as compared to the beheamoth American aircraft that had landed at the base, and yet it retained some of the characteristics of those planes too. It had a long high snout, but with twice as many cockpit windows. Its body was but a tenth as long as the huge jets, yet the fuselage was just as chubby. Its wings were much shorter too, but they were literally lined with what appeared to be engines—some of them jets, other smoking old propellers. Twang counted them and came up with four engines on each wing, no two of them looking exactly alike. The whole airplane was covered with wires, chains, tubes, and in some cases, even thick rope. There were so many strange appendages hanging off it, it looked like it would burst and break apart at any moment.

But it didn't.

The unearthly scream—or at least part of it—was being caused by the disparate group of smoking, unmuffled engines. Another contributing factor was the roar of gunfire coming from the strange aircraft. Like its predecessors, this airplane was armed to the teeth. Indeed there were weapons poking out of dozens of portholes and glass canopy blisters.

No sooner had the airplane moved out of the side of the mountain when all of these guns opened up at once. They were now pouring fire into the mass of soldiers surrounding the circus-colored airplane. There was instant panic. Soldiers were suddenly running everywhere again, jumping into trenches, hiding in craters, crawling over each other to get behind some piece of the broken circus airplane or the sandbag protectors they'd just torn down. The air once again was filled with tracer fire, all of it coming from the strange airplane as it moved along the dirt, gaining speed and heading for the littered runway.

It reached the end of the tarmac and there it stopped and waited for one long moment, its guns blazing, absolutely vaporizing hundreds of the black-uniformed soldiers, along with the circus-colored airplane. Twang felt another knife in his heart. He had become attached to the strangely colored airplane; like its crew, it had gone through so much. Now it was being shredded by the fire from the Americans themselves. The irony hit Twang right in the gut. Apparently only the Americans were allowed to destroy what they had created in the first place. Oddly this cemented everything Twang had ever heard about them.

Suddenly there was one long crashing roar and the strange airplane began moving again. Slowly at first, then picking up speed, the bizarre aircraft went streaking down the runway, right past him, right past the thousands of shocked black-uniformed soldiers, right past the strange, battered airplane and the empty sandbagged bunker. It was so close to Twang he could read the words painted in large sloppy letters on the side of its fuselage: *Big Plan—*

Bozo Two. He could plainly see a man in a pilot's suit and a lightning-flash crash helmet working the controls inside the huge bubble-type forward flight compartment. He could also see dozens of faces pressed against the airplane's haphazardly placed windows looking out—Americans, Legionnaires, mercenaries. Nearly all of them were smiling.

And never once did their guns stop firing. The streaks of tracer bullets, artillery shells and launched grenades poured out of both sides of the airplane, causing a noise so loud that Twang's ears began bleeding.

It continued to gain speed as it rolled down the runway, away from the attackers, away from the burning circus airplane, away from Twang's spider hole.

Then, to the amazement of all, there was a great burst of flame and smoke, and the plane lifted off the ground and slowly climbed into the air. Twang couldn't believe his eyes. It was almost scary to see such a strange machine actually fly.

But fly it did. Up and over the hills. Into the low clouds. Climbing. Flying.

Escaping . . .

PART THREE

Chapter Thirty-one

The sixteen-man long-range patrol was two hours from base when they found the airplane.

Their four-vehicle HumVee column came to a stop near the edge of a vast rice paddy. There was smoke rising above the treetops in the jungle beyond.

Leaving one Hummer behind for cover, the three remaining vehicles splashed their way across the paddy, their top gunners at the ready. They made the jungle and used a mule path to draw closer to the smoke.

They spotted it a few minutes later.

It was lying at about a forty-degree angle and a small clearing in the middle of the woods. The soldiers weren't quite sure what it was when they first saw it. It was obviously an aircraft of some kind—but nothing that was even remotely familiar to them. There were different kinds of engines, different kinds of landing gears, canopies of glass all over its fuselage, a lot of the important gear lashed down with chains, heavy rope and thick wire. It was what they once called a "Rube Goldberg"; a mind-boggling slapdash of metal, pulleys and wires, forming a machine that had no right being allowed in the air.

But here it was and it was obvious it had flown in from someplace, the clearing being completely surrounded by jungle.

Two Hummers unloaded their troops and a total of

eight men approached the strange machine. It was still smoking heavily—it probably hadn't been down but an hour, the soldiers figured.

They walked right up to it, and touched it, just to make sure it was real.

That's when they heard about a hundred weapons snap off their safeties.

The soldiers were stunned. They suddenly realized they were surrounded by more than 100 armed men. These men were all wearing different uniforms, carrying different weapons. They were all different colors. But there was one thing everyone of them had in common.

They were all smiling.

One of the men stepped forward. He was tall, skinny, with a long scar running down the right side of his face.

"I am Zouvette!" he declared. "Third Company, Third Division, Fifty Corps of the French Foreign Legion."

The soldiers were astonished. The man looked like he'd just walked off the screen of a bad 1930s movie. They turned and saw the fourth Hummer was surrounded by a smaller group of armed men. Somehow the armed gang had got the drop on them without making a sound.

The combination of the strange airplane and the hundred grinning faces made it slightly difficult for the soldiers to take the situation all that seriously.

Who the hell are you guys?" one of them asked.

That's when one man moved out from the back of the crowd and walked up to the soldiers. He was wearing a mud-caked flight suit and a battered crash helmet.

"We are from the First American Airborne Expeditionary Force," he said, evenly.

The soldiers all stared back at him wearing identical expressions of puzzled amazement.

"The lost guys?" one of the soldiers said.

Hunter paused for a moment to consider that one. Then he asked: "Where are we?"

"Twenty klicks north of a place called Da Nang," came the reply.

A second later all guns were lowered. A sudden cheer went up from the armed men. *They had made it!*

The man in the crash helmet shook each soldier's hand. "Take us to your leader," he said.

The road leading up to Da Nang city was so dusty, the HumVee driver had to keep his windshields wipers on.

Crammed into the back seat of the first vehicle were Hunter, Ben and Frost, his leg and hand wounds quickly on the mend. After ascertaining the city was under very friendly control, it was agreed they'd accompany the soldiers to Da Nang, while Geraci and Zouvette stayed with the rest of the escapees.

It took about an hour to get to the outskirts of Da Nang, and the closer they got the more astounded Hunter became. In all his years of combat, he couldn't remember seeing so many weapons packed into so little space. There were literally hundreds of large artillery pieces—American M-198s 150-mm cannons mostly—ringing the edge of the city's perimeter. There had to be hundreds of machine gun-posts scattered around too, sporting everything from big M-60s to Belgium-made M-249s to land-mounted GAU-8 Gatling guns. There were bunkers thick with rocket-launchers, recoilless rifles, AA-guns with their barrels leveled, grenade launchers, flame-throwers, and on and on and on.

And it didn't stop at the outer defense perimeter. After passing forests of concertina wires, they reached the mud and concrete wall of the city itself, finding more artillery, more machine posts, more leveled AA-guns.

And troops.

There seemed to be soldiers everywhere. All of different uniforms, different nationalities, different colors. Hunter knew many were mercenaries—but at the same time, he

251

was sure that they all weren't here just for the money. A good mercenary could get good work anywhere on wartorn planet Earth, certainly in places more glamorous than hot and smelly Vietnam.

Yet, here they were.

Why?

Was it because most of them must have believed there was actually something worth fighting for in the godforsaken place.

The jeep roared through the heavily armed gate, and headed for the center of the city. Some quick calculations told Hunter that Da Nang's current configuration was probably a mile and a half square, laid out in a slightly oblong shape. He figured there were at least 30,000 men under arms inside the city and around its defense perimeters, and a fifty as many civilians.

Most of these noncombatants were young women; the city was devoid of young kids and seniors, as it should be for a place where combat was so likely. Still it was jampacked with bar rooms, gambling dens, and cat houses, the obvious places of employment of many of the young women.

They finally reached their destination, the provisional headquarters building for the huge army-in-waiting. The place looked eerily like the Alamo; it was a dirty white, sandblasted limestone throwback to the French Colonial days. It was heavily fortified, with several perimeters of re-enforced barbed wire ringing gun posts and concrete barriers. More than fifty different flags were whipping in the hot dusty breeze from its ramparts.

The Hummer drove past the guards and into a small parking area which fronted the southside main entrance. Hunter, Ben and Frost climbed out and were escorted through the main door and into a huge hallway. Inside, the place looked like a movie set left over from *Casablanca*— slow whirling fans, bistro tables and chairs, and a long well-stocked bar. No surprise, the saloon was bustling with off-duty soldiers.

They were met by a young black officer with a Jamaican accent who led them up a marble spiraling staircase. At the top was a short hallway and a large oak door marked "City Command HQ." The young officer opened the door for them, saluted and left.

They peered inside. The room was large, brightly lit and cluttered with books, weapons, radios, and empty liquor bottles. It was also pleasantly air-conditioned. There was a large desk at its center. The man occupying the high-backed leather chair behind the desk had his feet up on the open top drawer, right next to the plaque that read:

Commander-in-Chief.

He was grinning broadly.

Hunter walked in, threw his helmet on a nearby couch and then wearily slumped down next to it.

"We can't leave you alone for a minute, can we?" he asked the man relaxing behind the desk.

The man frowned with perfect mock seriousness. " 'I saw my duty, and I did it.' "

It was JT. The last time they'd seen him, he had been behind the controls of the great gunship, *Nozo*, diving into the typhoon to escape the MiGs.

Now, he looked strange, from the braided, black camo uniform to the gold bars on the collar. The name plate reading "Commander" was hanging off his left breast pocket as if it weighed a ton or more. Yet he just couldn't suppress his lopsided smile.

"So," he dead-panned. "Where the hell have you guys been?"

The three of them ignored him; instead they were searching the place for a liquor bottle that had yet been drained.

JT was one step ahead of them. He was already pouring out four shots of dark red whiskey.

"They call this stuff *him-ham,*" he told them, as they each reached for a glass. "Not bad, considering."

They didn't even toy with the idea of a toast—the four shots were gone and four more poured out in the time it took to gulp.

"Our asses in the big ringer, and you're here in Partytown," Ben said, chasing his words with his second shot. "Why do these things always happen to *you?*"

"I live a clean life," he said, pouring out four more shots. "So, who first?"

Hunter drained his third drink, slumped down further into the couch, and then proceeded to tell JT everything: Losing their way in the storm, battling the MiGs, the crash at Khe Sanh, meeting Geraci, the Minx, the mortars, the snipers, the Legionnaires, the building of *Bozo 2,* and all the time spent in between trying to figure out how the hell to get out of the place in one piece.

"Sounds like the old days," JT said at the end of the story. "You guys can play yourselves in the movie."

Ben reached over and began pouring the shots himself.

"Just tell us what the hell is going on here," he told JT.

JT just shrugged.

"It's a short story, really," he began. "We went down low in the storm, took a lot of hits from the MiGs, but were able to put down here, probably just about the same time you guys went in. *Football One* was already here, and *Two* and *Three* came in right on our ass. I fucked-up the airplane pretty good on the landing—nothing but a pile of scrap metal now. But we all made it out alive. We were lucky that Jonesie's intelligence was good, because the locals already had this place pretty well secured and they were happy as hell to see us."

"So how'd you become God?" Hunter asked.

JT just shrugged again. "Their top dog is a guy named Yink. Nice guy; a rich guy. He paying all the free-lancers here, and he's getting more everyday. Well, the Yinkman needed someone to—how shall I put it?—steer the ship.

He needed organizing. He needed a can-do guy. And he was smart enough to, well, offer it . . . and . . . how could I refuse?"

JT was beaming throughout all this. He was, no argument, an operator's operator.

"So what's your situation?" Hunter finally asked him, turning the mood serious.

JT took his feet down and pulled the chair closer to the desk.

"We got about seven divisions of people out there in the jungle, somewhere, who don't like us very much," he said, motioning beyond the fortress walls. "They've been behaving themselves for about two weeks now. We get a few mortar rounds, every once and while, but that's about it. But they're not shitting me. They're just waiting to get paid."

"Paid?" Frost asked with a snort. "So these guys aren't in it for the old Red glory either?"

JT laughed out loud. "Are you kidding?" he replied, "They're just out there waiting to cash their paychecks, the bastards. Then they're going to crash this party—or try to."

He took the next ten minutes explaining what he'd learned about the Viet Minx and their screwy principles of Communist Capitalism. It fit in almost word for word with what the others already knew about the Minx.

"They're greedy motherfuckers, aren't they?" JT summed up. "I hear they bleed everyone dry, up and down the ranks. The top dogs sell the middle guys all their weapons, ammo, food, fuel—you name it. The middle guys raise armies and go off to carve of slice of the old Nam. They rape, they pillage, sell whatever they can back to the top dogs, then the whole cycle starts all over again."

"They sound like the old mandarins," Frost observed. "It's in their best interests to keep wars going."

"Well, they came to the right place," Hunter said.

"Any timetable for an attack?" Ben asked.

JT poured out another round. He looked authentically concerned. "Two weeks?" he shrugged. "Maybe three. Yink's intelligence guys tell me that the whole country is going to blow up pretty damned soon. The Minx have been planning this big offensive for a long time—they've got most of the countryside, and soon they'll be going for all the major cities. This pea patch included. That's why the good guys like Yink were sending out all those Maydays; they knew the roof was going to cave in at any minute."

"And what do you hear from home?" Hunter asked.

"I talk to Uncle Jonesie everyday," JT replied. "He was glad to hear you all made it in one piece, finally."

"Any mail wagons due to join us soon?" Ben asked.

JT just shrugged. "No way of telling," he replied. "They're busting their asses back at Edwards to get at least a few of them over. But you know we stole all the good stuff, and now they're working with leftovers."

Hunter ran his fingers through his long hair. He needed to eat, he needed to sleep, but most of all, he needed a bath.

And so did the others.

"There's a big empty room at the end of the hall," JT told them. "I'll have some bunks and clean clothes sent up. Pull about an hour or so and then we'll eat big time."

They spent the next ten minutes discussing the care and feeding of the beleaguered Legionnaires. Any of them who recovered to the point of carrying a gun would be given light duty inside the fortress walls. Then came the dispersement of Geraci's men. It was agreed that they would first strip *Bozo 2* of its weapons and useable equipment, just as JT did with *Nozo*'s guns. The New Jersey 104th could then use the weapons to establish yet another defense line at the far edge of the city's already heavily defended airport, located about a half mile away. Ben and Frost would head for the airport the next day too, to help the staff triangulate their defense control systems.

This left only Hunter with no real assignment.

The others got up to leave. Hunter looked at JT and asked: "Well, boss, what do you want me to do?"

JT's usually cheery face sank. Suddenly, he *looked* like someone who was in charge of a very precarious position.

"You can go save Crunch," he replied grimly.

Hunter knew it was too good to be true.

He knew that between the viciousness of the MiG attack and the monstrous typhoon, it was a miracle that any of the Galaxys of the First American Expeditionary Force made it.

But as JT told it, a total of six were now accounted for: *Bozo, Nozo, NJ104, Football One, Two* and *Three*. Plus, they'd heard a reliable report that the Cobra Brother's *Big Snake* had crashed on the island of Hainan in the Gulf of Tonkin, where all aboard were safe, but being held for ransom by the radical Eastern religious cult which controlled the island. Jones was currently negotiating via long range radio for their release.

But that left two C-5s unaccounted for: Crunch's *Crunchtime*, and the JAWs plane.

JT reported that no one had heard anything from JAWs. When last seen, they were being swarmed over with MiGs, their wings and fuselage aflame. The sad conclusion was that they probably went into the sea. Hunter felt a dull ache in his stomach every time he thought of Captain Cook and the guys from Jack Base being dead.

The fate of Crunch's plane was another matter.

Two days after JT and the other C-5s landed at Da Nang city, they'd received a report from a New Zealand mechanized division that was just barely holding on at Cam Ranh Bay, 300 miles to the south. The New Zealanders had processed a local militia's report that a large plane had been seen falling into the marshes 250 miles south of *them*. This put the rumored crash site deep down

257

in the Mekong Delta area, more than a 100 miles south of what was now known as New Saigon.

Could one of the C-5s have flown more than 500 miles away from the main pack after the MiG attack? It was unlikely. Yet Crunch's plane *was* carrying extra fuel on board in huge rubber bladders. Plus, the local militiamen, whose reliability the New Zealanders vouched for, reported the huge airplane was painted gray and red with scrolling on the wings and tailplane—a near perfect description of *Crunchtime*. They also claimed that there may be some survivors, at least they heard from the natives in the area that some Westerners had approached them for food and a radio. When the local militia passed through the area two weeks later, they reported the wreck was still there, but there was no sign of anyone around it.

The Mekong Delta was not a good place for an airplane crash. Bordered by the South China Sea on the east, the Gulf of Siam in the west, and what used to be Cambodia to the north, the area itself was just about total marshland and paddy area—rough going for airplane survivors. At one time, the Delta fed a lot of Southeast Asia with its rice crop; this was why the French came to Vietnam in the first place back in the nineteenth century. More than eight million people lived in the Delta during the last Vietnam war, but it was sparsely populated these days.

The only road servicing the Delta was old Route 4, a long, winding, serpentine highway which itself seemed lost in the almost-forgotten, marshy wilderness. In addition to the hundreds of miles of natural waterways—rivers, streams and lake—the Vietnamese had hand-dug more than 4,000 kilometers of canals in the area. Wherever these canals met in a major convergence there was usually a good-sized town, but these were all largely abandoned.

Oddly, the current enemy only seemed mildly concerned with the Delta these days. Viet Minx presence in the area was only rated as moderate, with several reenforced forts on the mouth of Son My Thou River, and a small port facility, twenty miles to the south at a place called Son Tay. Armed ferrys and tugs regularly plied the South China Sea between Haiphong and Son Tay, sometimes accompanied by helicopter gunships as escort.

Inside the Delta itself, the Minx were using small mine-sweeping type boats which featured heavy machine guns, rocket launchers and extensive flame-throwing equipment. Similar flame-throwing vessels used by the Americans in the first war were nicknamed "Zippos."

If anyone survived an airplane crash in the Delta it was probably just a matter of time before an enemy Zippo found them—or at least, it would seem that way.

But according to the local militia, and somewhat verified by the New Zealanders, something very different was happening down in the Mekong Delta these days.

After washing up and stepping into fresh clothes, Hunter, Ben, Frost, and JT feasted on a dinner of chicken stew, mashed peppers and the local gut-busting *him-ham* liquor.

JT played the perfect host. There was no end to the food and booze. He even arranged to have a half dozen local "hostesses" on hand, to "help with the arrangements." But most of the night was spent discussing the current situation in Vietnam. Basically it came down to this: In a strange way, the sudden arrival of the C-5s had postponed what seemed to be an imminent takeover of the southern part of the country. The key word was "postponed." For the Viet Minx forces had been simply delayed in their war of commerce and conquest, and if anything, the extra three weeks or so would give them addition time to bolster their armies and even add to them. This was especially true in the midlands where no less than 18 divisions of Minx were waiting, and around the New Saigon area, where an equally formidable force of fifteen reenforced divisions were said to be hiding. It didn't take a military genius to figure out that these forces—almost a half million men in arms—would not, could not, wait forever. If JT's estimate of three weeks before the attack on Da Nang was on target, then action in the rest of the country would most likely erupt at that time too.

The dinner debate lasted well into early morning, with dozens of strategies and wild ideas discussed. But on one point everyone agreed: if the Minx had their way, there would be no more democratic Vietnam inside of a month, no matter how many C-5s managed to show up.

When the day dawned, Ben and Frost reported to Da Nang's airport. The Legionnaires were transported to the city's hospital where they received a heroes' welcome. Geraci and his men began removing the vast array of weaponry from the carcass of *Bozo 2*, and trucking it in pieces to Da Nang to be set up along the far edge of the airport. And JT went back to running the paid-army that a man named Yink built.

As for Hunter, he was gone an hour before the sun came up.

Chapter Thirty-two

It had been years since Hunter had flown a helicopter.

But here he was, at the controls of an ancient Huey, carving a sloppy wake through the superheated tropical air above steamy South Vietnam.

Below him was the deceptively beautiful countryside. He saw a few examples of war sites left over from the last go-round—abandoned fire bases, deserted air strips, even the wreckage of aircraft, including two C-130s. The jungle had reclaimed everything else, he guessed.

Everything but the ghosts.

He'd refueled twice already, once at Quang Nai, which was now under control of First Italian Expeditionary Corps, and again at Cam Ranh Bay, where he spoke with the top commanders of the New Zealand contingent. They knew nothing more about the supposed crash in the Delta. The monsoons were absolutely flooding the area, as they were all of Southeast Asia, and reports of any kind were few and far between.

So Hunter was now heading for a place called Suk Deek. Located about 110 clicks south of New Saigon, it was on the northeastern edge of the Mekong Delta. It was the last outpost of the New Zealanders, a place so small it could handle one chopper landing site, and one boat dock facility and that was it. From here, two New Zealander scouts would escort him even further in the Delta, to the area where the big plane crash—as well as a number of other, unexplainable events—had supposedly occurred recently.

He reached Suk Deek just before sundown. It was even smaller than advertised, a black dot in a sea of brown water and green jungle. Located at the junction of two large canals, it consisted of two stucco-style buildings, a tiny dock, a metal net for the chopper pad and an antique 120mm howitzer.

The two New Zealander "Z-men" were waiting for him when he put down. They introduced themselves as Timmy and Terry, both sergeants, both friendly to a fault. They were at the end of a one-week sortie to the small base, and were looking forward to going back up to Cam Ranh. It wasn't that doing time at Suk Deek was dangerous or even boring for the New Zealanders. Indeed the Minx hardly ever came anywhere near the place—or at least they didn't anymore. The reason for this was not entirely clear.

The blokes laid out a MRE feast for Hunter, and then offered him a bunk to collapse on. He took to it appreciatively; they would leave early in the morning, and even he had to sleep every once and a while.

Lying back on the metal frame cot, staring out at the stars, listening to the water in the canal rush by, Hunter's thoughts drifted back to where they always seemed to go in his rare, idle moments: to his love, the beautiful Dominique.

He had no idea when he would see her again—he'd given up trying to forecast such things long ago. Instead, he simply took the small American flag from his breast pocket, unwrapped it to reveal the dog-eared picture of her, and stared at it for five long minutes.

Then, her haunting image seared into his mind for the next few hours, he fell asleep and dreamt of harvesting hay.

* * *

The next morning dawned hot and rainy; it reminded Hunter of the hellish weather he'd experienced at the Khe Sanh.

They set out after a quick cup of coffee, heading down river in the Z-men's small but heavily armed twenty-five-foot patrol boat.

Timmy and Terry couldn't have been more at ease. Their guns were loaded, and they were ready for any eventuality, but they knew none was coming. And they promised Hunter that when they reached their first destination, he would know why they were so sure there were no Minx in the area.

They traveled the wide canals for about an hour before they reached the place called Lok Song Ly. It was large for a town this deep in the Delta, and heavily fortified too—Hunter counted at least a dozen artillery pieces in the immediate area, and twice that number of machine-gun posts. The place was even flying the multicolored flag of the Viet Minx.

But there was nobody around.

No one but the dead.

They tied up at the small movable dock and cautiously approached the village. Timmy and Terry had their Uzis up and ready, Hunter had his M-16 on Full Auto. But they would not need them. The last battle to ever be fought at Lok Song Li had taken place two weeks before.

There were skeletons everywhere. For the most part they were devoid of clothing. They had been picked clean of dried flesh, and left to bleach in the hot sun. Hunter counted at least two hundred of them, many of those were scattered amongst the huts and dikes of the place. He'd seen battlefields before, but never one like this. Each of the skeletons had either been decapitated, disemboweled, or had one or two limbs chopped off. Those whose heads were still attached to their bodies had had their skulls crushed. Judging by the amount of dried blood powder surrounding these skeletons, it was easy for Hunter to determine much of the head-crushing had taken place while the victims were still alive.

"Your looking at a reenforced company of Minx, mate," Terry told him, surveying the grisly scene. "There's another half company out in those paddies beyond. All of them dispatched in the same, rather industrious manner."

Hunter could only shake his head. "Who the hell did this?"

The Z-men both shrugged back on cue. "That's just it, mate," Terry said. "We don't know."

They followed the river further south, leaving the bleached horror of Lok Song Ly behind.

Hunter couldn't get the vision of the skeletons out of his mind. No matter how despicable the Minx were—and stories of their atrocities were legion—they had obviously run into something worse. It was, he supposed, a case of just desserts. But getting one's head crushed while still alive was a gruesome way for anyone to go.

It was almost noon before they reached their next destination, a place called Bang Mi. It was an anomaly for the Delta, a high set of cliffs of rock outcrop and vines, rising out of the flat watery plain.

The small village was nestled against the northern edge of the small mountain, purposely hidden in the shadows which provided relief from the searing heat and the monsoon rains.

This ideal location was not being utilized at the moment though. Like the ghastly scene at Lok Song Li, the village was deserted.

They went ashore, and Hunter felt the same chilling feeling on the back of his neck—it was ice cold, despite the broiling sun.

Terry and Timmy led him past several well-kept, yet abandoned huts, to a larger, more military-style corrugated-tin building. This had a sign written in Vietnamese which identified the building as a subdistrict head-quarters for the Delta-South Command of the Viet Minx First Revolutionary Army.

Timmy expertly kicked open the building's door. Laying beyond was another disturbing scene. At first they looked like nothing more than a pile of leaves, scattered on the dirt floor, maybe numbering 200 or so. But Hunter didn't need a second look to tell him what the small leathery items were.

"Tongues . . ." he said. "That's a bad way to go."

Terry turned to him. "Who said anything about 'going' anywhere, mate?"

Hunter stared at him—then the real horror of the place began to sink in. The owners of the tongues were still alive, or presumably lived long enough to leave the building. Hunter grimaced at the thought of having one's tongue cut out while still alive.

"Cuts down on the chatter in the barracks, doesn't it?" he said.

Both of the New Zealanders laughed heartily. "Puts the dumper on the old appetite, too, don't it?" Terry howled.

They left the building, returned to the boat and started out to the south again. Suddenly the whole river seemed to become a very chilling place, like the set of a bad horror movie. Hunter half-expected to see dozens of hacked-up bodies come floating downstream at any moment. The Z-Men were right—something very strange was going on down here. And it had his powerful inner psyche crackling.

Who *was* the baddest motherfucker in the jungle? Hunter wondered. The Viet Minx, or the monster that was hunting them?

Hunter shook off an uncharacteristic chill. He wasn't too sure he wanted to know the answer.

They stopped at three more Minx outposts in the next six hours.

All of them were abandoned, all of them containing some evidence that an unspeakable horror had passed by recently.

One place, known as Cung Leek had a cemetery that contained nothing but dried human brains; more than 100 in all. In the nearby village of Sum Cung they found thirteen baskets filled with severed human digits—thumbs, fingers and toes. Once again, all indications were that the butchery had taken place while the victims were still alive.

Then at the bend in the river near a place called No Dinh they found a ditch where wild boars, birds and insects had been feeding. It contained the severed genitals of at least 150 men. Once more, they found evidence—a blood-stained butcher block, several broken hatchets— which indicated the atrocity had been performed while the men were still alive.

Thoroughly nauseated by this time, they skipped their evening meal and pressed on into the night, towards their ultimate destination: a place called Nieu Go. It was in this area that the large plane was reported to have gone down. Hunter had spent much time studying a topographical map of the place. Like the strange outcroppings at Bang Mi, Nieu Go seemed out of place in the flat marshy Delta.

It was an island really, spoon-shaped and built up with craggy brown rocks, stony beaches and a thick collar of jungle. Near its middle was a small rocky hill, elevation about 250 feet, which, according to the map, had a flattened top made by "unnatural means."

Hunter asked the Z-men what they thought "unnatural" meant. Timmy theorized the hill had its top razed by a large bomb blast, maybe a weapon gone astray during the last big war. Terry relayed the local myth that the place had been flattened thousands of years ago, by some obscure death spirit in some equally obscure Eastern religion.

Either way, it was easy for Hunter to see that neither man wanted to be near the place for too long.

They arrived just before midnight.

If the Delta was a strange place in the daytime, it was especially eerie at night. Sound traveled very well across the wet plains and rivers, and the starkness of the terrain seemed to amplify every weird noise from the jungles and beyond.

Twice, Terry and Timmy scrambled for their weapons, certain that *something* was either coming up the river towards them or swooping down on the boat from the dark, moonless sky. Hunter had stayed cool both times—his inner senses warned him of such things way in advance, certainly long enough for him to spring into action. But just seeing the two veteran Z-men rattled that way was enough to cause a shudder or two.

Hunter had checked his M-16 four times by the time the small boat pushed up on the dark beach at Nieu Go. Terry and Timmy were making sure their Uzis were on full load, too. They quietly yanked the boat into some tall reeds and then made for a line of mangroves just up from the beach. Although the place seemed totally devoid of life, Hunter's sixth sense was going off like a fire alarm.

"We better approach this very carefully," he kept reminding the New Zealanders, "There's something here that might not like us."

The two sergeants gave no argument.

They made it to the mangroves, pressing on through their thick roots, and made the swamp beyond. Off in the distance, Hunter detected a series of mechanical sounds—a thumping, like machinery working. He also heard voices.

They stopped at the edge of the swamp and hunkered down near a fallen tree. Hunter was buzzing with all kinds of warnings now. Beyond them was a very dark tract of jungle, probably a quarter mile wide, which led to an open field that ended at the base of the flattened hill. It was an infantryman's nightmare: if they don't get you in the jungle, they'll get you on the open field.

This is why the invented air support, Hunter thought.

If the key to the island was its flattened top, then that's where they would have to go. Just from a vantage point alone, they would be able to see for miles around them once day broke. If there was the wreckage of a large jet anywhere within twenty klicks, they would be able to spot it easily.

But as it turned out, they wouldn't have to look that far.

It was Hunter who saw it first. Just a glint of metal off about a half klick to their south. He stared at it for a long moment, his eyes getting seemingly conflicting signals. It was a huge dark shape, smooth in some places, jagged in others. It was definitely unnatural—just like the top of the hill on the island. He thought he could see wisps of smoke rising from it.

It hit him an instant later.

It was a C-5.

He nudged both Timmy and Terry and they soon saw the same dark shape in the gloom of the southern horizon.

"That's a motherfucker, that is," Terry observed. "We didn't have to look very hard for it after all."

"I've got to see this up close," Timmy agreed.

But Hunter was already ahead of them, somehow crashing through the thick mangrove swamp while still maintaining a semblance of silence. The Z-men were soon right on his tail.

It took them ten minutes, but they finally made it to the bottom of the rise which held the wreckage of the enormous C-5. Hunter climbed up on a piece of wing and ran his hand along the battered fuselage. Even in the near pitch-blackness he could clearly see the elaborate scrolling which dominated the design scheme of *Crunchtime*. There was no doubt about it now, this was Crunch's airplane.

"I guess everything we heard was true," Timmy observed.

"This must have broke some glass coming in," Terry observed. "Can't imagine anyone living to tell about it."

Hunter wasn't so sure. True, the monstrous airplane was definitely a total wreck. Its wings had been sheared almost completely from the fuselage, and the entire rear half of the airplane had been gutted by fire, and was now almost skeletal.

But the forward section of the airplane, while battered and twisted, was still intact.

He turned and looked out onto the marshy delta. It was open for miles around. No swamps, rock outcrops or spits of solid land. Suddenly the vision of the big airplane coming in appeared in his mind's eye. Flying low along the water, its engines smoking, overheated and running out of fuel, he saw it hit the water's surface once, then twice, then a third time. With a master pilot at the controls, this action would have served to slow down the flying behemoth, maybe enough to make its impact speed into Nieu Go relatively nonviolent.

He turned back to the wreck and once again studied it from end to end. Most of the damage was done by the fire, and that could have taken hours to burn out. Even now, there were still wisps of black smoke trailing up from it.

If the airplane had slid in, instead of crashing, there was good chance that there were some survivors—or even no casualties at all.

But how could they know for sure?

The answer came just a few seconds later.

Hunter saw the burst before he heard it. A huge, fiery red explosion went off no more than 250 feet above their heads.

Hunter yanked both Z-men down with him, all three rolling to the cover of one of the C-5's wrecked engines. There was another explosion, this one bigger and brighter, not 150 feet above them. Once more all three of them ducked lower, Hunter clamping his pilot's helmet tight around his ears.

But at the same instant, he knew something was wrong here. The aerial explosions were frighteningly bright in flame and intensity, but their corresponding sonics did not match the visual, like the flares shot at them over Khe Sanh.

When the third explosion went off just fifty feet above them three seconds later, Hunter had already figured it out.

These were gasoline bombs exploding overhead— frightening to the nth degree, but, for want of a better word, harmless at such altitudes.

"I think they's just trying to scare us, mate," Terry yelled over the muffled explosion.

"They're doing a damn good job," Timmy called out in reply.

But Hunter knew Terry was right: the bombs were more for show than anything else.

They crawled out from behind the engine, and managed to make it to the more protective burned-out frame of the fuselage before the next air-burst went off. From this position, Hunter could see just where the aerial bombs were coming from: not surprisingly, the flattened off top of the small plateau.

"They got the view on us, I suppose?" Jimmy said.

"Maybe got a NightScope up there," Hunter replied. His psyche was telling him that he was being "painted" by some kind of electronic detection device. "But if they wanted us dead, we'd been cooked by now, don't you think?"

The Z-men agreed. But that didn't solve their problem. As if to underscore it, another larger aerial burst was fired from the top of the hill, igniting just twenty-five feet above the burned-out fuselage. It was so close, they could feel a moment of intense heat tear right through their skin.

"Well, if they want us to leave, then, we might take their advice," Terry called out.

But Hunter knew it was already too late for that.

"Party's over, guys," he said, conspicuously laying down his M-16, and his .357 Magnum sidearm.

The Z-Men stared at him for moment, and then looked behind them. They found no less than 100 armed individuals staring back at them.

The soldiers were all dressed in black and wearing black jungle hats pulled low over their eyes. Many were wielding AK-47s, some of which were equipped with NightScopes. Others were carrying weapons of even larger caliber.

In a word, they looked vicious.

"So much for the notion of no Minx in the area," Terry dead-panned, dropping his weapons as well. "Looks like there's plenty of them to me."

While the two Z-men were braced for a fusillade, Hunter actually relaxed a little. He was sure they weren't going to be shot. He wouldn't have dropped his weapons if he had.

"I know this sounds like a bad movie," Hunter said slowly, "but I think they want us to go with them."

Sure enough, one of the soldiers stepped out and motioned the trio to come forward. Hunter and the Z-Men complied and they were soon being marched away from the wrecked C-5 and towards the flattened plateau.

"I just hope they kill us before they eat us," Timmy said.

Chapter Thirty-three

It was dawn by the time they reached the top of the plateau.

Hunter wasn't surprised by its layout. It was about ten acres in all, and was heavily fortified with mortars and high-caliber machine guns around a 360-degree perimeter, all hidden under expert camouflage. There were barracks for about 500 people, a mess hall, two small fuel storage tanks and a concrete weapons' magazine, again all of it concealed under top-notch camouflage.

The view from the top of the plateau was spectacular. He could see a slightly smaller island attached to the main part of No Gieu's "spoon," and it too had a high hill at its center. These two vantage points were by far the highest things for 100 miles around, and even the rising haze of the Delta morning didn't obscure the vista. They were the most militarily advantageous positions for as far as the eye could see.

At the plateau's center was a hut slightly larger than the rest. It was surrounded by a rather out-of-place white picket fence that appeared to be electrified. Standing at the door was a man much taller than the soldiers around them. He was bald, in his mid-forties, of hefty frame and wearing a long one-piece black gown. Hunter stared at the man now about fifty feet away.

It really was no surprise when he realized that it was Crunch.

They were marched right up to the larger hut, and then the guards were dispersed by Crunch clapping his hands once.

"Sorry about all this," Crunch said, authentically apologetic. "We can get carried away every so often."

Hunter studied his old comrade. He seemed a little older, a little heavier, a little less pugnacious. There was a moment of uneasy silence. They'd been friends for years. But it seemed as if Crunch had suddenly been dropped back on Earth. It was apparent he'd been out of touch with the rest of the world for a long time.

Finally he stepped forward and embraced Hunter, then they shook hands heartily. They were both extremely glad to see each other alive.

"It's been weird, Hawk," Crunch said, the gleam returning to his eyes. "This is a very weird place."

Hunter quickly introduced Terry and Timmy and Crunch led all three of them inside his hut. It was dark and rife with early morning shadows. The surfeit of mosquito netting was arranged to make the place look mysterious. Still, the place was fairly well-appointed, considering its location. There were several baskets of fruit sitting on ice, a barrel of rainwater, and a brace of recently killed chickens hanging over a spit. A large straw bed dominated the far end of the building. In the shadows they could see several young Oriental women were asleep atop it.

Hunter and the New Zealanders took a seat on the floor while Crunch collected four glasses.

"Not exactly a surprise visit, is it?" Hunter asked him.

Crunch just shook his head. "I knew someone would come—eventually."

"Who else got out?"

"We all did," Crunch replied, coming up with a bottle of rice wine and taking his seat next to them on the floor. "The crew hooked up with a passing River Assault Group.

273

A bunch of Italian mercs, armed to hilt, hired by someone to bust Minx. There were four injured of our guys; I sent the other three along with the wounded."

He poured out four glasses of wine, they did a quick air toast and downed the shots immediately.

"Why didn't you go with them?" Hunter asked him. "Surely you could have squeezed on somewhere."

Crunch slowly nodded. "Oh, they had room for me, all right," he said, his voice a little low. "But that's just it—they didn't have enough room to take *all* of us."

"All of you, you say?" Timmy asked.

Crunch nodded again, then smiled faintly. "Well, you know, you met my friends . . ."

Terry laughed. "The people with all the guns? They did a damn good job, they did."

Crunch's smile widened. "You'd be surprised," he said enigmatically.

He stood up and opened the hut's back door, revealing an exercise yard beyond. The area was filled now with at least 100 people, all of them doing a form of *t'ai chi*, the ritualistic morning exercise practiced by many in China.

But it was not the almost ballet-like movements of the participants that raised Hunter's eyebrows. Rather it was the fact that all of the exercisers were young women—and they were all topless to boot.

Hunter just shook his head.

"Well, Crunchman," he said, "you've finally managed to top JT."

It took the entire bottle of rice wine for Crunch to tell his story.

It was simple, really. After he brought the C-5 in for its incredible controlled crash landing, he and the others instinctively headed for the high ground at the top of the plateau.

The Chinese women were already there. They'd been

274

living in what used to be a Minx lookout post, having been abandoned there by slave traders, who, at the last moment, chickened out of a deal to sell the women as sex slaves to Minx high commanders in the occupied cities in the southern part of the Delta. When the Minx found out about the deal gone bad, they hunted down the slave traders and killed them.

Then they went to the plateau to get the women.

The Minx made their first mistake by sending only twenty-five men to collect the 150 would-be prostitutes. Having had at least an hour's warning of their approach, the women were ready when the Minx arrived on the island. Armed with sharpened tree branches, heavy rocks, and their own hands, feet, and teeth, they set upon the surprised Minx soldiers and killed all of them, losing only four of their own.

Taking their weapons and securing the landing craft the Minx had brought with them, the women were also ready and waiting when the second group of Minx arrived looking for the first. Appearing docile at first so the soldiers would approach unsuspectingly, the women then surprised the Minx river crafts, sinking them with hand grenades taken from their first victims, and then machine-gunning those Minx left floundering in the water.

Retrieving the weapons caches on both craft increased the women's arsenal to nearly 100 weapons. The next Minx rescue party approached the island more cautiously. They found twenty of the women on the island's small beach, completely naked, and waving the soldiers onshore. Like the Sirens of Greek myth, the women captured the Minx soldiers and then killed every one of them, further increasing their growing arsenal.

Within a month's time, the women became the most potent, and most crafty, military force in the basically anarchic Delta area.

But they didn't stop there. Having little hope of returning to China, and blaming the Minx for their current situation, the women—now collectively calling themselves Li-Chi Chi—began a campaign against the Minx with a vengeance. Soon, the word got around about the crazy women, and most of Minx units within twenty-five square-mile area pulled back to safer areas.

Some didn't make it.

"You guys saw some pretty gruesome sights on the way in, I assume?" Crunch asked them.

Hunter and the Z-men nodded.

"Bad stuff," Hunter told him, quickly recounting the atrocities they'd seen in the Minx villages on their way to the plateau island. "Some of the worst I've ever seen."

Crunch bit his lip and stared at his visitors for a moment. Then it finally began to sink in. Hunter looked back at him in amazement.

"They . . . did it?" Hunter asked, pointing to women still exercising outside.

Crunch nodded. "Hard to believe," he admitted. "But true."

He continued his story. Just about the time the *Li-Chi Chi* were butchering all the Minx in the area, Crunch's C-5 slammed into the island. Savvy right from the beginning, the women were quick to understand that Crunch and his comrades had come to help the people of Vietnam stave off the impending Minx domination of the entire country. They evoked the old axiom: "My enemy's enemy is my friend."

In other words, they greeted Crunch and his crew with open arms.

When the Italian mercenary force happened by about a week after the crash, they took Crunch's crew, including the wounded. But the women of Li-Chi Chi asked Crunch to stay. They needed some kind of military leader, and as they had witnessed his superb landing of the huge C-5, and his concern for his men afterward, he became their first choice.

"It was a tough decision," Crunch told them, retrieving

another bottle of rice wine, and pouring out four more drinks. "I wanted to find out what happened to everyone, of course, but on the other hand, these women were really on to something. Plus, there's a lot of very strange stuff happening out here—and not just with these ladies. Stuff that might turn out to be very important for us. And I figured that someday, the Minx would drum up enough balls to come out here in force—and, well . . . I guess I just thought, what would Hawk do in this situation? Or Fitz? Or the General?"

His voiced trailed off. There was really no further explanation needed.

Except, of course, for Crunch's hairdo—or lack of it.

He anticipated Hunter's question.

"Curious about the dome?" he asked running his fingers over his bald head.

"Very Brando," Hunter said.

"Well, it was a small price to pay," Crunch replied, motioning over his shoulder to the pair of sleeping beauties on his bed. "I guess they saw the movie, too . . ."

They drained their rice wine and Crunch poured another.

"What kind of 'strange stuff' are we talking about?" Hunter asked, taking a gulp of the bitter liquor.

Crunch reached inside his pocket and came up with a photo map. He spread it out on the floor before them.

"The Li-Chi Chi took this from one of the officers they killed along the way," Crunch explained. "It's a montage put together from about a dozen old high-altitude shots."

Hunter quickly studied the crude map and saw it was of the southern half of South Vietnam.

"This is the city of Song Tay," Crunch said, pointing to a pin point on the coastline. "It was a pisspot little town for years. But from what I can gather, it's been built up like crazy in just the past few months. See how the water appears darker here?"

Hunter studied the area Crunch was indicating. It did

appear that the water in the bay near the city was darker than the rest of the coast. It was in fact as dark as the water further out in the ocean.

"Recently dredged?" Hunter guessed.

"Exactly," Crunch said. "This little village is now a deep-sea port. It can handle the biggest ships, with enough room for turnaround, refueling, maintenance, you name it. They must have humped it to get it all dug in such a short time."

"Like they were surprised someone was coming?" Terry said.

"Bingo," Crunch said. "And what deep-water ships would they go through all this trouble for?"

Hunter shook his head. "The Cult battleships," he said bitterly. "It's got to them."

"It *is* them," Crunch replied. "I know. I've seen them."

Hunter looked up at him. "You've seen them?" he asked, slightly astonished. "How?"

"I went down there," Crunch declared. "Me and six of the ladies, took one of the river craft one night and sailed to within a mile of Song Tay. I saw one of those big bastards myself, with those Cult weirdos all over it."

"So the battleships *were* heading here," Hunter said.

"You made a good guess way back when," Crunch told him. "There's got to be some kind of alliance between the Cult and the Viet Minx."

Hunter felt a slight shiver go up his spine. "Now that's a scary proposition. But there must be someway to find out for sure."

Crunch refilled their glasses once again.

"Well, I got a plan," he said. "And maybe it will put another piece of the puzzle together."

Hunter had to laugh. "A plan? A plan for what?"

"To go after one of those battleships," Crunch replied matter-of-factly.

"By yourself?"

Crunch shook his head. "No, not now that you're here."

Hunter was amazed at Crunch's *chutzpah.*

"And what the hell are you going to do with this battle-ship?" Hunter asked incredulously. "Sink it?"

" 'Sink it?' " Crunch replied. "No way—we're going to steal it."

"Steal it?"

Crunch smiled again. "Sure," he said. "That way, we solve two problems. We get rid of one of them, and maybe we find out just what the hell they're up to. Plus, it's a way we can *all* get out of here."

Hunter just shook his head. Maybe his time in the hell at Khe Sanh had temporarily sapped him of that special kind of initiative that characterized the officers of the United American Armed Forces. But the *elan* was quickly returning. That idea that if you were in the right, then anything was possible—no matter how outrageous. It was good to feel that way again. Suddenly nothing sounded too crazy. Steal a battleship? Yeah, sure, why not?

"OK, I'm game," he told Crunch. "When do we start?"

Crunch poured out one last round of drinks. "Well, the sooner the better," he said. "But there is one thing we have to do first—and this is the really nutty part."

Hunter just shrugged. "What could be nuttier than trying to swipe a battleship?"

Crunch shook his head. "Well, Hawk, old buddy," he said with his trademark toothy smile. "You'll really have to see for yourself."

Through most of the conversation, Timmy and Terry had sat back and enjoyed the rice wine, and started a buzz.

But now, they were clearly puzzled.

"Excuse me," Terry finally said. "But did you chaps say you're going to steal a battleship?"

They were running.
Over the dry marsh, up small hills, down into gulleys.

The grass was bright green, almost emerald; the sun was incredibly hot, yet there was a brisk breeze in the air.

Hunter couldn't remember ever running so fast, but still he couldn't keep up with Crunch. The older, slightly heavier man was flying, his black flowing garment whipping behind him in the wind, the sun shining off his shiny bald head.

They were running west, along a path which served a network of canals, all of which emptied into the Mekong. Hunter had no idea that the plateau island was so large. A kind of land bridge ran up from the opposite edge of the plateau, down into the grassy marshes and then onto the smaller, connected island. While smaller than the plateau island, this spit of land also had a steep hill in its center, with a cliff on its southern side.

Crunch didn't stop running until he reached the foot of this hill, and then only to allow Hunter to catch up.

"What the hell have you been doing, taking vitamins?" Hunter asked him, pausing to catch his breath.

"I quit smoking," Crunch called back to him, starting to run up the hill. "I haven't had a cigar in weeks."

Hunter took a deep breath and continued the pursuit. He'd spent too many days and nights running back at Khe Sanh—from the snipers. From the mortars. From the ghosts.

Now here he was, hundreds of miles away from that hell, in a wide open space that was as opposite as you could get from the claustrophobia of Khe Sanh, and he was *still* running.

It took him ten minutes of humping, jogging and all out running to reach the top of the hill: Crunch made it in under five. He was waiting for Hunter at the summit, legs crossed Lotus-style, facing south. The wind was really blowing up here, and the heat rising from the Delta waters was almost condensed to hot vapor. It also smelled incredibly sweet.

It was now 1545 hours. The sun was beginning its descent.

Hunter half-collapsed beside his friend, sucking in the sweet air.

"You give up any more vices, you'll kill yourself," he told Crunch.

Crunch just sat back and let the sun wash over him. "Hey, there's something good to be said for a clean lifestyle."

Hunter suddenly froze.

"Don't you agree?" Crunch asked him.

Hunter didn't respond. He was sitting perfectly still, his eyes locked on the southern horizon.

"Something's coming," he said finally. "Something very weird."

Crunch opened his eyes quickly, sucked back to reality by Hunter's declaration.

"It's what I brought you up here to see," he told the Wingman. "It shows up almost every day at this time."

They both moved back from the cliff, and into the shrubbery, Hunter's finely tuned sixth sense still focused on the thin band of reddish clouds to the south.

"You're right," he half-whispered to Crunch, closing his eyes to better concentrate on what had his inner psyche setting off alarms. "It *is* something very strange. Flying at about two hundred fifty knots, if that. Maybe three hundred high, no more than that."

A second later, they both heard it. It was a highly-unusual whining noise, definitely that of a jet engine, or more accurately a pair of jet engines, but definitely not one of typical manufacture.

Then they saw it—Hunter first, Crunch about five seconds later.

"There it is, Hawk!" Crunch half-yelled. "See it? Coming in at about forty-five,"

Hunter did see it—and in the same instant, couldn't believe it. It was a jet. It was trailing two long white contrails, even though it was barely 300 feet off the deck. Its engine was whining, its mechanics sounding extremely foreign to Hunter's perfect pitch.

"Old bolts," Hunter said of the sound. "Old bearings and blades. This thing is antique."

It was now about fifteen miles away, and quickly taking some kind of distinct shape. It was tubular, with wings slightly swept back and a stubby tail plane. A disproportionately large engine hung from each wing, the thick vapor trail—actually exhaust and poorly spent fuel—underscoring their ancient manufacture.

Strangest of all, the damn thing was painted bright pink.

"Jeesuz," Hunter exclaimed. "It's a Me-262."

Crunch was nodding enthusiastically. "That strange enough for you Hawk?"

The Me-262 was the first jet airplane ever to see combat. Built and test-flown by the Nazis in the late Thirties, it was faster, more maneuverable and much more advanced than anything else flying at the time, including lesser-known British and American test models. If it wasn't for an incredible blunder on Hitler's part—he decreed that the speedster be used as a bomber—then the Me-262 might very well have turned the tide in the European theater. Had the Nazis used their brains and built hundreds of the jets to go against the Allied bomber forces, the entire strategic bombing initiative would probably have been halted, or radically reduced at the least. But a relatively few were ever built and they weren't used against the Allied bombers until the last few months of the war when it was too late. That was the Nazis for you: supermen who were superdumb.

But still, Hunter didn't think the Nazis ever painted their jets pink.

About twelve miles out, the pink Me-262 went into a long, slow turn towards the west. Hunter never kept it out of his sight.

"Do you remember me telling you about this thing, Hawk?" Crunch asked him. "Right after Okinawa?"

Hunter did remember. After the small United American task force defeated the hated Asian Mercenary Cult forces on Okinawa a few months back, Crunch was doing a long recon flight of the South Pacific looking for more enemy installations. Nearing the end of this mission, Crunch's F-4X nearly collided with an Me-262. His recollection of the incident was limited to a quick view of the old jet, and the distinct feeling that its pilot appeared to be out of it, not under his own control. One thing that was for certain, whatever reason it had for flying around, it was probably linked to the Cult.

Crunch's encounter with the Me-262 took place several hundred miles south of Okinawa, which was close to the Japanese Home Islands.

And now here it was, flying over the Mekong Delta, thousands of miles away.

"I tell you, Hawk," Crunch told him, "I think this thing is following me around."

They watched as the pink jet continued on its arc, slowly turning toward them.

"I've seen it about ten times in the past two weeks," Crunch told Hunter as they moved deeper into the foliage. "Almost the same time every day. Same flight pattern. Same speed, same altitude."

"What the hell is it doing?" Hunter wondered as the Me-262 passed overhead. "Can't be doing camera recon—he's too low for that."

"Doesn't look like it's armed," Crunch agreed. "They could obviously see us on top of the plateau if they looked hard enough. But they're not."

Hunter was baffled. The jet was breaking three cardinal rules of military operation: it was flying in a predictable pattern, at a predictable time of day, and doing so low enough to be picked out of the sky with small arms fire, never mind a surface-to-air weapon.

It didn't make any sense. But one word suddenly popped into Hunter's mind: *Ritual.*

"If we're going to do something about that battleship, we're going to have to deal with this thing first," he said as the jet disappeared over the southern horizon.

"I agree," Crunch replied. "But exactly *what* are we going to do?"

Hunter just shook his head as the jet's two white contrails slowly faded in the darkening sky.

"I don't know," he said finally.

Chapter Thirty-four

The Next Day

It was hotter than the day before—so much so Hunter was sweating himself right through his flight suit.

He was sitting on the edge of the cliff on the small island, looking to the south. He was waiting for his inner senses to start buzzing, the prewarning that would alert him of the pink jet's approach.

The last twenty-four hours had passed somewhat unevently. Upon returning to Crunch's plateau camp, the Li-Chi Chi laid out a huge feast of vegetables and fruits, with a healthy flow of rice wine. Terry and Timmy especially enjoyed themselves—the Li-Chi Chi made no pretenses as to their promiscuity or love of erotica. The younger members of the women's group seemed extremely anxious to dress up in their skimpiest outfits—sewn together from uniforms taken from the Minx they'd slaughtered—and parade around in front of the Z-men. Some resorted to X-rated dancing, others practically forced the rice wine down the visitors' throats.

No sooner was it dark when the randy New Zealanders were playing mix and match with about two dozen young beauties inside one of the communal huts; at least that many more were waiting outside.

Hunter had watched the whole exercise with a mixture

of amazement and amusement. The women were obviously starved for affection—and their sheer numbers dictated that not all of them could be satisfied during the course of the day and night. So they resorted to taking turns, and doing so in a very ritualized way. No wonder Crunch was in such good shape!

Though tempted to partake, Hunter had stayed on the sidelines. His head was filled with too much stuff to think about getting his oil changed. If he and Crunch were going to pull off their battleship heist, they would have to do it quickly. JT's estimate of the major Minx attack in the north of the country was three weeks. Once that campaign started, then the fate of Vietnam, and the United American air fleet's mission here, would be determined.

But before they even considered moving down the Mekong to the deep-sea port Son Tay, they would have to deal with this mysterious pink airplane. Not to do so would leave them open to aerial detection by the Minx, and that would put the kibosh on everything.

So that's what Hunter was doing on the cliff, studying the southern horizon. He had thought about it long and hard, and came to the conclusion that he had no other choice but to shoot down the pink airplane. And that he would have to do it alone.

As he sat waiting, the hot wind blowing across his face, he realized that there were few places he'd seen in his life that was so strange, so beautiful, so surreal as this part of the Delta. The marshes which stretched out endlessly before him looked like acres of well-manicured lawns rolling on top of the constantly rippling water. This oddly aquatic-pastoral scene was broken only by a handful of plateaus, which rose like gigantic mushrooms on the horizon. Some of them had small spoon-shaped islands attached, like the one his was sitting on now, others were fairly barren. It was like he was on another planet. Or seeing the earth at a different time; during a different age.

Soon other things began to cross his mind. As always,

the thoughts turned to Dominique. He missed her terribly. Solemnly he pulled the small, tattered American flag from his breast pocket and slowly unraveled it. Inside was the equally tattered photo of Dominique. His heart jumped upon seeing it—her lovely face, her long blond hair, her incredible inner beauty. It all came through even though the photograph was almost entirely faded.

This was another big reason he'd abstained the night before. It just didn't make any sense for him to be with another woman. Not now. Not with the way he felt about Dominique. He closed his eyes and imagined her sitting on the porch of their small farmhouse on Cape Cod, reading one of her books on the paranormal, and probably wondering when the hell he was going to return to her.

He opened his eyes and wondered the same thing.

That's when his spine started tingling.

He was on his feet in an instant, his M-16 up and ready. He saw the two white contrails first, about twenty-two miles dead south. The airplane was following the exact same flight pattern as the previous day; flying at the same height and the same speed. As before, the strange jet began a long arc about 18 miles out, first pulling towards the west and sweeping north and then eastward. Again, the one word that came to Hunter's was "ritual." For whatever reason, the airplane seemed to be following some kind of rite.

He waited patiently as the jet approached. At ten miles out, he had it in his rifle's telescopic sights. He expected the plane to pass within an eighth of a mile of him, just like the day before. It would take a perfect shot to hit it, but he had no doubt he could do it. And the question wasn't whether he could inflict enough damage on the airplane to bring it down—he was sure he could do that, too.

No, the question was: Did he really want to kill the pilot?

Something deep inside him was telling him not to—he didn't know why, but he'd always relied on his extraordinary perception before. Now was not the time to begin doubting it.

He waited for another full minute. Now the plane was about two miles due west of him, and beginning its long bank back towards the south. He was amazed—it was an exact recreation of the flight the day before, and according to Crunch, the path it had taken every day for the past two weeks.

But now, even as the pink airplane grew larger in his sights, Hunter's inner voice was telling him that valuable things might be contained inside the ancient jet. He was puzzled by this feeling, not that he was getting it at all—but *why* he was getting it. He suddenly felt like a hunter aiming a rifle at a magnificent golden eagle. One squeeze of the trigger and the rare creature would be gone forever.

The plane was now less than a mile away, and coming closer to him by the second. He tightened his grip on the M-16, keeping the pink fuselage dead center in his telescope. His inner psyche was flashing like crazy. It was a feeling unlike he'd ever felt before. He had to follow what it was telling him—and see what the consequences brought.

The jet was about 800 feet away when he squeezed the trigger. A long stream of tracer bullets streaked across the sky in a perfectly projected arc. Within two seconds, they found their mark, tearing through the pink jet at midfuselage and perforating it all the way back to the tailplane.

The jet predictably banked up, and ran right into the thick of his second burst, ripping apart its left side engine, and destroying the right-wing's control surfaces. It then began to slide to the left, exposing its cockpit to Hunter's gunsight—but he didn't continue firing. Instead he eased off the trigger.

The jet began smoking heavily and started to go down. He watched anxiously as it first dipped, then briefly rose again, then nosed down for good.

He was up on the edge of the cliff now, watching as it went right by him, both wings aflame. The plane hit the wet marsh a few seconds later, bounced up and then pancaked back down onto a nearby canal. Its momentum carried it across the narrow waterway and up onto the far bank. It was here it finally came to rest about a quarter of a mile away from him.

Before he knew it, he was running again. Down the hill, and across the marsh, heading for the downed airplane.

Two members of the Li-Chi Chi also saw the airplane go down.

They were at a lookout position on the far western edge of the plateau, placed there by Crunch to watch Hunter's one-man shoot-down mission and provide backup if necessary.

As soon as the airplane was hit, they made a quick call back to the base camp and then slid down the embankment and ran across the marsh. They got there just as Hunter did, and using the butts of their rifles, they helped him bust through the jet's canopy.

The airplane was nearly engulfed in flames by the time the hole in the glass was large enough to yank the pilot out. Hunter had to crawl into the blazing cockpit to unstrap the unconscious flyer; the two women fighters held tight to his legs, all the while fending off the flames as they totally consumed the wings and moved towards the forward fuel tanks.

The smoke inside the shattered cockpit proved to be Hunter's worst foe, but after several anxious seconds, he was able to cut through the safety straps and free the pilot. On his call, the women fighters yanked on his legs and Hunter and the pilot both came tumbling out. The women pulled them away from the flames, but they were startled to see Hunter scramble back towards the airplane, and once again dive head first through the hole in the shattered cockpit.

Before they could run to him, he was back out again, a large black, smoking box searing his hands.

He dove for a nearby ditch just a half second before the Me-262 exploded. When the fuel tanks finally lit off, it blew the jet's frame more than thirty feet into the air. All that came down were smoking pieces and sparks.

By the time the women fighters reached Hunter, he was already on his feet, examining the still-smoldering black box even as he was cooling off his burnt hands in a nearby marsh pool.

He looked up at them and surprised them with a smile.

"That was close," he said.

By the time Crunch and his Li-Chi Chi guards reached the crash site, Hunter and the two women fighters were marching the pink plane's pilot back towards the plateau.

Hunter ran up to him, the strange black box in his hands.

"Ever see one of these?" he asked Crunch. "I ripped it out of the 262's cockpit."

Crunch studied the box. It was about a foot square, six inches deep. It had a series of multicolored wires running out of its back—or was that the front? Other than that it seemed to be nondescript in every way.

"Some kind of autopilot?" Crunch guessed.

"Very close," Hunter told him excitedly. "It *is* a guidance system. But it was not originally designed for an aircraft. I think it's supposed to be on an ICBM."

Crunch stared at him and then back at the black box.

"You're kidding."

Hunter shook his head. "It looks like it might be part of a targeting system, probably used by a subsurface launched weapon."

Crunch looked back up at him. "Sub-launched?" he said, "You mean like in Fire Bats?"

Hunter nodded. The *Fire Bats* were the nuclear-armed subs that were known to roam the Pacific like moving pieces in a huge blackmail game. They were first used by the Fourth Reich, the cult of Super-Nazis who overran most of the American continent a year before, only to be run back out by the United American forces. At least one Fire Bats was sunk around that time; two others were on station off the Pacific American coast, working under orders of the Asian Mercenary Cult, and providing a nuclear umbrella for the Cult's occupation forces. When the Cult pulled out of California for the titanic battle at Pearl Harbor, the pair of mysterious nuclear-armed subs disappeared again. Their whereabouts at the moment was unknown.

"You think this is from one of the Fire Bats?" Crunch asked.

"Could be," Hunter answered, turning the strange black box over in his singed hands. "Could *very well* be."

Crunch scratched his head. "But what the hell is a nuke missile guidance system doing on that old jet bucket?"

Hunter just shrugged. "I can't wait to find out. I'll bet it will be a shocker when we do."

But they were both in for a more immediate surprise. One of the Li-Chi Chi guards was suddenly tugging on Crunch's sleeve. She whispered something into his ear and Hunter watched a puzzled look wash over Crunch's face.

"You're kidding?" he asked the woman in broken Cantonese.

She vigorously shook her head no, pointing to the pilot.

Two other women fighters held the still-helmeted pilot up straight. A fourth woman put her hand inside the pilot's flight suit and violently ripped it open.

Both Hunter and Crunch were astonished. Beneath the flight suit was a thin T-shirt and beneath that was a pair of breasts. They were small, young, pert—but breasts nevertheless.

They couldn't believe it: the pilot of the strange Me-262 was a woman.

Six hours later

Hunter was stumped.

He looked around the small communal hut, and suddenly nothing was making any sense. In one corner was the pilot of the destroyed Me-262. She was a woman, or more accurately, a girl. Probably no more than fifteen, sixteen at the most, and either Asian or Polynesian. She was absolutely terrified, shaking, possibly in a state of shock.

Just how she came to be flying the decades-old airplane, he had no idea. She couldn't speak English, and no one on the plateau could speak whatever language she seemed to speak in between the torrents of tears.

Resting on a small wooden table in the other corner was the strange black box he'd ripped out of the burning airplane. He had removed one of its top covers and peering inside confirmed that it was indeed a guidance system for a ballistic missile, most probably one that was nuclear-tipped, and fired from below the surface of the water.

In the third corner was Crunch. Half-asleep, half-fondling a pair of his favorite Li-Chi Chi. There was some connection to the three, and to the Me-262 jet that was still smoldering down on the marshes.

Crunch had seen the strange Me-262 months ago while on his recon flight prior to the pivotal battle against the Cult at Pearl Harbor. But he had told Hunter that at the time, it was definitely a man flying the jet and it was not painted in garish pink. At the time, Crunch had been over-flying some deserted South Pacific islands, and the Me-262, being of somewhat limited range, could have conceivably been heading for one of them, such as Tarawa, Kiribati, or maybe all the way to Fiji. If that was the case, that would explain the girl pilot's apparent Polynesian origin.

But what the hell was she doing flying the plane? And why was she here, now, in Vietnam, on the verge of a huge conflict, flying the same pattern, over and over? And carrying a fairly sophisticated piece of guidance equipment with her to boot?

Hunter closed his eyes and tried to dredge up some psychic prowess to help him put the puzzle together. He recalled the great axiom of Sherlock Holmes: If one eliminates the impossible, then what remains, no matter how improbable must contain the truth—or something like that.

So it came down to a basic question: How is it that a girl barely old enough to know better is flying an old Nazi-designed jet over Vietnam on the same flight pattern day after day, with a ICBM targeting device hooked up to the flight controls?

Hunter concentrated. Eyes closed, falling into a trancelike state, he began to hear voices. There were many as usual, but one stood out above the cacophony. It was the one that kept saying: *Just twist it around, dummy. . . .*

Hunter opened his eyes slowly. Twist it around? What did that mean? Girl flying airplane with ICBM guidance box aboard? Airplane flying girl with ICBM guidance box aboard?

No—wait a minute . . . How about: ICBM guidance box flying airplane with girl aboard.

Hunter was up in a shot—that might be it!

He quickly grabbed the black box and began ripping it apart in earnest. The first level was already unscrewed, it came off in a snap. The second level had no less than twenty-four tiny screws to be undone; it took him about a minute to do so. This level contained the black box's memory circuits. A quick glance told him they'd been rearranged recently; that was a good sign.

He went into the third layer, which looked like a nightmare of semiconductors, all crossbred and out of sync; more evidence that the box had been realigned recently, and not by any real genius.

He finally made it down to the fourth and final layer and it was here that he found the proof for his "twist it" theory. The actual guidance system itself—that part of the black box which sent signals to the key components of an ICBM's guidance apertures—had been recast big time. More than two thirds of the conducting units had been disconnected altogether, as had the computer terminal ducts. This was definitely the work of someone who was trading down in the world. They didn't want the box to guide anything as complex as an underwater ICBM; rather they wanted to dummy-it-up and fly nothing more than a simple, old airplane.

He sat back down in his corner and stared at the disassembled box. They wanted the airplane to fly somewhere, with the girl as a passenger. She could no more pilot the airplane than any schoolkid could. She was just along for the ride. But why? And where was she going?

The ritualistic daily flights up and around the Delta—what was the point of that? It wasn't for recon purposes, or prestrike stuff. Just going around and around—didn't make much sense, unless . . . He looked back at the black box's important fourth layer. Was there a chance that maybe the person rewiring the thing screwed up a connection? If they had, that might send the plane's controls into a constant circling pattern as the box's commands simply began repeating themselves.

He carefully scanned the fourth layer looking for any evidence of a semiconductor not sitting right or a connection not quite nailed down to a conducting point. To his dismay, everything looked properly connected, haphazard as it might be. Then he studied the third layer, the memory part of the box. Right away he noticed there was indeed not one, but two connectors that hadn't been fused correctly. They were laying bare as a baby's bum, their triangular plugs just begging to be coupled.

That was it—the black box had a case of Alzheimer's. Because of a bad circuit connection, it couldn't make up its mind what to do at any given moment—so it had just gone in circles.

Hunter closed his eyes again. He could just see the airplane taking off from a base down south—maybe even near the Cult battleship port of Son Tay—flying north, and coming around and back to the base again. The people at the base, for some reason compelled to launch the airplane day after day (now, that was a ritual!), saw it return each day, its flight another failure.

And if they had allowed it to go on long enough, the Mc-262 would have kept flying the same nonsensical pattern everyday, until it was too old to get airborne—or until someone shot it down.

It was a nice tidy theory, but it didn't answer three big questions: Why was the airplane rigged in the first place? Where would it go if the memory circuits had been fused correctly. And why was the girl on board?

Hunter opened his eyes. There was one person who knew the answers to those questions—and many more. And lucky for him, she was sitting right across the room.

It took more than seven hours before Hunter found a combination of languages with which he could communicate with the young girl.

As it turned out, she spoke a little Japanese, a little Korean, a trace of French, and a smattering of Bogonese—an obscure dialect favored by some of the more remote tribes on Borneo. Using these four tongues and a good deal of sign language, Hunter was finally able to get the skeleton of her story.

Her name was Ala.

She'd just turned sixteen by her calendar. She was born

on the island of Fiji, and most of her family still lived there. Two years before, the Asian Mercenary Cult invaded the island and killed off most of its male population; those who were spared were sold into slavery.

From the beginning, the Cult had considered the main island of Fiji as a sacred place, though none of the residents knew why. The actual military presence on the island was very small; if any Cult soldiers came at all, they tended to be high officers and their staffs. Typically, they used the most beautiful women on the island for sex; "comfort girls," they called them. The unattractive ones were put to work doing the menial domestic tasks.

Several months before, a man named Soho came to the island. He was flying a strange jet—the Me-262, as it turned out. He had come to Fiji from Okinawa, while it was being attacked by "white men in ships and planes," an obvious reference to the United American Task Force which first attacked Japan and then Okinawa, before taking part in the final defeat of the Cult land forces at Pearl Harbor.

Soho was immediately set up as a god on Fiji. The high Cult officers were very quick to kowtow to him and fell over themselves to get him anything he desired, from drugs, to booze, to girls for sex. As a result, Soho was intoxicated round the clock, making it very hard for the Cult officers to get him to make the decisions they needed him to make.

One day, Soho spotted Ala as she was placing flowers on the Me-262 which had been set up as a shrine to Soho, worshipping the "bird of his arrival." Soho immediately developed a liking to Ala; he told her it was because she was the only female on the island who had red hair. They spent much time together, mostly taking long walks along the island's miles of beaches.

During these times, Soho told Ala many stories about the Asian Mercenary Cult, and especially about its succession of divine leaders. One was a man named Hashi-Pushi;

when he was killed, his "spirit" passed control of the huge Cult to a woman named Aja, via the sex act. She in turn passed the crown to Soho in the final hours of the battle on Okinawa by way of a similar coupling. It was Aja who told Soho to fly to Fiji.

Although Soho more or less respected her during their time together, Ala saw that he was gradually getting sicker, both in mind and body. During their last meeting, he was a bag of bones, his consumption of alcohol and drugs had withered him away. He explained to her that it was his turn to pass on the crown of the Asian Mercenary Cult and that he had selected her to be his receptor. The next day, Soho called a celebration at the island's airport. In front of a large assembled crowd, including her parents, Soho raped Ala, and then put her aboard the Me-262. Terrified, she was helpless as the airplane took off on its own.

Thus began a very long odyssey. With the plane's flight controls being manipulated by the black box, Ala flew from base to base, all over the South Pacific, absolutely terrified. Each place she landed was under some kind of Cult control, either directly or through allies like the Minx.

Though she was treated like a goddess where ever she arrived, her hosts were very obvious in their haste to get her fed, washed, the plane fueled up and on its way again.

She'd been taking this remote-control trip for nearly a month when she finally set down at a small airstrip outside of Son Tay, the small port city which was now the calling place for Cult battleships. She and her hosts believed that this was just one more step on her trip to an unknown destination; like the others, the Minx officers at Son Tay were anxious to see her go. But something had happened to the airplane by this time—when she took off, she flew for about 40 miles and then inexplicably returned to Son Tay. Startled, her hosts sent her up again the next day, and the same thing happened. The next day it was the same, and on and on.

Each time she returned, her hosts would wring their hands and pray—literally *pray*—that the reputed supernatural powers behind the Cult would soon take the goddess-in-waiting off their hands, lest something happen to her on their watch.

She was on her eighteenth circuit when Hunter shot her down.

He sat and listened to her story, equally baffled and fascinated. What the hell did it all mean? Passing the crown of Cult leadership from person to person, via forced sex? It was crazy.

But then again, so were many of the people in the Cult.

Hunter asked Ala if she had any idea who she was supposed to meet at the end of her journey. She thought a moment; her only guess would be a man that Soho told her about once.

It happened during one of their first walks on the beach. Soho told her that it was important she know about this particular man. He came from a place in the Middle East, many years ago. He began preaching and soon gathered a small number of trusted followers. They traveled all over, and soon their number grew. This man had the ability to attract and influence ordinary people, and convince them that they could do extraordinary things.

Soon many people were talking about this man. They would walk miles just to hear him speak. Some people began praying to him—they were convinced this man had a vision for the world, one by which every person could live by.

Soho told Ala that this man's vision for a new way for men to live brought him many enemies too. Many people disliked him. Many tried to kill him. Soon many were waging wars against him, wars of struggle over men's souls. Soon these battles were raging out of control. This man knew that only by sacrificing himself could he really influence how others thought of him. So he was killed, murdered by those who disagreed with him.

But then, this man "came alive again," Ala said Soho told her, and walked among his people again, "like a ghost." And that he was still alive this day, possibly somewhere in the Middle East, possibly somewhere closer by.

And maybe that's where she was heading, to meet this ethereal personage.

Hunter was astounded. He asked her what Soho said this man looked like. She replied the man was supposedly tall, very strong, with long hair and a short beard.

"And did he tell you this man's name?" he asked the girl.

She nodded.

He stared at her for a long moment. "It's not Jesus, is it?"

She shook her head slowly. "No," she replied. "It's Victor."

Obsession takes many forms.

Love. Desire. Money. Drugs. Alcohol. Hate. *Revenge*.

The common thread was that, if taken to the extreme, obsession will eventually drive a person to madness. And at that point, the madness itself becomes an obsession.

Hunter was now a man obsessed.

He was in the cockpit of Crunch's crashed C-5, grabbing at wires, yanking at panels, tossing aside integrated circuit boards and LED switches—tearing out the heart of the cargo jet's flight controls in order to get to the brain.

Crunch was there, as were the Z-men, watching him rip through the battered control panel, looking for the small microprocessor which controlled the airplane's automatic pilot. The three men had given up trying to talk to Hunter—he'd answered all of their previous questions with little more than polite grunts, and sometimes uncharacteristic silence.

It was obvious that he was beyond conversation, and finally the three men just gave up trying to talk with him.

The match that lit the fuse for Hunter's rage was the name spoken to him by the island girl, Ala. The name was *Victor*. When he had her spell it out for him, translating the Borneo pidgen language into English characters, the word came out V-I-C-T-O-R, a slight variation on *Viktor*, by which Hunter had always known the supercriminal—but this made no matter. However it was spelt, the name was synonomous with evil, a culmination of all that was despicable in the world.

Hunter finally found the autopilot microprocessor.

It was a small unit, about the size of a cheap paperback book, and weighed less than a pound. But Hunter was sure that if he could graft the lead wires from Me-262's black box to the microprocessor, and then put the combined-unit into an adaptable airplane, then the coupled device would lead him right to the person who was now calling himself "Victor."

Hunter backed himself out of the torn-apart flight panel and was halfway surprised to see his audience was still there.

"I've got the sucker," he announced triumphantly. "Now, if I can just get a gap file, a micro-tandem wrench and some power, I can have this thing working in . . ."

He stopped in midsentence. Crunch was looking slightly askance at him.

"Hey, Hawk," Crunch said. "Are we forgetting the big picture here?"

Hunter just shrugged. "I don't know—am I?"

"We've a little problem right here, in this country?" Crunch went on. "Remember? We were going to swipe a battleship?"

Hunter stared at him for a moment, and then smiled.

"Oh, yeah," he said in perfect self-mocking tone. "The battleship. Right."

"First things first, mate," Terry said with a laugh.

The understatement was met with smiles all around. But then Hunter's expression turned dead serious again.

"But once we get this thing settled out," he said, his voice actually raspy with anger, "then I'm going to hunt down whoever the hell this new 'Victor' guy is.

"And then I'm going to kill him."

Chapter Thirty-five

Four Days Later

The Minx patrol had been walking for twenty-two hours straight.

All fourteen men were exhausted, tired, hungry, thirsty, hot and covered with bug bites of all shapes and sizes.

They'd left the Minx port stronghold of Son Tay almost three days before on a routine tax-collecting mission. They had been diverted to the small Delta village of Ko Lung by their regional commander: their orders were to contact the small garrison there and investigate if their radio gear was in proper working order.

What the regional commander didn't tell the leader of the Minx patrol was that the garrison at Ko Lung hadn't been heard from in nearly forty-eight hours.

The Minx patrol reached the outskirts of Ko Lung just before sunrise. The first thing they came upon was a small hut on the outlying edge of the village which had recently burned down. It was still smoking and its embers still glowing. The Minx patrol leader inspected the remains of the hut himself. There were a number of empty oil barrels thrown about as well as several lengths of singed, uncoiled electrical wire.

He ordered two of his soldiers to collect the wire—

cleaned and properly coiled, the patrol leader was certain he could get more than 100 *piestas* for it back at Son Tay.

The patrol moved on, passing several more abandoned huts, which were empty of booty, and entering the center of the village itself. It was eerily quiet—not that unusual for a fishing village, but strange nevertheless. The patrol leader sniffed the wind, and quickly reached up to hold his nose.

"Luc qway son toe!" he screamed. "something is a dead thing here—find it!"

Momentarily confused, the thirteen troopers quickly dispersed throughout the village, trying to find the leader's "dead thing."

They didn't have to look very long.

At the edge of the river was a long low building, used in the past as a fishing cleaning center. The far wall of this building was adorned with a row of three dozen five-inch hooks; on these the carcasses of fish were hung to dry.

The two troopers who burst into this building found thirty-six dead Minx soldiers hanging from these hooks instead.

The patrol soldiers couldn't believe it. The dead Minx had not just been killed, they'd literally been gutted. The contents of their stomachs—as well as the stomachs themselves—were spilled out on the floor in front of each corpse.

The patrol leader was called, and though he was a veteran of many battles, he immediately vomited all over his second-in-command. The rest of the patrol was almost as sick as their leader—they had heard the rumors of similar slaughterings further up in the Delta, brutal butcherings done by a mysterious band of flesh-eating "comfort girls."

Now, here, was proof positive that these stories were indeed true. And the patrol was twenty-four hours from nowhere.

The patrol leader regained his composure and ordered his men to take the safeties off their weapons—it was an order that he hoped would make them a little less shaky, but it had mixed results. He found his own hands shaking as he hastily loaded his Koch pistol. It took all his self-control to not vomit again.

The rest of the village was searched, but nothing was found; no guns, no radios, no more bodies. Nor where there any villagers: the garrison at Ko Lung had ruled over at least two hundred inhabitants. Now they were all gone.

It was the patrol leader's intention to get out of Ko Lung as quickly as possible—but his superiors at Son Tay had other ideas. When advised that the garrison had been graphically butchered, the regional commander ordered the patrol leader to cut down the bodies, go through them for personal effects, such as watches, rings or money and deliver such items personally to him.

Then, by orders of the regional commander, the patrol leader was to skin the bodies and bring the hides back to Son Tay. When dried, the skins would bring a good price on the exotic garment black market where they'd be sold falsely as "sharkskin."

The patrol leader did not have enough money in his unit bank to buy his way out of the gruesome order, so he set his troopers to rending their departed comrades.

He spent the time vomiting down by the river.

There were only five motorboats left in the Minx southern occupation patrol fleet.

When the Minx first moved into the area in preparation for their upcoming assault on the major cities of Vietnam, their river patrol fleet was twenty craft. Three had been lost to accidents, two others to maintenance. Ten others had gone out on routine patrol up the Delta—and never came back.

Boat #6 left the dock at Son Tay early in the morning; its captain was hoping to make the village of Buk Sik by four that afternoon. His mission was to check on a radio transmitting station at the small village, which, their commanders had told them was not in correct working order.

The captain was not looking forward to the patrol; like the other river force officers, he'd heard the rumors of what happened at the place called Ko Lung several days before. Thirty-six men of the garrison had been found butchered by a long-range patrol. When one of the Minx few helicopters was dispatched to the Ko Lung, they found all fourteen members of the long-range patrol dead, their bodies tied to pier supports where they had been fed upon by the fish, crabs, and other scavengers along the river.

All indications were that the men were still alive when they were lashed to the pier supports.

The scene at Ko Lung was so gruesome, the Minx commanders had shot to death the helicopter crew, lest the lurid talk leak out to the rest of the Minx forces at Son Tay. As it turned out, the chopper crew had died for nothing. News of what happened at Ko Lung was all over Son Tay within hours.

The river craft captain urged his motorman to coax as many rpms as possible out of the eighteen-footer's two Mercury engines. The last thing he wanted was to make landfall at Buk Sik after nightfall. Only an hour and a half downriver from Ko Lung, the captain wanted to be nowhere near the place once the sun went down.

As it turned out, Boat #6 made Buk Sik by 3:30 in the afternoon. Everything seemed peaceful enough as they floated in. *Too* peaceful. The captain's mission paper stated that Buk Sik had more than 120 citizens and a 24-man Minx unit watching over the radio transmitter. As the river craft motored up to the village's only pier, the crew couldn't see a soul.

Not wanting to make the mistakes his fellow officers obviously made in Ko Lung, the captain had all three of the boat's .50-caliber machineguns loaded, manned and ready.

This left himself and four crewmen to search the deserted village. They did so cautiously, slowly, with weapons up and ready, safeties off. They moved to the small radio shack first. Kicking in the door, they were horrified to find the two-room building was absolutely covered with blood. In fact, the reason the radio transmitter was not working was its booster units were literally sticky with blood.

They left the radio shack and moved into the village itself. Again, there was no sign of life—not even a bird calling or insect chirping. The stillness in the hot air was bone chilling.

The village was the typical collection of ramshackle straw huts and wooden or cinder block Minx barracks. None of the Minx buildings were occupied. Everything within them seemed in order—weapons in their lockers, ammunition in the magazines, and in some cases, food still on the table.

This left the civilian dwellings to search.

Normally the captain would have dispatched two, two-man teams to conduct the house searches, but under the circumstances, he decided it best they all stick together.

They went from hut to hut, finding nothing unusual. Several even had small baskets with coins in them—but the captain didn't steal the money, and ordered his crew not to do so either. They came up to the last hut, and the captain was almost breathing a little easier. One more search and he could return to the boat, his mission accomplished.

They kicked in the door to the small dwelling to find a table set at its center, four wooden bowls surrounding a metal cooking pot. There was a definite odor inside the hut—familiar, like meat cooking, but the captain could not place it.

His men routinely searched the three-room hutch and found nothing. The captain stood idly by, next to the table, sniffing the air and trying to identify the slightly sweet, slightly-smoked aroma.

That's when he casually lifted the lid of the cooking pot and discovered it was filled with human eyeballs.

306

Two of his troopers fainted dead away; the captain himself retched up water and phlegm. He thought himself in a state of instant shock. Try as he might, he couldn't stop looking at the bowl of bloody eyeballs.

It took both of his iron-stomach troops to lead him out of the horror hutch and lead him back towards the boat. But it was then they got their second horrible surprise: the boat was gone.

The gunners were floating face up in the river, their throats slashed, the swift current taking them away.

Crazed by the sudden, grisly events, and certain that the same horrible death awaited him momentarily, the boat captain pulled out his sidearm, placed the barrel in his mouth and pulled the trigger.

Leaderless and now mad with fear, the surviving crewmen did the same thing.

Chapter Thirty-six

Son Tay

It was simply called the Scream Hall.

Built years before by a contracting firm from Xmas Island, the large building resembled an aircraft hangar, except that it was located at the end of a long pier. Like many of the buildings in the port city of Son Tay, the Scream Hall was painted in garish hot orange. The dozen flags ringing its curved roof was of the same color, as was the bunting running all along its trim. These ornaments had been added just that morning, in preparation for the celebration scheduled at the large hall that night.

Next to the orange building were two barges, each supporting a huge crane. These machines were in constant use, keeping the surrounding port area deep enough to carry the huge Asian Mercenary Cult battleships which called with increasing frequency these days. The cranes too were painted hot orange.

Beside the crane barges was a strip of docks holding facilities large enough to handle up to 100 vessels. These docks were full. They were playing host to vessels of all shapes and sizes, from junks to seagoing luxury yachts. These were hooker boats, vessels which plied the waters from the Tonkin and the Gulf of Siam, stopping at the port cities and offering their services. Son Tay was one of the more popular ports-of-call; the Minx officers in the southern part of Vietnam were fairly wealthy, unlike their comrades in the north, who were too busy in combat or preparing for war to amass large bank accounts. The Minx officers at Son Tay were also inordinately sexual. This was because the Cult had provided them with *myx*, the superhallucinogenic, superaddictive drug which, among other things, raised the ingestor's hormone level as high as two thousand percent.

About 300 yards from this dock area was a small airstrip. It was here that the meager Minx helicopter corps was stationed. It was also here that the strange jet carrying the Cult "goddess" Ala had first landed, then taken off, only to land again, and repeat the process seventeen and a half times.

The huge festival scheduled that night at the Scream Hall was being thrown in honor of the flight of Goddess Ala. On the nineteenth try, the jet did *not* return. The relief felt by the top Minx officers at the port city was immeasurable. The goddess was no doubt not only on her way to her destiny, she was also finally out of their hair. And this meant they would not incur the wrath of the Asian Mercenary Cult for somehow queering the holy pilgrimage of their current "chosen one."

And this was cause for the celebration.

Only the top Minx officers at Son Tay were invited of course; they and every eligible woman or girl their legions could round up for them—voluntary or not—on the streets and docks of the city.

It was now seven in the evening, and the sun had disappeared.

Son Tay was lit up with strings of multicolored lanterns and even some gas-fire poles. The streets were mostly clear by this time. Son Tay's hundreds of unfortunate citizens were in their meager homes, imprisoned by a strict, shoot-to-kill curfew. The only people in the streets were patrolling Minx soldiers and the high command's prostitute procurement squads.

At the Scream Hall, there were already three dozen Minx officers gathered. They were awaiting three times as many women. Usually the females hired for these celebrations ranged in age from forty down to fifteen. They were provided free liquor and drugs, but had to pay for any antibiotics they might require as the evening progressed. Any food they consumed, either willingly or not, also had to be paid for.

The Minx officers were sitting at a long narrow table at the head of the vast hall, having just finished a sumptuous meal. They were now engaging kegs of red beer and rice wine that were placed on the long table well within their reach. Above the officers was a huge thirty-by-thirty-foot portrait of the Goddess Ala, a sloppily painted, overtly toady display commissioned by the Minx High Command for the pleasure of the frequently visiting Cult officers. Close observation would reveal that the girl's likeness was actually painted over a portrait of the man known as Soho, who in turn was painted over a portrait of a woman named Aja, who in turn was painted over an artist's rending of the enormously chubby, ex-God Hashi-Pushi.

The post-dinner activities had no formal beginning. Once the meal was eaten, and a quantity of liquor consumed, the women were led in. Fondling and foreplay followed, and soon all kinds of sex acts were breaking out. There was no word in the Minx dialect for "orgy," but that best described these rather frequent Scream Hall celebrations.

Usually, they lasted well into the night.

No one saw the Li-Chi Chi women arrive.

They slipped into the city under the cover of darkness, entered the Scream Hall unseen, and skillfully mixed in with the females already being ravaged by the drunk Minx officers. Most of them were dressed in black robes, which were quickly removed to reveal naked, and apparently willing bodies. To the intoxicated Minx officers, the infusion of new skin was a vision of delight. They immediately set themselves upon the late arrivals, especially excited when word passed through the hall that the women were Chinese, the perfect nationality for the ultranationalist Viet Minx to rape, both physically and symbolically.

The Minx guards surrounding the Scream Hall did not take much notice then of the yelps of apparent delight coming from the building. After all, that's how the place got its name. The screams *were* louder than other occasions, though; and possibly a little less joyful in tone. And more than once they thought they could hear the sound of gunfire within the building. But there was no way that an enlisted man would ever dream of entering the sealed building, unless it was the gravest of emergencies, and possibly not even then.

The screams of the Minx officers therefore continued uninterrupted throughout the night.

Chapter Thirty-seven

One day later

The battleship appeared on the eastern horizon shortly after sunrise.

A strobe light was flashing from the top of its radar mast, sending a message in Morse Code to the port of Son Tay, announcing its arrival. The return signals, from a similar strobe at the top of the taller crane, were a little ragged but readable. The battleship was to proceed at its leisure into the dredged-up harbor at Son Tay.

The battleship waited offshore for an hour, finally coming in at the height of hightide. As usual, the Cult crewmen could see the hills which lined the outer harbor area were covered with the natives of Son Tay, waving and displaying little orange flags in honor of their arrival. The Cult members knew that some of these people would be coming with them when they sailed again.

Dealing humans was an ongoing business for the Cult and the bootlicking Minx officers at Son Tay usually rounded up fifty or so citizens for purchase by the battleship captain—at *very* low prices.

The battleship finally passed through the outer reaches of the harbor and, slowing down, began to move towards its specially designated berth. Up on the hill to the south of the battleship dock, was a line of about two dozen Son Tay residents, waving their orange flags. Crouched behind them were Hunter, Crunch, and the Z-Men.

"You say it only takes a half hour to dock that damn thing?" Hunter asked Crunch as he peeked up and over the rise to study the enormous Cult warship. "It looks like it should take a couple days at least."

"For whatever reason, these Cult bastards have got this sea-faring shit down pretty good," Crunch replied. "They should, they ain't got no more ground troops."

The remark elicited a surprised laugh from both Hunter and Crunch himself. It was true, most of the Cult's ground armies had either been killed or isolated on the Hawaiian island of Oahu during the last battle of the recent Pacific war.

Hunter checked his M-16; as usual it was filled with a full magazine of tracer rounds. He had a dozen more magazines in his backpack, they were wrapped around the Me-262's black box/C-5 autopilot coupled device. He hadn't let the gizmo out of his sight since leaving the plateau a week before.

It had been a strange seven days. They had floated down the Mekong in the captured Minx river craft, but he was more of a passenger during the voyage than anything else. It was the women of the Li-Chi Chi who had run the moving operation; they'd manned the weapons, they'd charted the course.

And they had massacred the Minx garrisons at Sik Buk and Ku Lung.

Hunter didn't like their methods; he, Crunch and the Z-men had taken a backseat to the Chinese women fighters' post-battle activities. But Hunter did, to some degree, understand why the women used the grisly tactics. This was war; troops on both sides were going to die, whether it be from a bullet, a bomb, an artillery shell—or a razor-sharp knife.

A village full of dead enemy soldiers sends a message to the deceased's high command: a battle has been lost. Carving up those dead soldiers, and leaving behind gruesome calling cards such as gutted stomachs and eyeball stew left another kind of message: a battle has been lost and your soldiers met a grim end. Don't let this happen to you.

From a psy-ops point of view, it was a very efficient way of installing fear into your opponent. The Minx in the Delta region were absolutely terrified of the rampaging women, and understandably so. And that fear would rise proportionately when the Minx command discovered what had happened at Son Tay, especially inside the Scream Hall.

But Hunter and the others expected to be long gone before that happened.

The plan called for the Li-Chi Chi to get aboard the battleship in the same way they got into the Scream Hall to slaughter Son Tay's officer corps: by showing skin and a lot of it.

Crunch's recon had told him that the Cult battleship's officers and crew usually partook in Son Tay's hookers while still on board ship—as if the dingy, seedy facilities in Son Tay were below their dignity. This worked fine for the Li-Chi Chi's strategy. Once aboard, the women fighters would lure small groups of unsuspecting Cult sailors into isolated parts of the ship and kill them, like their unlucky Minx comrades before them.

The first part of the plan went fine. The battleship docked as usual, and was met by an army of slave workers made up of Son Tay's citizens who were now indebted to the Li-Chi Chi for liquidating the hated Minx overlords. A sizable contingent of these citizens, now well-armed, were guarding a collection of noncom Minx soldiers at a make-shift prison just outside of the city.

There were also 100 of the Li-Chi Chi's most alluring

women waiting on the dock. No sooner had the huge warship been secured to the pier when the captain motioned for the women to come on board. They did so, a variety of weapons hidden beneath their sahrongs. Ten minutes passed, the still, morning air punctuated by single gunshots and the occasional scream of horror and pain.

Within fifteen minutes, the Li-Chi Chi's gruesome work was done. They were already throwing the dead bodies of their latest victims over the side. Waiting nearby, Hunter, Crunch, and the Z-men got the high sign to come aboard.

That's when they spotted the *other* battleship.

It was Hunter who sat it first. Something inside him started buzzing, and his eyes were searching the eastern horizon for five minutes before he detected the tell-tale plume of stack smoke coming from a second battlewagon.

Then Crunch and the Z-Men saw it too.

"Damn, now what?" Crunch asked. "These guys are going to want to float in here and get laid. We can't run that scam twice."

The original plan called for Hunter and the others to man the most important command positions aboard the first battleship—not surprisingly, the controls to the Cult vessel were user-friendly, and mostly run on automatic. Once the tide began going out, they were going ride with the current and head for the open sea.

But the appearance of the second ship changed everything. Hunter knew that between himself, Crunch, the Z-men and the *Li-Chi Chi* they could probably sail the ship, and possibly fire one of its gun turrets, which were also highly automated.

But getting into a full-blown sea battle with a well-drilled sister ship was way beyond their means.

As usual, everyone turned to Hunter in the moment of crisis. As usual, he had to make up a life-saving plan on the spot.

* * *

The captain of the second Cult battleship didn't think it unusual that *Ship Number 57* didn't return his ship-to-shore calls.

He was friendly rivals with the captain of the *Number 57*, and they had raced here to Son Tay from the Thai island of Suangmayaya, which they had left in absolute devastation after brutally liquidizing its inhabitants. *Ship 57* had won the race, and now, he had no doubt they were sampling the best of Son Tay's "comfort girls," leaving the also-rans and rejects for him and his crew. No wonder he wasn't answering the radio calls!

But that was OK with him—he'd simply beat him the next time.

The tide had turned by this time, so the captain ordered his engine room to increase power for their approach to Son Tay harbor. He prepared to leave the bridge to go to his quarters to get into his dress blacks when his executive officer suddenly called out: *"Fifty-seven is away!"*

The captain looked at his junior officer. "What are you saying?"

The officer pointed towards Son Tay harbor. "It's true, master."

The captain yanked the binoculars from the XO and trained them towards the port. He was astonished by what he saw. It *was* true: *Ship 57* was pulling away from the dock.

The captain tried to fight down a swelling panic. The only explanation as to why *57* would be pulling out of Son Tay was that enemy action was imminent. Could he have missed a radio call from Cult Supreme Command?

He screamed to his communications officer, but the man came back with all negatives. There had been no comminiques from Supreme Command; no messages at all from anybody in the past two hours.

The captain was dumbfounded. Why then was *57* moving?

The entire bridge crew was looking at him. He had to do something—but what?

He grabbed the ship's intercom and demanded the engine room provide him with full power. Then he turned to his gunnery officer and told him to load all nine of the battleship's enormous sixteen-inch guns.

As the crew reported to their battle stations, the captain kept his eyes glued on the mysterious movements of *Ship 57*. The other ship was moving very slowly, obviously riding out of the harbor on the draining tide. What possible reason would have his colleague acting so strangely, the captain wondered.

He thought he had his answer a moment later.

It was his navigator who first spotted it. A glow at the top of *Ship 57*'s mast, where the Morse Code strobe light was usually installed. He trained his binoculars on the mast and gasped. With weakened voice, he called out to the captain:

"Our . . . lady. Our . . . leader . . . is . . ."

The captain immediately focused his glasses on *Ship 57*'s mast and he too gasped.

"By the gods . . ." he whispered, his voice equal parts of terror and wonder. "Is it true?"

He never took the binoculars from his eyes. He was transfixed by the vision before him. Standing on the service railing of *Ship 57*'s communications mast, arms upraised, red hair flowing in the wind, was the Goddess Ala.

Within ten minutes the two ships were but 100 feet from each other.

The captain of the second battleship had hastily assembled his crew on the bow of the ship, some dressed in their present blues. The ship's string band was out on the bridge railing, plucking out a barely rehearsed tune. The captain himself was standing next to the band—his dress blacks whipping in the wind.

The Cult religious officers had taught them that to gaze upon the face of Goddess Ala meant eternal joy both on earth and in the afterlife, a jolt of everlasting grace that could only fall on those who believed. Already the captain could feel his eyes tingling, his heart was beating through his chest. He could not wait to die now!

And he would not have long to wait.

For no sooner had the ships pulled even with each other did the captain and his crew see the trio of sixteen-inch guns on *Ship 57*'s second turret suddenly de-elevate.

What was this? the captain wondered, *a salute?*

The next thing he saw was three enormous tongues of flame. In the blink between life and death, the captain actually saw the huge, one-ton, high-explosive shell hurtling out of the middle gun and coming right at him.

He immediately raised his eyes to Goddess Ala—she seemed to be looking down at him. Her face was an expression of confusion.

Then the shell hit.

The Captain's last thought was: *At least I'll be happy*. . . .

Chapter Thirty-eight

Da Nang Air Base

The ancient Willys jeep screeched to a stop next to the nearly deserted runway.

JT jumped from the passenger seat, long range binoculars up and ready.

Frost and Ben were waiting there for him, their own spyglasses in hand.

"Where the hell is it?" JT asked them excitedly. "Can you still see it?"

"He's still up there . . ." Ben replied, his binoculars pointing almost straight up. "He's looking down at us just like we're looking up at him."

JT soon got the object of their attention in his field of view. It was an airplane—a C-5, slowly circling the airbase at about 25,000 feet.

"No radio yet?" he asked Ben.

"Nope, he's sticking to the rules," was Ben's reply.

The rules were based on radio silence. The rules were to check out where the hell you were landing, no matter what the latest intelligence told you. The rules were never to let a C-5 fall into enemy hands.

"C'mon down, you idiots!" JT was screaming, as if the people in the huge airplane could hear him five miles up. *"C'mon down!"*

But it was almost as if they *did* hear him. For no sooner were the words out of JT's mouth when the big airplane began venting fuel and turning into a slow descent.

JT was plainly delighted. He grabbed the jeep's radio and began ordering the air base's receiving crews into action.

"Any idea who it is?" he asked, putting the spyglasses back to his eyes.

Ben shook his head no. "We'll know in about ten minutes," he said.

It was actually eight minutes, twenty seconds later when the C-5 touched down at Da Nang.

By that time, more than half of the base's personnel had lined up along the runway to take part in the momentous occasion. This was the first C-5 to land in Vietnam since the 1st American Airborne Expeditionary Fleet arrived nearly a month ago.

It was the *Triple-X*, a converted New York National Guard C-5, previously named "The Empire State." The plane was nearing completion as an armed, long-range air carrier when the First Expeditionary left Edwards. Its wings were now adorned with four air-to-air Sidewinders on each side, plus two ultralong range Phoenix antiaircraft missiles. There were also a dozen weapons blisters poking out of the huge fuselage in the nose, above the flight compartment, along the fuselage and in the tail. Each weapons' station had a M-61 rotary cannon barrel sticking out of it.

The *Triple-X* taxied in from the main runway, rolled up to its hard stand and jerked to a halt. Its engines whining down, its access doors began popping open.

JT and Ben were waiting to greet the pilot as soon as he stepped off the extended access ladder. His name was Dave Morell, better known as ZZ.

JT put the bear hug on him. "ZZ, you son of a bitch," he said. "Did you bring any beer?"

ZZ was all smiles. "How about a razor?" he replied.

It was true—all of the base personnel were in need of shave and a haircut.

ZZ shook hands with Ben. "When did you leave?" Ben asked him.

ZZ shook his head. "Noon yesterday," he replied. "Or was it two days ago, your time?"

"Who knows?" Ben told him.

"Who *cares?*" JT said. "Just tell us how many are behind you?"

ZZ shrugged. "You're asking the wrong person," he replied. "We were first in line to go. Probably three or four are at eighty percent; the rest are at sixty or so."

JT's face sagged. "Damn," he whispered. "They might not get here in time for the big party."

ZZ looked at him. "How big a party would that be?"

Ben rolled his eyes. *"Too* big," he said. "We'll explain it to you later."

"Yeh, later," JT said. "But first, what the hell are you carrying?"

ZZ shrugged again. "Well, you better see for yourselves."

They walked around to the rear of the airplane. Frost was already there.

"We could have used some troops, or heavy weapons," he said, pointing to the hold of the *Triple-X*. "But these might come in handy."

JT and Ben looked inside the cavernous hold of the C-5 and saw a very pretty sight. There four jet fighters stuffed into the wide maw; three were ultrasophisticated Football City Air Corps F-20 Tigersharks.

The fourth was Hunter's F-16XL.

* * *

A half hour later, an informal briefing was in full swing in JT's fortress office.

In attendance were Ben, Frost, Geraci, and ZZ's crew. Three cases of beer, carried in by *Triple-X*, sat in a bathtub full of ice cubes in the middle of the room.

ZZ's men were drinking quicker than the others. They were coming around to the realization that they'd dropped in on a very bad situation—the "big party," JT was talking about.

"In a nutshell, guys," JT was concluding, "we've got about ten divisions heading right for us. Down in Hue, our allies are facing about fifteen more; the New Zealanders in Cam Ram Bay are looking at about twelve and the people around Saigon about the same. And there are a lot of smaller cities along the way.

"We talking about heavy tank divisions, lots of infantry, lots of mobile artillery, lots of rocket teams. The dust-up at Khe Sanh was just the preview. A warm-up—and a *damn* small one. When this tidal wave hits, its going to take anything that's not tied down with it. Us included."

Another round of beer cans were popped open.

"Jones and the Edwards guys are working day and night to get more people and equipment over here," ZZ told them. "But you guys know what they face. Most of these ships were stripped down to the cores when we got them. *Sheet*—I'm flying with hydraulics pinched from a 707, and the brakes from a C-141. It's like trying to stop a Caddy with the brakes of a Toyota."

JT just shook his head. "I'm on that horn next satellite pass," he said. "Fuck the radio protocol. I'm telling them to send anything that can fly over here—tomorrow."

Frost took a long swig of beer. "It's still isn't going to be enough," he said. "Not even close."

He had a point. Though they were well-entrenched in hardened, defensive positions in the big cities, they had only eight divisions of democratic Vietnamese forces, four divisions of trusted mercenaries, and two divisions each of

Australian, New Zealander and Italian regular troops. That was about 190,000 troops facing almost 750,000.

"We got the edge in airpower," Frost went on. "We can probably take care of any MiGs they might throw at us. But on the ground, pound-for-pound, man-for-man, gun barrel-to-gun barrel, they can kick our asses."

"Are we stuck again?" ZZ asked not entirely rhetorically. "Have we landed into another quagmire?"

No one replied.

The silence was broken by a lieutenant from JT's air defense staff who burst into the room.

"Sir, excuse me—but we've got a big problem."

Ten minutes later they were all gathered around a long-range radio set.

Its operator, a sergeant, was conversing with an Australian unit based at a small coastal village named Buk Ha, which was about 120 miles south of Da Nang. Their urgent message was simple enough: A Cult battleship was steaming north at full power, heading right for Da Nang.

After a series of confirmations, and position checks, the Aussies signed off. JT's usual confident facial expression had just hit a new low.

"Damn, we don't hear a peep from these floating assholes for a month, and *now* they're coming our way?" he cursed.

"And they're like rats," Ben said, "where there's one, there's usually a pack of them."

Frost and Geraci were equally concerned. "They could sit out over the horizon and lob those blockbusters at us all day and all night," Geraci said, "And there ain't a whole lot we can do about it."

"There's only one thing we *can* do about it," Frost said. "But it will never be enough."

"We've got to try it anyway," JT said. He turned to ZZ

and his men. "How long will it take to get those F-20s in flying condition?"

ZZ thought a moment. "Just got to gas 'em," he replied. "Fuse whatever the hell you're going to use. An hour, hour and a half, tops."

JT grit his teeth; he was definitely not enjoying playing leader now. "Let's do it in forty-five," he said.

Chapter Thirty-nine

The sensation hit him so hard, so violently, Hunter's head began to spin.

"What the hell . . ." he gasped. "What the hell is going on?"

He was sitting with Crunch and the Z-Men on the bridge of the captured Cult battleship, trying to find a friendly radio frequency on the mishmash of cheaply made, poorly maintained Japanese-manufactured communications equipment.

He was dizzy. He could hardly breathe. His body was shaking visibly and he couldn't control it.

Crunch looked at him. "Jessuzz, Hawk," he said urgently. "Are you OK?"

Hunter could only shake his head. "I don't know," he answered truthfully. "I'm not sure."

He tried to get to his feet, but almost fell backwards. He steeled himself and stood ramrod straight, his knees just begging to buckle under him. "I . . . I've never felt like this before," he mumbled.

He closed his eyes and did a quick self-diagnosis. The source of his malady was coming from deep down within. It felt like every element which provided him his extraordinary psychic powers were short-circuiting like crazy. He was in organic overload.

But for what reason?

It had been another strange day. After leaving the other Cult battleship in flames off Son Tay, they'd opened up the battleship's computer-controlled engines to full steam, and plowed the 450 miles up the Vietnamese coast in just under 24 hours. Now they were but an hour away from Da Nang.

Hunter was out on the bridge walkway in a flash, his eyes glued to the northern horizon. Then it hit him.

"I don't believe this," he whispered in amazement.

At that moment, Timmy the Z-man, who had been pressed into service as the battleship's radar officer, let out a cry.

"I've got something coming right at us," he yelled. "Fast and low! Out of the north."

Crunch hit the general quarters alarm and was immediately scanning the northern horizon. "How many?" he yelled back.

"Four," Hunter replied from the walkway. As always he'd "felt" the incoming aircraft before they were picked up on radar.

No sooner had he said it, when four dots appeared on the horizon. They were about twelve miles off the starboard bow, coming in at full military power no more than 500 feet off the deck.

"Bloody—are they MiGs?" Terry asked.

Hunter never took his eyes off the four airplanes. "They're definitely *not* MiGs," he replied quickly.

"Well, whoever they are, they're in attack formation," Crunch yelled.

He was quickly on the ship's intercom, urging all of the Li-Chi Chi to take cover below. Timmy and Terry were heading for the nearest AA-gun, a Bofors twin-barrel, but Hunter stopped them in mid-stride.

"They might shoot at us," he said, "but we can't shoot at them."

The New Zealanders were totally confused by now. "But, Hawk . . ."

Hunter looked them straight in the eye. "Better get below guys," he said firmly.

They stared at him for a moment, but then did as he suggested. Now it was just Hunter out on the railing, staring up at the rapidly oncoming airplanes.

"I still don't believe it," he whispered.

It had been so long since Ben flew anything fast he wasn't sure just where everything was.

The F-20 Tigershark was a rare and powerful flying machine, a high-tech, souped-up version of the F-5, itself a highly regarded, mass-produced jet fighter. These Football City Air Corps variants were armed with double 30-mm cannons, and capabilities to carry everything from a smart weapon to a dumb bomb. At that moment, Ben was carrying a Harpoon antiship missile, as was Frost's aircraft just off his left wing. ZZ Morell's aircraft, off his right wing, was lugging a Shrike antiradar weapon.

These were impressive weapons, but they were not nearly enough. The thick plating of the battleship would prevent wide damage by a Harpoon strike, and even a pair of good hits would prove nonfatal. So too the Shrike alone could not disable the battlewagon.

No, Ben knew their only chance was to hit the Cult battleship in the only place it would hurt: on the bridge. If they killed the commanders, then possibly the surviving crew would be leaderless to the point of calling off what was probably going to be a bombardment of Da Nang.

At ten miles out, he began checking the arming mechanism on his Harpoon. Everything came back green. Frost and ZZ reported the same.

"OK, me and Frostie first," he said. "Everyone else in back-up."

Ben kicked his Tigershark into afterburner and roared out in front. He switched on his cannons and fired a quick test burst. They were working perfectly.

Now it was time to concentrate on the target. He lined up the nose of the F-20 with the bow of the huge battle-ship. He planned to release the Harpoon at just one mile out, bank slightly to the right and then lay a double can-non burst along the entire superstructure of the enemy ship. Who knows? he might just get lucky and pick off an important person or two.

Six miles out Ben reduced his speed slightly and pre-pared to launch the Harpoon. He was surprised the battle-ship wasn't taking any evasive action. They had to have spotted them by now, yet there was no AA fire, no SAMs locking on to him.

No matter, Ben thought, let them make it easy for us.

At five miles out, the Harpoon was ready to go. His right hand was fingering the cannon trigger; his left was on the throttle, his thumb resting on the Harpoon throw-switch. Still the battleship was steaming right at them.

Four miles out, Ben did one last check of his systems. Everything was still ten-up. He did a final check with Frost and ZZ, they were right-on too. Still, Ben couldn't ignore the strange feeling that was rising up in his stomach.

At three miles out, he was feeling extremely anxious. Something was very wrong here—but he had no choice but to go through with the bomb run.

Two miles out. Ben could see the battleship clearly now through the haze. Still no AA. No SAM lock-ons. Why are they making it so easy?

One mile. His thumb moved to the Harpoon release. *Do it!* one side of his brain was telling him. *Don't do it!* screamed the other.

What the hell was going on?

He hesitated. Suddenly his eyes were focused on the

railing which surrounded the battleship's bridge. There was a lone figure standing on the walkway, his hand raised, not waving, simply raised. Ben stared hard at this figure, looming bigger within his sights by the second. Who would be crazy enough to do such a thing?

Then it hit him.

"Pull up! Pull up! Pull up!" he screamed into his lip mic, at the same time yanking back on the F-20's controls and putting the supersonic fighter into an inverted, full-afterburner climb.

He anxiously looked behind him. Frost had heard his warning and was veering off his missile run. ZZ wavered for a moment, but then he too held his weapon and zoomed off to the west.

Ben let out a long sigh of relief.

That's when he saw JT roaring in on the battleship.

His partner had been trailing the Tigersharks by five miles or so, his role in the bombing run to inflict as much damage as possible with cannon and also do a quick poststrike assessment. That was just about all he could handle. He was flying the F-16XL, and though he was a top-notch pilot, there were so many advanced systems inside the rocketlike, futuristic jet, just keeping it level and pushing the cannon trigger was chore.

Now Ben was screaming at him like there was no tomorrow, but typically, JT wasn't listening to his radio.

"Jesuzz, JT, pull up!" Ben was screaming, fearful he was about to see a disaster right before his eyes. *"That's Hawk down there!"*

It was almost like he willed it. Because suddenly, the red, white and blue delta-wing fighter jerked up and out of its strafing run. Ben watched as the Cranked Arrow turned over once, and then buzzed the ship from stern to bow.

Ben let out a second longer breath of relief.

"Another one for the memoirs," he said.

Chapter Forty

The battleship pulled into Da Nang harbor about two hours later.

A company of Omani Marines immediately went aboard and took up positions to the captured battlewagon. The Omanis were trained seamen, having operated in the Persian Gulf for years. Of all the mercenary units at Da Nang, they were deemed the best suited to operate the highly automated warship.

JT, Ben and Frost were waiting at the pier when Hunter and Crunch motored in. It was a happy reunion between Crunch and the others; they had feared that he was long dead. However, Hunter's usually pleasant demeanor was not in evidence. Instead he looked somewhat bewildered.

"Close call out there, eh, Hawk?" JT asked him after an attempt at a hearty handshake.

"I don't believe you actually did it," Hunter replied.

"Believe what?" JT replied with a wiseass grin. "Pulled up at the last moment? Sent an air strike against my old buddy, the Wingman?"

Hunter was almost beyond words. "I just can't believe it," he said again.

Now Frost, Ben and Crunch had taken notice.

"Believe what?" Ben asked him.

Hunter looked at them, shook his head, and pointed at

330

JT. "He flew my airplane. He almost shot my ass off—*with my own airplane.*"

The other burst out laughing. "The next thing you know, he'll be driving your Corvette," Ben told him.

JT didn't know what to do, what to think. It never dawned on him that no one had ever flown Hunter's souped-up plane before. "It handled great, Hawk," was all he could say.

Hunter just shook his head again. His sudden discomfit on the battleship had been caused by the approach of his own plane. Whereas he always knew when aircraft were coming in, his internal, organic radar had responded amazingly when it was the F-16XL involved. It was slightly unnerving to think that his psyche was so tied up with his airplane, that it would come close to making him suddenly ill when something was amiss. It was just another strange example of how melded he was with the Cranked Arrow.

At that moment several boatloads of Li-Chi Chi arrived at the pier. JT, Ben and Frost were all eyes as the women fighters climbed out of the service boats and onto the dock, their rifles and bandolier belts contrasting with their open-shirt, bosomly uniform tops.

"What the hell do we have here?" JT asked, his eyes almost popping their sockets. "Entertainment?"

Crunch opened his mouth, to begin to explain, but Hunter tugged him at the last minute. The Wingman had just arrived at the proper punishment for JT for having the *chutzpah* to fly the XL.

"They're *very* entertaining ladies," he told JT, who was succumbing to hormone overload. "Shy, though."

JT was rubbing his hands together like a teenager in a liquor store. "I'll take care of that," he declared as two more boatloads of the Chinese women fighters arrived.

"I'm sure you will," Hunter said with a wink.

Chapter Forty-one

24 hours later

Night had fallen on Da Nang.

The brutal heat of the day let up—but only slightly. A brief thunderstorm, nowhere near the intensity of the now-departed monsoons, had turned the air first cool, then muggy. The lights within the barricaded city were dimming considerably as hundreds of fans and even a few air conditioners were turned on to maximum power.

Hunter had walked the half mile from Da Nang air base to the walled city alone. He'd just spent the last twenty-four hours in one of the billets at the base, sleeping, eating, and then sleeping again. Such idle time was rare for him—but he was smart enough to take advantage of the situation. He knew he wouldn't have a chance of enjoying such luxuries as sleep and food again for a long, long, time.

His life had been the usual surrealistic exercise in the past few weeks, from the green and brown claustrophobic hell of Khe Sanh to the deceptive, eerie beauty of the Mekong Delta, and now in what was probably one of a handful of urban settings left in a country owned by jungles, swamps, paddies and mountains.

He felt like a foreigner here. The air itself was too thick for him, a very white man from a very white world. He might as well have been on another planet, a feeling he knew he shared with the majority of the hundreds of thousands of American troops who came here in 1960s and early 1970s.

What was the point back then? What was the point now? There was certainly a lot of dirty politics involved in that "police action," the result being the dreaded military-industrial complex looking on Southeast Asia as an open marketplace for testing and selling big-ticket weapons. Hunter abhorred the notion of sending Americans to die just so some fat-cat weapons manufacturer could see a new way to kill someone of the Asian race. He abhorred what the Presidents of those days did, to the people of America, to the people of Southeast Asia. And for what?

When it came down to it, for nothing.

So as he walked the dusty road from the base to the city, he looked out over the dried up paddies and weedy fields. Suddenly he imagined that he could see ghosts—not one, like the spirit that had haunted him back at Khe Sanh, but thousands, tens of thousands, rising up, uniforms tattered, their hands dirty, their faces bloody. American faces, all with the same expression: *Why?*

Ghosts, Hunter thought drearily, imagining he could feel the earth moving beneath his feet. *I'm walking in a land of ghosts.*

He reached the walled city ten minutes later, and passed through the heavily guarded main doors.

The city itself had a beauty of its own. There was still evidence of French architecture, as well as sixties-style American buildings. The garish bar lights and the neon come-ons of the bordellos made the place look a little like New Orleans. Except much hotter.

As usual, the streets were filled with troops. Different uniforms, different faces, everywhere. What was it about this place? What drew men from all over the world to fight here? *What drove men to become ghosts in this, the most foreign of places?*

He just didn't know.

He reached the Alamolike palace and passed by the three rings of sentries guarding the place. Inside looked like a Middle East bazaar. There were soldiers, merchants, liquor dealers, souvenir hawkers, and of course, hookers everywhere. He walked through the Great Hall and into the immense bar. JT, Frost, and Ben were sitting at a corner table; they waved him over.

Hunter sat down and studied the bottle of no-name booze on the table.

"They're selling Chivas out in the hallway and you guys are drinking this crap?" he chided them.

JT's ever-present grin grew even wider. "When is he going to learn?" he asked the other two. "You'd make a lousy businessman."

Hunter turned to Frost, usually the voice of reason in times like this. "Translate, please?"

Frost picked up the bottle. "It's Chivas in here," he explained, "and rotgut out there."

Hunter sniffed the open bottle; sure enough it was the good stuff. He poured himself a glass and took a slug.

"Heard a lot of Minx artillery up in the hills on the way down," he told the others. "Big stuff. Maybe 155s."

JT sipped his drink and shook his head. "They're just showing off, the dickheads," he said bitterly. "They've got two hundred thousand guys sitting in the jungle, with all their stuff bottled up underground, and yet they feel they have to shoot some of the big guns, just to let us know they're out there."

"In the old days, they'd send a company of Marines up there to take out those big guns," Hunter observed.

"Exactly," JT replied. "And ten jarheads would wind up in body bags—and for what? To take out one piece of artillery? That's insanity and it ain't going to happen here."

Hunter sipped his drink again. This informal meeting

was arranged so JT and the others could brief Hunter on their plans to thwart the impending attack on Da Nang. He was curious, to say the least.

"So," he asked his old friends. "How *are* you proposing we do this?"

JT leaned in over the table, and lowered his voice a notch. "I'll start by telling you what we *ain't* going to do," he began. "We're not falling for any of their shithead tricks. They live out in that jungle, and we'd be like rats in the water out there. No—we got what they want, right here.

"So that means no beyond-the-perimeter patrolling. No search and destroy crap. No preemptive strikes —hell, they got everything underground anyway, we'd just be wasting our fuel, our ordnance, not to mention risking our lives."

Hunter poured himself another drink. This was JT's show—and he liked what he heard so far. For once the shoe *was* on the other foot. The Minx might be good jungle fighters, but their present target was the very urban city of Da Nang and the wide-open spaces of the nearby air base. If they intended to take the city as part of the country-wide Minx offensive, they would have to come and get it.

JT produced a map from his sleeve pocket and unfolded it on the sticky table. It showed a three-dimensional view of Da Nang city, the airbase and the enemy-held jungle beyond the mutual perimeter.

"I don't have to tell you that we're outnumbered almost six-to-one," JT began. "There's no way we're going to win by standing and fighting it out with them. That's exactly what they want us to do.

"But instead, what if we give these guys a swift kick in the balls, something that will knock them cold right here—who knows what will happen in the rest of the country?"

Hunter just shrugged. "They're fairly predictable by never being very *un*predictable," he said. "If they get hit with something big time from out of left field, it could re-verberate, I suppose."

"Our thinking exactly," JT smiled.

He took the next ten minutes explaining his plan, the initial parts of which had been put into place over the past few weeks. Frequently indicating various points on the map, JT concentrated on the rather unique dual-defense plans for both the city and the air base. As it turned out, the arrival of Hunter, Crunch, and the battleship proved very fortuitous, it was "the last piece in the puzzle," JT said.

Like past United American operations against over-whelming foes, the emphasis of JT's plan was on survival, cunning, and, most important, the protection of innocents.

But it also called for one enormous sacrifice.

Hunter had JT go over the specifics twice more, just to make sure he'd gotten it all straight. Once again, all of the United American principles would have key parts to play. Once again, Geraci's men would be called on to complete a Herculian task in a short amount of time. Strangest of all was Crunch's role. In many ways it would be the most difficult.

Hunter considered the whole strategy for a few minutes.

Finally, he spoke. "It's innovative, I'll give you that," he told his old friend. "Needs split-second timing. And a lot of busting ass by Geraci's guys. But if it works . . ."

JT nodded grimly. "It's got to work, Hawk," he said. "If it doesn't, well . . ."

His voice trailed off.

Hunter studied his old friend for a moment. Suddenly JT looked older than his years. He was learning very quickly that being in command was usually an unenviable task. However, he had come up with an innovative, if bizarre plan against the Minx, one which would not only check them in Da Nang, but also might send shock waves right through the rest of the entire Minx corps. If it worked, it would be considered a stroke of military genius.

But if it failed . . .

"So what do you want me to do, boss?" Hunter finally asked JT.

JT's smile returned. "You do what we do," he replied. "Get in the air as soon as the balloon goes up and keep those bastards off the base. As for Da Nang city, well, again, it will really be up to the 104th to pull off their end as quickly as possible. Any delays and the bad guys will chop us all up into little pieces."

Hunter poured out another round of drinks.

"So when the shooting *does* start, how do you think it will begin?" Hunter asked.

JT just shrugged. "It will begin when all those assholes out there finally get paid from their blowboys in Hanoi," he declared. "Then they'll just launch a traditional attack. Mortars and big guns first. Katy rockets too. Then comes the infantry. They might feint here, feint there, but, in the end it will be two full-scale frontal attacks. One on the base, and a bigger one here. My guess is they'll want to capture the city first and then work on the base."

"We better hope they do," Hunter said, consulting the map again.

"Well, that's why Geraci's guys are working night and day," JT replied. "That's why we all have to be ready, every minute of every day. Ready for that first mortar round to drop. When that happens, we've got to go right down the line, doing the right things, at the right time. If we do, we might get lucky and be golden. If we don't? Well . . ."

Once again his voice trailed off.

"Don't worry," Hunter told him. "We'll do it right."

Chapter Forty-two

The next morning

The base at Da Nang was a whole new experience for the New Zealanders, Timmy and Terry.

They'd spent most of their lives rather isolated in Auckland, and during their military service, fighting in the bush in Malaysia, on Borneo, the swamps of Sumatra, and now, Vietnam.

They'd never been so close to really high-tech weaponry—NightScopes and choppers were about as advanced technology as they had seen. So they were very wide-eyed walking along the flight line at the base. They were especially amazed at the weaponry formerly installed on *Nozo* and *Bozo*, weapons now part of the defense of the base.

The LARS was the centerpiece of this long range defense. The massive rocket launcher was anchored at the end of Da Nang's main runway, its tubes loaded, a crew on duty around the clock. Although the base and Da Nang city itself were ringed with literally hundreds of machine guns and light-to-heavy artillery, the LARS would be the most important weapon when the inevitable Minx attack finally came. It could unleash an unholy barrage of thirty-six high-explosive rockets either individually or in staggered fashion at half second intervals. Each one of these rockets could carry a forty-pound charge an astounding distance of fifteen miles and hit just about any target right on the dime.

While the Z-men were amazed at the sheer brutal power of the LARS, they were also fascinated with the line of *Bozo*'s Gatling guns which now protected the west flank of the base. This was the most likely direction from which the Minx would come, and when they did, they would be met by these six awesome weapons, each capable of firing sixty rounds *a second*.

The Z-men contemplated the weapons and then the long stretch of flat ground and dried-up rice paddie over which the Minx would have to traverse when attacking the base.

"It will be a killing field," Terry said grimly. "Bloody better them than us."

They continued their informal tour around the base perimeter passing a *melange* of weaponry—from M-48 heavy tank emplacements, to Milan anti-tank positions, 155-mm howitzer pens to 20-mm antiaircraft gun mounts with their barrels cranked all the way down to level.

"Only madmen would do a frontal on all this stuff," Timmy said as they walked back toward the main runways. "How much can they be paying them to face all this stuff?"

"Not nearly enough," Terry replied.

They reached the aircraft parking area, and once again their eyes went wide at the sight of the rather exotic weaponry on hand.

The three Football City Special Forces C-5s were there, parked wingtip-to-wingtip, their red-and-blue, sports-logo-style striping gleaming in the hot sun. The Rangers were doing routine maintenance on their quick response vehicles which were lined up beside the huge C-5s. The most impressive of these were the FV101 Scorpion tracked vehicles. They looked like miniature tanks, complete with

76-mm gun turret, and two 7.62 machine guns, as well as various antitank or medium range rocket systems.

The Rangers however had souped up the engines to these Scorpions, and added everything from NightScope capability, to laser targeting. Now the minitanks could travel upward of 70 mph, while firing, even at night. When carrying a crew of six (double the normal complement) and massed for attack in number of twenty or more, the Scorpions could wreak havoc with any large attacking force, their capability to hit, run, hit and run again bordering on mind-boggling.

The Z-men passed the trio of Football planes and ambled up to the *Triple-X*. The crew was on break, and the airplane empty. The New Zealanders wandered into the huge cargo hold and out the back of the plane.

"How does it get itself up in the air?" Terry wondered.

"It must be like flying a building or two," Timmy nodded in agreement.

They moved on to the trio of F-20 Tigersharks. Though they'd been in action with jets providing air support, the Z-men had never seen anything like the sleek, sexy F-20s.

Terry put the tip of his finger on the end of the first jet's stiletto-like nose.

"It's bloody sharp," he cursed. "I swear I could cut me finger on it."

Timmy tentatively fingered the needle-nose and actually did nick his pinky. "Right, you could run a man through with that," he declared.

They passed the three jets and finally came upon Hunter's F-16XL. Of all the weapons they'd seen in the walk, this one was by far the most impressive.

"Look at it, will you?" Terry was near-shouting. "It looks like it's from bleeding out of space."

"It's like sci-fi on the old telly," Timmy agreed. "It's like Kirk and Spock . . ."

Hunter was in the cockpit, checking his avionics package for any damage JT might have caused. He saw the New

Zealanders approaching and climbed down to meet the pair.

"Never seen anything like this one, Hawk," Terry said. "Had a bunch of A-4s helping us out down in Borneo once. They were downright stuffy compared to this."

Hunter ran his hand along the XL's sleek fuselage.

"The A-4 is a good airplane," he said. "Built for something a little different than this one though."

"How did you get it?" Timmy asked. "Did you buy it? Build it from scratch?"

Hunter had to stop and think about it for a moment. He's always considered the F-16 *his* airplane. But did he really own it? The original frame was from his old Thunderbird demonstrator. He'd changed everything out from that long ago, and had help from a team of aerodynamics experts in converting it from a regular F-16 to the XL Cranked Arrow configuration. But was the airplane actually his? Or was it rightly owned by the government?

"I guess it's mine by reverse eminent domain," he finally answered. "I've been flying it for so long, I can't imagine not having it."

"Ah, you love it then," Terry said with a tooth-gapped smile. "Like a race driver likes 'is car. Or a hunter likes 'is gun."

Hunter smiled and nodded. He'd never really thought of it in that way before, but he *did* love the airplane.

"Like a woman," Timmy said. "Break your heart, and you go crawling back."

"Amen," Hunter replied.

The Z-men stayed and chatted for another few minutes. Hunter liked them both—it seemed as if he'd known them for years, and not simply a couple weeks. He knew they were virtually fearless, yet he'd never met anyone as down to earth as they were. Had they not been mercenaries, they would probably have been farmers or cattlemen. They were Hunter's kind of people, he could talk with them for hours.

They made plans to meet at JT's palace bar in an hour for a bottle of beer, and then the two New Zealanders ambled on, their baggy camouflage uniforms whipping in the hot wind, their weapons slung over their shoulders like fishing poles.

"Good guys," Hunter thought, returning to avionics package.

Suddenly he felt the hair on the back of his head go straight up. He froze, trying to ascertain from his psyche what was wrong.

Then he heard it.

The distinct sound of a mortar tube pop, echoing from the jungle beyond the end of the runway. He heard the whine and then the screech as the mortar shell rocketed out of its trajectory and came streaking back down. His computerlike brain was able to input the changes in the acoustics of the shell and tell him it was going to come crashing down very close by.

He jumped off the XL and ran to the front of the airplane. The screech was getting louder. He knew it was going to hit in about three seconds, and approximately forty feet away.

"Damn, no . . ." he screamed.

The huge mortar shell came down exactly three seconds later, exploding just beyond a line of ancient Huey choppers. As everyone around him was running away from the blast, heading for cover, Hunter was running full tilt towards the impact point.

When he finally got there, his worst fears had come true. There was a huge crater in the middle of the tarmac, still smoking, with sparks popping out.

Beside the smoldering hole, riddled and bleeding beyond recognition, were the bodies of Timmy and Terry.

Chapter Forty-three

Yet another war for Vietnam had begun.

With the opening round, the base at Da Nang came under a massive mortar and rocket bombardment. There were suddenly fires everywhere; smoke was obscuring the midday sun. Alarms bells and sirens were ringing; people were scrambling to the system of hardened shelters. Long range artillery was booming all over, the chatter of gunfire filled the air.

And in amongst it all, the angry sound of a jet engine screeching to life.

Not two minutes after the firing had commenced, Hunter's F-16XL was screaming down the main runway at Da Nang. Lifting off with a burst of power, he pulled the futuristic fighter back up on its tail, booted in the afterburner and shot straight up until he was out of sight.

He was loaded for bear. There were four points along the bottom of each of his wings, and each held some kind of exotic weapon.

On his right side inner he'd attached one KMU-351 Paveway smart bomb; next to it was a Durandal runway buster bomb. Third over on the right was an AGM-65A Maverick; beside it was a Mk-83 GP 1000-pound bomb. The tip of the wing held one of his two Sidewinder air-to-air missiles.

On the left side he had stacked from the inside out, a

CBU-528 bomblet dispenser, a larger CBU Rockeye dispenser carrying napalm globets, a Mk-117 750-pound GP bomb and a Mk 82 Snakeye bomb.

He was also packing a full house of ammo for his four M-61 nose cannons.

He screeched the F-16XL up to 15,000 feet in under ten seconds and then slowly flipped the fighter over. The war had started just as JT said it would—without warning, by mortar and rocket attack, as a prelude to a massive ground assault. Just as he was taxiing out for takeoff he heard the Da Nang tower confirm that fighting had also broken out down in Cam Rahn Bay, at Hue, at Bien Hoa, at Nha Trang, and inside New Saigon. He knew there were at least a dozen more coastal cities that were also probably under attack and had yet to report in. Just as advertised, the Viet Minx had paid of all their soldiers and were now trying to take all of Vietnam in a single bloody offensive— only the various mercenary armies and a small Vietnamese defense corps stood in their way. Caught in the middle were about two million Vietnamese citizens, who once again, had to stand by and watch others determine the fate of their country.

Hunter put the XL into a tight orbit and began studying the ground below. Just the smoke and flame spots alone gave away the enemy's previously hidden mortar positions; some of them were very near the wire at the Da Nang airbase, others as far as a half mile away from the perimeter. Behind the mortars were the 140-mm and 155-mm artillery and the Katuysha rocket emplacements. And somewhere in between, Hunter knew, was a huge enemy ground assault, poised for launch.

He was still shaking with rage over the deaths of the Z-Men. It was savagely ironic that the first shot of the war would kill the two happy-go-lucky New Zealanders, two soldiers who were far away from home, fighting on a foreign soil just so others they didn't know could remain free. Hunter had seen a lot of combat—and a lot of death.

There was only one way to deal with it: try to forget it. But he knew it would be some time before he would lose the memory of the two bodies of Terry and Timmy, perforated by Minx mortar fragments.

One of the cardinal sins of combat was to turn the fight personal; when a soldier's emotion got in the way, it opened up all kinds of possibilities for mistakes—and mistakes usually meant either getting very hurt or getting very dead.

But Hunter had stopped playing by the rules years ago, way back in the days of ZAP, when he was fighting the likes of the Mid-Aks and the Family. It got very personal way back then, and many times since, he'd followed his nose, not his brain.

Today would be no different.

The mortar that hit Timmy and Terry had been a heavy-duty job, maybe a dime-and-a-half or bigger. Judging by the way he heard it pop and how it came down, Hunter figured it was located about 1,000 meters beyond the edge of the main runway, and maybe 100 meters to the south. Sure enough, when he keyed his ground mapping radar on those coordinates, he could clearly see a staccato line of heat sources, the unmistakable glow of mortars being launched. He locked the image into the weapons control computer and then turned the XL over.

He was instantly into a screaming dive, booting in the afterburner at a heart-stopping 5,500 feet, cracking the sound barrier and issuing a mechanical scream that he was sure could be heard for miles. That was the whole idea—he *wanted* these bastards to know he was coming.

On the way down he saw that the jungles surrounding Da Nang were just lousy with Minx—big guns, tanks, mobile artillery, troops and mortars everywhere. In an instant he saw why it would have been unwise to launch preemptive strikes on this gang—the weapons and men had been so solidly dug in and hidden, it *would* have been a waste of precious ammunition and ordnance.

Beside, the only way to kill rats was to wait until they came out into the light.

He was down to 1,500 feet now and below he could see the hundred or so Minx mortar men scatter in panic at his supersonic approach. That was fine with him—he was giving them the opportunity Timmy and Terry never had, a chance to contemplate life before they lost it.

He finally pulled up at 400 feet, applying his airbrakes even as he began to level off. He lined up the long string of heavy mortars concealed on a ridge a few football fields away from the end of the main runway and quickly called up his weapons available readout screen. He touched the symbol for the CBU Rockeye dispenser, the one carrying 100 napalm globets.

The decision was thus made: Death by jellied fire would be the retribution for the killing of his New Zealander friends.

His bomb release light flashing like crazy, Hunter eased back on the throttles and squeezed the weapons' lever. Instantly he felt the right wing buck a little as the big dispenser dropped off and began its preguided path down to the mortar emplacements. Once the weapon computer checked off the Rockeye as dead on path, Hunter banked hard to the right, and then went into a screaming 180.

The Rockeye hit just as he was coming around. He saw it dispense inside two seconds, spraying the area with 100 baseball-sized, compressed napalm bomblets. The effect was like a wave of blue flame, washing over the line of heavy mortars. When the wave broke, it turned first red, then yellow, then bright, bright orange. He could see figures running through the inferno, clothes, skin, hair on fire—but his heart was hardened to all this by now.

When the smoke cleared, there was nothing left. No trees, no shrubs, no mortars. No Minx.

"Fuck you guys," Hunter muttered. "Hope you cashed your checks."

Beyond the now-scorched mortar line was a nest of

144-mm long-range artillery pieces. Like years before, this gun was favorite of the Vietnamese aggressors. The Minx had set up six guns in a rough semicircle, for the best in concentrated fire. It also made for a perfect aerial target—perfect for Hunter's 1000-pound GP bomb.

Unlike the mortar teams, the artillery men didn't hear him coming. Whether it was the booming of their guns, or possibly earplugs, they didn't see the F-16XL until it was almost on top of them. A glint of silver falling from the delta wing airplane was the last thing many of them ever saw. The huge bomb hit with such an impact that the concussion alone bent the barrels of two of the guns. The other four were simply vaporized along with their crews.

A quick twist to the left and Hunter found a traffic jam of enemy 150-mm Koksan mobile guns. Again, in the quest for concentrated fire, the Minx had typically jammed the mobile weapons bumper-to-bumper.

"Idiots," Hunter muttered, calling up the weapons available screen on his main computer. He touched the panel for the 750-pound Mk117 GP bomb, and then directed his laser sighting to the grille of the very first mobile battery.

A squeeze of the weapons release lever and the seven-five was on its way. Hunter pulled up and out—he didn't even see the bomb hit. He didn't have to. He knew the big 750 would not only destroy the first two mobile guns completely, but also the impact and exploding ammunition would kill the other four. He simply didn't have time to hang around and watch the fire works.

He banked hard right and went down to tree top level. The Minx had gathered their forces on the flank of Da Nang in a triangular fashion; the rear area being at the slimmest point. Though there were few weapons firing back here, experience told him that any high ground in the area was probably being used for observation and gun targeting.

Sure enough, as he passed over a small stream which marked the rear areas, he spotted a hill approximately a klick to the east. It looked like nothing more than a pile of rocks, and was about 700 feet high.

On top was a Minx chopper with a mobile radio unit.

He didn't hesitate a second. He simply swooped over the hill top his four cannons blazing, ripping into the radio set and Minx soldiers attending it. All it took was two passes. After that, everything on top of the rockpile—both human and electronic—was dead.

He twisted the XL over on its left wing and streaked back to the edge of the base's western defense perimeter. The airfield was still being peppered with mortar rounds and Katy rockets, but the defense forces had swung into action. He could see the Football City Special Forces Scorpions pinging around the no man's land separating the runway from the jungle, firing wide, interlocking barrages from their cannon and turret guns, and then dashing off to another position and repeating the process again. It was a tactic for which there was little defense; any Minx soldier or weapon caught in their cross fire was simply ripped to shreds.

The artillery units were also up and firing, their various sized guns working from behind the thick concrete barriers. Passing over the edge of the main runway, he could see the long streams of blue smoke which unmistakably marked the use of the late, great *Bozo*'s Gatling guns. Already the jungle at the end of the runway had been cut down as if a giant scythe had slashed through it. Actually, it was the combined fire of the Gatlings mowing down every tree, vine, shrub and Minx soldier within the quarter mile killing zone.

"Environmentally safe defoliation," Hunter thought. "Should have used it last time."

He banked back over the runway just in time to see the trio of Tigersharks moving out of the bunkers and onto the taxiway. His initial mission was now fairly complete. The Minx guns nearest to the runway had been silenced, at least long enough for the F-20s to take off.

He circled protectively overhead as the Tigersharks quickly edged out onto the runway and as one, lifted off in a burst of afterburner power. He immediately got on the radio with JT, who then patched him through to Ben and Frost. They quickly decided that the Sharks would go after targets immediately around the base perimeter.

Hunter meanwhile would head towards Da Nang city itself.

Chapter Forty-four

Da Nang City

Geraci was sleeping when the attack finally came.

He'd been up for thirty-six hours, putting the finishing touches on the 104th's end of JT's plan, a project which had come to be known as the "Jersey Tunnel."

It was a mission which dwarfed all their other accomplishments. By comparison, the assembly of *Bozo 2* at Khe Sanh was puny, a walk in the park. Working in shifts, the combat engineers had literally turned the Earth over, moving tons of rocks, sand and soil. And Geraci and his officers—Matus, Cerbasi, McCaffrey, and Palma—had stayed awake for most of the two weeks of the project, sleeping only when rain prevented work from continuing or when they were on the verge of collapse.

In the end, the 104th had never worked so hard to accomplish so much, in such a short amount of time. As it turned out, they'd finished just in time. When the final emplacements were poured, and all of the defensive obstacles in place, Geraci finally ordered his officers and staff to stand down—and get some sleep.

The Minx attacked just two hours later.

The 104th had bivouacked in the second floor of JT's Defense Headquarters, using the Palace's rather ornate ballroom as their temporary housing and it was here that Geraci retired to after standing down early that morning.

His first recollection that something was happening was waking up to a huge *bang!* and looking out the ballroom's window and seeing a Katyusha rocket go by. A second later there was an even louder explosion, one which shook the Palace right down to its sandy foundations. By the time he was up and into his combat gear, there were some dozens explosions going off all around the place—it seemed like a never-ending earthquake.

He finally made it to the grand hallway and was relieved to see the rest of his men and staff streaming down the stairs and out of the building. Tellingly, some of JT's men were grabbing the liquor bottles off the shelves of the palace bar and hastily packing them in bubble-filled rubber crates.

"Freaking fly-boys are always thinking," Geraci thought as he joined the flow of combat engineers and other evacuating the building.

It was total chaos in the streets of Da Nang when Geraci and his men reached the outer wall of the Palace.

Civilians and mercenaries were surging down the main avenue, under the firm prodding of the local militiamen. As part of JT's overall plan, everyone inside the city knew exactly what to do—and so far it was an orderly evacuation, amazing in the face of the dozens of explosions going on all around them. But Geraci knew it wouldn't take much to turn the moving crowd into a stampede.

He gathered his officers around him and took a quick headcount of the men. Everyone was present and accounted for. He turned back to the Palace just in time to see the last of JT's security men come charging out, their arms full of either weapons or crates of booze.

"Is everyone out?" Geraci yelled to their senior officer.

The man yelled an affirmative response and hurried on his way. Just then a trio of Katy rockets slammed down into the Palace courtyard, blowing out what was left of the intact windows and collapsing one corner of the structure's roof. More Katys went streaking overhead, as well as a barrage of the almost tracerlike 120-mm artillery rounds.

That was enough for Geraci.

"OK, guys," he yelled to his men. "That's our cue. Let's get the hell out of here."

The rest of the combat engineers needed no further prodding. Within seconds, the entire unit was also double-timing it down the main avenue, mixing in with the mercs and civilians, heading towards the Jersey Tunnel.

First Captain Luk So Sung was in charge of the first unit of Minx soldiers to reach the outskirts of Da Nang city.

So far, casualties to his 100-man force had been only moderate—thirty-two killed, half that many wounded, just about all to boobytraps or long-range artillery. This was far below what his commanders' had expected for Luk's unit, which was, in effect, a suicide squad.

Their mission was to take out the first line of machine gun posts that covered the main northern road to the walled city. His men had come out of the jungle with the opening salvos of the attack, twenty-pound TNT packs strapped to their backs. To their amazement, they found the line of machine gun posts had disappeared. There were no weapons, no gunners; only the trenches and the sandbags remained.

Not quite knowing what to do, Luk ordered his men forward. A quarter mile up the road was a string of heavy-caliber guns and TOW emplacemnets that another suicide squad back in the woods had been assigned to take out. Luk figured he and his men would simply complete their mission for them.

They cautiously rounded the bend and with their own side's Katy rockets going off all around them, spied the line of TOW emplacements. Using his binoculars, Luk counted twelve of the antitank, antipersonnel nests just within eyesight. He was sure many others were better hidden from view.

He called his fifty men up to his side, gave them a quick and final pep talk and then unleashed them. They were tentative at first, but finally they charged as ordered, running madly down the road and leaping into the TOW pits, igniting their dynamite-laden backpacks as they did so.

Five explosions went off, almost at once. Then there was two more, and finally another two. Then there was silence. Luk stuck his head out of his protective trench and was amazed to see at least two dozen of his men simply walking back towards him.

He jumped up and grabbed the first junior officer he could find.

"What are you doing?" he screamed at the man. "Go back and complete your mission. Those emplacements must be destroyed."

"There *are* no emplacements," the man answered, his tone shaky and puzzled.

Luk stared at the young officer.

"They're fakes," the man continued. "Props . . ."

Luk ran down the road, gingerly stepping over several puddles of gooey slime, the remains of his soldiers who *had* detonated their backpacks. He reached the first trench and found a TOW weapon—a Milan to be specific. Or at least it *looked* like a Milan. Luk ran his hand along the missile's body and fins and came away with two fingers covered in black paint. He scrapped some more of the paint off and discovered that the "missile" was actually a crudely-carved piece of hollow-out bamboo.

"What are these?" he cried aloud. *"Fakes?"*

Two of his men were suddenly beside him. "Yes, Captain," one said. "All of them, bamboo."

"What does it mean, sir?" the other soldier asked him.

Luk had to think quickly. "It's obvious," he finally said. "These weapons have been fakes all along. Props—set up by the cowardly white soldiers to fool us."

"They worked, sir," the first soldier said, ratherly foolishly.

"You'll be shot, after the battle!" Luk screamed at him.
He turned back to the rest of his unit. "Company up!"

The fifty men jogged up the roadway, all still carrying
their suicide packs. An eighth of a mile beyond was the
city's last line of defense—three trenches covered with concertina wire—and then the walls of the city itself.

Luk's heart was racing. His unit was originally intended
to be fodder, cut down in the opening minutes of the major attack. Now they stood on the edge of an authentic
achievement: capturing the entrance to the city itself. If
they could do that, Luk's star would rise like a skyrocket.

He stood up, sword in hand and dramatically pointed
towards the huge sealed wooden gates of Da Nang city.

"Onward!" he cried. "No slacking!"

His men gathered themselves up and began yet another
charge.

They ran as fast as they could even as artillery barrages
from both sides were crashing down all around them. Luk
cursed his comrade gunners, but understood too. There
was no way that the gunners expected any Minx units to
be this close, this soon to the entrance to the enemy-held
city.

They quickly reached the lines of concertina wire, and
found the trenches beyond to be as empty as the machine
posts and the *ersatz* TOW pits. Now they were but fifty feet
from the main entrance to the city, two huge wooden
doors thirty-five feet in height, and, Luk knew, bolted from
the inside with a series of six-inch steel rods.

"Continue!" Luk was screaming as his suicide troops
surged forward. "First squad, detonate on those doors!"

Three men in his squad obeyed him instantly. They ran
smack in to the large oak door, pulling their TNT fuse
cords and blowing themselves up. Luk's quick calculations
told him that it would take anywhere from fifteen to
twenty of his men to blow open the huge oak portals—but

this was by far within the realm of acceptable risk. After all, his commanders were expecting 100 percent casualties among the noncoms.

But then a strange thing happened. As soon as the smoke cleared from the three human bombs, Luk and the others saw the huge gates swing open, free and easy.

"They are not locked?" Luk said, quizzically. "How can that be?"

His remaining troopers stopped in their tracks.

"What does this mean?" they asked him and themselves.

It took a few moments for it to sink in, but then Luk finally realized the opportunity staring him in the face.

"It means . . ." he screamed at the top of his lungs, "that *we* take the city!"

By the time Hunter flashed over the walled city of Da Nang, Minx troops were pouring through the main northern entrance.

Tanks, APCs, mobile guns and literally thousands of soldiers on foot were streaming out of the jungle and into the city. Perversely, the Minx long range guns in the surrounding hills were still pounding the city even as their own troops were moving about. The advance enemy units had achieved their objectives faster than even their commanders in the rear could have imagined.

He buzzed the city once, then continued on his way. His main concern at the moment was the river crossing about five miles north of the city, located at a place called Go Minh.

Hardly known for getting their feet wet, the Minx did have a small navy consisting of armed junks, riverine gunships and ancient landing crafts. The river at Go Minh was about three quarters of a mile at its narrowest point, and deep with muck and silt along its edges. JT's intelligence men had spotted a large Minx force hiding in the jungle on the far side of the river nearly a month before.

The presence of these enemy troops had told JT's men two things: One, that the MInx were planning a weak flank attack on Da Nang city, and two, that to do so, they were planning a river crossing near Go Minh.

Recon photos of the area two days before showed unusual vegetation popping up along the mucky river edges; the intelligence men knew that foliage didn't grow that quickly even in the humid climate of Vietnam. The "growth" was actually camouflaged Minx boats, spirited in at night. Per the overall strategy, nothing was done preemptively about these river craft.

But now that the war had started in earnest, these troops had to be dealt with. Everyone involved agreed that the scariest link in the whole plan was protection of the weak flank. Because no more than a quarter mile from the far bank of the river was one end of the Jersey Tunnel—and if the Minx discovered that, a catastrophe would surely follow.

Hunter roared over the river and could clearly see the boats now, free of camouflage, and filling with Minx soldiers on the south side. Typically, the Minx were taking a blunderbust approach to a river assault. More patient commanders would have filled their boats and allow them to go across two or three abreast at a time. The MInx were launching their boats—more than fifty in number—all at once.

Hunter banked the F-16XL high over the river, the Minx troops vainly firing their small arms at him. He put the Cranked Arrow into a screaming climb, leveling off at 22,000 feet above the river. Even from this altitude he could see the line of approximately fifty-five boats launching from the northern edge, their weak motors churning up wakes of white foam on the dirty brown river.

"Fools," Hunter muttered.

He wasn't happy about what he was about to do. Combat was a strange thing; if a guy shoots at you, you shoot back at him. You kill him, well, that was considered self-defense; that was playing by the rules. Wholesale slaughter was *not* playing by the rules, though—unless you could rationalize it by saying that you were saving the lives of people on your side.

Still, looking down at the embarking Minx troops, Hunter felt uneasy about going against the rather unsophisticated enemy. The term "fish in a barrel" would not leave his mind.

He loitered over the river for another minute. That's how long it took for most of the Minx boats to reach the middle of the stream. Then he put the XL into a screaming dive.

He leveled out at just 150 feet and opened up with his cannons immediately. First two, then three, then five boats exploded. He turned over and came around again, pressing his cannons' trigger and trying not to think about the carnage he was causing below. Ten more boats simply disappeared in a ball of flame and smoke. Another turn, another strafing run, eight more boats sunk.

It went on like this for ten minutes. The defenseless Minx troops either dying from cannon fire or succumbing to the waters below. After all the boats were either sunk or sinking, Hunter performed the nastiest task of all: strafing the near shore, tearing into the Minx who had made it to the other side. Those not shot up on the narrow beach were forced back into deeper water and a death by drowning. Some of the estimated 900 enemy soldiers eventually figured out that only if they returned to the far shore, the one from which they came, would they be safe from the deadly fire.

But less than a hundred were that smart or lucky.

Stationed in a well-concealed observation post, Geraci had watched Hunter's one-man, lopsided battle on the river with much anticipation.

As grisly as it was, the combat engineer knew the

slaughter had to be done if the overall strategy for defeating the Minx was to work.

Now, as he saw Hunter's F-16XL rising straight up in the air and give off a long stream of white smoke, he knew at least one aspect of the plan had been accomplished.

Then he turned his attention to the city itself.

A conservative estimate would have placed the number of enemy troops inside the walls of Da Nang at close to 20,000, or a reenforced division. Another regiment or two was waiting outside the city gate while those inside searched every building, house and military installation.

Geraci knew they wouldn't find anyone—the city had been successfully evacuated during the first hour of the battle. Many of its defenders, and all of its citizens, were now safely hidden inside the Jersey Tunnel.

Though its shape was certainty tubular, the Jersey Tunnel wasn't a tunnel at all. It was, in fact, a very elaborate bomb shelter. Just a few feet short of a quarter mile long, and about a hundred feet at its widest, it reached more than sixty feet underground. It was nearly all concrete—mixed with local beach sand and petroleum-based binders—with air holes and ventilation shafts every 200 feet. These were covered with camouflage netting and real jungle growth, so from the air and from Da Nang itself, the top of the Jersey Tunnel looked like nothing more than another stretch of mango trees and tropical swamp growth, a terrain seen all over Southeast Asia.

One of the cornerstones of JT's bold plan was for the safety of the many civilians inside Da Nang city, numbering as high as 5,000. Obviously they couldn't have remained inside the city once the fighting broke out. But neither could they be evacuated to the air base—it was much too dangerous there, too. So, the solution was to build this place—and quick.

The ironic thing about the Jersey Tunnel was that it was originally laid out by the forerunners of the Minx, the Viet Cong themselves. It had been dug by the communists to stretch from the jungle to the east wall of Da Nang city and used to move fifth columnists in and out of the city. Never exposed or filled in, it was included on updated plans of the city during the first communist occupation—plans which JT and Geraci had access to when planning the defense of the city.

The project Geraci's men had faced was widening the original twenty-by-twenty passageway to accommodate the bulging population of Da Nang.

Even more important, they were tasked with reenforcing it for what was about to come.

The man with the unlikely name of Assass Asmad Asadd was now in charge of the walled city of Da Nang.

He was the top Viet Minx commander in the battle area, unusual because he was an Iraqi by birth, and therefore the only non-Oriental on the command staff of the Minx. He was a tall man, dark skinned, bald head and a thrice-broken nose. While he was widely disliked by other officers in the other various Minx commands, not to mention the Minx troops themselves, he nevertheless wielded great power. And not just in the field, but with the board members of CapCom too.

His well-armed, well-drilled, black-uniformed troops had moved down Route 9 from abandoned Khe Sanh and had carried out the main attack on Da Nang, leaving the stalemated battle at the nearby Da Nang airbase to other, less-impressive Minx units.

Now as he toured the city in the back of an open car, he felt extremely gratified—and more than a little confused. His elite troops had done bang-up job in capturing what had been thought to be the best defended targets in South Vietnam—even Assass was surprised when his free-lance suicide troops easily gained entrance to the walled city. Yet the place itself was deserted—except for the Minx soldiers themselves, there wasn't another person to be found anywhere inside the captured city.

The little parade accompanying Assass's touring car pulled up to the front of the Palace. It was now surrounded by Minx troops and equipment. Two Minx T-72 tanks had broken through the massive steel gates leading into the former defenders' headquarters and now they stood guard at the front of the large yellow building.

Assass waited until his underlings opened his door for him, and then he strutted out of the car, riding crop in hand. He surveyed the palace building, noting that even though more than a few Katy rockets had hit the structure, only moderate damage had been inflicted on the building. This impressed him; the place was obviously well-built.

"I want the complete architectural drawings and plans for this building within an hour," he demanded of his understaff handlers. "Failure to do so will result in death."

He walked through the palace gates and up into the main building itself.

The place was empty inside—absolutely stripped of anything of value, from lights, to furniture, to booze at the bar. Again, Assass thought this very unusual. Obviously the enemy had retreated—but maybe it hadn't been as hasty as those in Hanoi had been led to believe.

He climbed the long staircase, his entourage of junior officers behind him. Each room on the second floor had been similarly cleaned out; very little of anything of value remained. He proceed up to the more palatial third floor and walked into what had obviously served as the enemy commander's headquarters.

Assass came to like the office it right away. It presented an outstanding view of the entire city, as well as the ocean and the jungle beyond. He walked over to northside windows and could see the enemy airbase not quite a mile away. Several columns of smoke were rising from its northern end, and he could still hear the occasional booming of artillery, way off in the distance. At last report, the air base was still "under siege." This was another thing that puzzled Assass. CapCom's intelligence reports had told them that Da Nang city had been more heavily defended than the air base nearby. Why then had the city fallen without barely a shot being fired, when the air base was still in enemy hands?

Then there was the situation over at Go Minh. A flanking attack on Da Nang city by 900 Minx river soldiers had never materialized. Just where the soldiers were, no one seemed to know. They had been reportedly in position for weeks, yet when the jump-off call came, they disappeared. It didn't make sense to Assass; surely the enemy troops routed from Da Nang city couldn't have wiped out an entire company of Minx soldiers—could they?

He turned from the northern view and looked out to the south. He could see the ocean beaches—they were deserted, of course—and the thick jungle beyond. Since he was from the desert, Assass was unfamiliar with the type of foliage of this country. But there was a long line of trees about a kilometer from the outside of the city that looked very unusual—almost *too* green, *too* lush.

He made a mental note to investigate it later.

He finally made it around to the large oak desk in the middle of the room. He sat in the chair and tried the desk on for size. It fit perfectly. At that moment, his decision was made: this palace would be his headquarters from now on. From here he would oversee the conquest of northern South Vietnam. From here, he would communicate with his highest superior, a man totally unknown to the fools at CapCom.

He clapped his hands twice and two Minx officers literally ran into the room.

"Set up the long-range communication gear atop this building," he ordered them. "Install the satellite dish first."

The Minx officers shuffled right back out again, as Assass leaned back in his new, slightly squeaky, office chair.

With any luck, he might be able to call Baghdad by midnight.

Da Nang air base

The F-16XL came screeching in for a landing, its airbrakes and drag chute slowing it down to crawl seconds after touchdown.

Hunter taxied the futuristic fighter off the runway and into a hardened bunker which served as the base's aircraft ordnance—loading section. Two squads of flight mechanics were waiting to service the XL. Clad in flak jackets and Kevlar helmets, they would quickly refill its fuel tanks and load more weapons under its wings. Time was of the essence for the turnaround, a fact underscored by the bone-chilling background noise of Minx artillery and rockets crashing down all over the base.

Just as he was pulling into the thick-concrete service bunker, Ben and Frost were pulling out. Their F-20s recently bombed up and refueled, they were heading to hit Minx positions about a quarter mile south of the base perimeter. At the very same moment, JT's F-20 was off bombing Minx supply lines about five miles west of the air base. Meanwhile ZZ's *Triple X* gunship was orbiting the base, providing on-call air support for the friendly troops fighting all along the defense perimeter.

Hunter squealed the XL to stop and popped his canopy. As the flight monkeys went to work on the airplane, he gratefully accepted the cup of coffee handed up to him by the crew's sergeant. The plan's timetable was so tight, Hunter didn't even have time to unstrap from the cockpit, never mind climb down and stretch his cramped muscles for few minutes. He had to get rearmed and refueled and back in the air as quickly as possible.

Even as the battle raged out on the perimeter, he could see squads of mercenaries roaring by the bunker in all kinds of vehicles, towing artillery pieces and AA guns that had previously been protecting the outskirts of Da Nang city. Removed from their forward positions just the night before, these guns were now on their way to be added to the already awesome arsonnel of high-tech weaponry ringing Da Nang air base.

Hunter checked the time. It was now 1430; the battle had been raging for about four hours. So far NT's plan was working. The base defenders were successfully holding back the tide of Minx surrounding it, once again using to full advantage advanced weapons and sophisticated tactics to keep the strategically crude enemy at bay.

But Hunter could not help but feel a chill in his bones when considering the current situation: it was, as they once used to say, *deja vu* all over again. Though better armed and possessing more manpower, it was hard to escape from the fact that he was once again fighting from a position surrounded by the enemy. It was almost as if the bad dream up in Khe Sanh was just a warm up. There would be one big difference though: unlike Khe Sanh, there was no way they were going to fly out of Da Nang in a Rube-Goldberg aircraft built to fly twenty miles in five minutes and no more. There were just too many people for that.

No—for better or worse, the fight for Da Nang air base would be a fight to the death.

The crew chief called up to him that the XL was ready to go. Hunter's tanks were full of JP-8 and his cannons replenished with ammunition. Beneath his wings was another of array of ordnance: four 500-pound GP bombs, and six cluster bombs of various shapes and sizes. Also filled were the three cameras—one for film and two for video—located in the XL's nose cone. His next sortie would include a recon of the entire battle situation.

From this, they would determine if the second and most important step of JT's plan could be launched.

* * *

Hunter was airborne less than five minutes later, roaring off the base's main runway even as Minx artillery shells were landing at the far end.

Turning over the northern end of the base, he could clearly see that the battle was still in full fire. The Football City Rangers were sending up huge plumes of dirt and dust as they scurried back and forth in the small Scorpion tanks, stopping, firing, and moving on again. On their flanks were the telltale blue streams of smoke from the GE Gatling guns, mowing down what was left of the forest and the Minx positions within. Above it all, the air was filled with white contrails from the LARS, its continual barrage of high explosive rockets hitting Minx positions as far as 10 miles behind the lines.

Hunter clicked his front video camera on for about twenty seconds, capturing the most salient parts of the battle. Then he flipped over and headed for the western edge of the base. The terrain here was more hilly than to the north, and during the opening minutes of the battle, the Minx had opened up with a number of 88-mm field guns hidden on the high ground.

Now these hills were almost quiet. There were no enemy guns, only craters and plumes of smoke, rising into the sky. Hunter knew immediately what had happened. The place had recently been visited by ZZ Morell's *Triple X* gunship, it now carrying many of the Gatling guns formerly installed on the wrecked-beyond-repair *Nozo*. Hunter rolled off fifteen seconds of video strictly for poststrike evaluation. It was evident that the Minx would not return to this particular area anytime soon.

He then banked over to the southern edge of the base, a sector where the Minx lines were probably no more than 100 yards beyond the defense perimeter. What he saw made his breath catch in his throat for a moment. Back in the last Vietnam war, the U.S. forces used a tactic known as the "mad minute." Basically, this tactic called for a large force of soldiers to simply fire every gun they had into a confined area where they believe Viet Cong or NVA to be lurking. The thinking was that in sixty seconds such a wall of intense, concentrated fire would decimate any hidden enemy soldiers and/or scare away those who somehow escaped the carnage.

The tactic usually produced mixed results, but was, if nothing else, an impressive display of firepower.

Now the defending forces on the southern edge of the base—a mix that included some of *Bozo's* old crew, some of Geraci's engineers and even a few French Legionnaires— had adapted the basic idea of the "mad minute" and expanded on it in a rather mind-blowing way.

Using the level-barreled light artillery and AA guns quartered from the perimeter along Da Nang city, these troops were laying down a continuous, flank-to-flank barrage of high-caliber fire that stretched for more than a half mile from one end to the other. This nonstop stream of wasn't encumbered by a time restraint of a mere sixty seconds. Rather, Hunter knew the gunners were working on *ten*-minute intervals, or *600* seconds of blasting away back and forth.

Like its predecessor, this "Mad Ten Minutes" presented such an overwhelming vision of firepower, not even the most fanatical Minx would dare enter its awesome killing zone.

As before, Hunter recorded the action on his video cameras, and then moved on.

His next stop was over Da Nang city itself.

Chapter Forty-five

Da Nang City

The mysterious officer Assass looked out from the roof of the partially destroyed palace and smiled.

Convoys of Minx troops and weapons were flowing into Da Nang city at no less than four separate points. At the west gate, the largest entrance to the walled city, the troop trucks were actually backed up in a traffic jam so acute, many of the troops were being ordered off the vehicles and marched into the city.

It was a pleasant problem to have, Assass thought. It was not many commanders who could overwhelm such an objective as Da Nang city so quickly, that his conquering army was actually snarled in a traffic jam, so intent they were in claiming their prize.

Off in the distance, he could see the smoke and flames from the battle at the air base—but this was of little concern to him. The conquest of the air base was in the hands of other Minx units, and he supposed it would fall to them in good time. His main goal was the city. That was what CapCom had contracted him for, and the sacking potential was vastly superior than what he felt he would eventually find at the air base.

But it was more than that. Taking an entire city was not just a victory of military terms, it was a triumph of power.

And the first rule of conquest was to consolidate one's prize. Now as Assass looked out over the walled-in, urban sprawl of Da Nang, Assass imagined himself and his ancestors ruling the city for generations to come.

The fact that it was abandoned before his forces even reached the front gate didn't bother him anymore. The enemy was cowardly—it was as simple as that. He had recognized the tidal wave of Assass's force early on, and had simply left.

However, he *did* find it unusual that all of the city's civilians were gone, too.

Suddenly he heard a high-pitched sound above the hustle and bustle below him. He looked up and just barely caught glimpse of an aircraft flying extremely high over the city. It looked like a rocketship, its red, white and blue paint scheme gleaming in the setting sun. In a word, it looked *beautiful*.

"Someday," Assass thought, "I want to get one of those."

Da Nang Air Base
One hour later

It was a very nervous JT who hit the play button on the battered VCR.

"This is where the rubber meets the road," he said to the others gathered around him in the base's small, underground operations room. "If we fucked up, we'll know in a few minutes."

Hunter, Ben, Frost, and ZZ were crammed into the ops room along with JT. They waited anxiously as the front end of Hunter's recon videotape started to play on the small color TV monitor. It showed, in sequence, the battles on the north, west and south edges of the air base's perimeter. These illicited applause from those gathered.

Then the scene shifted to a bird's eye view of Da Nang city.

Through a light cloud cover they could see the city was absolutely filled with enemy troops. They appeared to be searching every building, even as their heavy weapons, such as towed artillery and mobile Katy launchers, were pouring into the walled city. The activity left no doubt that the Minx controlled the entire square mile of urban area.

Instantly a whoop went up in the ops room.

"We've got them right where we want them . . ." JT said triumphantly.

Everyone in the room agreed.

"But now," JT added soberly, "comes the hard part."

Ten miles offshore

Crunch was lighting his third cigar of the day when the radiophone started buzzing.

He picked up the receiver and heard a crackling burst of static.

Then Hunter's voice came on.

"Fourth quarter," the slightly echoing message began. "Third and goal. We're on the eight yard line. One minute to go in the game. Pass play."

With that the radiophone clicked off.

Crunch hastily wrote down the message and then looked around the bridge of the battleship.

"Where the hell is that 'general quarters' button?"

The dozen or so Omani sailors on the bridge with him immediately recognized his concern. They could speak very little English, and Crunch—pressed into service as the ship's commander—could speak no Omani. But he didn't really have to.

They only had one big job to do.

An Omani lieutenant stepped forward and hit the general quarters button. Instantly the entire battleship was reverberating with a high-pitch klaxon, calling the 300 or so Omani sailors to their battle stations. The message they've been waiting to hear for nearly two days had finally come.

Crunch showed the Omani officer the crudely decoded message. They were actually simple coordinates: Four, three, eight, one and the word "Pass" indicating zero. Crunch and the Omani checked the numbers against a specially drawn map and then double-checked them.

"It is clear," the Omani said.

Crunch puffed twice on his cigar and then nodded.

"OK," he said. "Let's get cracking."

Ten minutes later, Crunch was on the railing next to the bridge, high-powered binoculars in hand.

Off in the distance—more than ten miles away—he could see the twinkling of lights coming from Da Nang city. He could also see red streaks of light rising above the walled fortress, the result of Minx celebrating soldiers firing their weapons into the air.

He shifted his binoculars slightly north of the city and saw plumes of smoke rising from Da Nang air base. There were still explosions going off all around the perimeter of the sprawling base, but as far as he could tell, the defensive forces were successfully holding their own against the would-be Minx invaders.

And that was exactly all they wanted to do.

Three Omani officers appeared on the deck next to Crunch. Between them, they could muster up a passing semblance of English.

"Weapons are ready," one told him.

"Range is set," said another. "Shells are fused."

"Nothing on radar," said the third. "We have yet to be detected."

Crunch looked at his watch. It was one minute to 2100 hours. He checked the ship's position. They were cruising at five knots, heading north, maintaining a ten mile distance offshore. He did a quick mental check, making sure he'd crossed every *T* and dotted every *I*.

Then he turned back to the Omanis. "OK, boys," he said. "Let's open them up."

Not five seconds later, the three guns on the battleship's forward turret erupted in a trio of flames and smoke. The huge, 50,000-ton ship shuddered as three, massive, one-ton shells left the sixteen-inch barrels and screamed away into the night.

Crunch fixed his spyglasses back on the lights of Da Nang just in time to see the three high-explosive shells hit right in the center of the city. The explosions were so quick and so bright, they actually hurt Crunch's eyes. He blinked, and when he refocused he saw three huge fireballs rising above the city.

"Hit 'em again!" he cried out.

A moment later, the trio of guns on the second turret fired, shaking the ship again, and delivering three more one-ton shells to the middle of Da Nang. Crunch kept his eyes open this time and saw the shells hit, raising three identical fiery mushrooms above the city.

"Again!" he yelled.

Now the rear turret erupted, sending three more shells into the enemy-held city.

"Again!"

The forward turret fired again.

"Again!"

The second turret fired.

"Again!"

The third turret erupted.

Now all Crunch could see through his binoculars were fireballs and smoke. Crunch imagined what it was like inside the walls. At least 30,000 troops. Total confusion, panic, fire, smoke. No escape.

Death.

He grimaced and wiped his weary eyes. He was quite nearly tired of this combat stuff. Very tired of all the killing. He promised himself a good long drunk when all this was over.

Then he put the spyglasses up to his eyes once more. "Fire again!" he cried.

Inside the Jersey Tunnel

Geraci's ears were ringing.

He looked around the well-lit tubular concrete shelter and saw not one person who wasn't holding his or her ears. Small cascades of dust and mortar were falling from the newly poured ceiling. Geraci winced at each one—he knew every support, every stud, every metal beam in the place.

And if just one of them broke . . .

He didn't want to think about it, so he put his hands up to his ears, too. One hundred feet above them and too damn close by, the city of Da Nang was undergoing a fierce bombardment. He imagined he could hear the screams, the cries of panic and pain, the sound of death itself all around him. But at the same time he realized this was impossible simply because the sound of the massive sixteen-inch gun explosions were so loud, so violent on the eardrums, it was clinically impossible to hear anything else.

He looked up and saw his closest officers—Matus, Cerbasi, McCaffrey and Palma—all sitting nearby, scrunched in between various-uniformed mercenaries and the odd civilian, who more often than not was a hooker or some form of bar room girl. With each crash of a high-explosive shell outside, they all grimaced and shook their heads—but he also noticed something else. Between blasts, they were all smiling. But why? Relief that the previous shell had not come crashing through the ceiling? Satisfaction at the thought that the brutal Minx were finally getting their well-deserved comeuppance? Or was it a mixture of both? A kind of whistling in the dark.

He wasn't sure. But strangely enough, he soon found himself smiling after each shell crash—and then it hit him. They were in a well-protected bunker, theoretically out of harm's way, where just a few weeks before, they'd been scrapping the sides of a battered, very fucked-up airplane, withstanding massive Minx mortar barrages, and fighting off blood-curdling human wave assaults.

Now he knew the reasons for the smiles. These guys had cheated death so many times, death was no longer interested in playing the game. They had won. They were nearly invincible.

Hunter, JT and Ben were also holding their ears.

They all witnessed some massive bombardments before, but nothing like this.

They were holed up inside one of the concrete aircraft repartments, watching through binoculars the systematic destruction of Da Nang city. With each barrage of shells from the captured Cult battleship, it seemed like another piece of the city died. They correctly presumed that thousands of Minx soldiers, unprepared for such an onslaught, were dying too. Even if their commanders had ordered them into the cellars of the buildings within the city, there was no way anyone could escape the massive bombardment.

And even though the Minx troops surrounding the base itself were still shelling, it was now much more sporadic and untargeted; almost as if they too were in awe of the hell and fire their comrades were going through.

There was a row of radios and radiophones next to them in the bunker, and with these Hunter, JT, and Ben were keeping in close contact with the people inside the Jersey Tunnel, the front line commanders of perimeter defense forces and Crunch on board the captured Minx battleship.

From every perspective it was evident that the enemy

was being slaughtered—and with it, the city of Da Nang was slowly but surely disappearing from the map.

Aboard Battleship 57

The girl named Ala was also holding her ears.

The rumble and crash of the huge guns going off just two levels up and one over from her stateroom was so frightening and intense, she could not keep her teeth from chattering.

How had she come to this? By what devil had she changed from the simple island girl on Fiji, to this, a passenger on this massive warship, confused and terrified?

She pressed her hands closer to her ears and tried to think about her parents. How were they? Were they still alive? Or had the madman Soho killed them? There was no way she could know—or would ever know.

She began crying. All this fighting, all this warmaking—it made no sense to her. She no longer had any idea of time; the long stop and go journey in the pink airplane had taken care of that. And though the strangers under whose care she was presently seemed human enough, there was no way she could ascertain their intentions.

She felt then like a *poo-wa pow-wa,* a small piece in a game favored by her people which the players moved and tugged constantly as a way of seeking to defeat their opponents.

Another barrage caused her to scream out in pure fear—it was so loud, two of her Li-Chi Chi bodyguards burst into her stateroom just to make sure she was all right.

She quickly dismissed them—she wanted to suffer alone. The only regret she had was not telling them—or anyone else—that every time she closed her eyes, she saw the face of a man that looked like Satan himself.

Chapter Forty-six

The battleship didn't stop firing until first light the next morning.

Finally, after a one, last nine-gun barrage, the cannons fell silent. It was 0645 hours.

Geraci was the first one out of the southern end of the Jersey Tunnel. He emerged, his M-16 up and ready—but he quickly realized he wouldn't need his weapon.

There was nothing left. No buildings, no streets, no trees. Certainly no people. He was stunned. The massive bombardment have leveled every thing within a square mile. He couldn't see anything that was more than four feet high. Even stranger, there were no bodies—or at least none that could be seen out in the open. They too had been baked by the hellish temperatures and then snuffed to dust by the shelling.

Other members of the 104th and the civilians began emerging from the shelter. To a person, each stared out at the utter destruction, jaw agape, eyes nonbelieving. Just about everyone was of the same mind. The desolate landscape looked as if a nuclear bomb had hit it.

More than 5,000 people had spent the night in the Jersey Tunnel and now they were pouring out of the shelter. Within minutes a Huey helicopter appeared overhead and landed where the city square used to be. Hunter climbed out, followed by JT, Ben and Crunch.

They walked over to Geraci and shook hands.

"Everyone made it, OK?" JT asked him.

Geraci nodded. "Everything held together," he replied. Then, looking around him: "Thank God."

"Quiet morning, isn't it?" Hunter asked him.

Geraci took a moment to listen. All he could hear was the wind whistling through the rubble and the sounds of waves on the beach a short distance away. There was no gunfire, no mortar tubes popping, no artillery. No action at all around the massive air base nearby.

"They take their toys and go home?" Geraci asked the Wingman.

Hunter just shrugged. "Seems like it," he replied, looking back towards the heavy jungle to the west. "We did a dawn recon, couldn't see a soul down there. Nothing on infrared, nothing on the Jason module."

Geraci stared at the desolate vacant lot that a day before had been the city of Da Nang.

"Can't say I blame them," he observed quietly.

At that moment, Hunter felt a tug on his arm. It was Ben, motioning past the stream of civilians walking out of the Tunnel to a lone figure walking down what used to be a street. It was Crunch.

"Wonder what he's thinking," Ben said to Hunter.

Hunter walked over to his old friend. He'd been absolutely quiet during the chopper ride in from the battleship.

"I'm going to have to tell Jonesie to break out the medals," Hunter told Crunch. "You deserve at least a dozen or so."

Crunch just shook his head. "Not me," he said, his voice barely a whisper. "Not for this."

Hunter put his hand on the man's shoulder. "It's war, Crunchie," he said. "It was either them or us."

Crunch just stared straight ahead. "You know, Hawk" he began. "when I landed on Xmas way back when all this started, I couldn't imagine what kind of person would actually be responsible for that. Just total absolute destruction. I just couldn't imagine anyone living with it—having known that they were responsible for snuffing out the lives of so many people."

Then he turned and looked Hunter in the eye. "And now, the devil has become me."

Hunter began to reply something, but stopped himself. There really wasn't much that could be said.

Crunch started walking away, down the shattered roadway, looking at what the guns under his control had wrought.

"I should have stayed down in the Delta," Hunter heard him say.

Da Nang Air Base
One hour later

As always, it was Hunter who saw it first.

He was deep in work at the base ops room, studying the video shot not thirty minutes before by video cameras attached to a pod on Ben's F-20. The latest footage confirmed what the previous recon flights had discovered: the Minx units formerly attacking Da Nang air base had withdrawn, and were now in flight down old Route 7, heading no doubt for sanctuaries deep in the jungle.

The massive battleship attack had accomplished its twin purpose: it had destroyed one Minx army and had sent the other packing, its members no doubt concluding that no wage was worth facing certain screaming death from the skies, as their comrades inside Da Nang city had.

Hunter had just switched off the VCR/TV combo when when he felt a slight vibration run through his body.

He checked his watch. It was straight up 1200 hours.

"Right on time," he thought.

He walked out of the ops building and onto the vast tarmac. The base was already getting back to some kind of normalcy. Repair crews were patching the far runways, the fire brigade finally snuffing out the several inconsequential fires started by the Minx shelling. Though intense, the enemy attack had failed to damage any vital piece of equipment on the base. All of the aircraft—from the trio of Football City Galaxys to the F-20s—had survived in their concrete shelters. Even more important, there were few casualties among the defending forces, and most of those were minor.

Shielding his eyes, Hunter stared up into the brilliantly lit blue sky and immediately spotted a small speck coming in from the east. The speck grew quickly, a testament to its high speed, and soon was fairly distinguishable: a long snout, swept cranked wings, twin tail fins. The trademark dull black color. There was only one plane known on Earth like it.

It was the SR-71 Blackbird, the hyperfast, high-flying recon plane operated by the Sky High Spies, Inc.

There was a crowd of 100 or so gathered by the time the SR-71 came in for a landing. The Blackbird's ramjets engine emitted such a scream, many were forced to block their ears, so high-pitched was the distinctive whine.

The airplane rolled up to a stop right next to the crowd, its engines winding down. The twin canopy popped open and the two pilots climbed out. It was the Kephart Brothers, Jeff and George, the proprietors of Sky High Spies, Inc. They'd flown over from Edwards to do a high-altitude sweep of South Vietnam the day after the Minx offensive.

Bulked up in the high-altitude, spacesuit-looking outfits, they waddled over and shook hands briskly with Hunter.

"Nice place," Brother Jeff deadpanned, looking around the airbase and then over at the smoldering crater that was once Da Nang city. "But it looks like we missed the big party."

Hunter just nodded. "Did you ever," he replied.

Brother George produced a video cassette.

"Well, there's plenty more going on," he said grimly.

They hurried to the ops room where they were joined

by Ben, JT, Frost and Geraci. Quickly inserting the video-tape into the VCR/TV combo, within seconds the screen was filled with the crooked green shape of South Vietnam. Everyone in the room grew absolutely silent. The country's outline was barely visible, so intense was the smoke and fire. In fact, to Hunter, it appeared as if the whole country was on fire.

"When we did our first mission a few weeks back," Brother Jeff began, "we didn't believe it could get much worse. But obviously, it has."

The video rolled on, showing close-ups of such places as Cam Ranh Bay, Hue, Quang Ngai, and New Saigon. Each illustrated in the most graphic terms that incredibly intense battles were raging just about everywhere to the south of them. In fact, only the quick shot of the Da Nang area itself showed any semblence of peace.

"It was same up and down the coast," Brother George told them. "These Minx guys are everywhere. Troops moving, on foot or in trucks. Mobile guns. Tanks. Towed artillery. If you count them, you'll see there are more than three hundred big guns—81s up to big 120s—just around New Saigon alone. They're just pounding whoever the hell is defending that place. Same is true at all the major coastal cities. No wonder we were getting all those May-days."

Hunter felt his spirits sag to an all-time low. They had all been so caught up in their own survival, they had had no time to even ponder the situation in the rest of the country. Now it was quite apparent that it was all very grim.

As always, JT spoke for them.

"Jessuzz, we've been breaking our asses here," he began, his voice bitter, "just to save our own necks. But looking at this, it all amounts to a pee hole in the snow. We were just lucky. We can't beat these guys. They're overrunning the other ninety-five percent of the country."

No one argued with him. As the videotape rolled on, it

displayed with sickening accuracy, a country that was in its death throes.

"And once they get finished down there," JT concluded, "they'll all be back up here. And no matter what the hell we throw at them, it will never be enough."

The Kephart Brothers looked at each other and grimaced. It was up to Brother Jeff to deliver another slice of very bad news.

"There's more," he said simply, hitting the fast-forward control.

Within seconds, the fuzzy green shape of Vietnam dissolved, and soon the screen turned cloudy blue. The spy pilot returned the tape to normal speed and those gathered saw the new sequence was of the ocean from about ten miles up.

"We shot this about five hundred miles out from Cam Ranh Bay," Brother George began. "We started picking up microwave emissions and figured we'd check it out before coming in."

The room fell absolutely silent as they watched the scene's thin cloud cover clear away. Then an audible gasp went up. The screen clearly showed a group of ships sailing in three distinct lines.

"Damn," Hunter whispered. "The battleships."

Both Kepharts nodded grimly. "There's at least twenty of them," George said. "They appear to be under full steam, sailing due west."

". . . and heading right for us," Ben half-whispered.

JT flung his coffee cup against the far wall.

"That's the ball game," he said, teeth clenched. "It means we went through all this *for nothing.*"

Even Hunter had to agree. Staring out the window at the huge airbase, he couldn't help but think he'd been transported back in time, that his own recent past crazily mirrored the American effort in Vietnam in the 1960s. First, an encirclement by the shadowy enemy, saved only by a narrow escape. Then the deceptive beauty of the

Delta, that, like the rest of the country, hid unspeakable horrors committed by the most unlikeliest of soldiers—the Li Chi-Chi. Finally, the art of destroying a city in order to save it. And now, evidence of more enemy on the way—unchecked, uncheckable. And more enemy meant more fighting, more war, more death.

What was it about this place? It was a green jungle masked as black hole, sucking in more and more lives. And for what? Rice paddies? Oil?

He closed his eyes and tried to call on his psychic resources to provide him some clue, some little shred of truth in the whole bloody mess. Suddenly he found himself staring into a pair of vacant eyes. They were so lacking in life they were nearly white. That's when he realized they belonged to a ghost—the spirit of the Marine who had chosen to visit him in the foxhole back at Khe Sanh.

And what the ghost had told him then, suddenly made a lot of sense right now. *Don't make the same mistake again. Don't go about the thing the wrong way. Get to the heart of the matter!*

That's when it hit him. Get to the heart of the matter! He suddenly had a plan.

Chapter Forty-seven

The next day

Even at the height of the Minx attack, the air base at Da Nang had not been as busy as this.

There were four C-5s lined up on the main runway—the trio of Football City Special Forces Galaxys plus *Triple X*. The Football City planes were packed with paratroops; *Triple X* was bristling with weapons copped from the defense perimeter around Da Nang air base.

The past twenty-four hours had been spent on the radio with the commanders of the various defense forces in other parts of South Vietnam. To a man, they confirmed what the Sky High Spies recon video had shown: every major city on the coast was under tremendous attack; every major city was on the verge of being overrun by the Minx.

In all of the conversations, the United American officers in Da Nang had one message to their besieged colleagues: Hang on. Help is on the way.

Now each of the Football City planes was heading for a paradrop over a separate location—one to New Saigon, one to Cam Ranh Bay and one to Quang Ngai. The insertion of the three hundred elite paratroopers at each of these key locations would help the desperate defenders hold on just a little longer.

By the same token, *Triple X* meanwhile was heading for

381

Na Trang, where it would lend critically needed air support for the encircled mercenary troops there.

Behind the four Galaxys was the trio of F-20 Tigersharks, with Ben, Frost and JT at their controls. Their wings heavy with bombs, their cannons fresh with ammunition, the F-20s were heading for air strikes against smaller cities along the coast that had already been overrun by the Minx.

Waiting patiently at the end of this impressive line of aircraft was the SR-71 Blackbird. At its controls was Hawk Hunter.

Unlike the others, Hunter's mission this fateful day was to gather intelligence—information that he needed if his latest in a series of bold plans was ever going to work.

He was piloting the Blackbird alone—the mission he was undertaking was much too risky to endanger the lives of the Kephart Brothers, although they both insisted that one of them should go along, at the very least to work the spy plane's cameras.

But Hunter politely refused. All he asked for was use of their unique airplane, with a half-serious promise of full compensation if it was damaged or destroyed. Finally, they agreed.

At exactly 0700 hours, the Football City planes took off. Climbing slowly into the crystal clear morning sky, the gigantic airships formed up and slowly turned southward, their holds full of anxious, determined paratroopers.

Triple X was airborne a minute later, its fuselage absolutely bristling with weapons, from Gatlings up to light artillery pieces, shades of the old *Bozo* and *Nozo* gunships.

The F-20s went next. Their targets being hardened Minx positions, there was no need for them to carry anything other than big 1,000-pound GP bombs. Each Tigershark had four strapped to its wings.

Finally, it was Hunter's turn.

He'd flown the SR-71 on several occasions back when he was helping the Brothers Kephart reconstruct it after it was found hidden away in a hangar in Old Mexico. It was a very unique airplane, to say the least. With its awesome power and climbing ability, it was quite capable of reaching the edge of space—thus the need for the bulky space-suit and helmet. It could also fly at three, or four, or even *five* times the speed of sound, depending on load and fuel capacity. This mind-boggling performance was due to both the SR-71's pair of ramjet-adapted engines which Hunter and the Kepharts had souped up to 40,000 pounds of thrust each, and the airplane's titanium body which was light, yet capable of handling the high temperatures of near-hypersonic speed.

Possibly the most unusual thing about the airplane—at least from Hunter's present point of view—was that it was unarmed. The SR-71 couldn't carry a bomb or a cannon, nor would its baroque design allow for any weapons' adaptation.

No—the Blackbird sole weapon was its speed.

And that's exactly what Hunter would need where he was going.

It began as a slow day for the radar operators at the Dong Ha air base.

Usually the radarmen would run a drill around dawn every morning, to keep their senses sharp as well as check out their sophisticated airborne early warning equipment.

But there was no drill today—the radarmen and the pilots and mechanics for the squadron of 18 MiG-25 Foxbats also stationed at the base were in the middle of a work stoppage. They hadn't been paid in nearly two months now, and while their paymasters battled it out with the finance officers at Minx High Command in Hanoi, the base personnel had agreed not to perform any duty until the dispute was settled.

This was not the first time that High Command had screwed the men stationed at Dong Ha on their monthly payouts. Like many employers, the Viet Minx were long on demanding hard work and short on getting the checks in the mail. And everyone knew the reason for this latest indignation: with the big offensive now on in the south, CapCom was forcing the Minx High Command to concentrate its monetary resources there, and thereby stiffing its units in the north.

So there'd be little work done at Dong Ha today. Instead, the base personnel were gathered in the mess hall where a craps game was underway. Gambling was the common diversion whenever a pay dispute was happening at Dong Ha, though because there was a shortage of cash around the base, most of the players were betting with IOUs.

With the vast majority of the base personnel crowded into the mess hall, it was just a coincidence that one of the radar operators—a man named Vinh—just happened to be in the radar station when one of the air defense monitors began sounding its warning buzzer. He had gone to the station to retrieve a purse containing gold coins which he had hidden beneath one of the floor boards on the structure's first floor. Barred from using IOUs because of payoff discrepancies in the past, Vinh needed to use his small gold reserve to get back into a hot game. So it was more out of curiosity than anything else that caused him to disengage the alarm and check the long-range radar screen. He saw a tiny blip had entered the radar net at coordinates which put it about forty miles east of Dong Ha.

Vinh studied the indication with slight but gathering interest. With so many disparate Minx units under the CapCom umbrella, violating air space and failing to request proper crossover rights were commonplace. But this blip was unlike anything he'd ever seen. It was barely visible, a faint blink of static moving right into the center of the radar net. This told Vinh that whatever kind of aircraft it was, it was moving incredibly fast and at an incredibly high altitude.

And heading on a course which would bring it right over Dong Ha itself.

Vinh made a quick notation into the log book, retrieved his gold purse and then walked out of the radar station. Staring up into the crystal clear morning sky, he squinted long enough to spot a very thin white contrail passing directly overhead. He studied the long trail of ice crystals and exhaust for a few moments; the aircraft leaving the wake was moving so fast, and was so high up, it was nearly invisible.

Vinh had to think for a moment. He couldn't believe that this aircraft belonged to the Viet Minx or any of their allies.

Yet, what should he do about it? He was on strike.

Still, against his better judgement, he made a quick call to the next biggest Minx installation, the Long Dik railroad yards located about 55 miles to the west. He had a brief conversation with a junior radio officer there, telling him that an unidentified aircraft would be passing over their position with a few minutes time, Vinh hung up quickly, not bothering to wait for a reply.

Then, gold purse in hand, he headed back toward the mess hall.

It took another five minutes for the contrail high above him to finally fade away.

Long Dik Railroad Yards

There was a small crowd outside the administration building in the middle of the huge railroad marshalling center when the unidentified aircraft streaked over.

Most of the observers—Minx soldiers and civilian railway workers—could just barely make out the dark object riding the sky ahead of the long stream of white smoke. Even those with high-powered binoculars had a hard time focusing on the fast-moving, high-flying dark blue shape.

Just about everyone agreed they'd never seen anything like it before.

The Minx officers amongst the crowd were quick to point out that what ever the aircraft was, it certainly was part of the bulging Minx arsonnel, probably a secret craft of some kind, bought by CapCom to assist in the big offensive in the south. Why else would it be heading straight for Hanoi, some forty-five miles away?

But as the object finally faded from view, several of the Minx officers slipped into the administration building and quickly called the Viet Minx High Command headquarters in the capital city. Their message: alert your air defense units immediately. An unidentified aircraft is heading your way. And it is moving very fast.

Hanoi

There were three separate air defense systems protecting the myriad of Minx military installations in and around the city of Hanoi.

The first was made up of an infamous weapon: the SA-2 surface-to-air missile. This telephone-pole-with-fins missile was responsible for downing hundreds of American warplanes during the last Vietnam War. Under orders from CapCom, the Viet Minx High Command had bought up every SA-2 SAM on the world's burgeoning arms black market. Now there were literally hundreds of these weapons ringing the center of Hanoi in three concentric circles, the furthest being twenty miles out, the innermost placed around the city limits themselves.

The second line of air defense was made up of aircraft based at Xa Ho Ha air field, located on the southwestern edge of the city. The sprawling air base supported no less than seven squadrons of MiG-25 Foxbat jet fighters, each containing at least eighteen combat aircraft. But, as with many Minx units charged with protecting the capital city, six of the squadrons at Xa Ho Ha had been deployed south to fight in the Big Offensive. It was hoped that the remaining squadron would be adequate to provide air cover for the capital.

The third line of air defense was made up of thousands of antiaircraft artillery guns. These guns were everywhere the SAMs weren't. They were located on just about every high building, hilltop and even in some trees, surrounding and within the city. These weapons were of all calibers and in many cases had radar-controlled aiming devices and time-fused, high-fragmentation shells. They were spread out all over Greater Hanoi, and were especially thick around high-priority Minx installations including the extensive barracks and troop processing center north of the city, the enormous communications facility off to the city's west, and of course, the huge Xa Ho Ha air base.

But like many of the other Minx installations around Hanoi, a number of the AAA units were involved in a work stoppage. Some hadn't been paid in as much as three months—the majority hadn't received payouts for six weeks. The guns at these installations stood locked and sealed, their crews idle, their pay officers waiting in line at Minx High Command Headquarters to air their troops' grievances.

One of the AAA units that *was* getting paid—proof that the High Command was selectively compensating some units—was the 4518th Aerial Battery Company. It was no coincidence that this AAA unit was based the furthest out from Hanoi. Its string of six gun sites twenty-two miles due east from the city limits served as a tripwire for the inner defense sites. If an aerial intruder was bent on entering Hanoi's airspace from due east, they would be engaged by the 4518th Aerial Battery Company first.

It was 0900 hours when the 4518th got a hasty flash message directly from Minx High Command in Hanoi. They were to turn on their engagement radars and set them to the highest altitude possible. In most cases, this was 62,500 feet. They were told to look for anything flying near that altitude, possibly some kind of high speed jet or even an incoming missile.

But after three minutes of searching, the radar operators at the 4518th found nothing anywhere near that high altitude. When the Minx High Command was informed of this, they ordered the radar operators to search the skies around 40,000 to 45,000 feet. Again, after a few minutes of intense scanning, the radar operators could find nothing.

The third anxious flash message to the 4518th batteries ordered all of the gun crews out of their bunkers and to their gun posts. They were told to search the skies visually, at the same time loading their guns for possible action. Within seconds the highly trained, recently paid crews were pouring out of their revetments and manning their AAA weapons. Many were equipped with high-powered binoculars and they used these to scan all quadrants of the sky around them.

Still, they found nothing.

Not right away, anyway.

It was about twelve miles away, coming over the jungle due east of them, when the members of 4518th's Battery #6 first spotted it. It was a huge aircraft, painted all black, with a long snout and strangely cranked wings. It was flying so low, the exhaust from its powerful engines was setting the tops of the trees on fire.

The crew at Battery #6 ably loaded their gun and prepared to fire. But the black jet was moving so fast and so low, it was on them even before they got their elevation down low enough to hit it. It roared overhead, so close to the ground, the searing exhaust made their uniforms smolder. The noise from its jets was so loud, it made their ears bleed. Several of the gunners began vomiting, the sudden assault on all their senses being so massive it caused an instantaneous, acute nausea.

And then, just like that, it was gone. Streaking over the

western horizon like the angel of death vengefully looking for more victims—and heading right for Hanoi.

Hunter was sweating.

The leather straps holding his helmet to his chin were sopped with perspiration, shrinking the leather and causing it to tighten around his neck. The sweat was running so freely inside his spacesuit, it was seeping through his speed-johns and soaking his skin beneath. Even his hands were wet with perspiration, running down his wrists and into his leather flight gloves. The only part of his body to remain relatively dry were his feet.

It was not anxiety or fear or even apprehension which had soaked Hunter through. Rather it started with the eyeball-busting plunge he had made from 65,000 feet to just 150 feet off the ground in less than 45 seconds. The heat built up in the dizzying dive then combined with the heat generated by air resistance in the sluggish atmosphere so close to the earth. This caused the temperature inside the SR-71's cockpit to soar to 110 degrees, with no sign of letting up.

But Hunter didn't mind the discomfort. It was necessary if he was to complete this rather feverish mission. The plunge from twelve miles up had been necessary: he knew that Minx air defense systems would be searching for him at high altitude as soon as he passed over Dong Ha and Long Dik. This meant he had to get down on the deck so quick, they wouldn't have time to react, and thus allow him to complete his recon run relatively unhindered.

He saw the outline of the city of Hanoi ahead of him now. It looked as dreary and monolithic as he had been led to believe. At seven miles out, he banked to his right, and soon found himself roaring over a number of truck parks packed with military vehicles. Beyond these marshalling areas, he came upon a vast barracks and troop processing area.

A bank to the left found him just fifty feet above an enormous farm of satellite dishes and microwave antennas servicing a large communications complex located nearby.

A further turn to the left and he was able to skirt the far edge of the huge Xa Ha Ho air base. He could tell by the recent tiremarks on the base's main runway that a number of aircraft had taken off recently but had not returned. Hunter correctly guessed that these planes had been redeployed south to take part in the big Minx offensive.

But it was only when he banked thirty degrees to the left again when he began the cameras inside his nonsecone to whirring. Set on sideways angle fix, all six cameras captured, with reassuring mechanical efficiency, footage of the interior of Hanoi city itself, precisely the intelligence Hunter needed.

It took all of fifteen seconds, and when it was over, Hunter couldn't help but smile with the knowledge that he had gotten what he came for.

As he streaked out over Hanoi's city limits, he shut down the cameras and then put the SR-71 into a bone-crunching climb, rocketing straight up until he was out of sight from the ground.

He was passing through 65,000 feet in less than forty-five seconds. It was now imperative that he get back to Da Nang as quickly as possible. He had to send an urgent message to General Jones in Washington, requesting that he track down two individuals back in America who held the key to the ultimate success of Hunter's idea. At that moment, finding these two men was the most important thing in the world.

Leveling off at 70,000 feet, The Wingman buried the throttles of the big spy plane. The two ramjets exploding in a burst of pure hypersonic power, he turned south and headed for home.

Chapter Forty-eight

Boston
24 hours later

The blue, heavily armed Huey helicopter touched down at what was once known as Logan International Airport.

No sooner had it landed when six soldiers of the First American Airborne Division jumped out, their M-16s at the ready. Behind them a lone, smaller figure, was easing out of the chopper's passenger bay with a minimum of dramatic flair.

It was Yaz. He'd been sent to Boston by General Jones, handed a mission which, as unlikely as it seemed, might very well turn the tide in the war raging between the Americans and the Viet Minx half a world away.

There was little time for formalities with the officers of the Boston Militia, the group that ran the airport. Yaz and his men were looking for a particular airplane that was scheduled, he had learned, to leave Boston at any minute, its destination lying across the Atlantic.

Several jeeploads of Boston militiamen appeared as soon as the Huey set down, and Yaz quickly identified himself as a member of the United American Armed Forces Command Staff on a mission for the commander-in-chief himself. The soldiers demeanor instantly changed from understandable caution to alert compliance. Yaz explained they must find the target airplane and board it immediately. A quick check with their commander told the militiamen to assist Yaz and his men in everyway possible.

Though still functioning as a viable international airport, things at Logan were not run in the structurally compliant way as the old days. Planes landed and took off, almost at will, their only restraints being those mandated by safe operation. The control tower—which actually served more as a fuel broker—was in limited contact with most of the arriving airplanes, but few of the departing ones. This meant that Yaz and the militiamen would have to fan out across the huge airfield and look for the target airplane themselves.

Yaz checked the time. It was 1950 hours, and night was falling. The deep blue airport lights were blazing, giving the place an eerie look. Perched on the front seat of the lead militia jeep, he strained his eyes to see through the gathering darkness, looking for what had been described to him as the "strangest" Boeing 707 he'd ever seen.

As it turned out, he got lucky right away.

There was a 707 waiting in line on the airport's S6 runway, the strip favored by airplanes heading for Europe. The airplane was painted in dark purple and no windows save for the ones on the cockpit. The most unusual thing about the airplane—what had gotten Yaz's attention right away—was the nose had been custom-painted to look like, of all things, a dolphin.

"That has to be it," he yelled to the jeep driver. The man immediately kicked the vehicle into high gear, at the same time radioing the information back to the second jeep. In seconds, both vehicles were roaring across the tarmac, their headlights flashing in an attempt to get the attention of the pilots of the bottle-nosed Boeing.

It took some rather perilous maneuvering by the lead jeep driver to finally accomplish this, cutting in front of the big airliner just as it was beginning to taxi out onto the main runway.

It engines screaming, the 707 lurched to halt, the confused and stern faces of the pilots clearly visible in the blue light of the cockpit. The jeep rolled around to the 707's left side, just as the forward cabin door was opening. One of the pilots appeared at the opening and, even over the roar of the engines, Yaz could hear him scream: *"What the hell are you guys doing?"*

Yaz jumped out of the jeep and ran up underneath the door. Holding his UAAF Command Staff ID high above his head, he yelled up to the pilot: "I must come aboard. It's a matter of upmost urgency."

The pilot shone a flashlight down on the ID and convinced it was real, called ahead to his colleague in the cockpit to kill the airliner's four big engines. As these turbines were winding down, a pickup truck bearing a loading ramp appeared. Yaz waited for it to get into place, then he bolted up the steps, his ID still in plain view.

The two pilots were both in the entranceway now, and they studied his ID card closely. Finally they just looked at him and asked, "What can we do for you?"

Yaz took a deep breath. He looked around the small antecabin and into the cockpit itself and nothing looked unusual—certainly nothing that matched the strange color scheme on the outside of the airplane. But he knew behind the door to his right, things were probably very different.

"I must talk to your passenger," Yaz told the pilots.

The two men shook their heads. "You know we are on a tight schedule here," one said. "This guy wants to get across the pond by daylight tomorrow."

Yaz didn't have much time for discussion. "He's not going," Yaz replied definitively. "He's coming with me."

The pilots were slightly astounded. "Do you realize what this guy's got tied up back there?" one asked, pointing to the rear compartment.

Yaz just shook his head. "I have to see him, immediately," he replied.

The pilots just shrugged again, then one produced a key which opened the rear compartment door.

"OK," one of the pilots told him. "But you have to tell him . . ."

Yaz walked into the rear compartment and discovered it looked just like he'd expected. The cargo hold held a huge water tank made of welded-in glass and surrounded by air-filled cushion bladders. Inside the tank were two dolphins, now both staring at him.

Beside the tank was a small balding man, not quite into middle age. He was dressed in a lab coat and holding a small computer, which somehow was taking the water temperature of the tank. He seemed oblivious to the fact that the airplane had yet to take off.

He turned around a few moments after Yaz entered, and stared at him over the tops of his eyeglasses.

"Do I know you?" he asked Yaz.

Yaz shook his head. Their only thing in common was their mutual friend, Hawk Hunter.

"No—we've never met," Yaz replied. "But you are The Ironman, I presume?"

New Chicago
Two hours later

The bar known as Big Daddy Crabb's was full as usual.

The regular crowd was there—gun dealers, hookers, bookies, off-duty soldiers and militiamen. They had all gathered at the Loop watering hole to hear the best jazz—some said the *only* jazz—the Windy City had to offer.

Big Daddy himself was watching the door. An imposing man of six-foot-six height and offensive-lineman weight, his sheer size was enough to discourage any potential troublemaker from walking through his doors. Though famous for its entertainment and good, if expensive booze, fisticuffs or even occasional gunplay was not exactly unknown at

Big Daddy's. And this usually meant a visit from local constables.

But even Big Daddy was surprised when the UAAF armored personnel carrier pulled up in front of his place.

Big Daddy's eyes went wide as he watched a squad of soldiers pour out of the back of the APC. These weren't the local cops—their uniforms were that of the 1st American Airborne Division.

Crabb gently lifted the young Chinese hooker from his knee and pushed a hidden button next to the door. This warned his more regular clients in the club's back rooms that the law—or some extension of it—was on the way.

The soldiers were quickly at the door, a young officer walking in and standing before Big Daddy.

"Everyone's cool here, my man," Big Daddy told the officer. "No problems. No troubles."

The officer looked around the crowded bar and saw the hep patrons were trying their best not to look his way. But he knew, as they did, that the appearance of an officer from the elite First Airborne in what appeared to be an official capacity was not a normal occurrance on the rough streets of New Chicago.

"I'm looking for this man," the officer said, producing a photo of a middle-aged, short, squat individual with long black hair tied fashionably back in a ponytail.

Big Daddy recognized him right away. The man had once tried to sell him an airplane.

"He's in trouble?" he asked the officer.

"Not exactly," was the ambiguous reply. "Is he here?"

Big Daddy wasn't really sure what to do. Chicago cops he would take on, maybe even the local militia. But First Airborne guys? The same people who kicked the Nazis out of America? No way. That kind of trouble no one wanted.

Big Daddy flashed the photo to one of his bouncers, and within a minute, the man in the photograph was being escorted through crowd.

He looked stunned—until he saw the Airborne officer.

Then he simply rolled his eyes. "How the hell did you guys track me down?" he asked the soldier.

"That's top secret," the officer dead-panned.

"And what do you want me for *this* time?" the man asked.

"That is also top secret," the officer told him.

With that he nodded to the bouncers who released the man. Instantly two Airborne troopers were guiding the man out of the bar and into the APC.

The young officer gave Big Daddy a half-mock salute and then turned and climbed into the APC himself. With the roar of an unmuffled engine, the armored car rumbled away.

Big Daddy resumed his seat at the door. The hooker was soon on his lap again. The bartender came over with a bill in his hand.

"Hey Boss, that guy left on a seventy five dollar bar bill . . ."

Big Daddy examined the bill. It was a list of no less than twenty-five drinks, all of them scotch and waters. Printed in bold letters at the top was the name: "Roy From Troy."

"Put it on his tab," he told the bartender. "He'll be good for it."

Washington
Six hours later

The man named Ironman was not surprised to find himself at the Pentagon again.

Though he'd worked as an analyst for the U.S. Navy in years gone by, he'd never made it to the real seat of power during his time of employment.

Now, he'd been here twice in the past half year.

It was 4:00 AM, yet two sides of the five-sided gigantic building were ablaze with office lights. There was much activity going in and out of the building, and not a modest presence of United American military vehicles.

Ironman—his real name being Al Nolan—was escorted by the same UA officer who had fetched him from Logan Airport just moments before he and his beloved dolphins were due to take off. It was a quick Lear jet ride later, and here he was in Washington, in the middle of the night, still for reasons rather unclear.

Nolan was an accountant by trade, a number cruncher who had studied the Navy's procurement books, looking for errors of pennies which could add up to millions. After the world war and subsequent collapse, Ironman retreated to the old state of Maine where he began what would become another magnificent obesession for him: the study of dolphins.

He been at it for years now, working at a small research lab named the New American Aquatic Institute and spending upward of twenty hours a day, simply watching the institute's dolphins interact with each other. By sheer manhours alone, he was now probably the most learned expert in *Delphinus delphis* in America.

Nolan's life changed one night a half year before when his phone rang at the institute. The voice on the other end sounded staticky and far away. But it was still very distinguishable. It was the voice of Hawk Hunter.

Hunter and he had been friends for years and The Wingman had called him to work a miracle. Whisked to Washington—this being the first time—Nolan used his computerlike mind to wheel and deal with dozens of independent cargo ship owners and come up with literally hundreds of ships which were then used as the "phantom navy" in the climatic battle against the Asian Mercenary Cult at Pearl Harbor.

For that successful mission, Hunter had arranged for Nolan to use the services of a mothballed Boeing 707 airliner in his rather esoteric dolphin research, thus fulfilling one half of a promise he'd made to The Ironman in return for his help.

The other half was a pledge by The Wingman to help Nolan in his still-secret research project, the object of which was to find, of all things, the Loch Ness Monster. Where dozens of previous search efforts to locate the legendary creature had used everything from sonar, to radar waves, to submerged cameras, all to little result, Nolan had confided in Hunter another approach. Nolan had very quietly arranged to buy a pair of very rare Chinese river dolphins, animals adapted to living in muddy, fresh water. He'd been training these dolphins in endurance as well as other techniques for months, and it was these animals which were in the water tank aboard the Boeing 707. Nolan's idea was simple: he planned to set the pair of highly trained, highly intelligent dolphins loose in Loch Ness with small, light-weight video cameras attached to their heads. If there was anything lurking in the famous lake, Nolan was convinced the dolphins would find it—and find it quickly. He had sold Hunter on the idea, and once the world settled down again, Hunter promised he would personally assist Ironman in the quest. He was leaving for Britain to try out the dolphins in a smaller, similar lake when his flight was preempted by Yaz.

So now the Ironman was back in Washington, at the Pentagon, his research project delayed again.

He was brought to a basement office and led in. Behind the rather prolitarean desk sat the small wry frame of General Dave Jones, Commander-in-Chief of the United American Armed Forces.

Jones shook hands with him, and then introduced the other man sitting in the office. He was small, squat, dressed smartly and wearing a long ponytail. His name was Roy From Troy.

Ironman had known of Roy—he was an airplane broker with slightly checkered past. He was known for getting any airplane quickly and for fair price. He had been called on by the UA several times to come up with combat aircraft needed in their series of recent crisis-busting military campaigns. Most recently, Roy had provided the United Americans with a small air armada of carrier-adapted jets with which they carried out the daring raids on the Cult strongholds of Tokyo and Okinawa.

As it turned out Roy knew of Ironman, too. When they shook hands, Roy told him: "You're a freaking genius with the books. A genius with numbers . . ."

Jones invited them both to sit, and then he got down to business.

"Gentlemen, the reason we've brought you here on such short notice is that we need you—again," Jones began. "We need to tap your unique talents and we need to do it right away."

Twenty minutes later, both Ironman and Roy felt their heads in a collective swim. Jones had just laid the bombshell of bombshells on them. He had given them an almost impossible task to perform within an incredibly short timetable. Yet, after he explained the grave situation in Vietnam—an action that for many reasons was not common public knowledge—both men knew they had to try their best to fulfill Jones' critical request.

They stayed for four more hours working out the details. Then Jones had an armed escort bring them to their living quarters at a refurbished hotel about a half mile away. From here, Ironman and Roy would work their magic—or at least try to.

Jones had given them thirty-six hours to deliver. As their weapons, they had use of a bank of telephones, a massive Rolodex filed with secret coded phone—and radiophone numbers—and no less than 500 hundred bags of gold, supplied to them by Jones himself.

All that hung in the balance were the lives of more than 1,000 Americans in the First American Airborne Expeditionary Force, and the fate of the country of Vietnam itself.

Chapter Forty-nine

North Vietnam

The radar station at Dong Ha didn't see them coming until it was too late.

When its radar screens did start flashing, the operators—newly paid and back on the job—thought they had picked up a single indication, about twenty miles due east, coming in very low. An automatic alert signal went out over the base. Ground crews began scrambling for their MiG aircraft, the pilots soon behind. The eighteen-plane MiG-25 Foxbat squadron at Dong Ha was regarded as better trained and more efficient than most bases under CapCom's joint-subsidiary management. Being recently paid, the morale at the base was certainly on a high level too.

And one intruder would normally cause little problem for them.

But at ten miles out, the radar operators were stunned to see the single blip suddenly break into four smaller, speedier blips. In the blink of an eye, their intruder problem had just quadrupled.

The control tower senior official ordered the first four MiGs to initiate a "hot" take-off; no warm up, no instrument testing. Their sole task was to get the hell in the air—and quick.

But they would not be quick enough.

The Tigersharks came roaring over the base just as the lead flight of MiGs was lifting wheels off the runway. Flying *Shark One*, Frost had a tone on the first Foxbat before the enemy pilot even raised his landing gear. He launched his first Sidewinder and banked away just as the air-to-air missile impacted on the MiG's twin engine exhaust pipe. Maybe it was because the tailpipe wasn't hot enough yet, but the air-to-air just barely clipped the ass-end of the Bat, shearing off one of its tailfins. But the effect was the same as a direct hit. The MiG instantly went into an uncontrolled spin, careening into the jungle beyond the runway and exploding in a burst of flame and smoke.

The doomed plane's wingman immediately banked hard left—right into a prolonged burst of cannon fire from Ben's F-20. The 30-mm shells literally cut the Foxbat in two, even as its pilot was booting his "cold" engines into full afterburner. The cannon rounds found the raw fuel being dumped into the back of MiG-25's engines and instantly ignited it. There was one, big, quick explosion of orange fire, and then there was nothing. No smoke, no fire, no wreckage.

No more MiG.

Frost and Ben quickly exited the area. Their entire attack had lasted no more than five seconds. No sooner were they gone when JT's Tigershark flashed over the enemy base, his twin cannons typically opened up on full and shooting at anything and everything. He managed to rip up two warming MiGs, two parked MiGs, a Illuyshin supply plane, the base water tank, its auxiliary radio shack, its main generator, a ground crew barracks, the base mess, a guardhouse and the latrine. His work done, he pulled up just short of the tree line and exited hard left. His attack had lasted but seven seconds.

And right behind him was Hunter's F-16XL.

His wings were heavy with Durandal antirunway weapons. He was carrying twenty of them in all—more than twice the normal complement for a typical mission. The Durandal was an unusual weapon—and also a very effective one. Once released, a parachute deployed from the rear of the pipelike bomb, retarding its flight and pointing its warhead downwards. Seconds later, a rocket motor lit off, driving the weapon straight down into the concrete of the runway, where it detonated in the softer earth below. The result was a miniearthquake, cratering the runway beyond all quick repair.

Hunter spun over the base once, nimbly avoiding twin streams of fire from two Oerlikon 20-mm antiaircraft weapons hidden in the bush on the far edge of the enemy field. He banked hard, sprayed the pair of AA guns with his quad-pack of cannons and then came around on the MiG base's main runway. Calling up his weapons available screen, he saw nothing but Durandals.

Two Foxbats were just in the process of taking off when the XL roared over the runway, coming right at them at 10 o'clock. They saw the Durandals dropping off the XL's cranked wings but as they were committed to lifting off, there was nothing they could do.

The lead MiG made it into the air and immediately fled the scene. His wingman wasn't so lucky. A Durandal landed in the runway right in front of him, boring through the concrete and exploding just as the MiG passed over. A small storm of broken concrete was sucked into the Foxbat's engine intakes, instantaneously exploding them and driving their remains into the flight compartment. The MiG pilot was skewed with searing engine parts and high-speed pieces of concrete. He was dead before his MiG went out of control, toppling end-over-end and slamming into the weather lights at the foot of the runway.

Hunter continued on the runway-busting attack, dispensing all of his Durandals, and strafing the control tower for good measure. Flipping the futuristic jet over on its back, he could see the entire complement of antirunway bombs go off, tearing up more than fifty percent of the runway.

Though it took less than one minute, their mission was complete. The surviving MiGs had no way to take off and were thereby useless.

And another path was thus cleared.

Frank Geraci was anxious—to say the least.

He was sitting in the back of the C-5 known as *Triple-X*, no less than three restraining belts hooked to his legs, waist and shoulders. His four best men—Matus, McCaffrey, Cerbesi and Palma—were with him. They were similarly restrained.

They were flying at 21,000 feet, about sixty-five miles out over the Gulf of Tonkin. Before them sat an enormous dark shape, covered in black canvas. It was a bomb—a 35,000-pound bomb to be exact. It was bulbous, crude-looking and smelled of grease and cordite. Its nickname "Big Boy" was very apt.

Geraci and his combat engineers had done many missions in their careers, but nothing so strange as this. The *Triple-X* was heading for the massive railroad yards at a place called Long Dik. Just forty miles east of Hanoi, and stretching into the port city of Haiphong, the railroad lines not only carried weapons and supplies into North Vietnam, they were also the home of dozens of mobile antiaircraft guns set up on railroad cars.

Putting AA guns on moving stock was a trick that went way back to Hitler's Nazi Germany. Though the guns were usually low in caliber, due to weight restrictions, there were always plenty of them. Their mobility and their massed firepower was enough to bring down any size airplane—including a mammoth C-5.

A few miles east of Long Dik, there was a railroad marshalling yard, complete with a turn-around house and refueling facilities. It was here that the rolling AA guns were dispatched and rearmed.

And it was here that Geraci and his men would attempt to drop the Big Boy.

They flew along for another hour, waiting for the sun to dip below the western horizon.

They'd made the entire flight under radio silence, and there had been no contact at all between the NJ engineers and the *Triple-X* pilots way up in the C-5's flight compartment. The engineers passed the time mostly in silence; there were few windows in the fuselage, no way for them to look out and see where the hell they were.

What was taking so long? they wondered constantly. *Had something gone wrong?*

Suddenly, red lights began flashing all over the huge cargo hold, followed by a frightening number of warning buzzers. All five engineers would have left their seats in alarm had they not been wrapped in the restraining straps. A few seconds later, the huge vertical doors at the rear of the C-5 began to open.

A hurricane-force wind shot into the enormous hold; the change in air pressure caused the C-5 to dip with stomach-turning suddenness. When the engineers looked out of the rear of the airplane, they saw the three Tigersharks and Hunter's F-16XL riding right off the tail.

"*Jessuz,* this is it," Geraci yelled even though the others could not hear him.

The four fighter planes were so close to the rear of the C-5 he could clearly see the faces of Hunter, Ben, JT, and Frost. They seemed to be urging him to hurry up, to get this thing going.

The C-5 went into a wide bank; the huge airplane turned over almost 90 degrees, so that Geraci and the others were suddenly on their backs looking up at the Big Boy. The chains holding the seventeen-ton bomb started to buckle and Geraci horribly imagined what would happen if the weapon suddenly detonated. He closed his eyes and waited for the great airship to right itself.

When it did, they saw they were now over land. Below them was North Vietnam, the lush green terrain broken only by an occasional river, rice paddy, or small village.

The warning buzzers went off again, and ZZ Morell, the *Triple-X* pilot, climbed down into the hold.

He was characteristically all smiles.

"OK, guys," he said. "Time to get it on."

Geraci and the others reached up and unlatched the bolt that was holding their restraining straps to the fuselage wall. Suddenly they were free—relatively so. Though they could now get up and walk around, they were still harnessed in. Which was a good thing. With the wind whipping around the inside of the cavernous hold, it would have been fairly easy to get sucked out the back of the airplane to a long, terrifying death below.

It took all six of them to push the Big Boy back towards the open rear of the plane. The bomb was on a steel pallet which in turn was attached to a small rail. A series of levers served as the brake for the load, the squealing of these brakes was loud enough to hear over the scream of the C-5's engines, the roar of the wind and the racket of four jet fighters flying just a few feet off the end of the airplane.

After much pushing and pulling, they finally got the Big Boy to the last juncture on the rail. It was now but ten feet from the open back of the airplane.

ZZ checked his watch and then held up his right hand and showed four fingers. "Four minutes," he was yelling.

It would turn out to be the longest four minutes of Geraci's life.

The first indication that something was wrong came when Geraci looked up and saw that Hunter's F-16XL was gone.

Leaning forward, he could see the red-white-and-blue fighter spin straight down, a long plume of flame roaring from its tailpipe. Suddenly, both JT and Frost also dropped out—the two Tigersharks split and went into opposing 360s, lowering their altitude to about 1500 below the C-5.

"What the hell is happening?" Geraci yelled to ZZ. The *Triple X* pilot wasn't smiling anymore.

Before ZZ had the time to reply, the C-5 began shaking violently. Suddenly the sky beyond the open cargo doors seemed extremely dark; an instant later, they found out why. No less than 12 MiGs—Foxbats and Floggers—had suddenly descended on the C-5. They were all painted pale blue, indicating a coastal unit called to action inland. They massed so closely together they were like a huge mechanical cloud, blotting out what was left of the light from the sinking sun.

As the enemy formation streaked behind the *Triple-X*, the C-5 began dropping like a stone. Geraci and the others found themselves hanging on to the Big Boy, a dubious choice if there ever was one. Ben was still on their tail, his mission obviously to take care of the big cargo ship, no matter what.

As the C-5 continued to lose altitude, they could see off in the distance, Frost and JT streak right into the heart of the enemy formation. There was the sudden flash of cannon fire as the pair of Tigersharks opened up on the massed MiGs. The daring attack served one very important purpose: the MiGs began to scatter. Within seconds, the sky was filled with twisting, turning, high-speed fighters.

Suddenly it was every man for himself.

That's when they saw the XL again. One moment it was just JT and Frost battling the MiGs; the next, the Cranked Arrow was streaking through the buzzing enemy airplanes, its quad-pack cannons firing madly, even as it was launching Sidewinders.

Way below, Geraci could see five smudges of smoke and

flame, lining the paddies and jungle. That's when it struck him. The MiG formation had originally been much larger; Hunter had detected it before anyone else and had smoked five enemy airplanes even before they knew what happened.

But now the surprise was over—and an old-fashioned furball was in full swing. As the *Triple-X* still descended rapidly, those in the hold of the C-5 had a frighteningly close view of a high-tech dogfight, one which pitched three against ten.

Geraci was no expert in aerial combat, but he did know a few basic rules. One was, *Speed is Life*. The pilot who knew how to control his speed—as opposed to being the fastest on the block—was usually the winner in a dogfight. The second was *Lose sight, Lose fight*. A pilot had to keep his enemy in sight at all times; it was the one you missed who usually gets you.

The third rule was, roughly speaking: *If you ain't cheating, you just ain't trying hard enough.*

As Geraci and the others watched open-mouthed, they saw Hunter engage all three of these axioms, seemingly at once. He had somehow managed to get himself into position behind two Foxbats. Predictably, the MiG pilots accelerated and banked up and over the XL. But they did so way too fast, thinking that more power was better. Hunter on the other hand, *decreased* his throttles, causing the enemy planes to come out of their turns and streak by him. Two right-on barrages from his four nose cannons dispatched both Foxbats. They were spiraling down, all flames and smoke, mere seconds later.

The F-16XL then went into an incredible high-energy climb, rolling over on its back roughly level with the C-5. It paused there for a few seconds, an eternity in the middle of the supersonic dogfight—but Geraci knew exactly what Hunter was doing. He was surveying the battle—taking care not to lose track on any of the eight remaining enemy fighters.

At the same time, they could see JT's Tigershark spin over, and right on the tail of a climbing Flogger; it was obvious that Hunter had directed JT to the enemy's vunerable six o'clock position. A Sidewinder flashed out from the Tigershark's left wingtip and hit the MiG-23 square on the tail. The resulting explosion was so intense, it shook the air around the C-5, and thus the men inside.

Almost simultaneously, they saw Frost's Shark streaking in from a high altitude, its cannons blazing. At first it appeared as if he was shooting at nothing but the air. But soon enough, they saw the two Foxbats simply break up in flight, caught in Frost's incredibly accurate barrage. Once again he had been directed to the kill by Hunter; once again, the Wingman was able to exploit the enemy's weakness: They had completely lost sight of Frost's Tigershark, and they had paid the ultimate price.

Hunter dove back into the fray. Two of the remaining Foxbats had spotted him coming down at them and turned to meet him. But once again, Hunter used his speed—or lack of it—to best his opponents. He simply slammed on his brakes—flaps down, airbrakes up, throttles yanked back—and seemed to suddenly come to a complete halt in midair.

Stunned for a moment, the Foxbats instantly collided; Hunter had cheated—and the enemy pilots killed each other as a result.

Throughout the fight, Ben had stuck to the tail of the *Triple-X*, watching the dogfight over his shoulder. Suddenly a rogue Flogger came streaking up from underneath the C-5, its nose ablaze with cannon fire. Next thing Geraci knew, the inside of the C-5's hold was filled with sparks and shells, all too familiar from their days on *Bozo* during the Minx attacks.

This is crazy, Geraci thought even as he and the others held onto the Big Boy bomb.

Suddenly they heard a burst of power from Ben's Tigershark and it went straight up, pursuing the offending

Flogger. The C-5 hold was still full of smoke, and a few electrical lines were sparking, but it didn't seem like any critical damage had been done.

Seconds later, they heard a huge explosion and were treated to the sight of the Flogger coming down in pieces just behind them. Within seconds, Ben was back on station, guarding the C-5's rear.

The next thing Geraci knew, ZZ was right beside him, holding up one finger. The dogfight was over, the surviving MiGs pilots retreated and the pair of Tigersharks and the XL were pulling back into position alongside Ben. The combat engineer couldn't believe it. It seemed as if an hour had gone by—in actuality, it had only been three minutes and change.

Finally the C-5 leveled off and went into a wide left bank—they were now at about 7,500 feet. Down below, through the clouds they could see the gaggle of railroad lines, looking from this height like an unruly, multiarmed octopus. Once again the red lights in the cargo hold began flashing.

"There's the target!" ZZ yelled to them.

Sure enough they could see the middle of the octopus: the huge marshalling yard at Long Dik Ha directly below them.

"Ten seconds!" ZZ yelled.

Geraci looked up at his colleagues and took a deep breath.

"Five . . . four . . . three . . ."

They all secured their grips and got ready.

"Two . . . one . . . *Now!*"

With all their might, the six men pushed the 35,000-pound piece of iron and explosive. The brakes were no longer squealing as the huge bomb rolled out the back of the airplane, pallet and all. At that moment Geraci realized the true necessity of the restraining devices: his momentum very nearly carried him out of the airplane with the behemoth bomb. Only the straps, and a tight grip by Matus saved him from the long plunge down.

The Big Boy was floating right behind them for what seemed like a long time. Then its drag chute opened and it was jerked backwards. They watched it gradually start to sink into the cloud cover and towards the ground below.

The C-5 continued twisting to the left, its fighter escorts with it, thus giving those in the back of the big plane a distorted angle of the Big Boy's descent. It took about a minute for it to break through the clouds. When they picked it up again, it was falling even faster than before, its seventeen tons of encased explosive winning the battle of gravity against its drag chute.

Then it hit.

There was no noise—not at first anyway. There was only an incredible flash of bright light, followed by what only could be described as an instant hurricane of smoke and dust. To Geraci's amazement, a mushroom cloud began to rise up into the sky. He was stunned—they all were. It looked just like a nuclear explosion.

ZZ saw their expressions and laughed. "Scary, isn't it?" he yelled.

The combat engineers could only nod in numb agreement. Even the pilots of the fighter planes behind them were looking back at the explosion in awe. As the mushroom cloud rose higher into the sky, they got a glimpse of the ground beneath it.

And this might have been the most startling thing of all.

There was nothing left. The railroad turnhouse, the railway lines, the moving gun cars, were all gone, swept up in the flame and smoke of Big Boy.

The C-5 jerked to the right, turning sharply to the south. ZZ pushed a button and the big doors of the C-5 began to close.

"Time to go home," he yelled.

410

Chapter Fifty

Da Nang Air Base
Eight hours later

Hunter was eating a candy bar as he took off from Da Nang. It was a MRE concoction, a chocolate and almond combination, with maybe a raisin or two thrown in—or at least he hoped they were raisins.

It was way too sweet for his tastes—but he hadn't had time to eat anything in the past twenty-four hours, so the mushy confection would have to do.

He put the XL right on its ass and roared up to 20,000 feet. Leveling off, he did a surface radar scan of the perimeter around Da Nang. It was all clear—there was no indication of any enemy activity anywhere. Hunter let out a whistle of relief. There had been no Minx activity around the base for forty-eight hours.

He turned east, out to the sea. He checked the time. It was just 1400 hours. A fierce anticipation rose up in his bones. They were closing in on the final act of this play—he wanted to get it over with, and move onto other things. Specifically the pink jet's black box and where it would eventually lead him.

He increased power to 700 knots and soon the water of the Gulf of Tonkin was below him. He owed a tip of his hat to both Roy from Troy and Ironman. Though their merger was rather frightening—like two enormous insurance companies coming together to squeeze even more money out of their victims—it had apparently paid off in spades for the First American Airborne Expeditionary Force. It was just two days before that he sent the germ of his idea to Jones in Washington, emphasizing the major parts that Roy and Ironman had to play. Now if the coded message he'd received from Jones just thirty minutes before was only half true, then Hunter knew that the two "businessmen" had pulled off nothing short of a small miracle.

Timing was everything though—and if this timetable got screwed up, even by a few minutes, then Hunter knew the whole plan could go down in flames, literally and figuratively. He shook away thoughts of such a disaster. What he was trying to accomplish here had never been tried before—not in real combat anyway. There was no room for any negativity at all then. Worrying was just praying for things you didn't want.

Besides, the plan would be hard enough to pull off even if everything *did* go as scheduled.

He rose up to 55,000 feet and put his threat-warning radar to work. He had to make sure the airspace within 100 miles in all directions was clean. It took about five minutes to confirm this. He checked the time again. It was 1415 hours.

Time to get going.

He pushed the F-16XL up close to its maximum full military power; with thirty seconds he was topping 2,200 knots. The thin air at ten miles up provided little resistance as he streaked along at more than a half mile a second. The blur of the clouds were a comforting sight; the bright sun felt good on his face. He'd done a lot of flying lately, but he hadn't been enjoying it very much.

But now he was, despite the circumstances. He was free. Literally, free as a bird. *This* was the exact opposite of the claustrophobia of Khe Sanh, the exact opposite of the horror masked as beauty in the Mekong Delta. In the end, Vietnam *was* the land of angry ghosts. The farther away he got from it, the better he felt.

He reached the rendezvous spot with two minutes to spare. Reducing his speed back down to 400 knots, he went into a wide orbit and waited.

Already, he could feel them coming.

He saw them ninety seconds later. There were twelve of them in all, just glints in the sun, trailing long streams of vapor and ice. He held his flight pattern and watched their approach. They got bigger by the second. Soon he could discern wings from fuselage, fronts from backs. At twenty miles out they looked like silver pencils with long thin wings. He could see the individual engines now, spewing contrails that instantly turned orange in the high sun.

Suddenly the radio was filled with chatter: altitude checks, fuel loads, position confirmations. Finally, someone raised him on the blower.

"Cowboy One, this Calvary One, do you read?"

Hunter keyed his lip mic. "Ten by ten," he answered.

"Are we still on mission schedule, Cowboy One?"

"Roger, Calvary," Hunter replied. "On schedule. On time."

"Affirmative, Cowboy One," came the reply. "We'll follow your lead."

By this time the dozen aircraft were just five miles away. They looked huge, fierce, *awesome*. They weren't C-5s—this mission called for something more lethal than that. No, Roy and Ironman had certainly come through. They had secured the one aircraft that had been on this mission before. They had bought the services of twelve mighty B-52 Stratofortresses.

The *Second* United American Airborne Expeditionary Force had arrived.

Chapter Fifty-one

Da Nang Airbase

JT and Ben were sitting in their F-20s at the far northern end of the Da Nang runway, their engines running up to max power. Close behind them were two C-5s, the *Triple X* and *Football One*.

They were waiting.

"They're late," JT radioed over to Ben, his voice typically anxious.

"Not yet," Ben replied. "We've still got about a minute point five."

They sat in silence for another minute or so, watching an isolated rainstorm sweep over the hills off to the west of them.

"OK, they're late, now." JT called over exactly ninety seconds later. "Something must have got fucked up."

Ben just shook his head. "Listen, old buddy, you would think that after all this time, you would learn some patience," he told his friend. "Just relax. Take deep breaths. In through the nose, out through the mouth."

"If I start sucking on this pure O like that, I'll be high as a kite," JT replied, his tone a very model of unZenlike exasperation.

"That's the idea," Ben replied.

Suddenly their radios started crackling. "Mystery Ranch,

this is Cowboy One. Calvary has arrived. Repeat, Calvary has arrived. Over . . ."

It was the unmistakable voice of Hunter, giving them the unmistakable go-code.

"That's our wake-up call," Ben called over to JT. *"Let's go . . ."*

Together the pair of red Tigersharks roared down the runway, lifting off in a burst of pure afterburner power, their wings heavy with smart bombs and Sidewinders. The C-5s *Triple X* and *Football One* took off right behind them.

The four airplanes quickly formed up and, as one, turned north.

The waiting was finally over.

The B-52s were picked up on radar about forty miles southeast of Hanoi.

They were first spotted at a SAM base located on the edge of the city, but because it had been attacked earlier in the day by enemy jet fighters, it had no means to launch any of its missiles. All its surviving operators could do was watch the Stratofortresses roar over head at 50,000 feet and radio the news to Hanoi.

This and about a dozen other desperate messages alerted the MInx High Command that a major bombing attack was coming. The High Command was concerned but prepared. Hanoi was covered with SAM sites close in, as well as battalions of AAA units. Most of these units had been recently paid, and were reporting up and operational. Plus, it was three in the afternoon—what enemy would dare a major attack on such a large, well-protected city in broad daylight?

It was at this point, the Minx High Command made a huge blunder. Once convinced that an attack was indeed coming, the Minx defense officials determined that its target would not be Hanoi, but the large Xa Ha Ho airbase just outside the city limits. This made sense to them as in the past day or so, the enemy aircraft had been attacking airfields and antiaircraft sites. Why would they change tactics now?"

The Minx High Command ordered all available antiaircraft units to the area around Xa Ha Ho. If the enemy chose to attack the airbase with heavy bombers, then the Minx would make sure none of those bombers survived.

Xa Ha Ho Airbase

Colonel Nguyen Cao Li was angry.

"This is not the way to do business," he was telling the officer standing next to his MiG-25. "My men and I cannot simply fly on a promise of payment. We *must* have cash in advance."

The other officer, Major Sum Lu Buk, was nearly wetting his pants. It was his job to coordinate for air defense of the huge Xa Ha Ho air base.

"There is no time, Colonel," he pleaded with Li. "The enemy is approaching—in great force. High Command predicts that this airbase is their target. You and your men *must* get airborne or all will be lost!"

Li simply shook his head no. His men were sitting in their Foxbats, seventeen of which were lined up on the air base's main runway. Their engines idled down, their canopys up, they were watching with great interest the dispute between their commander and Buk, who was the base operations officer.

"I am certain," Colonel Li was telling Buk, "that if you checked with CapCom, they would support my point of view. This is COD—cash on delivery. It's a time-honored method of doing business. We cannot fly without being paid. It's as simple as that."

Buk was beside himself. He was sure he could already hear the low drone of the approaching enemy bombers.

"Colonel, I beg you," he said, his voice losing strength

with every syllable. "There is no time to contact CapCom. No time to argue. Our treasury is closed because of the pending air raid. It is impossible for me to get you payment in advance. Just impossible."

Li turned and waved his hand once. This was the signal for his men to taxi their airplanes back to their hardened shelters.

"Then, it will be impossible for my men and I to take off," he told Buk.

Buk was desperate. He reached into his pocket and came up with a handful of gold coins, stamped by the Royal Thai Empire.

"Colonel Li," Buk said, thrusting the coins into the pilot's hand. "This is my pay for the past month. Please . . . *take it.* Surely it is enough for at least three or four of your men to go aloft."

Li counted the coins and quickly calculated their worth. Then he laughed. "Major, this is barely enough for one airplane to go aloft for ten minutes."

Buk looked him straight in the eye. How could so many people get so greedy in such a short amount of time?

"Then do so, Colonel," Buk told him. "Take the money and go up for ten minutes and at least try to do something to save us."

Li stared back at him with some disbelief. Then he shrugged and pocketed the money.

"You must reimburse me for any ammunition expended," he told Buk as he ascended the access ladder and climbed into his Foxbat's cockpit. "And pay me a bonus for every enemy plane shot down."

"Done!" Buk yelled up to him as he motioned the ground crew to remove the airplane's wheel blocks. "Double for multiple kills."

"Triple!" Li yelled back over the increasing scream of his engines.

Then he closed his canopy and taxied away.

Buk watched him move to the end of the runway, the

only sounds now were the MiG-25 engines and the air raid sirens wailing above the base.

"I hope you die with that money in your pocket," Buk said through gritted teeth as the lone Foxbat roared up and away.

Then he ran for the air raid shelter.

"Calvary One, we are seven minutes from target."

"Roger, Cowboy . . . confirm seven minutes."

Hunter unkeyed his lip mic and did a visual check of the aircraft around him. Right behind him and slightly below were the first six B-52s of Calvary One, flying in a loose chevron pattern. Behind them was Frost's F-20, riding point for the second half-dozen Stratofortresses. Behind *them* was ZZ Morell's *Triple-X,* and *Football One,* with Crunch at the controls. Bringing up the rear were Ben and JT.

They were all flying at 42,000 feet, about 32 miles from the center of Hanoi. Hunter had to admit the small air armada looked impressive. The earlier path-clearing operations had been highly successful. Since turning into North Vietnamese airspace, they hadn't encountered a single MiG or any AA fire, or heard so much as a SAM warning tone.

Hunter could only pray the rest of the mission would go as smoothly.

He was certain the Minx knew they were coming—but at this point, it really didn't matter. He knew the Minx were undoubtably preparing to defend every major target in the city—every one, he guessed, but the one he was intending to hit.

"Cowboy One—this Calvary One . . . I read six minutes to target . . . clock for ECM activation."

"Roger Calvary," Hunter replied. "Engage in ECM now."

Hunter flipped a series of switches to the left of his in-

418

strument panel, activating his array of electronic-countermeasure devices. He knew the pilots of the B-52s were doing the same. They were sure to see some SAMs the closer they got to the city, but the radio/radar jamming devices inside his XL and the big Strats would reduce the problem significantly.

"Five minutes to target . . ."

Hunter checked his own weapons load. He was carrying four 1000-pound GP bombs, a pair of 750-pounders, plus a complement of six Sidewinders. As always, his quad-pack of M-61 cannons was full of ammo.

Behind him he knew each B-52 bombardier was checking his own weapons load. Each of the Strats was carrying an awesome payload of seventy 1000-pound HE bombs. Combined with his bomb load, as well as the push-off bombs in *Triple-X* and *Football One*, they were about to drop more than 500 tons of ordnance on Hanoi.

"Four minutes . . ."

Hunter couldn't help but think of the men so many years before who had done almost the exact same mission as they were attempting now. Linebacker One. Linebacker Two. Rolling Thunder One. Rolling Thunder Two. Mission names were all that remained now. Gone were the successes and failures of these missions. Gone were the screwy politicians on both sides which had made them necessary.

Gone were the men who had given their lives in carrying them out. . . .

And now here they were again. Approaching the same target, with some of the same planes, carrying some of the same type bombs, and trying like hell to avoid the same type of SAM and AA fire. Sometimes Hunter thought he was trapped in some kind of strange science fiction world or bad paperback novel, where everything just keeps repeating itself. Good versus evil—over and over again they battle. But no matter how many times the good guys win, the bad guys always come back to haunt them. Why? What did it mean? Were all their efforts in vain?

Hunter didn't know. These were questions for the ages. "Three minutes to target . . ."

He banked slightly and gazed at the city coming up below. He was certain it looked just this way to American pilots years before, blocks upon blocks of uninspired buildings, crossed by dull roads and railway lines, strung with power lines and telephone wires, and dotted with military installations, thatched houses—and SAM sites.

"Two minutes . . ."

Hunter activated his threat warning radar and soon was looking at a ghostly image of Xa Ha Ho airbase just outside the city. Oddly, he could still see the heat signatures of nearly a squadron of MiGs, yet he was sure they hadn't taken off. Not all of them anyway. Why would the Minx warm up eighteen airplanes and then not launch them? He hadn't the foggiest idea, but then again, there were few rational explanations for much of what the Minx did.

"One minute to target," he heard himself say into his lip mic. "Let's go through pre-bomb run checklist."

As he heard a call and reply of each of the airplanes' commanders checking with their crews, he kept his eye on the read-out from Xa Ho Ha. He knew they were expecting the bombers to go there—the place was obviously hunkered down, just waiting for an attack. Because there were few military barracks inside the city itself, and even fewer communications centers, he didn't blame the airbase commanders for assuming they were the target of the impending B-52 strike.

But they were wrong.

"Thirty seconds," Hunter called out, looking behind him and seeing the Stratofortresses tighten their formations. "SAM activity to the south. ECMs on high. Flares out. Chaff dispensers on high . . ."

Just as the words left his mouth he could see a trio of SA-2 SAMs rising up towards them from his left. The ancient weapon looked just as many American pilots had described it before: like a telephone pole with fire coming out the back.

"Hold positions . . ." he told the others.

Then, he deftly angled the Cranked Arrow thirty degrees to the left while still maintaining course, an aerial maneuver that could only be accomplished by the XL's unique shape and canard wings. He waited for the SAMs to close within 400 feet of the B-52s and then he squeezed off three precise bursts from his quad-pack cannons.

With incredible precision, his three streams of tracer rounds met the SAMs head-on. The trio of missiles blew up like three enormous firecrackers, sending three quick shock waves rumbling through the surrounding airspace. When the smoke cleared, the SAMs were gone.

"Hold positions . . ." Hunter repeated, pulling the XL's nose back to center. "We're out twenty seconds . . ."

Another pair of SA-2s were launched at them from the middle of the city, but these were instantly fooled by the small storm of metallic chaff and flares exuding out of the bottom of each B-52. Confused and overheated, the SAMs began corkscrewing and quickly plunged back to earth.

"Fifteen seconds . . . hold steady," Hunter told them. The air was now filling with the bright orange streaks of AA fire. But most of it was either way off target—due to the combined-effort ECM affecting the radar-controlled guns—or too shallow to affect the group way up at 32,000 feet.

"Ten seconds now . . ."

They were right above the center of the city, nowhere near the airbase, or the weapons repair shops, the communications building, or the Minx High Command headquarters.

"Five seconds to target . . ."

More SAMs were coming up through the thin clouds, but they were flying erratically and of no consequence. The skies below were simply filled with streaks of AA fire, reminiscent of bombing Baghdad, but just like then, nearly all of it was falling back to earth, not nearly as high as to affect the bomber force.

"Three seconds . . ." Hunter called out. As the group leader he was doing dozens of calculations in his head per *nano*second, concentrating on the target below and basically eyeballing it.

"OK . . . *two . . . one . . . Bombs away!*"

He pulled his own weapons release lever and felt the corresponding jolt as the two and half tons of bombs dropped from his wings. Cranking around, he could see the enormous stream of bombs falling from the Strats. Behind them, the pair of enormous, 35,000-pound Big Boy bombs came tumbling out of *Triple-X* and *Football One*.

He followed the bomb fall all the way down through the thin clouds to the center of the city below. They all seemed to hit at once, the pair of Big Boys providing the exclamation point to the massive carpet bombing. Almost immediately one huge sheet of flame arose from the target, the shock wave hitting the bomber force a few seconds later.

Though they would run a photo-recon for bomb damage evaluation later on, Hunter already knew the target had been totally destroyed. It would have been hard not to be. For the target was not a military installation per se, not an airfield, or barracks or communications center. Rather it was the one place whose destruction would most seriously disrupt the Viet Minx expansionist plans, and probably harken their demise.

What the American bombers had left in smoke and flame and ruins was the Central Bank of Hanoi.

"Group left and clear!" Hunter yelled into his microphone.

As one, the combined bomber-fighter force banked hard left and turned for home.

All except JT.

Hunter knew something was wrong as soon as he saw his friend's Tigershark dive down towards Hanoi.

The front of the sleek F-20 was alight with smoke and

fire, and following JT's tracers it was easy to see that he was strafing an AA gun atop of one of the dreary government buildings.

The gun post immediately exploded in a flash of fire and metal and bodies. JT immediately pulled up and typically did a low-altitude victory roll. Then he put the F-20 on its tail and booted his afterburner to rejoin the bomber group.

And that's when something went terribly wrong.

Hunter felt before he saw it. A glint of silver and black, streaking out of smoke and clouds, its cannons ablaze with gunfire. It was a Foxbat—and it was obvious that its pilot had been laying low waiting for the bombers to drop their ordnance and looking for something to pounce on. A distracted JT, showing off, was the perfect target.

The Foxbat's cannonfire raked the F-20 front to back, severing its left wing and igniting its fuel tank. The Tigershark immediately went into a spin, flames and smoke pouring out its perforated fuselage.

Hunter was on the scene in a matter of seconds; the Foxbat had already turned to escape. But it was too late. In an unusual moment of uncontrolled anger, Hunter unleashed two Sidewinders *and* sprayed the Foxbat with a long barrage of cannon fire from his quad-pack. Both missiles hit the Foxbat almost simultaneously with the arrival of the cannon barrage.

The resulting explosion was enormous; the fireball even bigger. When the debris blew away, only a few engine parts remained, tumbling to earth, trailing a few wisps of black smoke.

By this time, JT's Tigershark had already crashed onto the streets of Hanoi.

Chapter Fifty-two

Outside Hanoi
24 hours later

Never had there been such gloom inside the huge mansion that served as headquarters for CapCom.

There was no darker place than the mansion's boardroom. Those lights that had not yet gone out were certainly dimming. Less than a third of the huge TV sets were still online, and two of those were mostly static. Even the phones were dead.

The chairman of the board looked out on his once-propersous stable of members and saw nothing but death and profit loss. Two members had already blown their brains out, a third was soon to follow.

Where did they go wrong? the chairman asked himself. They'd undercut all of their suppliers and overcharged all their customers. They had neglected their own citizenry. With each new battle they had achieved the perfect balance between an evershrinking work force and higher rate of asset acquistion flow. This was supposed to be capitalism's Nirvana.

So what happened? the chairman wondered, pulling out his own Beretta and placing the barrel in his mouth.

He would never know.

The muffled sound of the chairman's gun going off

barely echoed off the sides of the cavernous boardroom. Two more members followed their leader to hell via pistol shots to the temple. Another man simply decided to slit his wrists and go slowly.

This left only two members who were afraid of ending their own lives.

So they made an agreement: one would shoot the other and them himself. A quick toss of a South African 110-mark gold coin decided who would be the triggerman. Grimly, the men embraced for the last time.

Without much hesitation, the shooter did his work, blowing half the skull off his colleague, and adding a bullet to the heart for good measure. He checked the pistol—there was one bullet left. Would it be enough? the man wondered.

It would have to be, he finally decided.

He put the pistol barrel in his mouth, and pulled the hammer back. Just as he was about to let go however, he heard a strange noise off in the distance. It was perculiar enough to cause him to take the gun out of his mouth momentarily and look outside.

The noise was coming from a quartet of huge helicopters landing just outside the mansion's east wing.

No sooner were they down, when scores of white-uniformed troops began pouring out, their weapons poised, their demeanor obviously one of shoot-on-sight. One chopper had landed in the middle of the other three, and from this aircraft a man in a black uniform emerged.

The last CapCom member squinted in an effort to get a better look at the man. He was extremely tall, maybe 6-10, thin but powerful looking. He was a white man, though his face was dark from the sun. He wore his hair long and bunched into a ponytail that reached halfway down his back. A small stiletto-sharp goatee adorned his face.

This man drew a long cape around himself and then began a quick march towards the mansion. The CapCom member wasn't quite sure what to do. Who was this? Who was *he* to arrive with such arrogance? The board member was curious—so much so, he felt death could be put off for a moment or two.

He watched as the tall man in black walked right up to the huge picture window anchored to the southern end of the boardroom and delivered a vicious kick of the boot. The huge pane simply shattered away, scattering thousands of small shards of glass all over the boardroom, the bright sun making them glisten like diamonds.

The man in black walked quickly through the hole in the window, followed by a squad of heavily armed soldiers. They stopped to study the boardroom itself. The man in black counted out the twelve dead bodies and then held back his head and laughed.

"Which one was Judas?" he roared with demonic delight.

The squeal nearly split the brain of the surviving CapCom member. He'd never heard a laugh so chilling, so fearsome.

The man in black then walked over to the CapCom member, who was now shaking with fear and confusion.

"Do you speak French?" the man in black asked him.

"Non . . . not enough . . ."

"English then?" the man in black asked.

"I speak it," the CapCom man replied.

The man in black looked around the room. "You are the only one left?"

The CapCom member nodded slowly. He was certain the man in black was about to order one of his troops to finish the job of killing himself.

"And were you were a senior member of this . . . this organization?"

The CapCom man nodded slowly again. He was lying, of course. He was barely a junior member.

The man in black stared down at him and then, strangely smiled.

"You are the sole proprietor remaining, then?" he asked him, almost gently.

The CapCom man nodded a third time, with more vigor.

"Then," the man in black said, "I have a proposition for you."

The man from CapCom was puzzled. "You do?" was all he could reply.

The man in black looked around the room. "Yes," he said with a huff. "I want to buy this, Or whatever's left of it."

"You want to *buy* CapCom?" the board member asked incredulously.

"*I do!*" the man in black replied heartily. "And as you are the only surviving member, you will be the one I shall pay. Now I'm a busy man. Will five thousand pounds of gold do?"

The CapCom man was astonished. He'd been a half a second from killing himself. Now, suddenly, he was a very rich man. Had there ever been anyone luckier?

He picked himself up out of his chair and stood tall on two unsteady feet. "I accept your offer, sir," he said in the boldest voice possible.

The man in black pulled a parchment document from his cape. He then made an old-fashioned ink quill pen appear out of thin air.

"Sign this, my good man," he said, thrusting pen and paper at the CapCom board man. "And our deal will be consummated."

The board member did so quite hastily. The man in black took back the piece of paper, studied it and then added his own signature, a large sign of a "V."

"Excellent," he whispered. "Now everything is legal."

The CapCom member straightened out his uniform and pushed back his rumpled hair. "And now, sir?" he asked.

The man in black smiled again. "And now, it is time for your golden parachute."

"Excuse me, sir?" the CapCom man asked.

"Golden parachute," the man in black repeated. "Aren't you familiar with the term? It means 'early retirement.' "

Suddenly there was a gun in the hand of the man in black. The CapCom member was astonished—it was *his* pistol. But he had no idea how the frighteningly-imposing figure before him had gotten it from him.

It made no difference. The man in black pulled the trigger and the bullet entered the CapCom member's skull right above the left eye. He was hurled back against one of the big picture TV screens, bounced off and fell to the floor. He was dead in two seconds.

The man in black dramatically blew the smoke from the still-hot barrel and then threw the pistol on the conference table.

"Another day," he sighed. "Another hostile takeover."

He turned on his heel and walked back through the hole in the window. His second in command was there, waiting for him.

"This is all in your hands now," the tall man in black told him. "Consolidate what is left, sell what we don't need, and keep what we do. I'll expect a full report in a week's time."

The man snapped an instant salute, then turned and and began barking orders to his vassal officers.

"Find any servants inside the house and kill them," he shouted in Arabic. "Locate any soldiers, disarm them and do the same. I want a complete inventory in my hand in less than one hour!"

As his troops scrambled to work, he turned back to the man in black.

"Your wardrobe is fully packed, sir," the second in command told him. "You will find it laid out in your sleeping compartment on the command plane.

The man was pulling on his long black gloves. "The best in artic gear?" he asked.

"The very best," the second-in-command replied with a lopsided grin. "It's pure 'shark skin.'"

They both laughed and then the man in black was off, walking briskly back to his chopper, and quickly climbing aboard. Within seconds, the huge aircraft was off the ground and turning to the north.

The troops left on the ground all watched it until it was completely out of sight.

Chapter Fifty-three

The next day

The huge Ch-53 Super Stallion helicopter touched down right outside the ops building at Da Nang airbase.

Its massive rotors never stopped turning. It had to pick up some passengers and then quickly be on its way. The chopper and its crew were from the Second Italian International Corps, based down near Cam Ranh. They were responding to a direct request from Hawk Hunter himself. The United Americans needed a heavy-lift, armed helicopter quickly.

The Italians were only too happy to help out. It was after all because of the United Americans that practically all Minx activity in South Vietnam had ceased nearly twenty-four hours before. Every major target throughout the country was on the verge of falling into enemy hands when the Minx suddenly stopped shooting, and quickly began to withdraw. A catastrophe was averted by mere hours. And everyone knew it was because the United Americans had bombed the Central Bank of Hanoi, and in one brilliant massive stroke, dealt the one blow to the Viet Minx military structure that could not be defended against: bankruptcy.

With the gold and paper reserves of the Minx's fortune

lying in cinders and dust in the middle of Hanoi, the Minx were suddenly devoid of all operating capital. The massive tap-out caused the immediate collapse of its management company, CapCom. No Minx meant no paychecks for the various military units in the field. An entire army had been handed its pink slip, and was now literally unemployed.

Democracy and Freedom had survived again in South Vietnam—at least for the time being.

So the Italians were grateful to the Americans, as were all of the foreign military units fighting for the people of South Vietnam. When the call came for a big chopper with big guns, they were the first on the scene.

Fourteen men emerged from the ops building, each heavily armed with M-16AX laser-sighted rifles and carrying a variety of small munitions, such as grenades and flash bombs. Each man was also wearing a Kevlar helmet, except for one, who was wearing a faded white crash helmet.

With the small army finally settled on board, the huge Sea Stallion revved its engines and slowly rose into the air. Once it gained altitude, it turned and headed towards North Vietnam.

His name these days was just Dong.

He was driving a truck—one carrying septic waste—on old Route 9, heading for a disposal center near the village of Quang Shau, which was located about 10 miles south of Hanoi.

The irony of driving a shitwagon on Route 9 was not lost on Dong, dull-witted as he was. Mere weeks before, he had commanded more than a division of men in a major battle fought for access to this very highway. He had lost.

Now he was back to doing what he supposed he did best—driving crap up and down the Minx lines.

Because his truck had no radio, Dong was one of the few Viet Minx troopers in either Vietnam who didn't realize that they were actually out of a job. For Dong, it couldn't have come at a worse time. The former multimillionaire had exactly three gold coins in his pocket, enough for a used pair of tire-rubber sandals, a pack of cigarettes and maybe a glass of *him-ham*, and that was it. And though he didn't know it yet, there would be no more pay slips coming from Minx High Command, simply because there *was* no more Minx High Command.

It was growing close to dusk now, and he was about two hours from his destination. Though he was hungry, he couldn't bear to eat, so great was the stench from the tank behind him. Instead he pulled out his last cigarette and attempted to light it. Rounding a corner which led into a thick forest, he had to take his eyes off the road momentarily in order to strike his match. When he looked up he found himself staring down the barrels of fourteen heavy machine guns.

Dong immediately hit the breaks, burning himself in the process and nearly getting ejected through the windshield.

The fourteen heavily armed men were around him in an instant, hauling him out of the truck's cab and throwing him to the ground. There was a bootheel on the back of his neck inside a second, many gun snouts on his nose not a second later.

"Did you speak French?" he heard someone using cracked accent say. "English? Chinese?"

"Fran-swa!" he screamed. *"Fran-swa!"*

"Where is the largest military unit from here?" the man with the bad French accent asked him.

Dong was petrified; he was certain he was about to be shot.

"There are many," he managed to blurt out, the boots on his back making it very difficult to breathe.

"Where's the camp of the nearest highest ranking officer?" was the next stern question.

Dong was inhaling sand and oily road gravel now.

"Hanoi," he gagged, "maybe some closer."

Another boot was added to the crunch on his back.

"Where the hell would they bring an enemy prisoner around here?" a new, angrier voice asked in a definite American accent. "Someone who was shot down?"

Dong was panicking by this time. He tried to come up with an answer he hoped his assailants would want to hear, on so thin a line he believed his life was hanging.

"There is a provincial police station on the edge of the city, right up this road," he nearly screamed. "They would take a captured pilot there."

"OK," a third, calmer voice replied. "You're going to take us to it."

It was two hours later when Dong literally burst through the door of the Hanoi police station.

Though charged with keeping law and order inside the former Minx capital city, the policemen now found themselves suddenly unemployed, just like tens of thousands of Minx soldiers. Like the troops, their pay slips came from the now-defunct Minx High Command.

The five policemen inside the station stared at Dong, astonished that he had entered in such an impolite manner.

"Leave here!" one of the policemen screamed at him, something a cop would never do in the old days. "Steal your food somewhere else!"

Dong was absolutely terrified, so much so he had trouble even opening his mouth, never mind forming coherent words. His main concern were the fourteen gun barrels he knew were aimed at his back at that very moment, their owners hidden in the dense growth on either side of the station's door. He was already shaking from the news these strange enemy soldiers had told him during the helicopter ride up to this place. These men claim—and he had no reason not to believe them—that the entire Hanoi government had collapsed financially and that the war in the south was very abruptly over. He was easy to convince for two reasons: tales of Minx financial woes were universal throughout the ranks, plus he hadn't received a pay slip in weeks.

Under these circumstances he knew the policemen would not be happy to see him—or any other Minx soldiers for that matter. Relations between the Hanoi police and Minx troops were always strained at best. So Dong had a very legitimate fear that he could get shot from the front, too.

The only bright spot—and it was a small one—was that he could see a Caucasian man through a glass partition sitting in an adjacent office. He did not look up when Dong burst in, but Dong could see that man clearly enough to recognize his pilot's uniform. The man's head was also covered in bandages.

"They have come for him," Dong heard himself mutter, pointing towards the white man.

The policemen were on their feet now.

"Who has come?" they demanded.

"His friends," Dong continued to stutter. "They are outside—in force. They want him back. If not, they will kill me—and all of you, too."

The policemen stared back at Dong, then turned towards the man in the nearby office and then back again. They were suddenly fingering the sidearms.

"Are you insane?" one of them screamed at him, no more than a foot from Dong's right ear; Dong could smell the *him-ham* on his breath. "This man is an enemy prisoner of war. We must fight to keep him."

"Are you sure," Dong somehow coughed out. "Even in these uncertain times?"

"He is to be held here until . . ." a second cop yelled at him.

Dong took a deep gulp. "Until . . . *when?*"

A third officer was soon in his face too. He looked to be the fiercest of them all.

"Until someone pays us to take him," this man growled.

Dong swallowed hard again. "That's just it," he replied, his voice down to a terrified whisper. "That's exactly what they want to do."

Six hours later

The sun was just coming up when the small patrol of Hanoi policemen reached the top of the small mountain.

This was the place they called Tienku. It was the highest elevation within twenty-five miles of Hanoi, lying due south of the dormant capital. From its summit, the policemen could see the smoke still rising over the center of the quiet city, the last vestiges of the massive American bombing attack.

They had both the soldier named Dong and the captured pilot with them. They were also all heavily armed.

The big helicopter arrived five minutes later. It landed gently on a flat outcrop of rock, a dozen heavily armed men inside deploying in aggressive fashion an instant after the chopper touched down.

The policemen were very much on their guard. Each one had his weapon up and ready.

Two of the chopper soldiers stepped forward; the only officer in the police unit did the same. The two white men were tall, rugged and sporting longer than military length hair and beards. One of them was wearing a pilot crash helmet, with two lightning bolts emblazoned on its sides.

It was this man who spoke.

"English?" he asked the police officer, "or French?"

"English," the cop replied.

"You are not regular Minx troops," the man with the pilot's helmet said. "This is why we can make a deal, right?"

The policeman nodded stoically. "We are businessmen, yes," he replied.

Hunter looked over at JT, who, though battered, looked none the worse for the wear.

"We have the money," Hunter told the enemy officer. "Give us our man."

The policeman turned back to his officers and gave a grunt. JT was led forward.

Hunter motioned back to the chopper and Frost and Ben appeared carrying a wooden box full of bags of gold coins.

The ransom—nearly $1 million—was raised in a matter of five hours from the defenders up and down the Vietnamese coast. Once more, they knew they owed the Americans a lot for the recent turn of events.

There was a tense moment of silence, and then the Hanoi cops let JT go. He walked a little unsteadily past Hunter, and over towards Ben and Frost. Hunter gave another signal, and two enemy policemen came forward and took the box containing the gold bags.

The exchange thus over, the American troopers began falling back into the chopper, Ben and Frost helping JT climb aboard.

Hunter took a long look at the police officer.

"Doesn't it bother you, trading with the enemy?" he asked the man.

The cop smiled for the first time. "Anything for a buck," he said, in grinning, broken English.

Hunter just shook his head. "You'll learn . . ." he said.

He motioned for Dong to get on the helicopter, and then backed up himself, never taking his eye off the policemen or their weapons.

"See you in another thirty years, guys," he said, climbing into the open bay door.

With that, the pilots gunned the chopper's idling engines and it slowly rose into the sky.

All of the Hanoi policemen resisted the urge to wave goodbye.

Thirty minutes later

Once again, Dong was on the ground, breathing in gravel and dirt.

There were no boots on his back this time. Rather the only thing weighing him down were the two bags of gold in the crotch of his uniform pants.

He was lying down to avoid the worst of the downwash from the ascending helicopter. His temporary captors had dropped him here, on a rise near his shit truck, still shaking but still alive.

His life had been twisted by fate again, Dong thought as he heard the helicopter slowly fly away. The Americans were a very strange bunch, of this he was now sure. They were fierce, obviously well-trained and determined, yet all in all, for the most part, Dong knew they were not out to harm him. They just wanted to retrieve their friend, that's all. In their faces he saw the looks of men who had seen too much war, too much death. So much of both, they were weary of it, and thus not inclined to do so frivilously.

But never, *ever*, did Dong expect them to pay him for his help.

However they did, with the two bags of gold they'd taken from the original ransom collection. Just why they decided to compensate him would puzzle him for the rest of his life. After all, he was certain that some of these Americans were the same men he'd faced at Khe Sanh, though he was equally sure they had no idea who he was. All he remembered was the American soldiers speaking in their unintelligible staccato sentences soon after the big helicopter had taken off, obviously discussing what they should do with him. Then one of them—the one with the pilot's helmet—threw the two bags of gold to him, cryptically adding French: "Go buy enough rope to hang yourself."

Then they dropped him off, bidding him a silent, gruff farewell. Now, as their helicopter was slowly flying away,

Dong felt a jolt of excitement run through him. He realized that next to the squad of Hanoi policemen, he was now probably one of the richest men in North Vietnam.

He looked up and watched the helicopter pass over the southern horizon and then he sat up and took out the pair of gold bags. He opened both and stared in at the dozens of gold coins.

He bit his lip and wondered, *What should I do with it this time?*

Chapter Fifty-four

Da Nang Air Base

It was the C-5 known as *Football City Two* that rolled out onto the main runway at Da Nang just before dawn the next morning.

A crew of 100 men—most of them being Geraci engineers—had worked for the past twenty-four hours stripping the huge Galaxy of all unnecessary weight. Gone were the plane's heavier loading systems, such as the motors in its huge cargo doors, both front and back. Its huge interior hold was torn away and now contained dozens of inflatable bladders, each filled with 500 gallons of jet fuel. An intricate network of hoses and plastic tubing rose up from the bladders, pumping JP-8 into the airplane's auxiliary fuel system, where it fed into the airplane's main fuel supply. With the Galaxy's regular tanks also full of fuel, *Football Two* now had enough gas to carry it at least 15,000 nautical miles, probably much more.

Hunter was in the pilot's seat of the sports-scrolled C-5—he was, in fact, the only crew member of the modified flying gas hog. In front of him was the black box he'd taken from the Pink Jet, it still being wired to the remains of *Crunchtime*'s autopilot. He had hooked this contraption into *Football Two*'s main controls and set up a crude flashing light warning system. If everything worked right, the flashing of the red light would determine which way the captured black box wanted to go.

Hunter had received some good news shortly before climbing into the C-5. A subsequent and intensive search of the Gulf of Tonkin by the Sky High Spies and their SR-71 Blackbird had failed to find any definite sign of the Cult battleship fleet. However, oil slicks and heat spots *had* been detected by the Blackbird's infrared cameras some 750 miles off Cam Ranh, indicating that a large force of ships had passed that way sometime within the past twenty-four hours, heading due east, away from Vietnam.

The report that the battleships were likely moving out of the area added to the fifth straight day in which there was no Minx activity anywhere in South Vietnam—the doors were closed and the Chapter 11 sign was just about hung out now as far as the Viet Minx was concerned. They were finished—absolutely *kaput*—as a military entity.

So Hunter was doubly grateful for the favorable turn of events. Now he had the time to pursue his own agenda.

He started powering up *Football Two's* systems when he heard someone climbing up the access ladder. Hunter turned to see it was JT.

His friend handed him a sealed blue pouch.

"Got maps in there for everything but the North Pole," he told Hunter. "Call if you need more."

Hunter took the pouch and put it under the pilot's seat.

"You've got your radio codes and the list of accessible friendly bases," JT continued. "Don't be afraid to call on these guys. Crunchie knows them all."

"How are the wounds?" Hunter asked him.

JT patted his head bandage and winced. "I won't be diving for anything, anytime soon," he replied.

"Go lay out on the beach," Hunter prescribed. "And talk to the *Li-Chi-chi*. They have their ways of treating such things."

"Well . . ." JT said, his voice trailing off. "I guess I'll see you when you get back."

Hunter nodded and yanked on his crash helmet. "See if you can get a card game together," he said, tightening his worn strap. "I haven't played poker in a while."

"Consider it done," JT assured him.

They shook hands and then JT started back down the access ladder. But then he suddenly reappeared again.

"Hey, Hawk," he said, his voice a little lower than usual. "Just one more thing."

"What? You need money?" Hunter asked him, only half-joking.

"No," JT replied, looking straight at him. "I just wanted to say thanks. Thanks for coming and getting me."

Hunter just shrugged. "No way we would leave you behind, old buddy. No one deserves to be left behind in this place."

"Amen to that brother," JT replied, his confident, cocky grin returning to his face.

They shook hands again, this time longer, then JT gave him a quick salute and departed for good.

It took another five minutes for Hunter to get all of the C-5's computers talking civilly to each other, and then he wound up its four big engines to full power. He began taxing, past the F-20s, past the other C-5s, past the deployment of 12 B-52s, past his own beloved F-16XL.

He felt a chill go through him as he rolled by the make-shift flag pole at the end of the main taxiway. There was a ripped Stars and Stripes flying from it, whipping, tattered but proud in the brisk morning breeze. They'd started out with nine C-5s, full of brave men, and lost some. The Galaxy fleet was now as tattered as the flag; there was no more *Bozo*, no more *Nozo*, no more *Crunchtime* or *NJ104*. *JAWS* had been lost, the Cobra Brothers' *Big Snake* was still missing.

But still, the air fleet had prevailed. Freedom was safe in South Vietnam—at least for the time being. And that, after all, had been the original purpose. They'd fulfilled their mission; no soldier could ask for better validation.

He pulled *Football Two* out on the main strip, and after a brief conversation with the control tower, gunned its engines and started an extra long take-off roll. Slowly, almost impossibly, the red-white-and-blue C-5 rose into the air. Nose pointing almost straight up, the airplane climbed steeply, gradually disappearing into the thin morning overcast, banking to the left as it did so.

It was gone from view in less than a minute.

Fifteen minutes later, the radar screens inside the Da Nang control tower started buzzing.

The operators quickly picked up a large airborne target flying in from the northeast—the indication was the size usually identified with a C-5. At first, all they could think of was that Hunter had turned back and was returning to the base for some reason. But as the blip came closer to the base, the tower officers knew Hunter was not at the controls of this plane. It was behaving too erratically. Plus, all attempts to raise it on the radio had failed.

The air raid alarm sirens stunned the base. In seconds soldiers were running everywhere, to shelters, to AA guns, to the armed and ready-to-go F-20s. But no sooner had the alarms died down, when the soldiers were actually coming away from their positions. They were staring up at a C-5 that was coming in from the due east, its engines smoking, flame spilling out from under its wings.

Ben and JT were out of the ops building, studying the incoming C-5.

"Who the hell is this?" JT roared over the din.

They knew less than a minute later. The wounded Galaxy fell out of the sky at a too-fast speed, its engines nearly exploding in flames. It hit the runway hard, bounced once, came back down, flattening its entire landing gear, and then skidded crazily, raising a tidal wave of sparks behind it. It screeched to a painful stop a full half mile down the runway.

Those that were there would later swear they didn't believe anyone on board the ship could have survived the crash, but miraculously, all of the crewmembers did. Even more astonishing was the plane itself. Obviously shot up before approaching the base, its airframe was now mortally twisted and broken. Still the Da Nang personnel who were running top speed towards the crashed and smoking jet could clearly see the large print letters adorning the airplane's bent left wing.

They read: *JAWS*.

The first group of base personnel to reach the crash site found all thirty passengers staggering out of the wreck. Ben and JT were at the head of that group, and to them it looked like a ghost ship had just crashed. Walking a little stiff, but briskly from the wrecked airplane was Cook, Maas, Clancy, Snyder, Higgens and the rest of the *JAWS* gang. It was all very spooky, as if it was a dream. *JAWS* was thought to have gone down in the sea weeks ago after the big MiG attack. Now it had just dropped out of the sky.

Cook was the first one JT and Ben reached. They didn't quite know what to do. It was as if they were looking at a spirit.

"I know, I know," Cook was telling them, instantly identifying their confusion. "But we made it . . ."

Ben, JT and the rest were simply dumfounded.

Cook looked at them all and smiled wearily. "And have we got a story to tell you . . ."

Epilogue

Hunter flew for twenty hours straight.

Over the border of North Vietnam into China, high across the Forbidden Kingdom, up into Mongolia, and then turning over Siberia itself.

All the while he kept his eye on the red light mounted on the control panel. The intensity of its flashing was guiding him perfectly, taking the huge C-5 where it was originally meant for the Pink Jet to go.

Throughout the long flight, day passed into night and began back to day again. His body and mind well-adapted to going long periods without sleep, he passed the time eating MRE candy bars, thinking of Dominique and wondering exactly where the flashing red light would bring him.

He had his answer at 4:00 AM on the second day.

He had passed over many miles of Siberian tundra and was now flying due east. Suddenly the red light began blinking madly, and after two minutes of this, it simply stayed on.

Hunter quickly checked the dark terrain ahead of him. Sure enough, on the far eastern horizon, almost hidden in the waning night, he could see the outline of a city.

He had already determined that he was deep inside what was once known as Russia. Now, after some quick, intensive calculations, he knew that specifically, he was approaching a place known as Baikonur or more specifically, "Star City."

This was once the Russians' version of Cape Canaveral. It was from here that Russian governments long ago past had launched their crude copy of America's space shuttle.

The red light still burning continuous and bright, Hunter knew Baikonur was his goal. He could see a huge airport on the edge of the city, one with a runway stretching six miles in length, more than enough to set down the big Galaxy.

He circled this airport once, and was not surprised to see it was totally abandoned. Ten minutes later, he was down and climbing out of the C-5.

The sun was beginning to come up, and to the north of the city, he could see the tops of the launch platforms formerly used by the Russian space programs. His heart pounding, a heavy parka wrapped around his body, he loaded his M-16 and set out for the towers.

It took him more than an hour of walking through the monolithic, abandoned city in subzero temperatures before he reached the edge of the rocket base.

And it was here that he got one of the biggest surprises of his life.

Unlike the rest of Star City, the base was very much alive.

He could see technicians hastily moving around the base's largest launching pad, attending to something hidden under a huge plastic cover. Fuel trucks were scurrying about, announcements in many languages were blaring out of the unsophisticated loud speaker system. It seemed the people at the rocket base were so busy with the object under the tarp they hadn't even detected his approach in the C-5.

The sunrise was about thirty minutes away now. He was huddled in a doorway of a deserted building with a clear sight into the base. His immediate plan was to observe, take as many mental notes on the situation as possible, and then figure out what he should do about it all—if anything. That the Pink Jet's autocontrol should bring him to what he thought was a long-abandoned space launch facility did not surprise him a whit. His many years of battling the forces of evil had taught him never to be surprised by anything an enemy did.

But just how was Victor connected to all this? And what was under the plastic covering that was getting so much attention? Could it be an ICBM? One aimed at America, to be launched in retribution for the inglorious defeat of the undemocratic forces in Southeast Asia?

Hunter just didn't know—and he felt he'd have to wait until morning's first light to find out.

But, as it turned out, it would not take nearly that long.

He figured it was about 0600 hours when it happened.

The dawn was just making its appearance. He was just munching the last MRE candy bar, biding his time, when suddenly, it sounded as if a hundred klaxons went off at once.

He had to hold his ears the noise was so intense. Through squinting eyes he saw a long black car emerge from a building way off to his left. This car—it was actually a Cadillac superstretch limo—roared right past him, and headed towards the launch tower. The scurrying technicians had all stopped by now and were standing at attention when the limo finally arrived. As the klaxons died away, more than six individuals reached for the limo's rear door. After a brief scuffle, it was finally opened and a tall dark figure stepped out.

Hunter felt his breath catch in his throat. Suddenly it seemed as if a bomb had gone off in his brain. He recognized the man emerging from the car right away. Tall, dark, wearing all black, long slick hair, and a sharp goatee.

446

It was Victor.

Or at least someone who looked exactly like him.

Hunter didn't hesitate an instant. He raised his M-16 and quickly sighted Victor's head in his crosshairs. But before he could squeeze off a shot, the supercriminal ducked behind an opening made for him in the immense plastic covering. He was followed through this hole by no less than six people dressed in what looked like very old-fashioned spacesuits.

What the hell is going on here? Hunter thought, his mind racing. *Could it be . . .?*

That's when the klaxons started blaring again. Then suddenly, a mobile crane appeared and in one, swift maneuver, yanked the huge plastic sheet from the launch platform.

That's when Hunter saw the space shuttle.

He was astonished—so much so he couldn't move.

It was an American space shuttle—there was no doubt about it. Hunter was an expert of the craft—he was, at one time, slated to be the youngest pilot ever to fly the shuttle for NASA, an appointment in outer space which was cruelly cancelled by the start of the Big War.

Now he was staring at one of the authentic items, and realizing much to his horror that it had somehow fallen into the hands of his archenemy, Victor.

So stunned was he, he didn't know how much time passed, but now people were running everywhere. Suddenly Hunter could feel the ground shaking beneath his feet. There was then a tremendous roar, and a burst of flame so intense, it nearly blinded him.

Then the shuttle began to rise.

He was out in the street against the fence in a heartbeat. His M-16 was up and firing, a long stream of tracers reaching out towards the ascending shuttle, carving their way through the flames and smoke.

But it was useless. In his rage Hunter knew he was way beyond the range of an effective shot.

But he kept firing anyway—over the noise, over the storm of smoke, over the billowing flame, firing nonstop even as the shuttle disappeared into the low clouds and climbed towards outer space.